CAPTIVITY

THE COMPLETE SERIES

SARAH BIGLOW

MOLLY ZENK

CAPTIVITY

CAPTIVITY BOOK 1

ONE

ONE

AIDEN

The gilded cage had been my prison for far too long. I grew tired of the cooing and fluttering of the beings that came and went. The one who always remained provided the basic necessities of my existence. The one with the wicked smile. I did not understand when she squawked at me, but there were things I could not forget.

I am the bird of rebirth. A phoenix. No matter how long freedom eluded me, I knew that fact deep in my bones. I waited day after day for that rebirth. A day I feared would never come. But, if I could not continue the path I knew I was meant for in this place, I would seek it beyond the confines of this prison. Sometimes, the one would leave the cage open. Today was one such day.

I had grown tired of waiting. It was time now. I would not get another chance. With the one distracted, I stretched my wings and gave them a weak flap. They still worked. The air smelled of burning as my wings flapped, straining to catch a current to carry me free of this confinement. It had been so long since I could fly, it was a marvel I recall the actions necessary. Sky—open and endless—loomed just ahead of me and I beat my wings harder. I was so close.

Pain zipped through my small frame and the sky no longer lay ahead of me. Despite the effort of my wings, and feathers catching warm swells, I plummeted toward the ground. Some part of me, deep down and forgotten, begged for me to close my eyes so I did not witness my painful demise. That deep part of me did not want to see death.

No, it was not I who feared death. It was *him*. *The other*. The strange being out of nowhere who now fought for freedom. The ground continued to rush up to meet me, but it took on strange tones as the sharpness dimmed. Gone were the lights and darks of my existence. Now the grass and dirt were shaded in something else. 'Color' the other's mind interjected.

Without warning, I felt the feathers that coated my body recede, replaced by something smooth. The pain that rippled through me as bones and cartilage stretched and expanded robbed me of breath and the stunning glimpses of color turned to blackness.

The jolt of my form connecting with the ground was shock enough to rouse me from the other pain. I blinked, colors flooding my eyes in an overwhelming kaleidoscope. They were still dimmed and dark. I opened my mouth—no longer a beak—to breathe and choked on vile, acrid air. I struggled to move on limbs that had not been used in far too long to support my weight. It was then I noticed the device clinging to my lower right extremity. It shot continual lances of pain through my body, but my relative size appeared to dull the effects. I slumped forward and clawed at the thing to no avail.

The more I labored to breathe, the less I liked my existence in this form. It was too cold and dark. I spat to free my lungs of the putrid tastes, but it did little good. I tried pulling off the thing on my leg—another word this form recalled—again and this time, the jolts jumped to my upper limbs.

"Argh." Vocalization emitted from my mouth. It had been so long since this form had spoken.

Sounds—high pitched and frantic—called from the direction I had come. This form's brain knew what they meant: danger and captivity. With every passing second, my brain regained control more and more. My feet remembered how to walk and then run. It was an inelegant manner of movement that propelled me forward and away from the oncoming danger. I gained speed as I crested a hill and I took a leap. For just a moment I felt like I could fly again. The thing on my leg snagged on some branches and I tumbled forward. A fresh smell hit my senses, this one metallic. I looked down to see the skin of this form marred by dark, oozing blood. The device had come loose. I clawed at it again, this time freeing myself from its confines.

The voices grew louder and I took off, running faster and more confident this time into the wild, rolling hills. My arms moved in coordination with my legs and my lungs grew used to the tainted air. This was freedom. My mind knew it and I needed to believe it.

My reflexes were not honed to alert me to the impending perils that lay ahead of me. My foot caught a rough branch and in moments I lay curled in a net suspended above the ground. The strands of the net bit into my flesh.

"Gotcha," a high-pitched voice said.

"Let ... out," I managed. Language seemed to be the last thing to return.

With a sharp 'snick' something flashed above me and the confines dropped away, sending me tumbling back to the ground.

"What do we have here?"

I blinked up at a small creature with pointed ears. Dark smudges marred her flesh. But her eyes shone bright. How I knew it to be a she I could not say. In viewing the 'she' I glanced down at my form and realized a distinction. A new concept—or perhaps an ancient one I only just now recalled—overtook me and I covered myself as best I could.

The 'she' moved around me, examining me. She prodded the wounds to my flesh and studied the angry marks to my legs. "Damn, I never thought I'd see another one of you. You got a name?"

Her words took a long time to make sense in my mind. It took even longer to find the words to answer. "Aiden," I said, my voice rough from lack of use.

"Mels." She bent and put her hand in mine. "Come on. I can take you somewhere safe."

TWO

TWO

LORELEI

This blows. Not that I mind the cushy job of just sitting around staring at a tracking monitor all day, but there are more exciting things to do with my time and life. I wouldn't even be in the Phoenix Location Agency if it wasn't for Kegan. He's lost. He's a phoenix. I need to find him. Enough said.

"We have a runner," my superior agent's voice announced, her voice piped into my ear through my com link. *Finally! Some action!* "Report to Madame Zemella Faberge's estate for further details."

I tapped the com link in my right ear to connect with my superior. I would not let any of my siren sisters in the PLA get a jump on what I was already thinking of as "my case." There was no way in hell I planned to sit at this desk for another day. I needed action. A running phoenix provided just that.

"Lorelei reporting in," I said. "I'm on the Faberge Estate runner. Be there in two."

"Be careful," my fellow PLA sister Aria's voice crackled in my ear. "Madame Faberge likes pets ... all sorts of pets."

"I can take care of myself." I opened my desk drawer and pulled out two long, pointed hair pins. I slid them all the way into my thick, honey colored braid. It's not a surprise if people know you have them. The gun at my hip was standard PLA regulation issue, but I didn't like using it. There's no art to self-defense if you just pull out a gun and shoot someone.

After readying my gear, I ran down the three flights of stairs to the parking lot. At least, that's what everyone called it even though there was nothing to park in the lot. Ever since the sky turned ever-dark from all the smog and pollution, individual transportation was outlawed. Now, it's public transport or walk. I liked walking, though on days like this when the rain burned, it could be a challenge. Lucky for me, even walking, Madame Faberge's estate was not far.

I dodged around the hover buses in the street and people clogging the sidewalk until my route brought me to the Faberge Estate. It was a typical

Booshie house, all stone white-washed walls and golden spires that stand out in the darkened climate. Even the ten-foot electrified security fence around the property was gold. How did her phoenix get out of this place alive? *Maybe he didn't,* I reminded myself. Maybe he sacrificed one of his lives to high-tail it out of here. I would if I were him. No one with an ounce of magical ability wanted to be kept in a Booshie cage. The Booshie just didn't see it that way.

I pressed my finger against the intercom button at the estate's front gate. "Siren Lorelei reporting for duty," I said after a short beep. "they told us you had a runner."

"Excellent timing," a woman's voice answered." Come in. Come in."

A buzzing noise sounded as the gates opened to let me in. I stepped inside, trying not to think of those same gates closing and trapping me inside. A phoenix might have wings to get away, but I didn't have that option. Siren fins would do me no favors if Madame Faberge decided she wanted another magical pet to replace her missing phoenix.

I took one last look at the closed gates behind me, before walking up the long, stone driveway to the house. A black car was parked in the open garage, flaunting the 'no personal cars' rule.

Booshies always thought rules applied to everyone except them.

The front door swung open before I even had time to knock. A squat woman with skin pulled so tight every expression looked like a grimace appraised me with glittering dark eyes. She'd been hitting the phoenix tears a little hard if *that* was the result. Usually, I'd tell her to her face she looked like a toad, but the PLA wrote me up for insubordination last week. I didn't need to give my superior any more ammunition to can me. Calling a Booshie client a toad would be like handing her the final bullet. Not going to happen.

I smiled, trying to look pleasant and helpful. "I'm Lorelei. Can you tell me what happened?"

"I can do better than that. I can show you." Madame Faberge motioned for me to follow. I trailed her to a room that looked like a giant concert hall, keeping my hands behind my back to calm the temptation to swipe some of her stuff to sell for credits later. I bet she wouldn't miss half the stuff in this hall if it went missing.

She stopped in front of a hanging gold cage, the door swinging back and forth. It didn't look forced which meant someone left the door open. Unbelievable. This Booshie lost her phoenix and now expected us to find him. It reminded me of the time I took a side job tracking a selkie that ran away to the boonies, because of her owner's neglect. I found her dancing in a slough in the northwest end of the territory. Booshies never learned. You leave a cage open, your magical creature escapes. How hard was that to understand? Sure, I'd be out of a job if they ever took care of their things, but freedom tended to be too tempting for pets to resist. They'd escape whether their owners kept the cage doors locked or not.

I smiled to cover up my disgust. "What was his name?"

"*Is*," she corrected me. "I can't bear the thought of my poor, dear, sweet Aiden being harmed in any way because of someone's carelessness." She pulled out a palm-sized clear object from inside the folds of her voluminous dress and tapped it twice. Flickering, holographic images appeared, hovering above the object. A phone. She owned her own phone. I had a government issued one. I could conference call any agent I wanted, but it didn't take pictures. Those phones were out of budget.

Madame Faberge flicked through the carousel of holographic pictures until she found what she was looking for. "There. Here is my Aiden. Isn't he a handsome bird?"

I spend most of my time tracking down rogue phoenixes with some side gigs of other creatures mixed in. I'd gotten to the point where I thought if you've seen one phoenix, you've seen them all. That theory went straight out the window the second I gazed at Aiden. His gold, red, and white feathers shimmered in a way I'd never seen before in my years working for the PLA. That meant he possessed powerful, powerful magic. Most phoenixes could only create the tears used for healing and to halt aging once, maybe twice, a month. Judging by Aiden's sparkle, I'd say he had enough magic in him to produce tears every week.

"I can see why he means so much to you," I breathed. "I'm gonna need to see a pic of him in human form just so I know I've located the right one," I added. "They like to be sneaky and hide in plain sight as human if they think they're being tracked. Happens all the time."

"Very well." Madame Faberge scrolled through more pictures before enlarging one toward the end of her photo carousel. "Handsome either way, don't you think?"

I sucked in my breath. Aiden—as she called him —was not Aiden. I knew him as Kegan. He'd been missing three years and now ... and now I found him. I'd been looking so long, I thought I'd never find him. *Kegan.* I made a big show of examining the picture so as not to give away my excitement. Aiden—or Kegan—was shirtless in the picture. His dark red hair stuck up in a natural spike like his crest feathers in bird form. Gold sigil tattoos similar to the pattern on his wings ran the length of his muscular arms. He stared straight into the camera, though didn't seem to see it. His vacant expression told me surer than anything that Madame Faberge drugged him, keeping him docile. She probably drugged all her pets. Good on him for escaping then. How long had he planned this? How long had he dreamt of freedom? Had he been trying to break free since he was stolen from me three years ago? Would he be looking for me just like I'd been looking for him?

"Do you mind if I bring a feather with me to aid tracking?" I kept my voice smooth and expression-less so she wouldn't guess that this was one phoenix I didn't intend to return to its owner.

She opened a drawer next to the tea table and extracted a large gold, red, and white feather. "Will this do?"

I held it in my hand, remembering the weight and feel of this same feather from when I tracked Kegan almost four years ago. I found him then—I always find my mark—but that job was different. I didn't expect him to plead for my help or my under-standing. I helped Kegan run away and escape the cage waiting for him. In the process, we fell in love. Then he was taken from me. Stolen by the Booshie bitch sipping tea with me now. I'd find Kegan or whatever she called him now, but that didn't mean I'd bring him back.

"And then, of course, there's the matter of payment," I added, playing her game.

"One million credits," Madame Faberge answered as if she was offering to buy my hover taxi fare. My hand twitched, but I tried not to show any emotion at her outrageous sum. One million was the highest bounty I'd ever heard of. I needed that money, but I also needed Kegan. We'd been apart too long already.

I forced a tight smile. "When do I start?"

THREE

THREE

AIDEN

The voices receded as Mels led me deeper into the underbrush. With every moment that passed, the instincts I'd clung to for so long faded, replaced by new ones. Human ones. The nagging fear that led me to cover myself with my hands developed a name: shame.

"Keep up, birdie," Mels snapped from up ahead.

Despite being smaller in size, she moved far quicker than I could on these new legs. I tried to move faster, having to resort to using my arms for stabilization again and again. Short dark hair the color of ash bounced against her shoulders as she marched onward. As we moved through the forest, I noticed something flicker on her back. I reached a hand out and brushed against something soft. Multi-colored, gossamer wings erupted from her back. I marveled at the beauty until she turned, sharp teeth bared.

"Touch me again and I will bite you."

My sense of smell was weaker in this form, but I could still pick up on the poison dripping from her mouth. I took an awkward step back and bowed my head. After a moment, she spat on the ground, leaving sizzling holes in the dry, dead brush near my feet.

"We need to keep moving. We're too exposed out here."

She took off at a clip and I had to run to keep pace. How I longed for the agility and speed of wings. I could see the markings on my skin reminding me of the beautiful glistening feathers that had once covered every inch of me.

"Where are we going?" I huffed as my lungs struggled to keep my body moving forward.

"Less talking. You'll waste air," she ordered.

Not keen to make her angry again, I did as she told me. I couldn't say how long we travelled, ducking behind thick tree trunks and racing through tall grasses. I still did not understand why she was helping me. Any smart predator would have seen me as a threat. Perhaps she was a dumb predator or simply prey. No, in this form I was little threat to anyone.

"What's going on in that head of yours, birdie?" Mels pressed when she slowed to a walk.

"Don't call me that," I answered.

"Sorry. Aiden was it? Question still stands. What's going on in there?"

I rubbed at the nape of my neck. "Why are you helping me?"

"You were cute and wounded." She smiled, the tips of her sharp teeth piercing her bottom lip. "Look, your kind is rare these days and it looked like you were running from something. I know a little something about running from things that want to hurt you."

Her words sounded genuine. I hesitated as another voice called out from nowhere and everywhere all at once. I couldn't understand the words, but it pulled at every ounce of my being. The world around me vanished and only the voice remained. It was comforting, calling me home again. It was like a melody I'd long forgotten, but knew was meant for me and me alone.

A sharp pain to my jaw broke the solace and the world flooded my senses. I tasted blood on my tongue.

"You can't let them in your head."

Her words triggered an odd vision in my mind

of a woman. No, not a woman. Not entirely. She sang and my kind flocked to her. To their deaths or worse; captivity.

"What do you know of my kind?"

"I know your only natural predator has ways of getting in your head. We've got ways to help you."

"We?"

"Me and some others. Some like you."

"You know more of my kind?"

She stopped walking and pointed to a structure ahead of us. "See for yourself."

Every instinct both bird and human told me that whatever lay within that place was dangerous. And yet, I couldn't help being drawn toward it. My feet moved of their own accord until I could rest my hand against the rough wood door. My ears picked up muffled voices from within and some spoke in words my human brain could still not understand.

Without warning, I felt a nudge between my shoulder blades and I staggered forward. My weight and momentum pushed the wooden door open and I stumbled into a large room. All eyes landed on me, some were the color of ash and others a deep purple or amber.

A large man approached me and I couldn't fight my instinct to cower. He let out a long sound between his teeth. "Well, hello there, handsome. You lost?"

I could see the red and gold markings of one of my own kind swirling over the muscles of his exposed upper arms. Our resemblance ended there. His hair—which should have been a shade of red—was dark as night. "I ..."

"Relax boys. I brought us home a stray," Mels announced. Somehow, she filled the entire entrance.

"For shame. Mels, get the poor thing some clothes," a high pitched, nasal voice said from behind a low table. The voice elongated the 's' sounds as it spoke.

I searched the gathered creatures and found a woman with clothing covering only the top half of her form. The bottom half shone with iridescent scales. They were entrancing. Her long brown hair flowed loose around her shoulders. Her sharp green eyes had slits like a snake. She slithered forward and I fought my hindbrain's command to flee. Snakes and birds are not friends.

She held up her hands. "I know, I must scare you. I'm Constance."

My gaze darted to the thick muscles of her tail and I took another step backward. "Snake."

"I'm not going to hurt you. Anyone who comes through those doors in need of help, gets it. No matter where they come from or their kind. If we don't look after one another, who will? Now, come with me. We'll get you cleaned up and sorted with some clothes." She glared at the other phoenix. "Xander, stop gawking like you've never seen a man before, you pervert. Make yourself useful and get him something to eat."

I looked over my shoulder at Mels. She nodded. If she believed I wouldn't be in immediate danger, I would trust her. She'd gotten me this far. I still wasn't sure I was safe. At least here, there were no gilded cages. As I followed Constance, careful to avoid stepping on her tail, the voice from the forest called again. It promised warmth and safety. But, Mels was right. It was a lure and I needed to resist it's pull. I couldn't let it ensnare me. If I gave in, I would be right back where I started. I had fought too hard for my freedom to turn back now.

FOUR

FOUR

LORELEI

The tracking part of my job was easy as long as the shifter kept his or her ankle monitor on. The second that puppy came off, the trickier my job became. Most shifters knew enough to dump the monitor as soon as they could. Bite it off … cut it off … You name it, I'd seen it. I tried not to get too attached to any of my bounties, because that made returning them to their gilded cages in the Booshie houses all the more difficult. Kegan was the one exception to that rule. I needed to eat, and PLA was good money. The only time I became attached—the only time I didn't do my job—was with Kegan.

Kegan. I tried not to think about him too much over the years, because it always made me want to go punch a tree or something. Kegan started out as a regular, straight forward bounty. Collect him, collect my reward. I tracked him via his ankle monitor and then, to lure him in, I sang my siren song. We're a phoenix's one known predator, thanks to our siren song. It subdues them, putting them into a trance where they'd do anything we asked them to. It worked for all men, really, but phoenixes were extra susceptible. It had something to do with the frequency of our song being potent to them. Usually with a bounty, it was easier for me if they stayed in shifted form. Returning a bird or other creature to its owner felt more like bringing a lost pet home. It felt like I was doing something good and noble. If they ever shifted to human, Gods help me, that's where it got tricky. Sending a humanoid home to be locked up in a gilded cage? Not as clear cut. I didn't know how many times Kegan escaped in the past, but he knew enough to shift into human form when I tracked him. Collecting a bird? Easy. Deciding what to do when faced with a gorgeous, naked dude who didn't want to return to captivity? Not so easy.

"Please," Kegan said the day we met. "Please, don't send me back there."

The please did it. I broke my siren song and let him convince me not to return him to his dotty old owner. The thing was, I ran off too. We ran off together and literally joined the circus. It was Kegan's idea. We called ourselves 'Phoenix & Siren.' I admit the act was a little cheesy, but most people had never seen any shifter up close and personal before. I sang and lured Kegan back to me a few times before we made a grand exit. It paid the bills at least … until the night Kegan was stolen.

I should have recognized Madame Faberge the second I saw her this morning. The memory of being knocked out after one of our nightly performances while Kegan was stolen, burned in my memory. It haunted my dreams to this day three years later. Since then, Madame Faberge's reliance on phoenix tears transformed her into a tight skinned toad of a woman instead of the face from my nightmares. I'd never send Kegan—or Aiden as she called him—back there. I just needed to find him first and then convince him I was on his side and not hers.

"Well, now, what do we have here?" I crouched down to retrieve a still operational ankle monitor. "Well played Kegan, but all this does is slow me down a little."

I closed my eyes and hummed. It was a tune older than any on record. It zeroed in on a male's basest nature and drew them to me. I didn't sense Kegan or any other phoenix nearby, but I sensed a male presence. An image flashed through my mind of a broad auburn-colored horse wading in some slough nearby. *Fuck.* A kelpie. Those Caledonian bastards never helped someone unless there was something in it for them. It made them great informants for the PLA, but not so great to do business with. My best informant was a kelpie named Douglas. We met just over two years ago when one of my siren sisters said he was the guy to go to if you were stuck on a case. He narked out fellow shifters for credits. I wasn't in the mood to part with any of my hard-earned credits so proposed a different payment system to Douglas. Being male, he welcomed my special brand of interrogation (read: seduction). We've worked together ever since. At least I called it work. He might call it something else. It was complicated. It was always complicated.

"You don't have to pretend," I called as I got closer to the water horse. "I know you're a kelpie." I flashed my PLA badge to show I meant business. "I'm looking for someone. Can you help me out, friend?"

"That depends," the horse's voice piped into my mind as if he spoke the words out loud instead of telepathically. "Are you gonna try to ensnare me in your siren song again?"

"Again?" I said out loud. "Douglas, is that you?"

The large horse shifted into a man with the same auburn hair and deep brown eyes as his horse form. He was of course naked. Not that I hadn't seen his particular brand of attributes before, but there was a time and place for it. In the middle of some Gods forsaken woods was not that time or place. "Good to see you again, Lorelei." He somehow exaggerated his already thick Scottish lilt. "You didn't get my last letter?"

"Letter?" I played dumb. "What letter? You know the mail system is crap, Douglas. If you want to get in touch, there are better ways than post." Ever since Kegan was stolen, my personal rule had been 'no strings.' There was no way in hell I'd be tethered to a kelpie of all creatures.

"Could you, uh, cover up or something?" I shielded my eyes.

"Why don't you come in?" he countered. "The water's fine."

"You know I don't like to shift while on a job." I kept my hand close to my eyes. "Just put some damn clothes on already, would you?"

"So, what's new?" Douglas stretched his arms over his head and did some weird leg press move to annoy me. "I thought you wanted to get out of the PLA."

"It pays the bills, okay? There are worse jobs to have."

"Sticking shifters back in cages is about the worst job you can have," he said. "Why don't you give it up? You talked about it the last time we were together."

"Because it's just about the only thing I'm really good at," I said. "You know that."

Douglas smiled. "I seem to recall something else you are really good at."

"Shut the hell up," I snapped. "And put on some clothes, will ya? This is pathetic ... even for you, Douglas."

"I like it when you yell my name."

I pulled one of my sharpened hair pins out of my braid and pointed it at him. "Say one more word and I will use this."

"The old weapons in the hair trick?" Douglas sighed as he reached for a pair of jeans and a t-shirt he'd laid across a bush near the slough. "You're so predictable, Lorelei."

I gripped the hair pin tighter. "No, I'm not."

"Yes, you are." He smiled, no doubt hoping he looked charming. "You never change. Same old Lorelei. Fight first, think later. What you failed to consider, though, is this may have been a trap from the word 'go.'"

I narrowed my eyes. "You wouldn't dare."

He lifted one auburn eyebrow. "Oh, wouldn't I? Try me."

I lowered my weaponized hair pin, confused. "What do you mean?"

Douglas stepped out of the water and walked toward me with deliberate, measured steps. The closer he got the harder it was to move or even think. My weapon fell out of my useless hand when he was two steps away. Fucking kelpie glamour magic! I should have known he'd try that old trick. I could bust out my own siren glamour to cancel his out, but pretending to be glamoured might be my best bet at finding Kegan. If I played things just right, I bet Douglas would lead me right to him.

Douglas lifted a hand and cupped the side of my face, fingers playing with loose tendrils of my blonde hair. "I'm almost sorry it was you they sent after the bird," he whispered. "I have no wish to hurt you. Mels was very clear though. Trap whoever comes looking for the bird."

"What do you know about the bird?" My lips barely moved as I spoke. The glamour was fading, but my limbs still felt heavy and useless from the persuasion magic.

"I know where he is," Douglas said. "I could take you to him right now if you wished. All you would have to do is renounce the PLA and all they stand for."

"It's my job," I said. "It's all I have."

"It's not all you have. There's more out there than the PLA."

Douglas' natural lilt seemed stronger—more persuasive. I wanted to give in. I wanted to tell him anything he wanted to hear if it meant getting to Kegan. I closed my eyes, trying to break contact with his mind games. Some kelpie magic bullshit would not control me. I was stronger than that. I smiled, deciding to play his old standby—act like you're glamoured then turn the situation to your advantage.

"Yes," I forced my voice into a sing-song, dream like quality. "So much more out there than the PLA. So much more for you to show me, Douglas."

He blinked hard, confused at my sudden turn-around, before grinning at his so-called 'success.' "Yes. Yes. So much more."

Douglas caressed my cheek, his fingers trailing a path down my neck and across my collarbone. My body gave an involuntary jerk as a jolt of something I will not name in connection to a kelpie coursed through my veins. I leaned into him, pressing a kiss against his lips. He tasted like seaweed and fish. Gross. He dug his fingers into my hips and pulled me closer. I let him, all in the name of playing along to get to Kegan, before I pulled away.

"Take me to the bird," I requested. "I want to help him, Doug, not hurt him."

He watched me through hazy eyes, trying to catch his breath, before nodding. "As you wish. I like it when you call me Doug."

I smiled, taking his hand as if we were some fucked up couple out for an afternoon picnic. "Duly noted. Lead the way ... Doug."

FIVE

FIVE

AIDEN

Constance led me deeper into the structure and I realized it was far larger than it appeared from the outside. I said nothing as she slithered around the space, filling a large basin with steaming water. The more time I spent in this form, the more words came back to me. She looked at me. "You got something on your mind? We don't hold our tongues here. You better speak up."

Even though the words were returning I still wasn't certain how to express my thoughts to her. "Your form ... you are a snake."

She smiled, her lips curling up past fangs I had not noticed before. "Nothing gets by you."

I shook my head. "No ... I mean you are only part snake now. Why?"

She cocked her head to one side, dark locks of hair falling over one shoulder. "Ah. I see. In this place, we are free to be who and what we want. For some, that means remaining in their shifted form. For others, they prefer their human guise. It allows them to move more freely throughout the world." She gestured to her upper body. "I happen to be myself like this."

I pondered her statement for a moment. I could not exist partially in one state and partially in another. I had not tried to do so, but something deep down told me it was not possible. Or at the very least, it was not safe for my kind to exist partially in either world. Constance pointed to the basin.

"Get in. I'll leave you to get cleaned up."

I shuffled forward and stared at the unbroken surface of the water now filling the basin. I wanted to hide my embarrassment about not understanding her instruction, but her hiss of laughter signaled she had seen it.

"They forced you to stay shifted, didn't they?" Her tone softened.

"Yes."

"How long?"

Time was still a foreign concept for my human brain. "A long time."

She slid around the basin and guided me into the water. I gave a hiss of my own as the heat scalded my flesh. She squeezed my hand tight until the sensation subsided. I let her run a soft cloth over the wound on my leg. Every movement was gentle. No one had shown me such kindness in a very long time.

"We will look out for you," she whispered as she passed me the cloth and gestured for me to clean the rest of my body.

Assuming I was capable enough to wash, she slithered from the room. I closed my eyes and let the warmth of the water wrap around me. For a brief time, I let my mind drift where it desired. A face flashed in my memory, fair haired and beautiful. I couldn't shake the sense there was supposed to be some other emotion tied to her face.

"Don't drown in there," the other phoenix—Xander—said, drawing me from the silence and away from the woman's image.

I opened my eyes to find him standing beside the basin, a bundle of clothing held in his arms. This time, I took the cloth and used it to cover myself. He smiled at me, as if he found all of this amusing. Perhaps it was because I had spent so long away from my own kind, but I could not recall ever meeting any bird like him. It was as if he was preening, trying to catch my attention.

"You look different." I pointed to his hair.

He set the clothes on a low table. "Consider it a

self-defense mechanism. I can cover up my markings and pass for straight up human." He laughed. "Well, human anyway."

"Oh." I couldn't hide the pain from the wounds on my back.

"Here. Let me help you," he said holding out his hand.

I blinked up at him, unsure what he wanted from me. After a moment, he grabbed the cloth from the water leaving me exposed. He bent behind me and ran the cloth over my neck and shoulders. I expected his size to translate to rough movements, but like Constance, he was gentle. He pushed me forward and trailed the cloth down my back. His fingertips brushed my bare skin and an unexpected emotion raced through me. It sparked feelings familiar in any form. Feelings I should not be feeling. I pulled away from his touch and staggered out of the basin, splashing water onto the floor. I reached for the clothing when Constance appeared.

"You, out," she snapped at Xander.

They shared a heated look before Xander tossed the cloth into the basin and stormed out. Constance shook her head. "He doesn't know what's good for him."

Her appearance had quelled the feelings within me. She handed me a soft towel and I dried myself before dressing. The simple mechanics of human existence were returning more and more.

"Do you have any family we should try to connect you with?" she asked as I pulled the shirt over my head.

Did I have family? I couldn't remember. And somehow, that made sense. There are some things innate for my kind. Fundamental aspects of what it is to be a phoenix. One such truth is that we may be gifted with many lives, but they are separate and distinct. "No. No family," I replied. Despite her kindness, Constance was still a stranger and one with whom I did not feel comfortable sharing this vital piece of information.

A commotion drew Constance's attention and she leaned out of the doorway. "Douglas is back. Come on, let's see what he's brought home this time."

I followed her back to the main room. Someone had laid out a bowl of food. My stomach rumbled, a painful reminder I had not eaten in this form in what was probably years. I reached for it, but stopped when the tall man stepped aside to reveal our newest guest. The woman from my memory stood before me. I had not imagined her. Now if only I could remember who she was and why she felt so important to me.

SIX

SIX

LORELEI

Even though Madame Faberge had shown me a photo of her pet, "Aiden" that I knew as Kegan, part of me expected it to not be him. I had spent so many minutes, hours, and years waiting for this moment—for this reunion—now that it was here, I didn't know what to do. Usually I would just bag and tag my mark, but Kegan was different. Kegan was always different. Here he was, though he just stared past me as if he didn't know me. I couldn't wait any longer. I needed to hold him and touch him again.

"Kegan?" I dropped my pretense of being glamoured. I ran past Douglas and threw my arms around Kegan. He continued to stand with his hands to his side. *Ok, not the reaction I expected.*

Wasn't he happy to see me? Maybe he blamed me for not coming to rescue him sooner. I pulled back and searched his blank face.

"What's wrong?" I asked. "I've been searching three years for you. I swear, I never gave up. No matter how many dead ends I hit, I kept looking." Tears sprang to my eyes when he continued to stare at some unknown spot over my shoulder. He seemed more interested in the door than me. "I kept looking. I swear."

"He doesn't remember you, Lorelei."

Douglas—all bravado, but secretly sensitive—sounded sympathetic before peeling my arms from Kegan. Douglas held me against himself with one arm across my chest in case I made a run for Kegan again. I didn't bother to struggle nor did I tell him to move his arm or lose it. All I could think of was the blankness in Kegan's eyes. Did he really not re-member me at all?

"You of all creatures should know how it works with phoenixes," Douglas continued. "Each new life means he forgets his old one. You're part of his old life, *M'eudail*."

I sagged against Douglas. "But we ... but we talked about it before. Kegan said he'd always re-member me, no matter what." I watched Kegan pace from foot to foot. He looked scared, broken, and confused. Is that what three years of captivity did to him?

"I ... I have one memory of your face," he offered. "That is all. I'm sorry. For your sake, I wish it were more."

"Nothing? Nothing at all?" Feeling lost and defeated my knees buckled. I would have fallen if Douglas didn't still have a hold of me.

"I'm sorry," Kegan repeated. "Nothing at all."

I DON'T REMEMBER LOSING consciousness. I remember waking up on a mattress thrown on the floor. It was away from the main room of wherever Douglas had led me to after leaving the woods. I sat up, rubbing my head.

"I'm sorry. I thought I should stay with you ... I felt it was my duty."

I turned to my right at the sound of Kegan's voice. "I can take care of myself."

He smiled. It was the same smile that still haunted my dreams, but now seemed to belong to a stranger. "I am sure you can. I merely wished to sit with you. That is all."

"Why?" I felt like I should cover up, even though I was fully clothed. I didn't want this stranger in Kegan's body looking at me.

He cocked his head to the side, the gesture looking more bird-like than human. "You were important to him. I know that, even if I don't remember being him. I'm Aiden, by the way. That's my name now."

I couldn't help the rueful laugh that escaped my lips. "Really, that's what your owner called you. What name would you pick for yourself?"

"Aiden," he said. "You say my owner picked it, but I picked it for myself when I was reborn. It is who I am now, Aiden."

I leaned forward on the bed, searching his face for any spark of recognition from his life before as Kegan. *Still nothing.* "Is that what happened when they took you from me?" I asked. "Did they make you rise from the ashes to ensure you'd forget everything?"

He was silent as he pondered the question. "I believe so. All I remember is Aiden, not him."

"Kegan." I lifted my chin, hoping it didn't betray my emotions by shaking. "His name is Kegan."

"Was Kegan," the stranger in Kegan's body corrected. "Again, I am sorry for your loss. That's what it feels like, doesn't it? A loss of someone you used to know?"

"A loss of someone I loved." I wiped at my damp eyes. "Ugh. It feels like the last three years of my life and career have been a waste. I have been chasing a ghost this whole time, haven't I? Someone I'd never find?"

"I'm sorry." He spread his hands in front of him, palm-side up. "I wish I had a better answer for you, but I do not. I *do* have one memory of his. It's of you. Your hair is loose, falling around your shoulder and down your back in waves. You are wearing a white, flowing gown with flowers in your hair. You smile at him. Your happiness makes him feel the same way. I'm sorry. I wish I could give you more."

"So, part of me stuck with you, even through the burning?"

He nodded. "He didn't want to let you go. Of that, I am certain."

"But you're not him?" I wanted to hear him say it one more time. Maybe if I heard it one more time, I might believe it.

"No," he said. "I am Aiden. I wish I could give you the answer you wanted."

I rubbed at my eyes again. "Yeah? Looks like I'm gonna have to come up with different wishes."

SEVEN

SEVEN

AIDEN

I left Lorelei resting in the back room and returned to the main hall to find Mels, Constance and several others. They all turned their attention to me as I stepped into view.

"She's got to go," Mels said.

"I don't understand," I replied, words coming more easily the longer I remained human.

Mels rolled her eyes and closed the distance between us. She placed one hand on either side of my face and squeezed. "You poor dumb birdie. Don't you know what she is? Don't you get why she's here?"

"She knows me. Or used to know the one I was before who I am now."

Constance slithered up beside me and with a

less than gentle nudge of her tail, sent Mels stumbling sideways. "Dear, that woman in there is a Siren. Their sole purpose in life is to hunt your kind and enslave them. She will send you back to wherever it is you escaped from and collect a hefty sum for her work. She is your enemy."

If that were true, why would she claim to care for me? "I don't believe you."

"I've known Lorelei a long time. They're telling you the truth. Hunting your kind is what she does. But I also know she went off the grid a few years back and the rumor was she fell for one of her marks. For you, I think. Whatever we do with her now should be your choice," said the tall man who smelled of the sea and horses.

His words carried a sense of logic, but, I knew nothing of this woman. How could I decide her fate? And if I told them to send her away, what would that mean for her and for me? I did not believe she would go without what she came for. As I stood there in silence, I tried to recall anything I could of our time together. Only that one memory remained and even now, it slipped farther and farther from where I could hold onto it.

"I ... I want to remember her," I announced.

"That isn't possible. It's like wired into your DNA that you forget everything that came before," Mels pointed out.

"I recalled her face as someone important before we met here today. I have one fleeting memory of her. It must still be there. If I make this choice for her, I want to remember her first."

Beside me, Constance let out a hissing sigh. "I may have a way, but I do not guarantee it will work. It is dangerous."

"Please try," I begged.

"Better make yourself comfortable."

WE RETREATED to a different back room, a short distance from where Lorelei remained hidden away. A part of me wanted to tell her what we were about to do, but I did not wish to give her false hope. With so many bodies, the room felt cramped and cage-like. Panic coursed through me and my breathing became shallow. "Too many people," I rasped.

"Mels, wait outside," Constance ordered.

"No way! I found him, I'm keeping an eye on him."

Constance bared her fangs in an all-too-snake-like manner. "You aren't who I need right now. Go check on our other guest and for the sake of all that is good in this world, don't kill each other."

Mels pouted, but turned on her heel and

marched from the room. I caught the tiniest flutter of her gossamer wings as she disappeared. That left the horse and Xander. Just thinking his name made me flush.

"I know, I should go too," Xander said before Constance could shoo him away.

"No. You stay. He will need his own kind to pull him out, if he goes too deep."

I said nothing as our eyes met. He smiled and patted my arm. That left the horse, Douglas. He remained sentry by the door, facing out into the hall. I suspected he would rather have gone with Mels, but given that Constance had not dismissed him, he stayed.

"Now, I will need you to lean back and try to relax," Constance whispered. She settled beside me on the bed.

"What are you going to do?" I pressed.

She took my right hand in hers. "I need you to look into my eyes. Nowhere else. Just there. Can you do that?"

I nodded and turned my full attention to her. I had marveled at the beauty of her scales before, but I had been blind to the mesmerizing shimmer of her irises.

"Good. Keep breathing. Now, think about her. Focus and think about Lorelei." Her words were miles away.

I brought the one image I had of Lorelei that had been *his* to my mind's eye. I could feel something in the back of my mind urging me to go deeper, to follow wherever that image led. She held out a hand and I took it. Our surroundings changed, but they were mostly a blur. Nothing else solidified until, for just a moment, I glimpsed us wrapped in an embrace. My lips pressed tight to her neck while we moved as one. I stared, taking it in. The intimacy, the connection. I needed to follow that back until I remembered what it felt like to hold her and kiss her.

And then it changed.

No longer was Lorelei's body wrapped in mine. A larger, male form had taken her place. He turned his head as the image of me continued to trail kisses along his throat. Xander's bright eyes sparkled as he smiled at me. That same smile he'd given when we'd first met. His hands clutched at my body, pulling tighter, a look of pure desire on his face.

"Pull him out now!" Constance's voice was sharp.

I felt pressure on the left side of my body and as I opened my eyes, the memory—or whatever it had become—faded, replaced by the trappings of the room. Xander sat beside me, my left hand clasped between both of his hands. His cheeks were damp and I could feel the cool, soothing touch of a tear as it pooled in my fist.

"Did it work?" Douglas asked from his post at the doorway.

I knew I needed to let Lorelei stay. It was the surest way to ensure my freedom, at least for a while longer. I did not wish to lie to these people who had so graciously taken me into their ranks and accepted me as one of their own. But I could not admit what I had seen. So, I would tell them what everyone expected to hear. I would give Lorelei a second chance with the man she'd loved.

"I remember her. I remember loving her. She stays."

EIGHT

EIGHT

LORELEI

This place smelled like a damn zoo. If the Booshies ever wanted more pets, all they'd need to do is find this place ... whatever this place was. Phoenixes were worth the most credits, but any shifter was worth something to Booshies looking to pay. The ultra-rich were so predictable. They loved to one-up their supposed friends and family. If their neighbor had a doxy, they needed a doxy. If their brother had a unicorn, well they wanted a unicorn. I liked to focus on Phoenix location, because of my personal search for Kegan. I could make a killing in the credits department if I ever branched out more.

The place smelled *and* the bed was uncomfortable. That's hospitality for you. I wasn't expecting some Booshie feather bed or anything, but not being poked by bedsprings would be nice. I sighed and flipped over onto my back. That was worse. I could feel the metal coils just under the surface of the mattress dig into my back instead of my side. I stared at the water damaged ceiling in the little cell of a room they'd put me in. It was night time—I could tell, because it was darker than usual and all the sounds of activity outside the door—I wouldn't think of it as *my* door—quieted. Could the others sleep like this?

I sat up and unzipped a pocket on the front of my black PLA vest. I pulled out the phoenix feather Madame Faberge gave me at the start of the hunt. Tracking was easy. All I needed to do was hold on to an object owned by the mark, hum my siren song, and follow where the song led me. I felt it like a pull, as if I were following an invisible thread to my mark. As long as I held on to the object, I could find anyone, anywhere.

I stroked the soft red and gold vanes of the feather. His name was Aiden now, not Kegan. I needed to remember that. He wasn't the bird I knew. He was a stranger. But that didn't mean I didn't want to know where they put him or if he was okay. I held on tight to the feather and hummed. The song pulled me to my feet, led me down a darkened hallway past a row of doors, before I stopped in front of the last door on the right. I let the song die on my lips before I pushed the door open a crack with my toe. It was unlocked. I doubted any of the doors in this rundown building had the ability to lock.

The room was bigger than the one I snuck out from. Two sets of bunk beds with a wooden dresser between them occupied the slanting, dirty floor. There were no windows and only one door in or out. The four occupants—maybe more—must share a communal bathroom. Aiden slept on the bottom bunk to the left of the door. He flung his arm over his face like a bird shielding his head under his wing. Old habits die hard, I guess. The good thing was he was asleep and, more than that, peaceful. I had forgotten what it was like to sleep without nightmares jolting me awake. Maybe now those nightmares could be replaced by the image of him peaceful. *Did he need me to find him? Had he ever needed me in the first place?*

I returned the feather to my zippered pocket. I pulled the zipper down the front of my vest and dug around in the hidden inner pocket where I kept secret crap-I didn't-want-anyone-to-know-I-had. I liked to swipe stuff from informants so I'd always have a way to lead me back to them. It was strictly for professional reasons, or so I told myself. How many times had I held the little coppery coin with the hole in the middle in my hands and thought about tracking its owner for non-strictly professional reasons? Once or twice or, okay, maybe half a dozen times I had broken down and hummed my siren song while holding this coin, but I'm not proud of it. When you tell yourself, you're looking for someone else, you don't want to keep showing up at the same damn shifter bar with paper thin excuses. I don't need the coin to lead me to the bar this time. I just needed it to show me which room was Douglas' in this crap hole shifter base.

"Stupid kelpie," I muttered before humming. "This doesn't mean what you think it means."

My feet jerked me back down the way I came before making a sharp left. There were less doors down this hall and spaced further apart. I counted four before I stopped short in front of number five. My song died on my lips again. I debated if I wanted to knock. Knocking was polite and I wasn't exactly known for my politeness.

"Doug?" I called. "You awake?"

No answer. I nudged the door open with my toe. A shaft of light from the flickering overhead light in the hall illuminated a single bed and dresser with a lamp and chipped wash basin on top. The room was around the size of the one I left, but it had a second door leading to a private bathroom. Huh.

Douglas must be moving up in the shifter world if he had his own room with a bathroom.

I stepped into the room and shut the door behind me. The only light now came from underneath the bathroom door. I heard water shut off. *Shit.* I had terrible timing.

Douglas entered his bedroom from the bathroom, toweling his coppery hair dry. At least he wore plaid pajama pants this time. Thank the Gods for small favors.

"Lorelei?" Douglas' hands stilled, towel on his head. "What are you doing here?"

I shoved the coin back in my secret crap-I-don't-want-people-to-know-I-have pocket before he could see it. "Don't get all excited, horse face. I'm just here to talk."

"About what?" He threw his towel toward the bathroom before turning back to me. "I stuck up for you, you know." He cocked his head to the side, considering his own words. "Well, more like I was diplomatic on your behalf. Mels wanted you gone outright, but, in the end, Aiden decided you should stay."

"Is Mels that doxy bitch just itching to bite me?" I asked. "You could do better than her, Douglas."

"I'm not doing anything with her, Lorelei," he said. "You know where my loyalties lie."

"With yourself?" I guessed. "I mean, why else turn informant and give up your fellow shifters? You like a payday just as much as I do."

"We all gotta eat," Douglas drawled, his Scottish lilt more pronounced. "Isn't that what you like to say, Lore?"

"Don't call me that." I sat on his bed without bothering to ask if it was okay with him or not. I didn't really care how he felt one way or the other about me being here. Judging by his reaction, though, I made him nervous. Douglas stuck his hands in his pockets before taking them out and crossing his arms over his bare chest. He repeated his fidgeting a second time before asking, "What do you want, Lorelei?"

"I told you, Douglas. I just want to talk."

"About what?" He repeated himself and sat down next to me. The narrow bed shifted under our combined weight, making me slide into him. Douglas wrapped an arm around my waist, fingers splayed possessively across my hip, to steady me. I blinked, my mind going blank. Why wasn't he letting go? He should let go.

"I'm not sure," I admitted. "I mean, I thought I knew but now I don't anymore. This has been a weird day. I couldn't sleep. I guess I just wanted to see a semi-friendly face."

A grin spread across his face, his teeth a little

more pronounced than what was considered normal thanks to the water horse side of him. "You couldn't sleep, so you came here? *M'eudail*, if you want to stay over, all you need to do is ask."

I punched his shoulder. "Don't get any ideas, horse face. When I say talk, I mean talk."

"Of course you do, fish fins."

If I could punch that smug grin off his face, I would. Instead, I diverted back to the question I remembered I wanted to ask. "So, where are we?" I gestured at the darkened room. "What do you call this place?"

"The Magical Creature Underground," he said. "It's an abandoned hospital from before the wars, but more than that, it's a place where shifters and all forms of magical creatures can gather in peace for the better good of all. There's no judgement here. It's a safe place for all who need it."

"How noble of you." I did a terrible job of keeping the sarcasm from my voice. "When did you go all good instead of neutral, Douglas?"

"Since I found out how bad it was for the ones kept in captivity."

Douglas watched me in the dim light. I couldn't quite figure out the emotion that flashed across his brown eyes before it was gone. Regret, maybe, or pity. Did he pity me for continuing to do my government job? A shifter hunting other shifters for money didn't exactly fit the Magical Creature Underground's mission statement.

"Do you want me to go?" I asked.

"Do you mean tonight or for forever?" He shrugged one shoulder. "Neither, but it's not up to just me. Mels, Constance, and Xander have a say as well. Aiden is the ultimate voice of your fate, though."

"Do you think the Kegan I knew is well and truly gone from him, Douglas? Don't lie," I added. "You have never lied to me yet. I don't want you to start now."

Douglas cupped my face between his hands. "Yes, *M'eudail*, I think Kegan is gone. My advice is to learn who he is as Aiden and ... see from there."

See from there. I let the suggestion roll around in my mind. It's not like I knew Kegan that well before we ran off together almost four years ago, either. Aiden was a stranger, but he didn't have to be. Maybe I could learn to love him like I learned to love Kegan.

What about Douglas? My stupid mind betrayed me. I placed my hands over where his still rested on my cheeks. I squeezed, hoping that conveyed a little of what I didn't dare say or even think, before I removed his hands. I pressed a quick kiss into his palm before letting go. "Hey, Douglas, can I stay here tonight?" I asked. "You know I don't like the dark. That's when the nightmares come."

"I remember." He laid on the bed in answer, pulling me down until my back rested against his front. "Good night, fish fins."

"Good night, horse face."

NINE

NINE

AIDEN

My first sleep as a human made me wish for the dreams of a bird. Then, at least, I could not recall the terrors that haunted me. In my mind, I was back in the cage, but this time, in my human form. The woman who'd kept me caged against my will, laughed and mocked me. I tried to free myself, but the bars remained locked, solid against my efforts.

I woke with a start, slick, cool sweat covering my body. I shivered in the darkness, grateful to be free of the nightmare. I wasn't certain what roused me until I heard muffled voices beyond the room. I dragged myself from beneath the thin blankets and followed the sounds out the back of the building to find Mels, Douglas and several others in an open field wreathed by tall trees. The sky was pitch dark as it always was, day or night. But, just below the tree line, I spotted a majestic bird. At first glance, it appeared to be a phoenix though as it swooped low and took a pass above our heads, I could see its plumage was solid gold with thin strands of vibrant orange at the tips of its feathers.

A sunbird.

"Welcome to the party, birdie," Mels said, her lips parted into a smile that bared all of her sharp, poison-covered teeth.

"What is going on?" My voice was sluggish.

"Most nights, when the humans have gone to sleep, we come out and run free," Douglas answered.

Lorelei trailed him. She kept her distance from everyone, although our gazes met. She quickly let her eyes drop. I was still new to reading human emotion, but I could swear she appeared guilty. I couldn't fathom what would have brought out such a reaction.

Before I could speak, the sunbird let out a wild screech and its feathers glistened with radiant light. Light none of us had seen in years, possibly decades like before the wars turned the atmosphere to ash. Constance slithered up next to me and smiled.

"Micah reminds us of what it used to be like in this world. Now, enjoy his gift. Feel the sun on your wings." With barely a hiss, her upper body shrunk down, melting into the thick trunk of her snake's body. The clothing she'd worn pooled to the ground. Her tongue flickered at me, as if she was giving me an encouraging smile before she darted off among the grasses.

I had spent so long in my shifted form, fear rooted me to the spot. I could only watch as Mels shrunk to no larger than my smallest finger. She zipped around my head, buzzing with glee before she too, took off into the woods.

"Come on, fish fins. Let loose," Douglas called to Lorelei as he took off at a gallop. He shed his shirt and pants, leaving himself naked.

I'd never seen anyone transition forms mid-motion. Douglas' spine lengthened and his arms turned into the front hooves of a horse. A sleek coat of copper covered his entire body and as he approached a shallow pool of water by the edge of the trees, he let out a neigh. Lorelei remained where she stood. My own apprehension didn't seem so out of place now. I should go to her and make her feel less unwanted. But I still couldn't move.

"You aren't alone anymore," Xander said, approaching from the far end of the clearing.

"Forgive me if I don't wish to be in a form, they forced me to keep," I whispered.

Xander's chin dipped as my words hit him. "I

didn't think about that. I ... I've never been in that situation."

I blinked at him. "Never? In none of your lives?"

He shook his head. "I've been lucky that Mels and Constance found me when I was young. They've kept me safe during my risings. I've always been free. I've met others of our kind who weren't so lucky, but they've come and gone. And they never flew with me. I just want to fly with one of my own. Just once."

The sadness in his tone touched me and I knew if I refused him, it would break him. And in some small way, it would break me too. And I could not be afraid of my other self. I was as much a bird as a man. If I could not be comfortable in feathers and flight, then I wasn't truly *me*.

"I will fly with you," I said.

Xander beamed and tugged his shirt over his head, exposing a well-muscled abdomen. He caught me looking and flashed that flirty smile. I turned my back to avoid watching him completely remove his clothing. The wind against my back signaled he transformed and now waited for me to join him. Lorelei crossed the short distance between us.

"You okay doing this?" The concern in her eyes begged me for some recognition. Like somehow, she understood my trepidation.

"If we cannot be our true selves, then how can we ever be free," I answered and removed my clothing.

She had the decency to avert her gaze as I prepared for the transformation. Before I let the shift take me over, I saw her shed her pants and wade waist-deep into the pool. She shivered from head to toe and then beautiful fins appeared where legs had been a moment ago.

Lorelei's acceptance of this activity spurred me onward. I closed my eyes and stretched my arms out to the side, calling to beak and feather to engulf me and make me whole. Even before my life of confinement, I could recall the ease with which I could change forms. Now though, the shift fought me. Bones refused to melt into their proper shape, sending tendrils of pain through my core. Above me, Xander whirled in a lazy circle, waiting for me. He swooped low and nudged my shoulder with a large wing.

"I'm trying," I said, knowing in his current state he couldn't understand me.

I felt a drop of something damp against my bare skin and a warmth spread through me; a healing tear. This was the second time in as many days he had given me this gift. He shouldn't be wasting them on me. I would need to remind him of that when we both walked on two legs again. For the moment, I let its power guide me and in moments I, too, took flight, letting the invisible swells in the air carry us both higher.

We darted together amongst the trees and chased one another just below the sunbird's warm glow. It had been so long since I had felt able to enjoy my existence in this form. Xander let out a loud call and I answered him in kind. We were a matched pair and he was beautiful.

Without warning, my wings grew sluggish, unable to keep me aloft and I plummeted towards the ground. Having so recently been human, that brain kicked in and I transformed. My legs lengthened and the feathers receded, but I could not stop the momentum and tumbled to the ground with a pained grunt.

"What happened?" a flurry of voices called.

My head throbbed and the world blinked in and out of existence. I could make out Xander and Lorelei crowding around me before they too, vanished.

TEN

TEN
TEN

LORELEI

I hated waiting. It didn't matter what for—pay day, new case assignment, food ration delivery— if there was a wait, I always ended up feeling like I was one second away from stabbing someone in the eye with my weaponized hairpins. Now, I sat alone in the hallway outside of wherever they took Aiden. This cold, plastic chair made me want to punch someone and *then* stab them. Hell, I'd settle for kicking someone in the face. I needed to get some energy out and violence was always my best medicine.

I closed my eyes so I didn't have to see the flurry of activity in the room behind me and imagine the worst for Aiden. What did they call the room again before bringing him back? An operating room? An examination room? I couldn't remember. The only thing that kept replaying in my mind was watching him shift from phoenix to man midair and falling. That couldn't have been on purpose. Which left the question: What went wrong?

Douglas sat down next to me. Oh great. Just the person I didn't want to see right now. He reached for my hand before thinking better of it and pulling back. "I have an update for you," he said.

"Unless you have answers, I don't want to hear it."

"Micah is a doctor." This time Douglas put his hand on top of mine and squeezed. "He ran some scans and thinks he has pinpointed the issue that made Aiden, well, that made Aiden fall from the sky like he did."

"You seriously want me to believe whatever Dr. Sunbird says?" I scowled and yanked my hand free. I pulled my knees up to my chest and wrapped my arms around my legs to stop Douglas from trying to touch me again.

"Don't you want to know what he found?"

"I don't care what he found," I said. "Aiden needs real doctors in a real facility in the City. Whatever's wrong, you don't have the resources to take care of him here. He needs the best. I doubt the sunbird is the best."

"Micah found something called 'blood graft' in

Aiden's system," Douglas continued as if I said 'sure, tell me all about what the bird's scans showed.' *Asshole.*

"Blood graft?"

"It's a poison. Micah says he knows Booshies feed their magical pets—especially shifters—the blood graft to keep them drugged up and docile. He says it's to cut down on escape efforts. It's faster acting when they're in animal form. When you're bigger—when you're human—it's slower. Micah thinks that's one reason Aiden has been so foggy since we found him. The blood graft is working through his system."

"Is there a cure?" Knowing Booshies, the poison was more than likely fatal, but I needed to ask. I needed to know.

Douglas spread his hands out in front of him, palms up. "Only one. The Khalas root, but it only grows in one place."

"Then we go get it."

"It's not as easy as that, *M'eudail,*" Douglas said. "Khalas root only grows in one spot—the shifter haven town of Sanctuary. We're not even sure that place exists. It's a bit of a myth. It's the sort of place everyone talks about but no one has ever seen."

"What about the black market?" I asked. "You can buy anything on the black market. We have to try *something,* Douglas," I insisted when he continued to sit silent next to me, not even bothering to offer placating comforts. "We can't just let him die."

"We'll do everything we can, Lore, but prepare yourself for the possibility of losing him twice."

I shifted until I was curled up against Douglas' side instead of balled up in my own anger and helplessness. The damned kelpie may be an opportunist with a far too high opinion of his skills with the ladies, but being near him made my mind shut down. Everything went quiet, and I could relax. Gods help me, I needed that right now.

"Do you think the doctor will let me see Aiden soon?" I whispered.

"He's still asleep." Douglas tested the waters by putting an arm around my shoulders. When I didn't punch or stab him, he relaxed. "Xander is keeping watch over him right now. He's safe. He's in good hands."

I frowned. "How much do you know about this Xander bird?"

"He's free range," Douglas said. "Never been in captivity. He's been part of the MCU a helluva lot longer than I have. I *think* Mels found him as a hatchling, but don't quote me on that, *M'eudail*."

"May-dal." I said the word like he pronounced it instead of I'm guessing how it was spelled thanks to his crazy, ass-backwards native language. "You keep calling me that. You have since we first met. What does it mean?"

He squirmed, seeming uncomfortable with the fact I called him out on his secret code word. "That's unimportant now. Let's focus on Aiden's health."

Aiden's health. I already lost him once. I didn't want to lose him again.

ELEVEN

ELEVEN

AIDEN

I woke to the feeling of a soft pillow beneath my head. The evening's activities rushed back to me and my heart hammered in my chest at the memory of plummeting to the ground again. My lungs burned as I tried to suck in air and failed. I sat up, clawing to get free of the blankets when a firm hand gripped my shoulder.

"Slow down, there. You need to rest," Xander said.

"What happened?" I said through ragged breaths. I was growing tired of not knowing what was happening in my own existence.

"You fell." The shortness of his answer told me there was much more he wasn't saying.

"I remember that. Why did I fall?" I looked him in the eye.

"That Booshie bitch who locked you up, poisoned you with blood graft."

"Poison?" My throat went dry.

Xander nodded. "Micah says it's better if you stay in human form. It's slower acting because of your size. Eventually it will get to your heart and ..."

I tried to remember anything about being fed poison, but nothing came to mind. Could this vile substance alter memories in addition to forcing me out of my shift? I wanted to pepper Xander with questions, but the fear that made his eyes shine with tears warned not to press him. The fact he couldn't finish his sentence also signaled my prognosis was grim.

"You worried the siren," he muttered.

"She still thinks I'm her lost love."

He let out a harsh laugh. "You sure about that? She's awfully cozy with Douglas. I saw her slip into his room earlier tonight. She may say she's all about getting you back, but she sure doesn't act like you matter worth a damn."

I considered Xander's statements. If they were true, the guilt I saw on her face earlier made sense. Her actions only confused me. Sure, she'd appeared ready to take me back to the woman who'd kept me, but she also expressed happiness at our reunion. I may not remember much about her, still I couldn't find a reason to doubt her feelings for me. I also decided to try and rekindle things with her, even if I hadn't shared that with her, yet. Shouldn't I be jealous of the time she spent with another man? Was I jealous?

"She can spend her time with whomever she pleases," I answered, my heart returning to a normal rhythm. I wanted to believe my own words.

"You really think that?" he challenged.

I sighed. "I am not the man she loved. I am willing to try if she is. I have to accept what we had was tied to who I used to be, not who I am now."

Xander grew quiet and pulled his hand away from my shoulder. I took the break in the conversation to study him. I could see hints of red poking through the dark locks on his head and he was still bare chested, despite having retrieved his pants. My confusion over Lorelei's actions paled compared to my confusion over his. Not that I could remember interacting with many of my own kind, but I felt certain I had never met a male phoenix who made passes at another male.

"Why are you here?" I whispered, afraid of his answer.

"Because this is a safe place for us. I'm with people I trust and they allow me to be who I am, no matter who that is."

"I meant here with me."

"Micah said you shouldn't be left alone. Mels and Constance had other things to attend to and they didn't trust leaving you with *her*." Xander said the last part with disdain.

"I'm fine, now. You don't have to stay." Part of me wanted to be alone to contemplate my impending death. Still part of me wished he would stay. Glimpses of the image of him from Constance's hypnosis danced in my vision.

"I can tell you have something you want to say to me. So, just say it. We don't keep secrets here."

"I don't understand you. You act like you want to be my mate or something but that makes no sense. That's not how it works."

He smiled and for the first time it wasn't flirty. I couldn't quite put a name to it. "Funny thing about being reborn; it changes things you wouldn't expect. I've been told on more than a few occasions after my risings, I've been attracted to women, although I feel like my most honest self when I'm attracted to men."

Had I felt that same attraction before now? I silently cursed our kind's inability to recall our past lives. Before I could speak, he leaned forward. Breath caught in my throat as he pressed his lips to mine. His tongue fought to slip between my lips. My shock allowed the moment to last longer than I intended before I pushed him away. I felt heat burning in my cheeks. I wanted to believe it was embarrassment, but that look of desire I'd seen in my hypnotic state pointed a different direction.

"Go. Please just go." I couldn't feel this for him.

Anger turned his facial features sharp and angular. "You can't hide who you are forever."

"I need to see Lorelei. Send her in. Now." I would prove to myself and to Xander that there was no real attraction between us. There was a woman who desperately wanted to love me and I would let her.

TWELVE
TWELVE

LORELEI

"Hey, Aiden, how are you feeling?" I was proud of myself for using his name now instead of slipping back into the past. "That was a nasty fall you took outside."

"And an even nastier poison is coursing through my system."

He struggled to sit up in the surprisingly clean hospital bed before giving up and collapsing against the pillows. I picked my way across the floor around the scattered medical equipment. Before the shifters claimed this place as their home base, it looked like someone left in a hurry. Either that or someone looted it looking for a fix or something valuable to sell on the black market. Medicines didn't come cheap. You could make credits hand over fist selling them on the black market.

"Sit." Aiden patted a spot next to him on the narrow bed. "You said you never gave up looking for me over the years, yet we have barely spent any time together now that you found me."

"I thought you might need some space to adjust." I sat where he indicated, my feet dangling over the edge of the bed. "You seemed confused. I wanted to give you time to clear your mind if you needed to."

"Tell me something you remember from our previous time together," he requested.

I watched him while trying to decide what story to tell. His fiery hair stood out against the white of the pillow. The blood graft must have worked quickly while in Phoenix form. Hours ago, he was vibrant. Now his eyes were sunken and rimmed with dark circles, his skin ashen. He breathed through his mouth as if even keeping his chest rising and falling was an effort.

"What don't I remember?" I answered. "You loved to laugh. Even if the joke was terrible, you'd still laugh. Maybe, it was more you liked to be happy. You liked being free. That's what I remember most. How happy you were to be free."

"But then it ended."

"Not by choice," I said. "I would have tracked

you the second Madame Faberge took you, but that's not how my tracking skills work. I need to hold an object you own. After that, I sing and it leads me to the owner. Madame Faberge kidnapped you and took everything I could have used to find you."

"So, you returned to your old life?"

"I returned to my old job," I corrected. "I was lucky the Phoenix Location Agency took me back after I pulled a stunt like that." I waved a hand, trying to organize my thoughts. "I never forgot about you, Aiden. My plan was to keep tracking and hope that one of my bounties would be you."

"When exactly did the horse enter the picture?" His breath hissed through his teeth as if it was painful to ask about another guy. Maybe there was still a piece of my Kegan in there after all.

"Douglas?" I attempted to play dumb.

"Of course, Douglas." Aiden forced himself to sit up. He swayed in place, looking like he might throw up, before the nausea passed. "Are there others?"

I shook my head. "No. Just him." I held up a hand to stop any accusations when Aiden opened his mouth. "Hear me out, okay? If this is how we get to know each other again, so be it. I'll be honest with you. Kegan would deserve that and so do you, Aiden. What do you want to know?"

Aiden grabbed onto the plastic bedrail to steady himself. "Xander said –"

"Xander?" I almost laughed, but slammed a hand over my mouth before any sound came out. "Xander put you up to this? Oh, yeah, sure, he has no ulterior motive at all."

Aiden frowned. "What do you mean?"

This time I laughed. "Forget it. If you don't know, I won't tell you." I toyed with my braid, hoping Aiden would forget about the Douglas line of questioning. He didn't.

"Back to the kelpie," Aiden said. "Start at the beginning. Tell me everything."

"Everything?" I raised an eyebrow. "Kelpies are kind of into kinky shit."

His pale cheeks flushed almost the same color as his bright hair. "You know what I mean. If he's the only one since I was Kegan, tell me why. Why him?"

"It's a work relationship," I said. "I was working a case a little over two years ago and heard about an informant at this Shifter Bar called Slide. Douglas was the informant. He had intel I needed to complete my case. The best way to get it from him was, well...you know. I call it interrogation. You probably have a different word for it."

"You slept with him so you could get information, that in turn, put another shifter in a cage?"

"Well, when you put it that way ..." I sighed before running a shaking hand through my hair. "Look, it's not my proudest moment, I admit, but you asked how I met him and there you go. He's a work friend."

Aiden's laugh was cold, bordering on cruel. "Hardly. Was it just one time?"

"One time?" My eyes widened until it felt like they'd pop out of my head. "Oh, Gods, no. Kelpies have stamina." I twisted my hands in my lap, feeling like a little girl being scolded. "Do you, uh, want me to give you an accurate count on how many times we worked together?"

Aiden did an 'after you' hand gesture. "By all means. This should be amusing."

I scowled. "Xander putting a bug in your ear turned you into a judgey bastard, you know? If you mean 'This should be upsetting', just say upsetting. You wanted me to be honest with you, and I am. If that hurts you, I'm sorry. I could deny everything. I could make up stories, but I'm not. I'm telling you the truth, Aiden. Sometimes the truth hurts."

He closed his eyes, breath rasping as he struggled to stay calm. "Please continue."

I rewound my mind over the past two years of knowing Douglas in, well, every sense of the word. If Aiden got this upset over hearing how I worked, he did *not* need to know any specific details of what

I liked to call my interrogation sessions. *Handcuffs were super versatile.* I pinched the bridge of my nose between my thumb and second finger. What the hell was wrong with me? Kelpie kink should be the last thing I wondered about right now. I was trying to build up trust with Aiden, not tear it down over stupid horse face.

"We worked together six—no, wait—eight times over the years." I did a quick count on my fingers to make sure it was accurate. "Yup. Eight times."

Aiden sucked in his breath, but recovered seconds later. As much as I hated to admit that Douglas was my go-to guy for work related intel and all other needs, it was good that Aiden found out now instead of building up some sort of illusion of who he thought I was versus who I really am.

"In those eight times you worked together, you felt the need to 'interrogate' him—"

"On average three times per work session, but that's an, uh, conservative average." I shrugged as if to say 'Hell, I don't know why I did it either.' "Stamina, remember?"

"For you as well, it seems." Aiden cracked a wry smile. Did he think this was funny? Maybe there was less Kegan in there than I thought.

"Look, Aiden, I'm not going to apologize for my choices," I said. "I am who I am. You knew that before and you should know that now. Doug is ... well,

I'm not exactly sure what Doug is, but it's never been all that serious with him. Not like it was with you. I mean Kegan."

Aiden smiled again, this time a mixture of sadness and exhaustion. "Spare me the line where you say business and pleasure shouldn't mix, Lorelei. The horse is more than a work friend to you."

Was he making fun of me? *Damned foolish, bird.* "Douglas may still want to get in my pants, but have you seen how that free-range phoenix moons over you? It's, like, a murder-suicide in the making if you ever turn him down."

"Xander is a friend," Aiden said, voice firm.

"A work friend?"

He nodded his appreciation. "Well played, Lorelei. Well played."

THIRTEEN

THIRTEEN

AIDEN

I hadn't expected the conversation to take this turn or that I'd feel so jealous over a woman I didn't really remember. And yet, it had. Still, I had committed to trying to make this work. Her mention of the way Xander acted around me only made me more uncomfortable.

"Tell me about how we first met," I said, setting the empty bowl aside.

Lorelei smirked, but didn't look at me. "You'd flown the coop. I guess that's something similar between you and Kegan. Your owner was this mushy old windbag who gushed over you like a baby. It was nauseating. I tracked you down. You'd shifted back to human."

"Another thing he and I have in common," I offered.

"He wasn't dying from blood graft," she said, a hard tone in her voice. "I had every intention of bringing you back, you know and collect my bounty. Your owner—I mean Kegan's owner—was offering a big pay-day. 300,000 credits. That would ... That would pay a lot of bills."

"But you didn't bring me back," I prompted.

She shook her head and toyed with the end of her braid. "You talked to me like a person. You wanted to know what I wanted in my life. No one had ever taken the time to give a fuck about me like that. And, you were easy on the eyes which made saying no even harder for me. So, we ran away to the circus."

I laughed a deep belly laugh. "You're serious?"

She nodded and smiled wide. "It was your idea. We put together an act where we'd both shift and I'd lure you back a few times and then we'd pull a vanishing act. The humans ate it up. For a while at least."

Her face fell, a hardness settling over her features. I suspected this is where the happy couple became decidedly less happy. I was almost afraid to ask what happened, but I did so anyway. "What happened?"

"We had six months together, Kegan and I. It

was fun and freeing. I'd never really appreciated that type of freedom before. I may not be locked in a gilded cage, but even sirens aren't free. Our last show was a big success but there was someone waiting for us. They knocked me out and took you. I don't know if Jarron was in on it, but I quit that night, just walked out, and re-joined the PLA. I vowed to find you." Lorelei held her hands out, palms toward me. "It took three years, but here I am."

"Who is Jarron?" The name stirred another memory hidden deep in my subconscious, but it was gone before I could grasp it.

"The son-of-a-bitch who ran the circus," Lorelei said. "Maybe he got tired of the novelty of shifters in his caravan. Then again maybe someone offered to pay him a fuck-ton of credits for you, but the performance that night was the last time I saw you until yesterday. So, that's how we met."

It was a sad tale. One I couldn't quite recall, though I really wanted to. I had left this woman heartbroken and I wasn't helping her. Kegan had helped her find freedom, however short-lived. What did I offer her? I wasn't the lover she remembered. Still, just maybe I could be.

"I want to remember what it was like. Our first time together," I said, reaching for her hand.

She arched a brow at me. "Are you sure you can handle it ... in your condition?"

I sat up straighter and put on a brave face. "Maybe it will make me feel better," I countered.

She shifted her weight and leaned in close. I could feel her breath against my cheek as she kissed me. I wanted sparks to fly and everything to feel second nature, like we were supposed to fit together, but it was just a kiss.

She pulled away and said, "Is that bringing anything back?"

I swallowed. Did I lie to her, stroke her ego or did I come clean? "Maybe if we just keep going ..." I opted for vagueness.

She slid into my lap, wrapping her arms around my neck and straddling my legs. Without a word, she leaned in again and kissed me. The proximity of her body to mine ignited my libido. Her lips were soft and her kisses gentle. I could almost see a fevered exchange in my mind's eye, but I didn't want to ruin what was happening in the here and now. I made the move to deepen the gesture, parting her lips with my tongue. She sighed and pulled away, tugging her shirt over her head, exposing bare breasts. I rested my hands on her hips, but she pulled them off, one finger at time and moved them to cup her chest before returning her lips to mine.

Lorelei ground her hips against me and I let the sensation build, giving in to the arousal. But still that image in my mind's eye vied for attention. It wanted to be seen and acted upon. I was so focused on letting my erection build I didn't notice when she was no longer kissing me.

She pressed her lips to my ear. "Now was about the time you got frisky," she prompted.

She didn't elaborate on what 'frisky' meant and I had to swallow a lump in my throat that whatever I did next wouldn't live up to her memory. She moved off of me and slid her pants off, leaving her naked before me. I kicked the blankets down to give myself room to move and pinned her to the pillow. I kissed her cheek, her neck, but stopped at her breasts.

"Keep going," she urged, her voice husky.

Licking my lips, I pressed a gentle kiss to the hollow between her breasts, making my way down her belly. I stopped at the bare skin just above her pelvis. She had one arm thrown over her head, her chest rising and falling with rapid, shallow breaths. I moved to her inner thigh, eliciting a soft moan. I felt the throb in my groin grow painful as the clothing I wore restricted it. But I wasn't ready to shed my clothing.

"Stop teasing me," she rasped when I stopped my kissing.

I paused, the image that had been fighting for my attention forming as I closed my eyes. I wasn't on the verge of pleasuring Lorelei. Another figure lay before me, prone and on the cusp of orgasm. *Xander.*

Cold sweat trickled down my neck and panic overtook me. "I can't do this," I said and backed away from her. I turned my back to her, trying to hide my shame. How could I admit to her that after all of her time searching, not only hadn't she found the man she remembered, but he was imagining sexual encounters with another man?

The bed shifted and she sat up, placing one hand on my shoulder. I flinched at her touch, but she didn't back down. "Look at me," she said.

I didn't want to do as she instructed. I couldn't meet her gaze if I did. A soft melody escaped her lips, drawing me in and I had no say over my actions. I turned and looked her in the eye.

"We don't have to do this if you're not ready. I can just get you off instead."

"What?" I croaked.

She placed a hand over the waistband of my pants and slid her fingers beneath the fabric. "Let me do this for you. Please."

FOURTEEN

LORELEI

Aiden watched me, confusion instead of desire clouding his eyes. Did rising from the ashes mean he needed to relearn everything? I admit, there's a bit of a learning curve when it comes to sex, but it should be a little bit instinctive, shouldn't it?

"You don't know what I'm talking about, do you?" I pulled my hand from his waist band and rocked back on my heels. "Kegan—"

"Aiden," he corrected.

I swore under my breath at my lapse into the past. "Sorry. Aiden. You have his face. It's easy to forget sometimes." I found my clothes and pulled them back on, feeling self-conscious about my nakedness with Aiden staring at me all blank like that. "I know you asked about our past, but it's probably weird for you with me remembering and you not. It's weird for me, too. I'm not sure how to act or what to say around you. You should conserve your strength anyway. I don't want to be responsible for the blood graft working faster through your system."

He frowned. "I don't think ... activity ... causes the poison to move faster."

"See! You can't even say it!" I crouched over him so my hands and knees were on either side of his body, well aware my shirt gapped open for him to enjoy the view. Aiden bit his lip and turned his head away. I sighed and returned to sitting. "It's just sex, Aiden. There's nothing to be afraid of. If you don't remember, I can show you. That's what you wanted, wasn't it?"

"I'm ... I'm not ready."

"Which is where the blow job comes in." I motioned at his pants and current non-existent erection. "Or hand job. Whichever. I'm not particular. We could do both and then you tell me which you prefer."

Aiden was silent for long, tense minutes before shaking his head. "I have some things I need to ... sort out ... before I can be who you wish me to be. I'm sorry, Lorelei. I think you should go."

"Excuse me?" I blinked, shocked. No one had

ever told me to go away before. I was a siren. Seduction was in our DNA. "You're asking me to leave?"

"Yes." He closed his eyes so he wouldn't have to see the betrayal, I'm sure was etched all over my face. "I'm sorry. I need to rest. It's been a trying few days."

"Fine." I hopped off the hospital bed and made sure I had my boots in hand. "Enjoy your *nap*, Aiden."

I turned around one last time at the door to check if watching me walk away changed his mind about my offer, but he was asleep. Or at least he wanted me to believe he was asleep. *Fucking phoenix*. I slammed the door behind me. It didn't ease the humiliation I felt at being turned down, but it helped a little.

Douglas strolled around the corner, whistling that annoying Caledonian tune of his. Leave it to the damn kelpie to show up at the most inopportune moment. I didn't want him knowing Aiden turned my offer down. It was embarrassing enough in the moment, I didn't need Douglas teasing me about my failure, too. I smiled when a bad idea popped into my head. What I needed was a distraction. I knew just the perfect type .... and the perfect person to distract me.

The tune died on Douglas' lips when he saw

me standing alone in the hall. "Did things not go so well between you and our phoenix friend?"

I tilted my chin up. "What's it to you?"

Douglas took a step closer, reaching his hand out until he cradled my cheek in his warm palm. "Don't think that I don't care, because I do. Very much. You fight so hard to keep people out, Lore, that you let no one in."

"If someone offered you a blow job, would you say no?"

He covered his surprise with a choking cough. "Is that, uh, a trick question?"

"No. I'm serious." I stepped back until he was no longer touching me. I had trouble thinking when Douglas touched me. "If someone offered help in the—" I motioned at his crotch "—fun department, would you say no?"

"Is the 'someone' you?"

I narrowed my eyes. "Why does that matter?"

"It matters loads." He grinned. "If some random slag offered, my answer would be no. If *you* offered. Well, if you offered ..." His grin widened. "You'll just have to ask and find out now, won't you?"

Gods, that shouldn't be as tempting as it was. "Not here. Even I'm not that much of an exhibitionist."

"My room?" Douglas countered before I realized what I'd agreed to.

I shook my head. "That Xander bird is just looking for shit to report to Aiden. I wouldn't put it past the doxy either."

"Mels is overprotective," Douglas said. "She found Aiden and thinks he's her responsibility."

I toyed with the end of my braid. "You found me. Does that make me your responsibility?"

He grinned again. "Something like that."

It was my turn to step toe to toe with Douglas. I lifted my hands to his face, winding my fingers into the ends of his hair. I chewed on my bottom lip, thoughtful, as I studied his sharp, wiry angles, trying to decide on my next move. I'd spent the last three years searching for Kegan. Yet, here I was standing in a hallway with another man. Aiden turned me away. Would Douglas?

"Let's find a room. Not yours. Not mine. Something that can be ours." I stepped back. There. I offered. I held my breath waiting for his response.

Douglas extended a hand to me. "As you wish, *M'eudail*."

He led me through the winding hallways until we were far enough away to feel like we were the only ones in the building. Douglas tried a door labeled 151. It swung open to reveal a large, dusty room. Dormant medical equipment lay scattered around the floor and countertops. There was an uncomfortable looking padded examination table in the middle of the room.

"Well, it's not perfect. No one, but us have been in here for years." Douglas looked over his shoulder at me. "Wanna give it a go?"

"You or the room?" I joked.

"Both, but mostly me." He kissed me, pulled me into the room, and shut the door all in one fluid motion. "Is this supposed to be a quickie or are you up for our usual standard?"

My hands were already on his belt buckle. "Just shut up and kiss me, horse face."

"Gladly, fish fins."

My mouth was already parted, ready to welcome him, as he slanted his lips across mine. His tongue delved deep, echoing what was to come as we fumbled with buttons and snaps. He lifted me onto the nearest countertop, stepping between my legs. I unzipped his pants, my fingers growing more confident as memories of our last "work meeting" at the shifter bar played through my mind.

"Did you take preventatives?" Douglas asked, breath ragged.

Did I? The government issued pregnancy preventatives to all employees in case we needed to use unconventional tactics in our cases. The only other way to get the pills were through the black market. With shifters, you could sleep with whoever you wanted to just like humans do, but only compatible elementals could create life. Most shifters stuck to their own breed for family planning, but hybrids happened. They were rare, but they happened. At the start of this case, I didn't plan to be gone overnight. That meant, I didn't pack my preventatives. So, did I take them? Yes. Did I take them today? No. Douglas and I were both water elementals. I'd be taking a huge risk if I said yes.

"Did you?" he asked again.

I nodded yes, sending up a prayer that I still had an emergency preventative waiting in my backpack just in case.

DOUGLAS and I lay together on the examination table, sweaty and spent. He dozed, breathing slow and even. I couldn't sleep. What I had meant to be a quickie turned into one of our marathon "work" sessions. I stretched, storing away the new memories. I hated to admit it, but the kelpie had skills.

"What are you thinking about?" Douglas mumbled into my back.

"I thought you were asleep."

"Just recharging." He kissed my shoulder blade. I shivered at his touch, which only seemed to embolden him. He reached one hand up to the valley between my breasts, fingers stroking lightly before he pinched one of my nipples in between his thumb and forefinger.

My breath hissed through my teeth, my body betraying my need as his other hand stroked between my thighs. "Doug, we shouldn't ..."

"I hate to break it to you, *M'eudail*, but we already have."

"You know what I mean." I arched against his hand, my body disagreeing with my words. "We should stop."

"You sure?"

I bit my lip until I tasted blood, pin pricks of light building behind my eyes as the wave of desire his touch elicited rose to near its breaking point. "No ... No, don't stop. Don't stop."

"Mar is miann leat."

I gave myself over to the physical sensations racking through my body. I didn't want to think. I didn't want to feel guilty over what happened with Aiden earlier. I just wanted to be wanted.

After, I turned in Douglas' arms so we were facing each other. I curled up against his bare chest, breathing in his unique scent. "Doug? I wasn't exactly honest with you earlier."

He stroked my arm; a lazy half smile a permanent fixture on his angular face. "What do you mean? *Did* something happen between you and Aiden?"

"No. No, nothing like that. I promise." I burrowed myself deeper against him. "I just ... I didn't bring my preventatives on this job. I only skipped a day so it shouldn't be a big deal but I ... but I thought you should know."

"Thank you, *M'eudail*."

"For what?"

Douglas kissed the top of my head. "For trusting me. You wouldn't have said 'yes' if you didn't trust me to stick around in case of ... well, you know."

A hybrid felt so foreign, I took a while to figure out what he meant. "I might have an emergency preventative pill back in my room."

"Do you plan to take it?"

I shrugged, my walls going up again. "I should."

"Is that a no?"

I screwed my eyes shut tight, not wanting to think about it. "That's a 'shut up and go to sleep, horse face.'"

Douglas chuckled, his chest rumbling against my cheek. "There go the walls again, right when we were doing so well. Sleep now, Lorelei. I'm here. I'll always be here."

"Stop being so nice to me," I mumbled.

I didn't hear his response. I was already asleep.

FIFTEEN

FIFTEEN

AIDEN

A week of rest did my body well, but my mind still warred with itself. I had pushed Lorelei away and she hadn't been back to see me since. I knew she was still here, because every time Micah came in to check on me, he was muttering about the "bounty hunter" making everyone nervous. I didn't know many of the people here well, but his comments sounded more like they should come out of Mels' mouth. And then there was Xander. He, too, had been conspicuously absent.

I made my way outside to the back of the structure where we had all shifted and this whole ordeal began. In the day's dimness it looked like an ordinary stretch of forest. I settled on the ground and looked up at the sky. I could almost feel my wings aching to be set free.

"Hope you aren't thinking of flying the coop, birdie," Mels said from behind me. She moved to sit beside me before I could answer.

"I couldn't fly, not unless I wanted to die," I commented.

"At least you look less like death warmed over. Whatever Micah's been doing is working."

"I feel more like myself, but I can still feel the poison working its way to my heart. Even remaining in human form, it will eventually kill me."

Mels nodded, picking at a blade of grass between her knees. "If we ever find that bitch who did this, remind me to bite her head clean off."

I arched a brow and looked at her. "You can do that?" I had a hard time believing Mels capable of such an act, given how small she became in her shifted form.

She grinned, the sharp points of her teeth visible. "Might take me a chomp or two but I'm resourceful."

I leaned back, bracing myself on my hands and studied the tree line surrounding our little enclave. "How is it that humans haven't found this place?"

"We're careful about who we bring back here. So far, we haven't had any errant mortals intruding on us. No unwanted characters busting down our doors. Well, until your girlfriend showed up."

"She isn't my girlfriend. I'm not sure what we are to one another now."

"You know, I don't get it. She chases you all over fucking creation, claiming to be in love with you and what does she do when she gets here? She shacks up with Doug."

Breath caught in my throat. I thought I had gotten over the realization she had been with someone else in the intervening time between our shared past and now. To know she was still in his bed bothered me. Again, I couldn't put my finger on why. "I am not the man she knew me to be before. If she finds comfort with another, then she should be happy."

"You really don't feel anything for her?"

"I feel a fondness toward her and I think I care about her. But, if there was love, real deep love, I don't think it's there now. I think I pushed her into his arms."

"Well, if you want the fish bitch gone, just say the word. She's only here because you wanted her to stay."

I shook my head. "We both know she can't leave. You would never let her compromise the security of this place. And I will not let any harm come to her."

Mels pouted. "Fine."

I listened to the sounds of nature around us. It should sound like freedom, but even here, I was feeling like a prisoner. Still where would I go? I couldn't make it far on my own, not with this blood graft stealing my future with every beat of my heart. And even if Lorelei didn't turn me in, I knew the woman who had caged me would send others to hunt me down.

Has she done so already?

"You got some serious thoughts going on in there," Mels commented, poking the side of my head with the tip of her index finger.

"The woman who kept me ... who poisoned me. I was thinking since Lorelei hasn't brought me back yet, maybe she has sent others to find me. I could put you all in danger by staying here."

"Let those bitches come. We aren't afraid of some fish," Mels scoffed.

I appreciated her bravado, but I didn't quite buy it. Sure, she could hold her own in a fight, but some of the others who resided here? They did not appear to be the fighting type. Maybe Xander. There he was again, co-opting my thoughts without being present.

"You have been with the underground for a while," I said. It came out more statement than question.

"Constance and I started it. I know, it seems odd a snake and doxy teaming up. But we had mutual interests."

"So, you know Xander well?"

Mels snickered, hiding it poorly behind her hand. "Been making passes, has he?"

"Is that normal for him?"

"He's been a lot of people. But he's always been a shameless little flirt. He's a good guy, but he can be pushy."

I swallowed the lump in my throat. I didn't want to think about him being pushy. Or think about him at all. And yet, the image of our naked bodies intertwined and the memory of his lips on mine came unbidden to the forefront of my thoughts. I was very grateful for the lack of daylight. It hid the blush I felt creep up my neck and onto my cheeks.

"He hasn't been around this week," I said.

"He's on a mission."

"What does that mean?"

"Oh, boy. Don't tell me I have to define the word for you. I know you were all beak and feathers for a while, but you know basic language, right?'

It was my turn to roll my eyes. "Yes, I know what the word means. What mission?"

Mels averted her gaze and focused on picking at more blades of grass. Drops of poison fell from her mouth, hitting the ground with a 'hiss' as she tried pretending she hadn't let something slip she shouldn't have.

"Mels, please tell me what is going on?"

"You'd want to help and you can't," she mumbled.

"How do you know I can't? I may be dying but I'm not dead yet," I snapped.

"Because it's dangerous and if you get hurt or killed, that's on *me*."

"No, it isn't," I argued.

She jumped to her feet with lightning quick reflexes. I was slower to join her on two legs and she was already pacing back and forth in front of me. "Look, I brought you here. You're my responsibility. I vouched that you were safe to be here. I always keep my word. Understand?"

"No. I don't understand. I am a grown man. I am no one's responsibility but my own."

"That's not how it works here. You bring a newbie in, you look out for them. It's how we survive."

"Does it have something to do with me being hunted?"

"Oh, for fuck's sake. Fine," she huffed. "You want to know? Xander's been off putting out feelers. There's been some chatter a long time ago, like years, that there might be a cure for the blood graft.

None of us have ever seen it. He is on his way back now and I don't know whether he will be successful."

"Why wouldn't you want me to know that there is a cure and you've been trying to find it? You're damn right I would want to help," I snapped.

Mels bit her lower lip, acid sizzling against her flesh. She didn't seem to mind though. "Because if you're not sick, there's less reason for her to not drag you back and collect her payday."

"Lorelei? No matter whether we are together or not, she has made it clear she isn't bringing me back to that woman. So, try again."

"Look, birdie, I like you. Despite myself, I've sort of grown attached. I don't want you to suddenly be cured, change back into a bird and fly off and leave, okay?"

I stared at her open-mouthed. Of all the things I'd thought she would say, this was not even on the list. I didn't know how to respond to her. I didn't get the chance, because the door behind us opened and Xander strode out. I tried not to look like I was relieved he was in my presence.

"We need to gather everyone. I've got news," he said.

SIXTEEN

SIXTEEN

LORELEI

I sat in one of the semi-comfortable padded chairs in what once must have been the waiting room when this place was still a hospital instead of a shifter base. I watched the group I called the inner circle—Doug, free range phoenix, the doxy bitch and the naga chick—whisper in a huddle in a spot where the large room met the dusty hallway. They wanted me here even if they didn't tell me why.

"Relax, they're not talking about you." Aiden sat down next to me. He nudged my shoulder playfully that reminded me so strongly of Kegan I blinked back tears. Aiden noticed and frowned. "Have I upset you?"

"No. It's just ... that's something *he* did." I pulled my legs up to my chest and wrapped my arms around them. "Kegan's bad puns were legendary. He loved nudging my shoulder after a particularly heinous one to see if I got it." I took a deep, ragged breath to stop my mind from hurtling into the past. "I never told him I ignored them on purpose. I always laughed even if it was the most fake-ass laugh you've ever heard."

"You talk about him as if he's dead."

"He is." I looked long and hard at this near-stranger in Kegan's body. "You told me so yourself."

"A part of him will always be with me." Aiden tapped his chest. "It's small, but it's there." Now it was his turn to study me, eyes narrowed as if trying to figure out a game where the rules kept changing. "Why did you stay away for a week? Was it because of how we, uh, left things before?"

I didn't tell him the truth. I didn't say my anger had turned to embarrassment and I needed to put some distance and time between us. I couldn't face him until now. Yup, I avoided him and spent way too much time in Douglas' company, but that's not anything Aiden needed to know or hear. Instead, I broke my promise never to lie to him.

"I was exploring the base." I unwrapped my arms from my knees and planted my boots on the ground. "Besides, you needed time to rest. I gave you that by staying away."

"Was the kelpie your tour guide?"

I caught the spark of jealousy in his words. A laugh burst out before I could stop it. Aiden's cheeks burned at my reaction. "You've got to be fucking kidding me. You wait til *now* to be jealous of Doug? Seriously, Aiden, rethink your priorities, because Douglas is not the issue here. You are."

"What do you mean?"

I laughed again, the sound harsh. "Ever since I met you-as-you and not you-as-Kegan, you've been running hot and cold on me. One second, you're asking me to recount *very* intimate memories, and the next you're freaking out like the PLA is on your tail. Well, the PLA besides me is on your tail." I shook my head. "Forget it. That's not the best analogy. All I'm saying is you need to figure out what you want. From me. From that strange bird Xander. Hell, from whatever life you have left. Figure it the fuck out, Aiden. No one else will do it for you."

The red stain of embarrassment darkened on Aiden cheeks. "You're ... You're one to talk, Lorelei. You entertain two men."

"It's only one, thanks very much," I bit back. "I'm not a whore."

"No, but you're unfaithful."

"To who?" I kept my voice low. I didn't need or want the MCU's inner circle to overhear us. Douglas wouldn't be able to wipe the smug smile from his face if he knew I just admitted to being faithful to him. "Who am I unfaithful to, Aiden?" I pressed, partially to stop myself from thinking of Douglas' smile, smug or otherwise. "I'd like to know. Do you think I'm unfaithful to Kegan's memory? That's all he is now—a memory."

Aiden sat up straight in his chair and did a shake thing that reminded me of a bird ruffling its feathers. "Did you move on to the kelpie the next day or wait a week out of respect for your kidnapped boyfriend?"

I jumped to my feet. My knees shook, threatening to topple me onto the cold floor, but I forced the mix of emotions swirling inside me into determination. I would not fall. I would not cry. I would not give Aiden the satisfaction of seeing any weakness. "Don't you dare pretend to know how I felt about Kegan. I never gave up looking for him. Never."

"Some tracker you are if it took three years." Aiden cocked his head to the side. "Or maybe you didn't want to find Kegan." His gaze flicked to Douglas still deep in discussion with the inner circle. "You'd already moved on."

"Fuck. You." I whipped out one of my steel hairpins and flung it at Aiden. It found its mark, pinning his shirt to the back of the chair. "That's a warning. Next time will be something vital."

I stormed out of the waiting area. I made it most

of the way down one hallway before my legs refused to hold me. I collapsed onto the floor. Still, I refused to cry. I had cried too much already for Kegan over the years. I wouldn't cry for Aiden.

"Lorelei?"

I didn't need to look up to know Douglas followed me. As confused as I was over Kegan rising from the ashes into Aiden, Doug held even more mixed emotions for me. I wanted to pull him close yet push him away at the same time. There was a war waging inside me and I didn't know which side would win.

"Go away," I muttered, refusing to look at him. Refusing to need him. "I have one hairpin left, you know."

"Two." Douglas held out the one I used on Aiden. "I thought you might want it back."

I plucked it from his hand and stuck it back into my hair. "Thanks."

Douglas slid down the wall until he was sitting next to me on the floor. Uninvited. He sat silent, waiting for me to explain myself. When I didn't, he asked: "What happened back there? Why'd you attack Aiden?"

"I didn't attack him," I insisted. "He provoked me."

"What, hit a nerve?"

I shook my head, not wanting to answer. "Just

go away, Doug. I don't want to be around anyone right now."

"You stormed off before we could tell you about the plan," he said. "Xander came up with the idea after his latest intel mission."

"I thought intel was your department."

"I asked to stay behind on this one."

I frowned. "Why?"

Douglas' mouth crept into a half smile. "You know why. I can say it if you like, though."

"Save it." I gave in and leaned against him, resting my head on his shoulder. "You'd make a terrible poker player, you know? Your face gives away your emotions every time."

Douglas wrapped his closest arm around me. "Only regarding you, *M'eudail*."

"So, tell me about this plan," I requested. "Is it to heal Aiden?" Talking strategy would distract me from other thoughts that insisted on creeping in whenever I was near Doug.

"Yes." Douglas squeezed my arm, acting as distracted as I felt. "Xander found a seller on the black market who claims to have a supply of Khalas root. He's willing to trade it for a vial of fresh phoenix tears. Aiden's already agreed to it. Xander and Mels are going along for support."

"What happens if the plan falls through?" A

memory of Kegan being dragged away flashed in my mind. The one that replayed in my nightmares.

"We find a way to Sanctuary," Douglas said.

"But we don't know if Sanctuary even exists," I reminded him. "It could be just a legend. You said so yourself."

"Better to try than let the blood graft work its way to Aiden's heart."

We fell silent. It wasn't an uncomfortable silence. Words just weren't needed. A sense of calm washed over me. I'd never admit it out loud, but I liked that Douglas and I could sit in complete silence and still feel peaceful.

"Hey, Doug?" I nudged him with my elbow. "Don't you dare repeat this to anyone, but I would have missed you if you'd gone on the intel mission."

He laughed, pleased with my attempt at being honest about my feelings. "I would have missed you too, Lore. And thanks for not calling me horse face."

I grinned. "You're welcome ... horse face."

Douglas leaned in to kiss me. No words needed.

SEVENTEEN

SEVENTEEN

AIDEN

To say I was nervous about our mission was an understatement. I knew little about our destination or the identity of Xander's contact. And then there was the fact I would need to spend prolonged time in Xander's presence. Mels' presence was a small consolation. At least she could act as a buffer.

"You ready to go?" Mels asked, sticking her head through the open doorway of the room they had given me.

I made a show of looking around the small space. "Remind me how we are getting there?" I followed her out to the back wooded area behind the compound. I quickly learned regulars didn't use the front entrance to come and go. Less conspicuous that way.

She glanced over her shoulder at me and grinned, the points of her incisors creating small indents in her lower lip. "We fly, birdie."

I tried not to let the panic show. "I don't think that is a good idea."

"Don't worry, you won't be shifting," Xander said as he appeared from around the side of the compound.

"It may have escaped your notice, but in human form I'm not exactly made to survive heights and thinner air," I quipped before I took in his appearance.

Xander had darkened his hair again and despite the lack of sleeves, his markings were gone. Or so they appeared. I resisted the urge to touch his skin to find out how he could have hidden his true nature. He caught me looking and smiled.

"Sometimes, it pays to live with a bunch of chicks. Constance gave me a make-over. You like?"

"Keep it in your pants, perv," Mels spat and patted my arm in what I hoped was a reassuring gesture. "Don't worry, I won't take you too high and I've got excellent grip strength."

Cold sweat prickled along the nape of my neck as I watched Xander strip down, stuffing his clothing into a pack that he tossed to me. I tried to avoid watching as he shifted, partly so I wouldn't commit the contours of his frame to memory and so the jealousy I felt at being confined to one form didn't flare. Beside me, Mels shrunk, flitting around my head. I did not understand how she would be strong enough to lift, let alone carry me. She gave me little time to wonder. She dug her tiny hands into my shoulders and in an instant I was airborne. The compound vanished beneath us and we were soon moving through the air at speeds I could only dream of in my shifted form.

Xander beat his wings to keep pace with Mels' tiny form. I turned my attention to the land below us, spotting larger gilded mansions beneath us, sprawling across more land than should be allowed. I didn't think we were close to the woman who had imprisoned me, but every time the golden exteriors caught my eye, anger burned hot and acidic in my chest. We had to succeed.

EVENING SETTLED around us as we landed in a copse of trees outside a small tent city. Mels set me down and I slung the pack off my back. I pulled out the clothing, tossing it to Xander once he was bipedal again. He pulled the clothes on and took the lead, marching us through the collection of tents to one near the far edge.

"You should let me do the talking," he said, looking Mels in the eye.

"Why are you looking at me like that?" she snapped.

"Just try not to bite anyone and wait out here. We'll be back," he answered and clamped a hand on my shoulder.

"Who exactly are we meeting?" I asked, my throat parched.

"A broker. He goes by Fabian. It's probably not his real name but he claims he's got the cure we need."

"And why exactly am I here?"

"All brokers have a price. His is phoenix tears. So, get ready to cry on command."

I stopped walking and Xander got a few paces ahead of me before he turned and looked at me. I crossed my arms over my chest. "Why can't you give him the tears?"

"Because, he doesn't know I'm one." Colored flushed his cheeks. "He thinks I'm human and that I traffic in shifters."

The plan was beginning to not sit well with me. Why wouldn't Xander admit he was a shifter to this broker? "Is *he* human?"

"Look, just relax, okay? We will meet him, give him the tears, he gives us the cure and we are back to headquarters in time for supper."

I lacked his confidence and I doubted the success of our plan as we moved toward the tent. Mels had kept her distance, baring her teeth at random strangers. We stepped through the tent's opening to find a wiry bald man with skin the color of an oil slick lounging in a chair. His gaze slid over me, assessing me for my value and I repressed a shiver of revulsion.

"I brought what we agreed on," Xander said and nudged me forward.

"You haven't brought me anything," Fabian answered.

"You wanted a phoenix to cry for you. I brought you one. Now, give me the item we agreed on."

"What do you want with Khalas root?"

"That's my business," Xander answered, his temper rising.

Out of the corner of my eye, I caught something small flitting around the edge of the tent. At first, I assumed it was an insect. I realized Mels had ignored Xander's warning and had snuck into the meeting unnoticed.

"How do I know you brought me the genuine article?" Fabian gestured at me with an arched brow.

I tugged the shirt over my head, exposing the sigils on my arms and back for him to see. They sparkled in the pale light of the lantern hanging from the tent pole above us. Xander handed me a tiny vial from his pocket. I hadn't shed healing tears in this form in a very long time. Any emotion that would trigger tears now would be bitter and somber. They could affect the potency, but I couldn't conjure anything joyful to ensure he got what he wanted. So, I focused on the feeling of being kept against my will, drawing on the anger inside for the humans who had done this to me. Hot tears trickled down my cheek into the vial. I put the stopper in and held out my hand.

Fabian pushed himself to his feet. He closed the distance and ran a hand over my skin, sending uncontrollable shivers down my spine. He palmed the vial, but continued to circle me like a predator stalking prey.

"You must think me a fool," he spat, his face mere inches from Xander.

"You're stalling," Xander snapped.

I suspected our broker lied to Xander about having what we needed. By the flash of anger in Xander's eyes, he was arriving at the same conclusion.

"Whatever magic you used to dress your pet up is good. I'll give you that. But, unless I see a phoenix in this tent on the count of five, our deal is off and our partnership is over. And believe me, *friend*, you do not want me as your enemy."

Panic set in and heat flushed my entire body. I couldn't shift without risking the blood graft making it to my heart and killing me before we even had a chance at laying hands on the cure. And Xander made it clear he couldn't break his cover. It left us with no options.

"One ... two ... three ..."

Before either Xander or I reacted, Mels returned to her full size and landed a solid punch to Fabian's jaw. He staggered to one side and she grabbed us both by the shirtsleeves, hauling us out of the tent before the broker could recover. We took off at a mad sprint out of the encampment until we reached the copse where we'd set down.

"I told you to stay outside!" Xander howled.

"I saved your asses. You should thank me," Mels replied, flipping him off.

"You may have saved him but I'm still dying and that was our only chance to get the cure," I reminded her.

She shook her head and held up a rolled-up leather tube. "Not the only way. That fucking swindler had a very nice map to Sanctuary. As in, the one place we know we can get you cured," she answered.

"We can't be sure that actually exists," Xander argued.

"It's worth a shot. We should bring it back to

Constance and the others, then decide what we do next as a group," I said. I took the tube from her, stowed it in the pack and gestured for Xander to hand over his clothing. The sooner we got back to headquarters, the better.

EIGHTEEN

EIGHTEEN

LORELEI

I lay on the sagging bed in my room trying not to listen to the commotion going on outside in the hallway. Aiden, the doxy, and the other phoenix were back based on the doxy swearing up a blue streak about how she saved their sorry asses.

"If it wasn't for me, you'd both be in a fucking cage sold off to the highest bidder!" she screeched. "Just admit it, Xander. Your plan was fucked from the start."

"We don't need a fairy flying in to save the day," Xander shouted back. "You should have minded your own business and stayed put. I had it under control."

"Under control? Under control? The only thing you had under control was how fast that bastard Fabian planned to turn on you. And I'm a doxy not a fairy, you complete and utter fuck-face."

"That's enough. Both of you."

I sat up when I heard Douglas' voice. He sounded tired, possibly discouraged. Their big Khalas root plan went south. That was clear. I could have told them trading for anything useful on the black market was a waste of time, but did they listen to me or even ask? Nope. The government had trained me my whole life to find things, but don't ask the siren. No. Come up with a half-assed plan instead and then meltdown when it imploded. Amateurs.

I stood. It only took three steps to reach the door. My hand hesitated, hovering over the knob. Did I really want to help them? Most of the members of the MCU treated me like a spy at best and a prisoner at worst. If I helped, I'd expect that to change. An image of Kegan being dragged off by Madame Faberge's goons flashed through my mind again. Kegan—no, Aiden—needed my help. I didn't find him in time before. I could make up for that now.

"You're doing it all wrong." I stepped into the hallway. "Your plan was doomed from the start. For every one legit black-market dealer, there are one hundred charlatans. Your mistake is you went looking for someone else to help you instead of helping yourself."

The inner circle swiveled in my direction. Aiden wasn't with them. I hoped he was resting and not captured.

The doxy bared her teeth at me, the poison glistening. "Oh, look, Douglas, your girlfriend has an opinion on the fucking matter. Imagine that."

I didn't bother to correct her. I would not argue semantics in the hallway as the poison spread closer and closer to Aiden's heart. If letting them call me Douglas' girlfriend got me into the inner circle, I'd be Douglas' girlfriend.

"Let her speak, Mels." Douglas raised one coppery eyebrow at me as if to ask 'since when are we ok with labels?'

I rolled my eyes and mouthed 'later' before switching gears to outline a plan to save Aiden that would actually work. "The first rule they taught us in PLA training is the only person you can rely on is yourself. In this case, that means us—" I motioned at everyone gathered in the hallway. "The more outside people you bring in, the more chances the plan will fail. We have a common goal. Saving Aiden. Outsiders don't care whether he lives or dies. We do."

The prissy Phoenix Xander who looked like he

covered his hair in fresh mud, crossed his arms over his chest. "You're an outsider."

I shook my head. "Not really. There are people on the inside I care about. I'm loyal to them. You may not think so, but I am."

"What's your plan?" The naga, Constance asked, the 's' hissing.

"The only way to get legit Khalas root is to go to the source," I said. "That means heading to Sanctuary. We find a map--"

"Already done," the doxy interrupted. "I'm one step ahead of you, siren. I doubt that black-market bastard ever knew the real value of the map. He won't miss it."

I nodded. "Good. One less thing to slow us down. Now, we just need credits. The easiest way to get that is to return Aiden to his owner."

"You bitch! Giving up Aiden is your plan? No fucking way!" Mels lunged at me. Poison dripped from her teeth, burning a hole in the dusty linoleum tiles at my feet. I would have been next if Douglas hadn't jumped forward to hold her back.

"Calm down, Mels," he ordered. "There's always a rhyme and reason to Lorelei's plans. Just listen to her."

"I don't trust anyone who thinks hooking up with you is a good idea, nark." Mels shifted into her tiny fairy-sized form, leaving Douglas holding on to nothing, but air.

Xander snorted with laughter at Mels' dig. I ignored that one, too. As much as I wanted to stab half the inner circle with my hairpins, I needed them to help put my Save-Aiden plan into motion.

"There's a one million-credit bounty on Aiden's head," I reminded them. "That's more than enough to get to Sanctuary. We return him, collect the bounty, and steal him back."

"How?" Mels buzzed close to my face.

"That's where you and your doxy strength come in," I said. "We smuggle you in to Madame Faberge's estate, you pick the cage lock, and free him. Open a window and you're both on your way back here. Think you can handle it?"

"Of course, I can." Mels shifted back into human size, her gossamer wings shimmering in the light from the overhead bulb. "When do we leave?"

"Aiden needs to rest," Xander said. "He wasted his phoenix tears and needs to recoup." Some emotion flashed across his face at the mention of Aiden's name. Fear? Worry? Doubt? I wasn't sure. Maybe he blamed himself for not getting the Khalas root as planned. I would if I were him.

"I'll ask Micah when he feels it's safe for Aiden to travel." Constance slithered away in search of Doctor Sunbird.

That left Xander, Mels, and Douglas still standing around. I didn't need to convince Douglas to trust me. I knew he already did. That left somehow making nice with the free-range phoenix and doxy. I leaned back against the wall, studying them to find an in. I sighed. The best in would be the truth. *Damn it!*

"Look, I know I need to earn your trust," I said. "Let me do that. No false promises or anything like that. Just a sincere wish to save Aiden's life. I couldn't save him before. I can try now."

Mels pointed two fingers at her eyes and then at me. "I'm watching you, siren. You fuck the MCU over and even your boyfriend won't be able to save you."

I let the second reference to being Douglas' girl-friend slide. "Understood."

"Just don't hurt Aiden, okay?" Xander ruffled a hand through his dyed hair. "If you do, I'll let Mels bite you."

I nodded. "Hurting Aiden is the last thing I want to do."

They looked to Douglas, as if expecting him to add something about not screwing over the MCU. When he remained silent, Xander and Mels wandered off to wherever they went when there was no inner-circle pow-wows needed. That left me alone with Doug.

"You not in the mood to stick up for the Magical Creature Underground?" I asked.

"I'm in the mood to figure out when we started using relationship labels," he countered.

"We're not, they are." I pushed myself away from the wall and headed back into my room. Douglas followed. "Did I invite you in?"

He grabbed both my hands. "Enough with the walls, Lorelei. You don't have to pretend with me. Remember that week we spent together outside of Drysdale? And the other time outside of Merriman? And then Pemberton. And—"

I pulled my hands away. "I get it. We took some time off work together. It happens. Don't read too much into it. Maybe I just needed a change of scenery."

"No. It wasn't just time off, it was time to—" Douglas shook his head, deciding against saying whatever he planned to say. "See there. You're pulling away again. No matter what you want to call it, those times were the realest I've ever seen you be, Lorelei. No walls. No guard up. Just you. The real you. The one you let me catch glimpses of now and then but never for long."

The panicky, trapped feeling I got whenever anyone expected me to talk about my *feelings* descended, wrapping around me like a suffocating blanket.

"Why is that?" Douglas pressed. "Why are you so afraid of letting me in?"

"It's easier to push people away."

He wasn't going to let me get away with that lame-ass answer. I had used it too much already. "Why? Just tell me the truth, Lorelei. After all we've been through, and seen, and done together, don't I deserve that?"

I closed my eyes and counted down silently from ten, my anxiety fading with each number. *Ten, nine, eight, seven....* Douglas deserved the truth, but was I ready to tell it? *Six, five, four, three...* I never wanted strings attached and, without realizing it, strings were what I got. *Two, one, zero.* I opened my eyes. "Fine. But don't go spreading it around, okay?"

He raised both eyebrows, looking hopeful. "I'm listening."

"Every time I let someone in, they get hurt. My parents. Kegan. Maybe it's misguided, but I thought if I kept you at arm's length as much as possible, I could stop that from happening. Earlier in the hallway, I said there were people I cared about in this base. One of them is you. Just don't let it go to your head, horse face."

Douglas flashed his bright grin. "I won't." He swiped a quick 'x' over his heart. "Cross my heart."

I stepped forward, playing with the button holes on his plaid overshirt so I wouldn't have to look him in the eyes. "Maybe you can stay here tonight."

"If you want me to, *M'eudail*."

"Are you ever going to tell me what that means?" I glanced up. "You've been calling me that stupid Gaelic word since we met."

"My darling."

I squinted at him, not sure I heard right. "What did you say?"

"*M'eudail*," Douglas repeated. "It means 'my darling.' Not so stupid anymore, is it?"

I shook my head. "No. No, I guess not. It's not stupid at all."

NINETEEN

NINETEEN

AIDEN

Even from my room I could hear Mels berating Xander long after we got back. I'd picked up on Lorelei's voice entering the conversation, too. Producing even the small number of tears had tired me out more than I expected. No doubt, because of the poison coursing through me. We failed to obtain the cure. I had no idea how we planned to halt my impending demise now.

I peered out into the hallway to find it empty. My stomach rumbled with hunger and I made my way to the front area where I'd first met the Inner Circle in all of my naked glory. I ducked behind the bar and rustled through the contents. I found left-over breads and meat. It would have to do.

"You're not going to find much back there," Douglas said.

I stood up, food still in hand. "This is fine."

He smiled and for a moment I wondered what Lorelei saw in him. That spark of jealousy lit again in my belly. I had to stop lying to myself that I didn't have feelings for Lorelei. I would be dead soon. This might be my last chance.

"You know Lorelei well," I broached. I wasn't sure why I was seeking his advice. *Because he has more experience in what she wants.*

"I suppose I know her as well as anyone can. She's quite private."

"Yes, but, um, you know her ... likes and dislikes," I continued, stumbling over how to convey what I meant.

He laughed this time. "It is true we have shared quite a few nights together. Why, what's on your mind?"

I tore off a bit of bread and chewed, hoping the stall would give me time to plan an answer that didn't sound ridiculous. "It's no secret I've been having trouble connecting with her. Our attempts to rebuild our previous relationship have been less than successful." I caught a knowing smirk pass over his lips. "I want to show her that I want this to work. But I haven't been human in a long time and I haven't been the man she knew for three years. If I wanted to win her over, what would you suggest I do?"

Douglas rubbed his chin in thought and I continued eating. He didn't seem to mind. Finally, he leaned on the bar with both hands and looked around us as if concerned about eavesdroppers. "You really want to win her back?"

"Yes," I replied.

"Get some flowers, make her a nice meal. Show her you put in the effort and she'll see you mean business."

In this form I had very little experience preparing food, let alone elaborate meals. But if that was what it took to show Lorelei that I wanted our relationship to work—even if it took up whatever time I had left—I would do it. "Thank you."

"Sure. Good luck."

He strolled off, whistling a tune I hadn't heard before. I downed the rest of the bread and meat as I headed toward the back of the compound. I could pick some flowers from the enclosed area. I was halfway there when Lorelei appeared from her room.

"I was just coming to look for you," she said upon spotting me.

"Oh," I said, unsure of what else to say. I knew I needed to ask her to have a meal with me, but I wanted to surprise her.

"We need to talk."

"Can we do it later? I'm still feeling tired from the mission," I lied.

Her face fell. "Right, of course you are. I'll let you rest."

"Come by my room in a few hours," I said.

"Sure."

I watched her turn on her heel and march back into her room, closing the door with more force than seemed necessary. Now, I just had to hope I could win her over.

I'D SWIPED an extra cup for a vase and set the flowers I'd picked on the makeshift table. Food had been more of an endeavor than I'd realized. I'd earned raised brows and thinly veiled gags from some of the other MCU members. I wiped the back of my hand across my cheeks, picking up trails of tears and sprinkled them over the flowers. At least they perked up a little from the healing effect of the tears.

"What's all this?" Lorelei asked, stepping into the room before I was ready.

"I wanted to surprise you," I answered and gestured at what I hoped was a romantic dinner for two.

She eyed the food and flowers, toying with the end of her braid which fell over her right shoulder. "This is a surprise."

I stepped around her and pulled out the single chair for her to sit down. "Hope you're hungry."

She sat, but remained silent. I settled on the bed, the other side of the makeshift table. "Go ahead," I prompted.

Lorelei poked at the food on her plate before taking a bite. She couldn't mask her reaction. An uncomfortable heat crept up my neck. "I know I don't have a lot of experience cooking but I'd hoped it was better than that."

She coughed. "What is all this about?"

Better to come clean so we suffered no further bouts of miscommunication. "I wanted to show you that I still want this to work."

"And that meant flowers and dinner?"

"I thought you liked that sort of thing."

She burst out laughing. "What gave you that idea?"

The competition, I realized. It made sense Douglas would try to push Lorelei and I apart. With me out of the way he had a better chance of being with her.

"Your boyfriend. That was my mistake trusting him," I answered, my words laced with anger.

"Douglas is not my boyfriend! And you're right,

it was stupid to take his advice. He doesn't know the first thing about what I want in a relationship."

"He's kept your attention for the last two years so is clearly doing something right."

"I told you, it was work. He was an informant. He helped me track other escaped shifters. So that I would have a job where I could find you," she shot back.

"How long did you really look for me? For *him*."

Lorelei opened her mouth, but didn't speak. "I never stopped," she said.

"That doesn't answer the question. How long was it? A few months? A year? Clearly at some point you just gave up," I accused.

"I loved Kegan with everything I had. I've never felt that way about anyone before. I let down my guard with him and I failed. I looked for you, but yes, okay, after a while it was easier to bury the pain of that loss in work and other things."

My appetite soured at her admission. If I wasn't the man she'd loved and I was accepting I never could be, this had no hope of working. Especially since she had been so hurt by being with my previous identity. "I'm sorry you got hurt. And I'm sorry I'm not the man you fell in love with. I can't be that person no matter how hard I try or how much we wish it. I appreciate you not turning me in but I think we should accept that we aren't meant to be."

She chewed her lower lip. "Maybe you're right. But, about the not turning you in part. That's what I needed to talk to you about. I know the mission went south and you didn't get the cure. I've proposed a new plan to the Inner Circle and if I get you on board, I think they'll fall in line."

"What are you proposing?"

"The doxy got the map to Sanctuary. If the Khalas root is anywhere, it's there. But we will need serious credits to travel under radar. You've got the biggest bounty I've seen in a while on your head."

"I don't like where this is going."

"It would be a controlled situation. The doxy would go in with you and let you out as soon as the credits hit my account. She opens the cage, then a window, and off you go. You're back here before you know it."

"Did you forget the part where I can't shift or it might kill me?"

"I know. That's why you don't shift until we get there. You're shifted for a half hour, an hour at most."

In theory, her plan could work. And Mels having my back gave me some comfort. But being in bird form for an hour scared me. "The last time I shifted, I barely made it back and that was only a few minutes."

"I know. But this is the only thing I can see working. If you don't agree to it, we won't do it."

"We don't have a choice," I answered.

She plucked one hairpin from her braid and toyed with it. I tensed, a memory of it hitting me in the arm made the muscle ache. She wouldn't meet my gaze, but I could sense she wanted to say something else.

"What is it?"

"I think you might be right about us not being right for each other."

"Okay. There's something else on your mind."

She looked up, her eyes sparkling with unshed tears. "I think I'm pregnant."

"What?"

"It's not like I planned this. You think I want to be a parent? But I can't deal with it now. Our priority is getting you better."

"It's his, isn't it?" Not that it's really any of my business.

"Please don't say anything. I don't know why I even told you. You're the first person ... the only person I've told. It makes it real."

"I won't say anything but the others need to know, Lorelei. Even if you don't think it matters, they will. He deserves to know he's going to be a father."

She stabbed the hairpin into the tabletop hard enough for it to stick. "They already don't trust me."

"They have a reason to look out for you now. This baby makes you one of them. You can't tell me the government would welcome you back like this."

She shook her head. "No. Will you go with me to tell them?"

I reached across the table and took her hand in mine. "Yes. Just because we can't recapture the past doesn't mean I don't still care about you."

She blew out a breath and stood up, retrieving her hairpin. "Thanks. I appreciate that. Let's get this over with."

TWENTY

TWENTY

LORELEI

Aiden and I went around knocking on doors to alert the Inner Circle to another, what we called, emergency meeting. I didn't think it was an emergency to reveal some damn hybrid accident, but Aiden insisted.

He reached down and squeezed my hand in support once everyone with any decision-making power in this crap hole base were gathered in what must have once been the office of a prominent doctor. The furniture was swankier. Gold and green paneling peeked out from under the dust on the walls. The desk was wood and filled up most of the office. I focused on details so I didn't have to reveal truths.

"Why are we holding another meeting?"

Xander frowned at Aiden and I's entwined hands. "Can't this wait? I'm wiped from this morning's black-market adventure."

"You mean the black-market failure." Mels grinned at Xander, her sharp teeth glinting in the fluorescent light. She made her thumb and index finger into the shape of a "L" and placed it against her forehead, mouthing "loser." Xander scowled, swatting at Mels, who jumped just out of reach.

"How did your ... meal prep go?" Douglas nodded toward Aiden and I's show of solidarity. "Good, yay?"

Aiden flushed. "Not quite. Lorelei needs to tell you something ... tell you all something," he added in case Douglas thought it was all about him. "But first, I've agreed to return to my owner to collect the bounty. Lorelei is correct that we need credits to have any chance of making it to Sanctuary. This is the only way to collect." He glanced at Mels.

"How do we know the siren won't stab us all in the back after she collects?" Mels glared at me and did her 'I'm watching you' hand gesture.

"Because 'the siren' can't go back to work for the PLA." I sighed. "Not in my condition."

Everyone stared at me, blank faced, trying to process my vague-on-purpose news. Constance was the first to figure it out.

"A hybrid baby." She slithered over and patted my stomach. "Congratulations."

Oh, hell, no. I didn't need or want anyone being nice over this. It wasn't nice. It wasn't a happy event. It was the scariest thing I'd ever faced before in my entire life—and that included losing Kegan. Hybrids were one step below phoenixes in value to the Booshies. It was better if I ignored everything associated with this shit-show instead of thinking about how the baby would always have a price tag on his or her head.

"I didn't plan this. I didn't want this." I blinked back tears, refusing to show my fear of my now uncertain future. "I didn't think this job would last as long as it did. I didn't expect to run into the MCU. I left my preventatives at home. I found an emergency one in the bottom of my backpack, but it was so old. I ..." I looked up at the ceiling so I wouldn't have to look at any of their faces. "I didn't take it. I knew the risks, and I didn't take it."

"I bet you didn't stop having sex either," Mels spat. "Whore."

Douglas grabbed Mels wrist and twisted. "Take that back! You know nothing of Lorelei or what she's been through. Apologize now or else—"

"Or else what, nark?" Mels landed an impressive roundhouse kick to the back of Douglas' kneecap. He crumbled to the floor, swearing a long stream of what I assumed were Gaelic curse words. "Why are you even defending her? I bet she was whoring it up behind your back this whole time." Mels nodded toward Aiden, his hand still locked in mine. "Playing one against the other. Classic whore-move."

I pulled my hand free and crossed the small space to Douglas. I kneeled in front of him, and checked to make sure his knee wasn't broken, before putting my palms on either side of his face. I leaned my forehead against his. I was still terrified, but I knew I could trust Douglas to be a standup guy about our little predicament. Despite the bravado he liked to show the world, I knew underneath, it hid insecurity and a deep desire to be loved. Maybe that's what all my walls and pushing people away hid, too. Underneath everything, I just wanted to be loved.

"Only you, Doug," I whispered to him. "I swear it."

"I know, *M'eudail*." Douglas hugged me briefly before using me as a crutch to stand. He leaned against me, unable to place weight on his left leg. I wrapped one arm around his waist in a show of more than physical support. I made my choice. Gods, help me, I made my choice.

Xander looked around the room from me to Douglas to Aiden. "Wait. I'm confused. Who exactly is the siren screwing? And how do we know she's telling the truth about the hybrid? It could be some government plot to infiltrate the MCU."

Mels clapped her hands together. "I didn't think about that! Great job, birdie. She's a whore and a liar. You really know how to pick them, don't you, Dougie?"

"If I would lie about something, it wouldn't be this." I surprised myself by being able to keep from yelling a big "fuck you" at the inner circle and storming out of the room. Either that or kicking the doxy in the face. "I'm not into faking pregnancies. Especially hybrid ones. You all know where hybrids stand in the list of desirable Booshie pets. Why would I put a target on anyone's back, let alone a baby?"

"To collect the bounty." Xander crossed his arms over his chest. "What other reason do you need? A phoenix hybrid would net a mil easy. Probably more."

Aiden had the sense to look embarrassed. It seemed like no one explained the shifter elemental rule to the free-range bird before. Constance stepped up to the plate.

"Fire and water don't mix, dear," she informed him. "You need compatible elemental ... participants … to create a hybrid. In this case that means water and water."

The truth slowly dawned on Xander. He swiveled toward Douglas. "Fuck, man. Seriously?"

"We're in a relationship and have been for almost two and half years. Before you stop me, just hear me out." Douglas rattled on before I could correct him. *More feelings.* Ugh! "I know you call it 'work', Lore, but it's never been just work. Not for me. I hope not for you either. I've been patient. I've waited for you to realize what I've known all along. It's complicated, I know, and messy and a million other things you never want to talk about but a hybrid baby—*our* baby—is just the natural progression of our relationship. Why didn't you tell me the second you suspected the possibility?"

"If I don't talk about it, I don't have to deal with it," I mumbled.

I was happy when Mels interrupted whatever Douglas planned to come back with by sticking her finger in her throat and making gagging sounds. The doxy was good for something after all. "Yuck. We get it. Take it somewhere else, mom and dad. We have better things to spend our time on."

"The plan for returning me to my former owner goes forward as soon as we're prepared," Aiden got the conversation back on track, to saving his life.

"But you spent so much time getting out of that

hellhole," Xander argued. "We can find another way to get the money. I'll fill as many vials as I can with Phoenix tears and sell them to the highest bidder if it means keeping you out of that cage."

Aiden shuddered at the thought of the gilded cage he escaped from almost six weeks ago. "This is the only way. I know I won't be in any true danger if everyone plays their part."

"But what about the blood graft?" Constance asked. "The Booshie woman is expecting a bird, not a man. You can't shift without the graft working overtime in your system."

"That's why I only shift right before reaching her compound," Aiden repeated the plan as I had told it to him. "Mels, if you agree, you'll be with me the entire time in tiny form. Pick the cage lock and we're free. It's hazy, but I remember my owner leaving the window open before my first escape. With luck, that will remain the same for my second."

"And if it doesn't?" Xander asked.

"I bust the window lock too." Mels seemed on board which was a huge hurdle. "If I can't pick it, I'll smash the glass." She grinned at Aiden. "A little vandalism sounds like a fun way to spend an afternoon."

Aiden's shoulders sagged as all the tension left his body. "You'll help me?"

"We all will, dear." Constance squeezed Aiden's hand in support. "We're not going to let you die on us. Not after your first real taste of freedom in three years."

"Thank you," Aiden whispered. "All of you."

TWENTY-ONE

TWENTY-ONE

AIDEN

I didn't have much to gather, given all I had was the clothes the Inner Circle had given me. I'd be shedding those soon enough. I ended up in the front bar area where Constance lounged, the thick coils of her serpentine body curled beneath her.

"You look troubled," she said, patting the chair beside her.

I sat and studied my hands. "I was just getting used to this place and now we have to leave ... because of me."

"It's kind of you to worry but this isn't our first home and it won't be our last. The people we are leaving behind will carry on the mission and protect those who seek our help. Just like you."

"Finding Sanctuary is a long shot," I muttered.

She slid one finger under my chin and tilted my face until our gazes met. "That attitude will not get you there. We keep fighting, no matter what. Even you."

"I suppose after everything I've been through, it is harder to keep hope alive than I realized."

"You are taking a great risk to secure your continued freedom. But I admire you for it. Few men would put their lives in danger for the prospect of bringing about a better world for others." She tapped my chin. "You're not the only one hoping Sanctuary is real."

Her slit pupils diminished, turning far more human than I had ever seen them. The added humanity brought with it a sadness I hadn't seen before, either. "If you'll excuse me, dear, I need to finish preparing."

"Thank you for the pep talk," I said.

She smiled, her tongue darting out between her lips. As she slithered away down the hall, I could almost swear her tail shortened and split, turning into legs. If we had to run, it would be easier on two feet, but it hurt to know this venture to save my life forced her to take a form she didn't want.

"Can we talk?" Xander's voice came from the opposite direction. The front door stood ajar.

"Sure," I replied. If our plan went off without a hitch, we would spend a lot more time in close quarters. Whatever there was between us, we needed to resolve it now.

"Did it upset you when you found out about the baby?" He leaned on the table beside me.

"I was relieved, actually," I admitted.

He laughed. "Is that so?"

"Lorelei and I reached a point where it became obvious, we are not the people we used to be and are not the ones we are meant to be with."

Color warmed his cheeks, fighting to bring out the red of his hair underneath all of the dye. "And who are you meant to be with?"

It was a loaded question and I knew he expected a certain answer. Part of me wanted to give him that answer, but I couldn't keep lying to the people around me. I didn't have time for that. "I don't know. That's the truth."

"You have got to be joking. Stop lying to yourself, Aiden. There is something here."

Every fiber of my being wanted to deny his statement. "You might fall in love easily but I don't."

"You fell for her pretty damn fast," he quipped.

"I'm not Kegan. I have a fragment or two of his memory but I'm not him. I stopped being him the moment they took me and forced me to rise. You of all people should understand that."

"You think it's going to happen again, don't

you? I'm telling you it won't. You didn't have backup then. You've got us now."

"I truly do appreciate that support. But, be realistic, Xander. I'm dying. We all know it. Whether I'm human or bird, the blood graft will reach my heart and it will kill me. Even if I accepted that there was something between us, it isn't fair to you."

"You don't get to decide what's fair to me or what I can handle," he argued, pushing himself away from the table and pacing.

"You really would be okay with falling for someone who has a high probability of dying and leaving you?" I yelled.

"If it means getting to experience some happiness in this godforsaken world, then yes, I'd be okay with it. It may have escaped your notice but we aren't exactly living the high life here. We're barely surviving. And the more shifters we help, the higher the risk someone actually finds us. So, do I want to believe that we will save your life? Absolutely. That means everything we've been doing isn't for nothing." He closed the distance between us and kissed me.

It didn't catch me off guard like the first time. A tiny voice in the back of my head had warned it was coming. We'd been doing this dance of avoidance for weeks and time was up. I didn't pull away. Instead, I let the feeling of his lips on mine wash over me. If it was possible to channel all of one's feelings and intentions into one gesture, Xander managed it. It was as if he was sharing his hopes and desires for a future where our kind weren't hunted—where we could explore this thing between us—and begging me to take on some of the burden.

Letting my heart take control, I kissed him back, doing my best to tell him I accepted his burden. All of these people believed I would survive and we would find a better place for our kind away from the harsh treatment of humanity. We parted and my breath came in ragged gasps. I sunk back into the chair. Maybe the exertion was more than I could handle.

"Whoah, what just happened?" Xander kept one hand on my shoulder.

"I think maybe it took more out of me than I realized." My pulse pounded in my ears. Not a good sign. "And I think we may run up against the clock sooner than we expected."

He brushed a stray strand of hair off my forehead. "I promise I won't let anything happen to you. We will find Sanctuary and we will save you. End of story."

I shook my head. "No."

"Don't make me go over this again."

"It isn't the end of the story. It's the beginning. If we succeed, we have an eternity to figure this out.

If we find Sanctuary, no one will force us to rise if we aren't ready."

"I like the sound of that."

"Hey, love birds," Mels called, a pack slung over one shoulder. Given how flat it was, I deduced it would hold my clothing while I shifted and we enacted our ruse.

"Is it time?" I asked.

"So says the siren. Reserve your strength. You will need it," she said and gave me a plaintive look. She didn't want me to risk the poison working faster.

"I'm ready. Let's go."

TWENTY-TWO
TWENTY-TWO
LORELEI

Me, Aiden, and Mels alone together on a day long journey to the City was not my idea of a good time. I didn't like leaving the others behind, but too many people meant too much attention. As it was, Mels needed to travel in tiny form. If the light hit her wings just right, we'd be screwed. The people in the poorer, rural areas around the City loved turning in shifters for credits. We couldn't risk it. Aiden wore a long sleeve shirt despite the heat to cover his sigils and a stocking hat over his bright flame-red hair. My PLA gear might give me away, but it also got us a wide berth from any humans in the Podunk towns looking to nark out rogue shifters. Everyone respected federal agents. We may not get to the City unnoticed, but we'd get there undisturbed.

We walked half a day before we reached the train hub. High-speed trains zipped up and down the tracks going to and from different areas of the City. I didn't like the crowds, but it may work to our advantage. The more people, the less likely someone would notice us. I bought tickets from the automated kiosk, hoping that using the rail system for the last leg of our trip was a smart move instead of our downfall.

"How are you holding up?" I asked Aiden as we waited on the platform for the next train. None of us had slept since leaving the MCU base. Sleep could wait. We needed to focus on the mission at hand.

Aiden found an empty bench and sunk onto it. "It feels as if this journey is taking twice as long as when I left."

"That's because you were flying before," Mels piped up from her perch on his shoulder. "Everything takes less time with wings."

"Enough talk about wings," I hissed. "Do you want to out us as shifters?"

"Birdie and I will just fly away." Mels shrugged her tiny shoulders. "Not my problem what happens to you."

I sat down next to Aiden, but directed my

words at the doxy. "Look, I don't like working together any more than you do, but for this to have any hope of success, we need to put our differences aside. You can hate me again in the morning."

"I plan to." She flashed me a miniaturized version of her lethal poisoned-smile. "If you double-cross us, siren, I'll bite Doug."

The old me would have said "go right ahead, see if I care." The new me—the one who wanted to do the right thing instead of just survive in this crap world we called home—didn't answer. Not right away at least. "If we all get out of this alive, do you want to call a truce?" I asked.

Mels frowned, not expecting that answer. "That depends on the outcome, now, doesn't it?"

"It's a simple yes or no."

"Nothing is ever simple," she said. "I'll give ya a 'maybe.'"

It was better than a no. I nodded. "I'll take it."

I helped Aiden onto the train once it pulled up to the platform. He was fading fast even in human form. At this rate, he might die before we made it back to the MCU base, let alone all the way to Sanctuary. I didn't tell Mels my suspicions. She only needed to look at him to know he was going downhill faster than we thought.

"Hang in there, Aiden," I whispered. "Don't you dare die on me a second time."

We found seats in a car at the back of the train. I bought tickets fair and square, but wouldn't put it past Madame Faberge to put out an APB on me for taking so damn long to deliver her bird. The longer it took the ticket taker to reach us, the more time I had to plan in case there was now a bounty on my head as well as Aiden's.

"Tickets ... tickets ... tickets ..."

I dug around in my backpack until I found my black hooded jacket. I pulled it on as the ticket taker entered our train car, making sure the hood hid my hair. I bet I looked suspicious as hell, but I couldn't worry about that now.

"Tickets?" The man—a human and not a bot or shifter hiding in plain sight—stopped in front of our seats.

I held out our paper tickets. He scanned them and moved on before circling back to our row.

"Is anything wrong?" I looked him in the eye. People with something to hide don't make eye contact. I needed to convince him we were just travelers returning to the City after a vacation or some shit.

"You feds?" He gestured at my PLA gear.

"Phoenix Location Agency." I jerked a thumb at Aiden. "We're going home after two weeks off. My boyfriend partied a little too hearty in Absecon if you get my drift."

The ticket taker smirked at Aiden, taking his inability to open his eyes as drunkenness instead of the blood graft winding its way through his system. "If you're PLA, maybe you can help me with something." He pulled out his phone and tapped a few buttons to bring up the photo feature. "This was beamed over to us about a month ago. Seems like this siren went rogue and skipped out on a gig. Pocketed the finder's fee first, of course, the little cheat. Madame is out a Phoenix and credits. We're supposed to bring both bird and fish in if we see them. Have you seen her around the PLA office? The guy is what the bird would look like if he shifted."

A holographic image of Aiden and I popped up from his phone. I leaned forward to study it more closely. No. No, not Aiden and I. *Kegan* and I. We were standing just behind the circus curtain in costume waiting to start our act, not aware of anything, but each other. When did Madame Faberge have time to take a picture of us? Had she been trailing us, waiting for just the right time to kidnap Kegan? She planned it. I never stood a chance of rescuing him.

"They don't look familiar." I tapped the screen of my phone against his to transfer a copy of the picture. "I'll keep this on file just in case I run across them."

The ticket taker tipped his hat toward me. "Thanks, miss. I appreciate the effort."

"Not a problem." I used my no-nonsense federal agent voice. I held my breath and waited for him to move on. After a brief hesitation, he did just that.

"Almost there," I whispered to Aiden. "Hang on."

MADAME FABERGE'S estate was just as gaudy and gilded as I remembered. I stopped Aiden and Mels just outside the range of the security cameras. It was better if no one knew we were coming.

"This is it, then?" Mels hovered in the air just above Aiden's shoulder. "You ready to shift, birdie?"

Aiden attempted to stand up straight. He took off his clothes without help, folded them, and placed them in the empty pack. Before shifting, he looked over his shoulder at me. "He loved you, you know," he said. "Kegan. I may have forgotten everything else, but I remember that."

"Thanks," I said, self-conscious. "That sounds suspiciously like a good-bye."

Aiden smiled. "I never got the chance before."

"No one is dying or rising or anything else, ya

here me?" Mels ordered. "We get in, we get out, we go home."

"I hope you're right." Aiden took a deep breath before he willed himself to shift. The sigils on his arms and back glowed gold before feathers sprouted where skin had been. His legs grew spindly and toes became claws as the transformation claimed the last bits of his humanity. He was now bird instead of man. I held out my arm when it was over. Aiden cocked his brightly feathered head my direction, as if trying to decide whether or not to trust me. I hummed a bit of siren song to entice him to cooperate. The notes wove their invisible spell around him. He blinked once and hopped onto my arm.

"Get this right, siren." Mels tucked herself into the underside of my jacket's hood. She'd transfer to Aiden's cage as soon as we were inside.

"I plan to, doxy."

I marched to the estate's gate and pressed the intercom. "Yes?" a guard's voice crackled over the system.

"PLA," I said. I lifted my arm to show off Aiden perched near my wrist. "Returning Madame Faberge's runaway phoenix."

"It's about damn time." The guard buzzed us in.

"We got this," I said to Aiden. "I won't let you die."

"FRANKLY, my dear, this is the worst service I've ever received from the PLA." Madame Faberge said, alternating between sipping her tea and sniffing into a handkerchief. Cages line the parlor. Fairies, selkies, sunbirds, dryads. Hell, why didn't I notice them all before? I was so focused on collecting a paycheck and my own agenda, I failed to see all the shifters and magical creatures suffering right in front of me.

"Six weeks and not a single check in with your superior?" Madame Faberge continued. "That is unacceptable. I have a mind to call the PLA and cancel the payment."

"Your Phoenix was crafty." I held my tea cup, but didn't drink. If she feeds her pets blood graft, I don't want to find out what she might slip into my tea. "He knew enough to head straight for the middle of nowhere. My phone didn't work in those conditions. If I went somewhere with proper reception, the trail would have grown cold. It already took me longer than I'd expected to find your bird. I didn't want to keep you waiting any longer."

She bought it, or at least pretended she did. "That's very thoughtful of you, my dear. How is my little Aiden-waiden?"

"See for yourself." I stood and walked toward

the cage. Mels hopped out of my jacket's hood and crawled under Aiden's water dish when I got close. "No worse for wear after his little adventure. I understand you're disappointed in the time frame of return. I'd be willing to offer a one-time 10% discount off the bounty."

Madame Faberge's eyes narrowed. "20%."

We needed credits and fast. 20% off a million credits would still get us to Sanctuary and the source of the Khalas root.

I stuck out my hand to shake. "Deal. As you can see, your Aiden is home safe where he belongs. Transfer the credits to the PLA. I'll wait."

I watched as Madame Faberge took out her phone and punched some numbers into the keypad. I acted as nonchalant as possible as I waited for my phone to ding to alert me to the bounty being transferred from the main PLA holding to my personal account. I could liquidate the funds later. We didn't have time to hang out in the City until morning. Once Mels sprung Aiden, we were hopping right back on the train for the boonies.

Ding.

"It's been a pleasure doing business with you, Madame Faberge." I smiled. "Keep me in mind for future projects."

I left before anyone could stop me. I got the money. The second part of our plan was up to Mels.

TWENTY-THREE
TWENTY-THREE

AIDEN

The world became fuzzy as I settled behind the gilded bars of my confines. Weariness set in and I could not focus on the one in front of me. I sensed another presence, one I should find comforting, but the urge to sleep was strong.

"Don't go," a tiny voice called.

Blinking, a tiny creature appeared in front of me. The human part of me fought to claim some control. To remember what was happening. What was supposed to happen. I shook my head and ruffled my feathers to rouse myself.

There was another presence here I should find calming. I focused on the creature just beyond the cage. She was important. I knew this no matter what form I took. She left, the one trailing after her.

"Time to go," the tiny creature called. She flew free of the cage with no effort, darting amongst the creatures that sat confined around me.

Their cages fell open and as if roused by the sudden scent of freedom, they fled. One by one they crawled through openings in the room. Larger creatures forced their way out of high spaces. The creature that had been my comfort returned and my cage door swung open.

Freedom.

The human part of me urged me forward. I could not stay in this form. It was too dangerous. My body was sluggish as I took to the air. The other creatures raced out of the space, leaving me to trail them. My guide darted in and out of my range of vision, calling me onward. We would be free. Finally.

SANCTUARY

CAPTIVITY BOOK 2

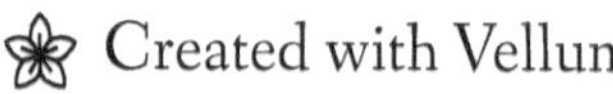 Created with Vellum

ONE

ONE

LORELEI

I paced back and forth in our designated meeting spot two miles away until I was positive I'd wear a hole in the grass. Where were Mels and Aiden? They should have been here ten minutes ago. If we wanted to save Aiden's life before the blood graft stopped his heart, we needed to move as fast as we could to the shifter haven of Sanctuary to get the khalas root cure. No one knew if Sanctuary was a myth or not, but we didn't have time to be picky at this point. Traveling undetected wasn't cheap—especially for a group of shifters. We had the money now, thanks to a plan I'm still not sure how we pulled off without Aiden's Booshie former owner turning us in to the feds. Still, we were safe. Or at least I was. Now Mels just needed to hold up her end of the plan.

"Come on. Don't screw this up, doxy," I muttered. "Where are you?"

"Miss me?" Mels shifted into girl-sized form in front of me. "I got a little side-tracked."

"Doing what?" I demanded. "Where's Aiden? We agreed to stick to the plan."

She wagged a finger at me. "One question at a time. One: I couldn't leave them all behind, so I sprang the whole lot. Everyone in a cage in that witch's parlor of horrors is now free. Two: Aiden landed on that tree over there." She gestured off to my right. "It's okay now, birdie. You can shift."

Aiden fell out of the tree, still in bird form. *Shit.*

Mels and I ran to him. I reached him first. I cradled him in my arms like I would any dying animal. *No. No, no, no, no, no.*

"What's wrong?" Mels asked. "Why didn't he shift?"

"He can't," I said. "The blood graft is moving too quickly. He's lost his ability to change form."

"But that means—"

"He'll be dead before we get back to base the regular way." I passed Aiden to Mels. "Fly. Fly as fast as you can. See if the sunbird or someone has any ideas on how to fix this. I'll catch up with you when I can."

Mels, tough as nails Mels, cried. Bluish tears tracked down her dirt-streaked face. "Douglas will murder me if you're not with us."

"Tell him I..." I shook my head. This was no time to get sentimental. I needed to think about how to get back to base undetected. *They* needed to go now before the blood graft stopped Aiden's heart. "Just tell him whatever you think he'd want to hear." I paused, straining to catch the hint of a song I heard carried on the wind. To most men, and even magical creatures, it would sound like nonsense words, but I could translate. It was siren-speak. They were calling to me. More than that, they were tracking me.

We're coming. We're coming. We're coming for you. Siren-sister, beware. The tide is turned. We're coming. We're coming. We're coming for you.

"Go now," I urged Mels. "Go, before it's too late."

She swiped at the blue streaks on her cheeks before nodding. "Just try to make it back, okay? I don't like leaving anyone behind. It's not the MCU way."

I tilted my head to the right, listening as my sisters' siren song grew closer. Given the strength of the song, there were at least three. Enough to be considered a shiver. Like sharks, but far more dangerous to shifters. It wouldn't be hard to get a personal item of mine to aid in tracking. They'd just need to swipe something from my desk at the PLA and they'd have an instant link to me no matter where I was.

"Go," I repeated. "Trust me, I'm not going down without a fight."

Mels shifted to tiny doxy form with no further protests. She picked up Aiden and zipped away before I could tell her to go a third time. I took a deep breath and double-checked that my government-issued taser and small throwing knives were all within easy reach in my PLA vest pockets. I pulled one of my sharpened silver hairpins from my braid. I didn't want a fight, but there was no way I would wait for a shiver of my siren sisters empty-handed.

I didn't have to wait long.

"Hello, Grady. Hello, Aria. Hello, Darya," I called as three of my co-workers emerged from the woods on the outskirts of the capital. "I see Macy sent the best. Should I be flattered? I'm not scared, if that's what she hoped for."

"Shit, Lorelei, what are you playing at?" Grady planted her staff—more like a cattle prod—into the ground. She was a fan of 'go big or go home' for weapons. More power to her if she could take down people with an electrified staff. I preferred the hidden but deadly mode of combat.

"I don't know what you mean," I stalled. The

longer I distracted them, the longer Mels had to get Aiden back to the Magical Creature Underground. "The job took longer than I expected, but I still brought the bird home."

"Aiding and abetting an escaped phoenix?" Grady continued as if I'd said nothing. "I thought you got over that, like, a couple years ago."

"What can I say?" I held one hand behind my back so they couldn't see my steel hairpin. "Old habits die hard."

Aria narrowed her eyes. "You don't deny it?"

"If I did, would you believe me?"

"We don't want to hurt you, Lorelei," Darya—the most sensible of the group sent to hunt me down—said. "We need you to come back to face the charges."

"Charges? What charges?" I asked. "Since when is it a crime to take six weeks to close a case?"

The last time I helped Aiden, who was Kegan back then, I came back and claimed I was ambushed and held against my will by a crooked circus owner who forced me to shift to siren form and perform in his show. The circus part was true. The rest was not. I did nothing I didn't want to. Still, I needed my job back to find Kegan, and faking a kidnapping was easier than faking amnesia. They'd never charged me with any crime. This was new.

"Escaping from captivity is a crime," Darya

said, voice flat as if she was reciting the boring laws they taught us all in PLA siren training. "You aided an escaped criminal. You're an accomplice to the phoenix's crime."

"Do you really believe all that bullshit they fed us at the Institute?" Out of the three sisters Macy sent for me, I had the highest chance of flipping Darya. Two against two was a fair fight.

Darya's fingers tightened around the handle of her taser. "Come with us, Lorelei. Make this easy on everyone." Her voice held just a hint of glamour. Where did she get off trying that mind-control shit on me? We all had the same training in resisting.

"And if I don't?"

"You give us no choice but to use force."

Grady, always itching for a fight, flung a shuriken at me so fast I almost didn't have time to block it. I retaliated with a sharpened hairpin toward her leg. It found its mark, lodging in Grady's upper thigh. She howled in pain, crumpling to the ground when her wounded leg refused to hold her. Felling Grady bought me some time to think, but she wouldn't be down long. Darya and Aria wouldn't wait around for me to come to them, either.

Aria grabbed Grady's staff and charged. I sidestepped her attack at the last second, throwing her off balance when she needed to stop short and change direction. The next time she came at me, I swept her left knee out from under her. The Academy discouraged sirens from having any close relationships because emotion equaled weakness, but these girls were the closest thing to family I had in this crap-hole world we called home. I didn't want to hurt them, but I would defend myself.

Instead of attacking, Darya knelt next to Aria to check on the status of her knee. I doubt I broke it. I held back with the force of the knee sweep. With two sisters down and one more interested in assessing health statuses, I saw my opportunity to escape. I knew they must have an object of mine to track me. Even if I somehow figured out who had it, and snatched it back to disrupt their tracking ability, all they needed to do was go back to the office and find another object. Getting close enough to pick their pockets didn't appeal to me either. There was one other way to disrupt the magical binding between hunted and object: Water. The trail would grow cold the longer I was in water.

"Darya, just do yourself a favor and tell them you couldn't find me."

She shook her head, close to tears. For a brief second, I felt sorry that our supervisor Macy got her mixed up in all of this. Darya had always been too sensitive for a job like ours. "I can't do that."

"Just think about where you want your loyalties

to lie," I said. "When it comes to a fight, who do you think will have your back? Me, or the government?"

Darya slid her taser from its holster. I stepped closer to the river bank, preparing to jump in if she came at me. Water and electrical current didn't mix, but I could swim fast enough to only get a slight shock if she charged the water. Instead, Darya held the taser against Aria's neck and zapped her into unconsciousness.

"Darya! What the fuck are you doing?" Grady yelled as Darya advanced on her next.

"We didn't see Lorelei," Darya said. "Say it, or I'll do the same to you."

Grady, unable to walk thanks to my handiwork, threw every small weapon hidden in her boots and vest pockets at Darya. In her haste she didn't bother to aim, just throw. Darya deflected any object that came close.

"Say it!" she repeated. "We didn't see Lorelei. We lost the signal at the river." Darya pressed the taser button until blue sparks crackled between the prongs. "Say it, Grady. Say it."

"We lost the signal at the river." Grady glared at me. "You'd better run, Lorelei, because this is the only head-start I'm giving you."

"The PLA froze your account," Darya added. "You can't access the bounty you collected, or anything else you saved up. They'll use it to track you."

I nodded. "Understood. Thanks. I'm sure I'll see you around sometime."

"Count on it," Grady answered.

I wouldn't hang around and wait for them to change their minds. I bundled everything I didn't want to get wet into my waterproof PLA pack and dived into the water. The contaminants stung my eyes, but it was a small price to pay for freedom. I didn't doubt my sisters would regroup and continue the hunt. Until then, I planned to take advantage of every second they afforded me. Every second they held off on tracking was a second closer to saving Aiden's life.

TWO

TWO

AIDEN

Darkness and numbness—two concepts my human brain understood—enveloped me. I could still sense the swells of the air currents buoying me onward. To where, I could not recall. My mind—the one that belonged to the other—tried to remember what had led me to this point.

"Hang on," a tiny voice called.

The swells dipped and I had enough sensation to feel the plummet as I descended. *Shouldn't my wings work?* I tried to flap them, but their response was sluggish.

"I know you want to help, but save your strength," the voice spoke again. It was only by sheer force of will that the human part of me comprehended what was said.

The voice carried me onward and I let the darkness take me. It was nice within that void, nothing to worry over. No fear of the gilded cage. Just empty. I had no concept of how long the currents and the voice carried me, but from out of nowhere a cacophony erupted around me. I was too tired to make sense of the sounds around me. Sounds rose and fell, and rose again. I tried to open my eyes, to take in more than darkness. Fuzzy grey forms took shape and I knew I should know them, understand what they represented, but the numbness was trying to reclaim me and it was all I could do not to let it win.

All at once the sounds faded and something warm wrapped around me. It called me to rest. Not in the same way as the numbness. This was hot and fiery, and sang on a level only my kind could understand. It called for me to live, not to give in to the ashes trying to burst into flame inside me. To claim all of what I had become. Dampness touched my feathers, and the world took on more focus. Faces peered at me from above. My human mind understood the expression to be fear and worry.

"We have to get him out of shift," the owner of the warmth said. I could feel his voice rumble against my body.

The voices argued over one another, too quick for me to follow. How I longed to be in human form. To warn them of what was coming. I could feel the burning beginning at the core of my being. It wouldn't be long now before I couldn't contain the fire. The warmth of the one holding me receded and another being appeared, bent close. A soft hand stroked the plumage on my head and whispered something my animal brain was incapable of understanding. The stroking continued and I became lost in the being's gaze. The dampness that had awoken me from the numbness continued to keep me afloat as the lull of the being before me called to the deeper part of me. The one hidden beneath wing and feather and beak. The one who could stop the burning from turning into a raging fire.

Moment by moment, the urge to become the other strengthened, less easy to ignore. Wings lengthened, and pain sizzled along every nerve in my form. This form did not want to give in, no matter how much my mind willed it. The stroking grew more intense, more fevered, and I found myself pulled deeper into the gaze. It gave me no choice. The change cascaded over me and feathers became flesh. My legs and torso lengthened, and again I was standing on two feet.

Or I would have been standing if they had borne my weight. I collapsed sideways, falling naked into Xander's arms. My mind reeled from the change and my head throbbed. I could still feel the embers burning in my chest. Begging to ignite and take over, to give me new life. Rising would quell the poison in my veins, but I had given up so much to stay who I was now.

"I've got you," Xander whispered in my ear. His arms encircled me and held tight.

"Get him to Micah," Constance hissed. I recalled how she had shifted into her human form when last I'd seen her. She was now more snake than woman, her entire body covered in scales.

"Did ... we do it?" I asked, my throat parched.

"We got the money," Mels answered.

"Where's Lorelei?" Douglas demanded.

Micah burst in before anyone else could speak. He took one look at me and his naturally mocha skin went pale. Pale was not a good look for someone who could burn as bright as the sun. "It's gotten worse."

I nodded. "I could feel the rising coming. If I hadn't shifted, I think it would have taken me."

"That will *not* happen," Xander said, still not letting me go.

Mels vanished, reappearing with new clothes. I struggled into them. There were gaps in my memory. No doubt from the blood graft working faster in shifted form. Douglas' point still stood: We weren't going anywhere without Lorelei. For one she had the money, if Mels was telling the truth and we'd succeeded.

"I need to know where Lorelei is. You'd better not have left her behind," Douglas snarled, towering over Mels. I had only known him for a few weeks, but in that time I never witnessed his temper flaring like this. I could only imagine the anger fueled by the body and power of a horse.

"She gave us time to get away. It wasn't as clean we thought. There was a little ... hiccup."

"Define little."

"I had to get them out. If you'd seen them all in that bitch's golden prison, you couldn't have left them behind either," Mels answered.

"I ... I remember that," I said.

"We got to the meeting spot, but Aiden wasn't doing so hot. She sent me on ahead. She wanted to make sure he was okay, and she swore she'd be right behind us."

"You didn't look, did you?"

"She's a fucking government-trained operative. She's a resourceful fish. Besides, she told me there's no way she's not making it back to you."

A little of his anger faded. "She said that?"

Mels nodded. "She's not giving up on you. On any of us. Like she said, she's got no one else to turn to. We're her best shot at survival. We have to be patient."

"How soon can we move Aiden?" Constance asked, scales receding from her upper body.

Micah hovered over me, checking my pulse and feeling for what I assumed was a fever. "An hour. Maybe two. Getting more food into him with some fluids wouldn't be a bad thing."

"I'll be okay as long as I don't have to shift. I'm feeling better already." It was a lie. I could still feel the embers of a rising calling, urging me to give in and be reborn. But I would *not* slow down the group. Not when they were taking these risks just for a chance to save me. I hated being a burden to them, but if they weren't giving up on me I couldn't give up on myself.

Constance slithered off to fetch me food and drink, when the front door burst open and Lorelei staggered in—drenched head to toe with murky water. Her eyes darted around the room before landing on me. Her shoulders dropped a fraction of an inch. She, too, had worried about my failure to shift back at the meeting point.

"We need to move, now. My sisters are coming for us and I've bought about as much of a head-start as we're likely to get."

THREE

THREE

LORELEI

I took a deep breath, willing my fight or flight instinct—well, fight instinct—to calm down. I made it. I was back with the MCU. Bonus, Aiden was out of bird form. How did they manage that?

Douglas rushed forward once he got over the shock of me appearing out of nowhere. He touched my face, my wet hair, my arms, everywhere, as if to make sure I was real. "Never scare me like that again." He pressed his hands against my cold cheeks before kissing me. "What if something happened to you or the wee bairn? If you don't care for your own safety, think about the baby."

Right. The baby. I forgot about the baby. I'd been trying to forget about the baby since I first suspected I could be pregnant with the little hybrid siren/kelpie accident. There was no way I would tell Little Accident's dad that, though. Instead, I squeezed sludge out of my waterlogged braid and changed the subject. "How long until Aiden is strong enough to be moved?"

"Two hours," Dr. Sunbird said.

"Good. I'm washing this muck off and then we throw everything we can into whatever travels easy and get the hell out of here. And it won't be as easy as we thought. Turns out the PLA expected I might run off with the credits, so they froze all my assets. We'll rough it."

"Hold up. First off, you're telling me we risked birdie's life for no fucking reason?" Mels hissed.

"It wasn't for no reason," I replied, my voice dipping a little. I should have realized the PLA would take measures like this.

"Guess my plan wasn't as stupid as you thought," Xander muttered.

I resisted the urge to stab Free Range. "Look, you can be mad at me all you want. But we need to move."

"When did you start making the decisions for everyone?" Mels protested. "Last I checked we're in the inner circle, not you. Any plan that affects the MCU needs a majority vote."

"We have two options." I emptied every drawer in the room of medical supplies while I talked. "We stick around here and wait to be arrested by three sirens who are very good at their jobs, or pack what we can carry and head out as soon as Aiden is strong enough to travel. Have you ever been in a Booshie-run prison before? It's worse than being kept in a cage."

Aiden struggled to sit up. I appreciated his attempt at rallying. "Lorelei knows what we're facing. I vote we leave tonight."

Mels threw up her hands in defeat. "You're not inner circle, either! No one votes anything except us!"

"Then put it to a vote already." Xander's eyes never left Aiden as he spoke. "All those in favor of following the siren's plan to get out while we still can, say aye." A chorus of 'aye' votes came from Douglas, Constance, and Xander. "Those opposed, say nay."

"Nay!" Mels raised both hands and waved them around, as if that somehow made her vote count more.

"The ayes have it." Xander dragged a chair next to where Aiden rested. "You guys throw whatever crap you think I want to take with me in a backpack. I'm staying with Aiden until we leave."

"You don't have to do that," Aiden protested, voice weak.

"I know I don't have to." Xander squeezed

Aiden's hand, not seeming to care who saw his clear affection. "I want to."

Constance slithered over and patted my grungy arm. "Go wash up, dear. We'll handle the packing."

"My room," Douglas said when I looked over at him, unsure where I would clean up now that the inner circle had agreed on a plan. "That way you won't have to use the communal washroom. I'll pack while you're in the shower."

I followed Douglas down the hall, even though I already knew the way to his room. "Just make sure packing is all you have planned, horse face."

He grinned. "Is it my fault I'm happy to see you?"

I ignored him. Instead, I walked into the bathroom and turned the shower on. I let the steam from the hot water fill the room before I stuck my head out the door to check on Douglas. He looked up and flashed his bright grin at me again.

"Want me to join you, fish fins?"

"The only thing I want is for you to pack our shit so we can get the hell out of here. Macy sicced Grady, Aria, and Darya on us. I think we have a chance of flipping Darya to our side—she didn't attack when she could have—but the others are committed to the PLA. It wouldn't surprise me if there's a bounty on Aiden and me now."

"Grady tried to break my arm once." Douglas

pulled a backpack out from under his sagging bed and set it next to where I'd dropped my pack on the floor. "She's got a temper, that one." He shrugged. "She may not like how I deal in the exchange of information, but she's also the one who told you to find me for that first case we worked on together. I'm grateful for that."

"Don't get sentimental on me now, Doug."

"I like when you call me Doug."

"Pack!" I reminded him before shutting the bathroom door.

FOUR

FOUR

AIDEN

X ander hovered nearby, not taking his eyes off me. Like, if he blinked, I'd disappear altogether. I couldn't blame him. I hadn't told them how close to death I'd been. And I wasn't in the mood to see if this relationship would work if I were yet another new person. I sipped the tea that Constance brought me. "You don't have to stay here. You should go pack your things," I said, and set the cup down.

"I told them to pack for me. Besides, it's just clothes. Not like I've got anything sentimental here."

"I doubt that. You've lived here your entire existence. There have to be things that mean something to you," I countered.

He shook his head. He'd reapplied his hair dye , turning it almost jet black. I hoped one day I'd be able to see him as he'd been born. "You know as well as I do that we don't hold on to our past. It seemed unnecessary to keep things that meant something to someone I no longer am and can't remember. Besides, someone has to make sure you keep up your strength."

I spooned the soup someone had rustled up into my mouth to appease him. The burning in my chest was receding, but the memory of it still haunted my mind. It wouldn't go away. I was certain of that. Not until every bit of poison left my body. "You were worried about me, weren't you?"

"Of course I was worried about you. I thought I made that clear before you left."

"I could have died if Constance hadn't been able to pull me out of the shift. I could feel the poison fighting her. I almost wasn't strong enough to stop it," I admitted.

"You're stronger than you give yourself credit for," he muttered.

"I'm not sure about that."

"I promise you I'll get you there and we *will* find the cure."

Dampness and healing warmth still tingled on my skin. "You used a tear, didn't you?"

He shrugged. "It wasn't a big deal."

"Xander, that's three times in six weeks you've shed tears for me. You know how dangerous that is.'

"You gave them up at the black market."

"And look what happened. I wasn't able to shift back on my own. It weakened me."

"You didn't say anything."

"Because I assumed you understood the consequences!" I slammed the bowl down on the table and stood up. To the surprise of us both, my legs held my weight.

"We're doing all of this—leaving our home and risking our lives—to save you," Xander shouted, "If that means I have to give up a tear or two, so be it. I will *not* lose you."

I let out a harsh laugh. "That's quite the about-face from earlier. You said you could handle being with someone who might die. Yet now, when it was almost a sure thing, you couldn't deal with it."

"I don't have to explain myself to you."

"I never asked you to save me," I snapped.

"That is enough." Constance's tone was sharp and crisp. She approached on two legs, looking human. Only the barest hint of slit pupils gave her away as something other than a mundane. She turned and placed a hand on Xander's shoulder. "Go help the others finish packing. We leave within the hour."

Xander shot me an angry glare but stormed off.

The anger that had brought me to my feet ebbed as soon as he left the room, and I sank back into the chair. I wiped sweat from my forehead and turned back to the soup. The sight of it turned my stomach. Constance sat beside me and rested her hand on mine.

"You have every right to be angry with each other, but we need to stay focused on the task ahead of us. We will only survive if we rely on one another."

"I don't know why you're helping me," I whispered.

"Because every creature deserves a chance to live free. And if Sanctuary is a real place, then perhaps there is hope that our kind can live free of the fear of bondage and torture at the hands of the human minority that seeks to oppress us because they do not understand what it is to be one of us."

"This isn't just about me. It's about finding a new home for all shifters," I said.

"Precisely."

"So, you don't regret letting me cross your threshold?"

"Oh my dear, of course not. You have given us a chance at salvation. One we did not know we needed. I've been guiding and protecting shifters for a long while now. I forgot that there was another way to be. And don't be too hard on Xander."

"He told me he would be fine if I died."

She patted my hand like one would a small child. "You did not believe his words, did you? He would care if you died. He may be rather open with his preferences, but I've known him for a long time and I know that what he feels for you is rare. He's not one to love lightly."

I considered her words. They made sense, but I still couldn't let him put his own health and safety at risk just to keep me going. If this was about finding a safe haven for our kind, they would need to keep going even if I didn't make it. "I need you to make me a promise. If along the way I don't make it, you need to keep going. If finding Sanctuary is about the wellbeing of all shifters, then you can't give up. Make it there. Xander and Lorelei will argue, but you need to make them see it's bigger than me. Lorelei is right that her child will have a target on its back. Sanctuary may be the only safe place for it to grow up."

Tears sparkled in her eyes but they remained unshed. "I promise I will do everything in my power to keep them going if anything were to happen to you. But sweet bird, I pray we will all see this journey through to the end. Long ago, I made a similar promise I could not keep. It cost my children their lives and my mate—" She blinked back tears before continuing. "My mate Charles forced me to keep going while he stayed behind to face those that harmed our eggs. I am unsure of his fate. I prefer to think of him dead versus the alternative."

"Could he be held captive like I was?" I asked.

Constance frowned. "I haven't the strength to find out. If he has been held captive all these years, will he even be the same man I knew?" She sighed before patting my arm, back to being the maternal figure I knew. "Now, eat up, Aiden dear. We haven't much time."

FIVE

LORELEI

I don't know how Aiden kept one foot in front of the other on our first day traveling, but he did. As a group, we stayed in human form versus shifting. A group of humanoids walking would draw less attention than a group of various animals traveling together. Walking may not be the fastest way to get to Sanctuary if the black-market map was to be believed, but it was the safest. There were too many stops on a train, which meant too many chances to be recognized. The map Mels nabbed from the black-market seller was old. It looked like no one had used this mode of travel since before the wars. Blue and red lines crisscrossed the page, with the words "interstates and highways" across the top. The town names were unfamiliar. Anything pre-wars was wiped off the map, or had reverted to its oldest name after the bombs stopped falling. Someone, somewhere, drew a star at our location on the far eastern part of the map and drew a dark line through what they considered the best route. They wrote "Sanctuary" on the corner on the far western part of the map. No wonder no one knew if Sanctuary existed or not. Anyone who took the time and effort to make it out there wasn't coming back. I wouldn't travel that far only to turn back around.

"What does the map call this place?" Xander stepped over something metal which looked like it had rusted off one of the abandoned cars littering our route. He reached for Aiden's arm out of instinct to help him navigate the clutter on still-unsteady legs. "A highway?"

"An interstate, whatever that is," Mels said. We took turns with who read the map so no one blamed anyone if we got lost. It was her turn in the lead. It rotated back to me next.

"It's how humans traveled by car before the wars," Constance said. It was weird seeing her walk on two legs instead of slithering in naga form, but I was getting used to it. "Cars weren't outlawed then. Anyone could own one if you had enough credits."

"It was called money back then, not credits," I added. "Everyone had different kinds before the universal system took over."

"You mean before the Booshie elite took over." Mels held out the map to me. "Tag. You're it." She stuck a dirt-smeared thumb on a dot next to something—or somewhere—called 'Palisades'. "We're here. Try not to screw things up."

"I'm a trained tracker," I snapped. "I'm the most qualified out of the whole damn lot of us to find this stupid shifter safe-haven."

"Pregnancy hormones making you testy, huh?" Mels dodged out of the way when I tried to punch her in the face. She beat her shimmery wings, only able to rise to her tiptoes while in girl form. "Uh-uh-uh. Think about the baby."

Douglas laughed before trying to turn it into a cough when I glared at him. I balled the hand not holding the map into a fist, but restrained myself from punching anyone. I kicked random debris instead. "Why are you laughing, horse face? Do you think this is funny?"

"No, *M'eudail*, I think it's hilarious." He leaned over and kissed me on the temple. "Relax. Think about the baby."

"Oh, ha-ha. You're lucky I lo—" I stopped short and shook my head. "You're lucky I don't punch you in the face." *Love* was a word I never said, and it came too close to slipping out right there.

Douglas laughed again before whispering close

to my ear, "Don't push everyone away. I know what you meant to say."

My fingers found his and twined around them. "Fine. Just keep it to yourself, okay?"

He nodded, his fingers squeezing mine. "As you wish, *M'eudail*. As you wish."

IN A WORLD OF PERPETUAL NIGHT, the only way to tell the difference between day and night was the sky growing darker than usual. We left the interstate and found a clearing in the woods when the murky half-light we call "day" disappeared. So far, the map had proven accurate. It at least had the right names for roads, even if the towns had long since disappeared or been renamed.

I sat down next to Aiden after Dr. Sunbird finished taking his vitals. Once he gave the thumbs-up, he followed the others into the woods. Somehow, Aiden and I were the only two not on firewood duty. "How are you feeling? Sorry I didn't check in with you all day. If you're tired you can say so, and we'll rest, okay?"

He nodded, smiling weakly. His chest rose and fell with effort. He didn't have to say anything for me to know he'd exhausted himself almost past the point of recovery. "When I was Kegan, before the rising, did you ever think we'd end up here? Me fighting for my life. Bounties on both our heads. You pregnant with someone else's baby."

"Does it bother you?" I asked. "The baby, I mean." I was so focused on my freak-out, I hadn't given a thought to how Aiden felt.

He shook his head. "Xander asked me the same question. It feels like a lifetime ago but it must have only been two days, maybe three. I told him it relieved me. We were trying to recapture emotions between us that just weren't there anymore. It feels like the baby gave us both permission to find new happiness with whoever is our present instead of our past."

I dug a hole in the ground with the toe of my boot. "I don't believe in happy endings or anything like that, but when we—Kegan and I—were together, I could see a happy ending. It felt so real. Almost like I could reach out and touch it. When Kegan was kidnapped, my world shattered. I hid it well. I went back to work and pretended like I wasn't dying inside. I never thought of it in this way, but maybe we both rose from the ashes. We both needed new lives. The only difference is that *I* remember my old one."

"I wish I could remember being him," Aiden said. "If it makes it any easier on you, I wish I remembered."

My mouth quirked into a half-smile. "I know you do. Thank you."

"When did you move on to your present instead of staying in the past?" he asked.

"I'm not sure," I admitted. "It kind of happened gradually, I think. One day thoughts of Kegan were gone and Douglas was there instead. Don't tell him I said that, okay? I don't need his ego getting any bigger than it already is. He acts like he's the first guy in creation to knock someone up."

"Hybrids are special."

I touched my stomach. "Hybrids are accidents."

"You don't believe that." Aiden leaned back against a tree and closed his eyes. "The kelpie cares about you very much, you know. I wish I had someone in whatever time I have left to look at me like he looks at you."

"*Hello?* Have you seen how Xander falls all over himself to get close to you?" I elbowed Aiden in the ribs, our relationship evolving from former lovers to friends. "You must not be paying attention, because that bird is crazy for you."

Aiden cracked an eye open. "What should I do about ... that?"

I spread my palms out in front of me. "That's not my call, Aiden. It's yours. Though, one thing we all could use more of in this world of ours is happiness. Do whatever makes you happy."

Before Aiden could answer the inner circle returned, arms loaded with firewood. Xander busted out impressive survival skills by arranging the wood into a pyre and lighting it with two sticks and a flint rock. We gathered around the fire, lumping ourselves into groups of two: Aiden and Xander, Douglas and me, and Constance and Micah. Mels was the only odd one out.

"I know a way to get this campfire jumping." Mels pulled out a silver flask from her backpack. "Who's up for some Shine and a little game?"

SIX

AIDEN

I wasn't sure what compelled me to look at Lorelei as Mels waved around the flask, but I did. She looked at once amused and irritated. I almost thought Mels suggested a drinking game just to annoy her.

"What game?" Xander asked, rubbing his hands together in front of the fire.

"A little truth or dare," she said with a wicked smile, pointy teeth on display.

"We are not children," Constance whispered.

"Oh, come on, have a little fun. Besides, laughter is good for the soul," Micah said.

"You'd better have something else to put that in. I'm not drinking your venom," Lorelei muttered.

"Not for you anyway, Fish. Only those of us not carrying new life," Mels replied.

"Her point still stands. We don't need to end up paralyzed from accidental exposure to your venom," Douglas added.

With an exaggerated eye-roll, Mels pulled out a second flask. "I brought extra." She took a long swig from her flask and smacked her lips. "Best batch I've made."

I turned to Xander. "She makes her own alcohol? Since when?"

He smirked in the firelight. The light picked out the streaks of red already showing through his dyed hair. It also picked up on the uncovered sigils on his arms. "She's been making that stuff for years. It's strong as shit, so be careful. It'll make you puke if you aren't careful."

"Noted," I said as I took the first flask she had produced.

"Rules are simple: you drink and ask truth or dare of whoever you want. They can't change their mind after they pick," Mels announced. She pointed a slender finger at me. "You're up first, birdie. Make it a good one."

I took a small swallow of the moonshine and choked at the taste. To say it had flavor would do a disservice to the word. It was foul and strong, and it burned my throat as it went down. But it invigorated me in a way I hadn't felt in a long time. I coughed to get my voice back and looked around our small circle, trying to decide who to pick. I settled on Constance. There was so much I didn't know about her. "Constance, truth or dare?"

Even this far away I could see her eyes take on a more snakelike appearance, as if narrowing her pupils conveyed her annoyance at the whole situation. She let out a hiss before replying, "If I must play, fine. I pick truth."

"Why did you start the underground?" As questions went it wasn't that deep or probing, but it was the one thing that came to mind while the alcohol burned through me.

"To give our kind safe passage out of bondage at the hands of the human minority," she replied.

"But what happened that you felt you had to do it?" I pressed. No one seemed to mind the follow-up question. "Was it because of what you told me earlier about your mate?"

"I lost more than I ever thought possible at the hands of cruel men who did not understand my kind. I already told you that." The others looked around the circle as she spoke as if this was new to them. "I vowed I would not let it happen to anyone else. Charles would be proud of me. I hope my children would be, too. That is all I'll say on the matter."

Micah gave me slight shake of his head, no doubt a signal to back off. So I passed the flask around the circle to her. She took a small swallow and made her own selection.

"Lorelei. What do you choose?"

I watched her face as she considered her options. I didn't know her as well as I once had, but something told me she would opt for a dare over getting personal with the group. We may have both argued our case for why we should be in the Inner Circle, but she was a private person.

"Truth," she answered.

"If you could go back and change one thing in your past, what would it be?"

Across the circle, Mels gave a big yawn. "Boring. Do something exciting," she complained.

"You were the one who set the rules, remember? Can't change it once I've chosen," Lorelei parroted back to her.

"Fine. But if someone doesn't do the daring, I'm going to just claw my own eyes out from boredom."

Lorelei flipped her off. "If I could go back, I'd save Kegan. He's my biggest regret." She gave me an apologetic look. "I'm sure you wanted to hear I'd go back and leave the PLA, but I didn't have a choice. The government took me from my parents and turned me into a weapon. Even if I wanted to, I don't have the power to change that."

Douglas took the flask from her before she could take a drink. He took a long swig for them both, I suspected. She looked around the circle and landed on Xander. I could already feel my nerves getting the better of me. "Free Range. You're up."

"Truth," he answered.

"For fuck's sake!" Mels groaned with a hiccup. She took another swig from her flask and frowned. "Damn, empty."

"Have you ever screwed someone who wasn't a phoenix, or are you only into the pretty boys?"

"He'll screw anything that's shiny," Mels sniggered.

There was an awkward glance between Xander and Micah that I wasn't sure how to read. My mind filled in the blanks with what I hoped wasn't the truth. I know I had no right to question his past relationships, but it still made me uncomfortable.

"Yeah, I've been with other birds. Not into fish or things with scales."

I made a mental note to ask him in private what that meant. He swiped the flask from Douglas' hand and took a sip, his eyes glittering in the firelight. "Mels. I know you're up for a dare."

She set the empty flask aside and clapped her hands. "Finally! Let's see what you got."

"I dare you to kiss Douglas. Not just a friendly peck. Really go at it."

"Hold on a minute," Lorelei protested, but Mels had already darted around the circle and thrown herself into Douglas' lap.

For a winged creature who prided herself on biting people she didn't like and being tough as steel, she wrapped herself around him with a sensuality I didn't think was possible. She pressed her lips to his and didn't let go. I could almost see Douglas turn white at the gesture—whether from embarrassment or paralysis was unclear—until Lorelei got up and yanked Mels away.

"Game over," she snapped.

"Oh relax, it meant nothing," Mels said.

"I'm done. We have a long way to travel. We need to get some rest. We need to be far from here when morning comes. Our head-start won't last forever."

SEVEN

SEVEN

LORELEI

"Just accept Douglas' apology already so he can stop repeating himself every damn hour," Xander said the next day as we traveled. "It's annoying. He didn't even do anything wrong." Walking was still slow going, but we couldn't risk hopping onto a train or commandeering a wagon from some hick in the rural areas away from the tech of the City.

"Aiden, did you hear something?" I ignored Xander, too. He was the asshole who dared Mels to kiss Douglas. I wasn't into all that forgive and forget bullshit.

"Perhaps you should apologize to Lorelei," Aiden told Xander. I was a little surprised he took my side over Free Range. Maybe there was a touch of Kegan still in there.

"For what?" Xander raked both hands through his hair in frustration. "It was a game. We bored Mels with everyone taking truth so I livened things up a little. If you can't handle a little fun, don't play."

"Aiden, tell Free Range I wasn't given a choice as to whether I wanted to play. Mels decided for everyone."

"Then be mad at her, not me," Xander said

"Lore, can we talk for a minute? Alone? At the back of the line?" Douglas caught up to where the phoenixes and I walked at the front. It was Aiden's turn to be in charge of the map. "Please, *M'eudail*. I hate misunderstandings between us."

I looked away. "Aiden, tell Douglas there's no 'misunderstanding' watching him kiss the doxy in front of me. It was clear what happened."

"Oh for fuck's sake, just talk to the kelpie," Xander snapped. "You've already put us through your childish nonsense for three hours straight. Just end it now, will ya? And stop dragging Aiden into your mess while you're at it." He turned to Aiden. "Seriously. There was an incarnation of you in love with this chick?"

"Xander, be kind. Lorelei, talk to Douglas," Aiden ordered, never raising his voice or acting agitated. "I need to focus on the map, and you're distracting me."

"Fine." I rolled my eyes before grabbing Douglas' arm and dragging him to the back of the line. "Talk fast, horse face, 'cause I'm not sure how long I want to listen."

"I have no control over Mels' decisions. It's unfair that you're blaming me for them. Do you think I enjoy being paralyzed by doxy venom? No. It's hideous." He obliged me by talking fast, words slurred and accent harder to decipher.

I cracked a smile. "Don't let Mels catch you calling her hideous."

Douglas let out the breath he was holding in an audible sigh. "I swear, I had no time to react. If I did, the game wouldn't have turned that direction."

"I believe you."

He relaxed even further. "You do?"

"I do." I looked around to make sure no one was watching us before I reached up to caress his cheek. "And to be fair to Free Range, I've treated none of you very well today." I patted my stomach. "Pregnancy hormones."

Douglas laughed. "So now you're blaming the wee bairn? Brilliant. You know kelpie bairns come out in horse form, don't you?"

I felt the color drain from my face at the

thought of birthing a horse instead of humanoid or siren. "You're joking, right?"

"Plus, they're wee right kickers." He grinned. "My mum said I kicked so much she thought I'd open up her stomach and fall out before my time was due."

Pinpricks of multi-colored light danced before my eyes. A wave of nausea and cramping hit, forcing me to double over in pain. I fell to my knees, my vision going grey around the edges, and then nothing.

WET DROPS OF SOMETHING—TEARS maybe—hit the back of my hand, warming my skin. It gave me the strength to claw my way out of the darkness surrounding me. I opened my eyes, looking around in confusion. I tried to sit up, but another wave of dizziness and nausea rose to knock me down again. I got enough of a look around to know we'd moved off the interstate to the safety of the woods and my head was cradled in Douglas' lap. He kept muttering something in Gaelic which my fuzzy mind didn't even want to comprehend.

"You shouldn't have done that." Xander's voice was half-accusation/half- warning, but not directed at me. I opened my eyes again to see who he meant.

Aiden turned away, but not fast enough for me to miss the tears still glittering on his cheeks.

"Aiden, no," I whispered. "Don't you dare waste your tears on me."

"They're mine to give." He balled his hand into a fist at his side, determined. "You couldn't save me once. Don't tell me I shouldn't try to save you now."

I struggled to sit. I swayed in place, but stayed upright. "What ... what happened?"

"I believe it's a case of Hyperemesis Gravidarum," Micah said. I didn't even realize he was checking my vitals until he spoke. "Extreme morning sickness. The baby is growing rapidly. Too rapidly for your body to keep pace. Because of the hybrid nature of your pregnancy, the gestational time is sped up. Your eight weeks gone is the equivalent of sixteen weeks in a standard pregnancy. By my calculations, you only have four months at most before the baby is born."

Four months? I was barely used to being pregnant in the first place and now Dr. Sunbird tells me I only have four months until the kid is here?

"Can we do anything for the illness?" Douglas asked.

"Rest. Hydration." Micah loaded his medical equipment into his backpack. "We must slow our pace to Sanctuary. Stop more. I can't guarantee another episode like this won't happen."

"We can always leave the fish behind if she can't keep pace," Mels piped up. She scowled when everyone glared at her. "What? I'm just saying what everyone is thinking."

"There's no bloody way I'm leaving Lorelei on the side of the road like some damn wounded animal," Douglas snarled. "I'll tear your wings off if you dare suggest something like that ever again."

Mels crinkled her nose. "Touch-y."

"No one's leaving anyone behind," Aiden decided. "I know I'm not in charge here—we're a collective group—but we're only making this journey to save my life. My opinion should matter more. I say we follow doctor's orders. We slow our pace until Lorelei and I are well enough to move faster. End of discussion."

"But my siren sisters won't care about our health issues," I protested. "You're just making it easier for them to find us."

"Then we fight if we need to fight," Aiden said. "There are more of us than them."

"I for one would *love* the chance to kick some siren ass." Mels flashed a thumbs-up sign. "If we stay ahead of them, great. If not? No big deal."

"We should rest for at least thirty minutes," Micah advised. "After that, we can re-evaluate our needs."

The baby gave a kick so strong it took my breath away.

"What is it? What's wrong?" Douglas noticed my distress.

"Nothing's wrong." I grabbed his hand and placed it on my stomach. "The baby just showed off its kelpie kicking abilities, that's all."

Douglas grinned as Baby thumped his hand. "That's my wee nipper. Good on you, bairn."

"Can I feel?" Mels approached, voice hesitant. "No one's ever been pregnant in the MCU before. We all just show up fully grown. Well, unless you count Xander as a hatchling, but that's different. That's not something growing on the inside."

I nodded. Mels felt around until Baby rewarded her with a kick. "That is so cool." She leaned close, talking to my mid-section. "Hey there, little one. I'm your Auntie Melisandra, but you can call me Mels. We're all a family here."

Family. I hadn't had a real one of those since the government took me from my parents at age six. The Magical Creature Underground was a strange, rag-tag group of shifters, but they were feeling like family. No matter what happened on the way to Sanctuary, we were in this together. That's what families did.

EIGHT

EIGHT

AIDEN

I hadn't thought stepping up would work to get their attention, but we'd rested long enough for Lorelei to get her bearings again. And I couldn't deny the rest had helped me, too. The tiny inkling in the back of my mind—the bird within me—was still calling, whispering of the promise of a new life free of disease if only I gave in. I couldn't give in. Constance had taken the map from me and was leading the way.

"Do you need to rest more?" Xander asked, hovering over me like a concerned parent.

"I'm fine for now. Like I told you the last three times you asked," I reminded him.

"Sorry, I'm just worried about you."

"I know." I grabbed his hand and pulled him to

a stop. The others moved past us, eying us long enough to make sure we would still keep up. I leaned in and kissed him on the lips. "I appreciate you looking out for me, but I'm not as helpless as I look."

"It's nice to have someone to look after," he whispered, and squeezed my hand.

We rejoined the group, falling into step behind Mels and Micah. Lorelei and Douglas remained in the middle of our little pack; the better for any of them to step in and catch or defend Lorelei if the need arose. Not that she'd let them fight on her behalf. The sky was as bright as it ever got during daylight hours, but I could sense an oncoming storm. We had no discernable destination for the day, and if the electricity I could feel in the air was an omen of what was to come we were about to be caught in a storm.

"What's on your mind?" Xander asked, nudging my shoulder.

"There's a storm coming," I answered.

He tilted his head skyward and his nostrils flared. "Smells like rain, all right. We don't want to be out in it when that happens."

Rain had become somewhat acidic since the wars tore the world apart. Most shifters could survive in shift long enough to get somewhere safe and dry. That presupposed one could shift without fear of immediate death.

"We need to find a place to take shelter!" I called to the front of the group.

Constance stopped walking and looked up at the sky. "You would be correct."

"A little rain never hurt anyone," Mels scoffed.

"Not all of us enjoy the feeling of poison on our bodies," Lorelei snapped before pressing one hand to her belly. Even from this distance I could see it protruding, swelling as the baby within grew.

Without a word, Micah discarded his clothing and shifted before taking to the sky. Constance bent to gather the items as we waited for him to return.

"What happened between you two?" I asked Xander while we waited.

"Oh, uh, it isn't important."

"It was important enough to admit in the game."

"Are you jealous?"

There was that word again. And the feeling that brought with it such confusion. It had literally been another life for the both of us. It wasn't who we were today, and yet I still felt the need to know. "No. But if we're traveling with him, I'd like to know what happened."

Xander's cheeks flushed. "It was nothing. I only know it happened because he wrote me a letter to remind me, so I wouldn't forget or do it again. I was young, like first-life young. I'd gotten into Mels' moonshine and nearly poisoned myself. Micah found me on the verge of rising, but he saved me. I guess I was still out of it and I kissed him and, well … we had sex. It was once, and it was over quick."

"He wrote you a letter to tell you not to have sex with him?"

He shook his head. "Warning me off the moonshine. Nothing ever developed between us, I swear. His kind mates for life and … let's just say he's not in the market for one."

I considered his explanation, and instead of feeling the pangs of jealousy I expected all I felt was sympathy for Micah. I knew so little of the man keeping me alive. "Thank you for telling me. And he was right about the moonshine."

Xander cracked a smile. "Yeah, he's right about a lot of things."

Just then a shot of bright, blinding golden light descended from the clouds and Micah returned, transforming midflight to land on his feet. Constance handed over his clothing and he dressed frantically.

"The storm's nearly upon us. There are buildings a few miles up the road. If we hurry, we can make it there before the skies open up."

Mels glanced between Lorelei and me. "You two had better keep up."

Before Lorelei could respond, Douglas scooped her up into his arms. "Put me down! I can walk my-self," she groused.

"Forgive me, but this is rather urgent," Douglas said, and took off at a sprint. Even on human legs, the kelpie could move.

Xander raised an eyebrow at me. "Care for a ride?"

"Don't you dare," I replied.

The rest of the group took off at a jog and I did my best to keep up with them. Breathing was diffi-cult, given my compromised state, but I did my best to power through. I could see the others getting far-ther ahead of me, and the world faded at the edges as I gasped for air to fill my lungs. And then I heard it.

The tantalizing melody I knew meant death as certain as if I had shifted to feathers and beak in-stead of flesh and bone. They'd found us.

"They're coming!" I rasped, praying the others would hear what the wind carried with it before I fell to my knees, landing face-first in the dirt.

NINE

NINE

LORELEI

We found a half-falling-down barn to take cover in just as the first drops of burning rain fell. It sizzled and popped as it hit the ground. Mels stood on tip- toes to look out the boarded-up window, watching the grass smoke.

"Love it. This is my kind of weather." She bounced on her toes in excitement.

Constance looked around, mouth moving as she did a head-count. *One, two, three, four, five, six...* "Wait. Where's Aiden?"

I struggled to sit up straighter. Little Accident gave me a swift kick that made me rethink my decision. I breathed deeply until my vision and head cleared. "If he's not here, it means he's still out there," I said. "Didn't any of you stop to check?"

"He said he would be fine." Xander tilted his chin, not willing to take responsibility for leaving Aiden behind. "He was right behind me the last time I looked over my shoulder. He seemed fine."

"Well, he's not." My knees wobbled a little when I stood, but I stayed on my feet. "He's stuck in a burning rainstorm, with my sisters closing in, 'cause no one could pay attention to see if he needed help or not." I pointed a finger at Xander. "And don't pretend like you didn't hear the siren song, either. If they're close enough for us to hear their song, they're close enough to capture Aiden."

"What are we going to do?" Constance's forked tongue flicked out to lick her lips.

"Not 'we'. Me." I rummaged through my pack and pulled out my rain-proof poncho. My PLA jacket and pants were armored to withstand rain. To protect our heads, the government issued ponchos. It was heavy, but effective. "I'll get Aiden and deal with my sisters."

"Absolutely not," Douglas vetoed my plan. "There's no way in hell I'm letting you risk your life more than you already do on a daily basis. You got lucky Darya wasn't looking for a fight the first time you faced them. Grady and Aria may have changed her mind for this go-around."

I crossed my arms over my chest, ready for a

fight. "Then what do you suggest? And talk fast, 'cause Aiden needs us."

"I'll go," Douglas said. "I'll shift if I need to, or use the poncho if shifting is too conspicuous. I've worked with Grady, Darya, and Aria before. They know me. The bounty is on Aiden and you, not me."

"The nark has a point." Mels turned to face us instead of continuing to watch the rain. "The shiver is less likely to attack someone they know."

A mix of emotions rose in my chest at the thought of Douglas facing my sisters alone. Anxiety. Fear. Panic. He refused to let me put myself in danger, but I didn't want to okay any plan that did the same for him. Little Accident needed a father.

"Fine. But you're not doing it alone." I pulled my PLA comm-link from a small exterior pocket of my pack. I clipped one end to Douglas' top button hole and positioned the signal receiver in his ear. I kept hold of the palm-sized video link. "Tap the comm once to turn on video when you find Aiden. We'll be able to see everything you see on the vid-link. You'll hear us through the comm in your ear. Micah can talk you through any medical things Aiden might need, and I can help with my sisters. Mels?" I looked at her with wide, pleading eyes. "Go with Douglas. Hide under the poncho in tiny form. If any of you are in any danger at all, I give you permission to bite the shit out of my sisters."

Mels grinned, doxy venom glinting on her sharpened incisors. "Biting sirens sounds like my kind of afternoon. Let's go, nark."

I handed the rain poncho to Douglas before burrowing my face in his chest, allowing myself one brief moment of weakness. "Make sure you come back, horse face."

His lips tipped up into a wistful half-smile. "I plan to, fish fins."

I HEARD "OKAY, WE FOUND HIM" in my earpiece before an image popped up on the receiver. I relaxed my grip on the monitor, my palm sporting red marks from where I held on too tight. Constance, Micah, and Xander gathered around the small screen.

Douglas turned Aiden over and checked his pulse. Red, circular splatters where the rain had hit peppered his exposed skin. "Still alive. Can we do anything for the burns?"

"I have silver sulfadiazine in my bag," Micah said. "He'll need a day to rest. Maybe more."

I relayed the message to Douglas. "Any sign of my sisters?"

"No," he said. "I don't hear the song, either. Wait a sec ... I spoke too soon."

We watched him throw the poncho over Aiden before the feed turned jumpy as Douglas climbed to his feet. Constance's breath hissed through her teeth as Grady, Aria, and Darya came into view.

"Don't do anything stupid," I warned Douglas. "You don't have to be a hero, you know."

If he heard me, he was ignoring me. He trained all his attention on the trio of sirens in front of him. They watched him, as if unsure what to do with this new development.

"Ladies!" Douglas called. "Fancy meeting you in the middle of a rainstorm. Lucky, lucky me."

"Douglas." Grady nodded acknowledgement. "How'd your arm heal after our last meeting?"

"Despite your best efforts, the doc said it wasn't broken. Thanks for asking."

Grady jammed her staff into the wet ground. "I'll try harder next time."

"If there is a next time."

"Enough with the fucking small talk already." Aria didn't even bother to play nice. "Where's Lorelei? Is she with you?"

"Why would she be with me?" Douglas asked. "She didn't answer my last letter. I assumed she was on a job. Now, what brings you three to this neck of the woods? Do you need information? I'm always willing to swap what I know with the lovely ladies of the PLA. You know my price. Two hundred credits. I'll admit I give Lorelei a deep discount, but she's the exception not the rule."

"Shut the fuck up, you stupid love-sick kelpie, and just tell us where Lorelei is." Aria pulled her taser out of its holster. *Mixing electricity with rain water? What was she thinking?*

"Pay me my fee first."

Grady hit the button to charge her staff. We could hear the crackle of the electricity jumping between the prongs even over the vid-link. "Be useful or I'll do more than almost-break your arm this time."

"As charming as that offer is, I must decline." The video feed bounced as Douglas bowed to them. "Now if you'll excuse me, ladies, I need to be going. When you're ready to pay my fee, perhaps we can chat again. Until then, I have no intel to give you."

"You're doing good," I whispered into the earpiece. "Just turn and walk away. Act like you have nothing to hide."

The view over the link turned from the sirens to Aiden, still a motionless lump under the poncho. I held my breath, hoping my sisters wouldn't question why Douglas had government-issued anything with him or insist on checking under the poncho.

"Hey!" Grady yelled. "Show us what's under the poncho!"

My sisters were in front of Douglas and the unconscious Aiden in a heartbeat.

"Not so fast," Aria said. "Grady, you know what to do."

Grady slammed her staff down on the center of the lumpy poncho. Aiden moaned, rolling over. His foot peeked out from the cover.

"You trafficking humans now, kelpie?" Aria puckered her lips, which either meant she was confused or truly curious.

"Of course not." I caught the glamour in Douglas' voice. He should know that wouldn't work on the shiver, but desperate situations called for desperate measures. "Who pays for humans?"

"Shifter?" Darya, silent until now, asked.

"Finding runaway shifters is your job, not mine. Now if you'll excuse me, ladies..." His voice shook as he cranked up the level of influence he was attempting to exert over them. "Good day to you all."

"You still didn't show us what's under the poncho. Stand back, kelpie. You know I have no issue using force." Grady kicked the poncho.

The last thing we heard was Douglas muttering "Oh, shit" under his breath before the video and audio links both went dead.

TEN

TEN

AIDEN

The jolt to my stomach roused me more than the hissing of the rain. I could hear voices above me, ones I didn't recognize, all female. The memory of the siren song hit me. Panic sent shivers down my spine and cold sweat popped out on my face and arms.

"Easy," a tiny voice whispered in my ear. *Mels.*

"What do we have under here?" one siren asked, and kicked at my foot. I tried not to move. I could feel the acid burns already peppering my face and hands.

"Nothing that should concern you," Douglas answered, his accent thick. Not a good sign.

"Stay down," Mels hissed, and I caught movement as she darted out from under the protection of the poncho. I had just enough of a view of the scene to see three blonde sirens who looked both similar to Lorelei and nothing like her towering over me. One held a large electric staff.

"Hey, fish bitches! Over here!" Mels called, shifting to human size in the process and landing on her feet.

I had never seen a doxy look so pleased to have acid falling all around her. Her dark eyes flashed brightly and her smile was treacherous. She was ready for a fight, and the sirens had no idea what was coming to them. I couldn't say I wanted them to get hurt—they're just as much victims of our corrupted reality as the rest of us—but, given how they put our freedom in danger, I was rooting for the scrappy fairy.

"Trafficking a pixy?" the staff-wielding siren asked, looking at Douglas.

"I'm a doxy, you fucking traitor," Mels snarled, and lunged.

"Grady, look out!" one other shouted. She was less assertive than the others. *What did Lorelei say her name was? Darya?*

Grady's staff crackled with electricity and I held my breath, waiting for the pained look on Mels' face when the current hit her wet body, shocking her into submission. Grady never had a chance. With the beat of her wings, Mels zipped over Grady's head and wrapped one arm around her throat. Mels squeezed tight, and even though I couldn't see Grady's face I could hear her sputter. The staff fell from her grip, landing in a puddle and sizzling. Mels used her own weight to topple Grady forward.

"So sorry about this, ladies," Douglas said, out of my field of vision. I heard bone on bone, and another female figure hit the ground.

I heard someone moan, and lifted the poncho enough to see Mels sink her teeth into Grady's throat. Her mouth came away bloody.

"You're going to kill her!" Darya wailed.

Mels wiped her mouth, teeth still glittering with venom. "If I wanted her dead, I'd have just snapped her neck. Now it's time for you to go night-night, little fish."

I saw a blade flash and held my breath again. Mels had shown she was fast, but was she quick enough to dodge a knife? I mustered enough energy to stagger to my feet beneath the poncho's protective layer. The weight of it was more than I expected, and my balance wavered, but it was enough to hold me upright. It also gave me a better vantage point on the situation. The third siren—Aria, if memory served—was laid out on her back in the rain, blood trickling from her nose where Douglas had hit her.

Darya flicked the blade in Mels' direction. I was too slow to stop it, and Douglas stood motionless. Maybe my sudden appearance in the fight had caught him off guard. Not my intention. "No!" I yelled.

The blade landed in the meat of Mels' left bicep. She growled, teeth bared, and ripped the knife free, flecks of blood splattering her shirt. "That wasn't very nice of you, fish. I think now I'm gonna have to gut you like one."

"I let Lorelei go before. I can't just let you walk away again," Darya said, her voice shaking.

"Oh, you won't be *letting* us do anything," Mels replied, brandishing the knife.

I had to make a move before Mels killed one of our pursuers. I moved as quickly as I could—given the fact that the acid burns were prickling with pain, it wasn't as easy as it could have been—and wrapped my arm around her throat, tightening my grip until she sank down to the ground unconscious.

"I had her!" Mels yelled at me, knife still gripped in her hand.

"And you would have killed her," I answered, the exertion leaving me winded.

"Easy, there. Let's get you back to dry land," Douglas said. He wrapped a solid arm around my torso, slipping beneath the poncho, too.

THE BARN DIDN'T LOOK like much from the outside as we approached it. It was run-down and I could see large gaps in the siding. The roof looked shaky, but when we stepped through the air was dry and no longer tasted of acid. My lungs still burned from the exertion, and I leaned against a pile of moldy hay to catch my breath.

"Out of the way; let me look," Micah said, more forceful than I'd ever heard him. He bent in front of me and studied me, prodding around the acid burns. "I can treat this, but it will hurt."

"Can't hurt more than it already does," I wheezed.

"Don't say I didn't warn you," he said with a sad expression, and dipped a cloth into a dark brown container from his pocket.

I braced myself against the hay, but it did little good to stop the agony searing into my brain as he dabbed each spot with ointment. I took slow, shallow breaths to keep from passing out as he moved to my arms and hands.

"I've got you," Xander said, his voice soft.

"Don't you dare waste a tear on this," I warned.

"I hate seeing you in pain when it's my fault," he replied.

Now wasn't the time to lay blame or assess

guilt. I looked at Lorelei, who was busy checking Douglas for burns. He seemed better equipped to handle the rain. He had a few small marks, but he brushed them off. "Your sisters caught up with us," I said.

"I know. It's why we sent Douglas and Mels back to get you."

"They won't be following us for a wee bit," Douglas said.

Lorelei's gaze narrowed at Mels. "What did you do?"

"You said I could bite them!"

"The one with the staff, she bit her," I explained.

"Grady. She's tough," Lorelei muttered.

"I only gave her enough venom to knock her out for a few hours. Besides, she tried to electrocute me. Naughty bitch."

"We subdued the other two," I added, and pointed to Mels' bleeding shoulder. "Someone should look at that."

Mels eyed the wound and sniffed. "Doesn't even hurt."

Micah moved to examine her and she let out a growl at his touch. "It isn't deep. At least let me clean it and bandage you up."

She gave an exaggerated sigh. "Fine. But I'm keeping the knife."

"You're lucky you got away with that little prize," Lorelei said with a smile that radiated pride.

"Luck had nothing to do with it. I earned it. She was lucky I didn't slit her open with it."

"As colorful as I'm sure your retelling would continue to be, we need to rest and wait out the storm before we move on. Take the time to sleep," Constance interrupted.

Lorelei and Douglas shuffled off to one side as Constance passed out rations. Mels swatted Micah away as he tried to add extra bandages to her shoulder, leaving Xander and me to sit on the hay.

"I swear I thought you were right behind me," he said, tears in his eyes. This time there was no healing held within them, only sorrow.

"I don't blame you. And I'll be okay."

He leaned over and kissed me. "I won't let it happen again."

"You don't have to take care of me, you know. We have a doctor for that. Just be here with me."

"I can do that."

Micah moved to the middle of the room and gathered up some dried bits of wood. He shifted just enough of his hands to feathers and emitted sunlight to catch the debris on fire to keep us warm. I should have realized that was a bad idea. We were in the middle of nowhere, but the shiver had tracked us down. It would be foolish to think we were alone out here. Smoke curled up and out through the walls, and in the distance I thought I spotted movement. Lightning crackled high above us and illuminated a pair of figures approaching.

"We've got company," Xander announced.

The door to the barn slid open and two very human-looking men appeared, bundled against the storm, with old-style guns in hand. "Well, what do we have here?"

ELEVEN

ELEVEN

LORELEI

"Looks like we got trespassers." One man rested the barrel of his gun against his shoulder. "You think these folks know what we do to trespassers, Earl?"

The human named Earl grinned, revealing black spaces where most of his teeth should be. "Naw, Jimmy. If they did, they wouldn't be trespassing on our land." He cocked his gun and aimed it at Micah, still standing near the fire. "Whatcha got to say for yourself, boy?"

I stood and stepped into the light. Douglas tried to grab my arm and pull me back but I side-stepped his attempt. "I'm a federal agent with the phoenix Location Agency." I flashed my PLA badge toward

227

the men to look more official. "I commandeered your barn for official government business. Everything is under control here. Thank you for doing your due diligence and checking on the safety of your property. It makes my job so much easier."

"What sort of official government business?" Earl spat something dark and tobacco-smelling toward one stack of hay. "You got any phoenixes with ya since you're PLA?"

"The PLA focuses on phoenix location, but we retrieve all lost or runaway shifters." I used my 'I'm a fed and know what I'm talking about' authoritarian voice. "I'm returning this group to their owners in the City. We needed the safety of your barn during the storm. Thank you, gentlemen. We do not need your services. We will be on our way as soon as the rain stops."

Jimmy's beady eyes surveyed the occupants of the barn. "All them shifters?"

"Yes. Myself included." I tried to arrange my jacket to hide my growing abdomen. Pregnant shifters were like a buy one get one free to Booshies. These men were far from the Booshie elite, but everyone knew you could make credits by selling shifters. "Thank you for the use of your barn, gentlemen but, like I said, we do not need your assistance."

I waited to see if my bluff worked. Earl and Jimmy glanced at each other before raising their rifles to their shoulders. There was my answer. We must be in the part of the country that thought the only good shifter was a dead shifter.

I pulled a knife out of my boot and flung it at Earl. It connected with the end of his rifle, jerking the barrel upwards. He shot a hole in the roof instead of in one of us. Mels took my lead and threw her own knife at Jimmy. The only difference was, I aimed at the rifle. She aimed at his abdomen. Jimmy laughed as the knife bounced off the armored protection of his rain gear.

"Nice try, little shifter. How much do you think I can get for them wings of yours on the black market?"

"Come try to find out." Mels pulled a pair of brass knuckles from her back pocket and slipped them on. I had no idea where she got them, but I didn't doubt she knew how to use them. Jimmy was outmatched and didn't even know it yet.

"Lorelei, get out of range." Douglas pulled me back into the shadowy corner of the barn, away from the light of the camp fire. "You're an open target out there."

"I can defend myself!" I snapped. "What part of 'lifetime of training' are you having trouble remembering? I'm not some helpless chit, Doug. I can handle this."

Before he could answer, Micah shifted so fast he didn't even bother to remove his clothes. If Douglas or Xander tried that, their clothes would have ripped to shreds. The sunbird was small enough, though, that he was just buried in a pile of clothes lying on the barn floor. At first I thought Micah was abandoning the fight before realizing it was a distraction technique. A damn good distraction technique.

Jimmy stopped trying to catch Mels and Earl forgot to reload his rifle as they stared at the spot where, only seconds before, Micah stood. A gold, red, and orange swallow-sized sunbird emerged from the clothes and flew to the ceiling. Micah gave one loud caw before illuminating the barn with his sunlight.

"What the hell?" Jimmy sputtered.

"I can't see! I can't see!" Earl shouted before both fell to their knees, hands over their eyes.

"Oh, you're making this far too easy on me." Mels fluttered over to the writhing yokels. "If anyone asks remember to say I'm a doxy, not a fairy." She chomped Earl's wrist, holding on until his movements stilled, before repeating the process on Jimmy.

Micah glided down from the rafters. He shifted

right before he reached the floor, landing in a crouch. Constance handed him his clothes.

"Nice work, Micah," she said, hissing the 'c' in nice.

"Thank you." He dressed quickly. "I wasn't sure it would be as effective at subduing our ... friends ... as it was. I'm glad I was wrong."

"Does anyone have a rope?" Xander nudged the unconscious men with the toe of his boot. "We can tie them up and deposit them somewhere in the woods far away from here."

"Are they even alive?" Aiden asked.

"Relax, birdie; I only knocked them out," Mels said. "It's no fun if you kill them. Then you can't play with them later."

"Remind me to never get on your bad side," Xander muttered.

"I might bite you even if you're on my good side." Mels grinned. "Right, Constance?"

"Do not drag me into your games," Constance warned. She pulled the asked- for rope from the barn wall and made quick work tying up our yokel friends. They moaned, and mumbled under their breath. Maybe they weren't as knocked out as Mels thought. Once finished, she half-shifted to naga form. Her eyes turned to slits and she whispered hypnotic suggestions, the rattle of her cobra tail keeping time to her words. "Sleep. You will not return to this barn. Bandits attacked you. You will remember nothing you witnessed here. Sleep. Sleep. Sleep..." Constance repeated "sleep" until Earl and Jimmy were snoring. She whispered "sleep" one last time before slithering over to the fire. She stared unseeing into the flames, not bothered by the heat.

"Constance?" Micah sat next to her. "They're not the ones who took Charles and your family."

"No, but someone like them did." Her forked tongue flicked out. "Someone take those two far from us. Please."

"Aiden and I will do it," Xander volunteered. Free Range even raised his hand for good measure.

I rejected the idea. "Take Mels. Aiden just got trapped in a burning rain storm. He's injured, not to mention already weak from the blood graft. He doesn't need to be dragging a dead-weight yokel through the woods with you."

"No, I'll go," Aiden said. He shrugged when I shot him a look that said, 'Why are you contradicting me?' "Thank you for your concern, Lorelei, but I believe I'm strong enough to pull my weight in the group. Or, in this case, pull *their* weight into the woods."

I couldn't stop the laugh that escaped. "That, Aiden, is a Kegan-worthy bad pun. You must feel better."

He grinned, and for just a moment I felt as if

Kegan was standing before me instead of Aiden. It took my breath away. The moment passed, but it reminded me again of how I couldn't save him. I'd lost Kegan forever and, no matter how much he denied it, time was running out for Aiden.

TWELVE

TWELVE

LORELEI

We waited until the rain let up to haul our human captives out of the barn. I didn't admit it to anyone, but I was grateful for the additional time to rest. There'd been a little too much excitement in the last few hours for my taste. I suspected, however, that this was about to become our reality—running and fighting our way to a place that might or might not be real.

"Come on; you ready to get these assholes out of here?" Xander called, pulling my attention from my inward thoughts.

I nodded and we each freed them from their rain gear—we could use the extra protection for our group after all—and dragged them out of the barn by their collars. Even though I'd been locked away in a cage for so long, their bare existence was a surprise. Had I assumed all humans lived as lavishly as the woman who'd imprisoned me? "How do you think they survive out here?"

"They probably turn in anyone who passes by, shifter or not. I bet they assume they can get a few credits out of it," Xander answered.

The ground squished beneath our feet as we hauled Jimmy and Earl toward the woods. It seemed a little cruel to leave them here, exposed to the elements, but I knew if I tried to bring it up I'd get voted down. They were a threat to our survival and we had to deal with them.

"I never thought it would be like this," I huffed, and leaned Earl up against a tree.

Xander flung Jimmy across Earl's lap and dusted off his hands. "Like what?"

I gestured at the unconscious men. "Hiding out, fending off attacks. Let alone having to deal with a hybrid child that's growing too fast."

"None of us ever expect life to be as shitty as it is. But that's what they've dealt us and we'll get through it. All of us. Like a family."

"You're lucky you've had people around you to look out for you, remind you they love you even when you can't remember their names," I whispered.

"Well, you don't need to worry about being alone anymore. We've all got your back."

I held my tongue. It wasn't worth the argument to remind him that there was every possibility I wouldn't see our journey through to the end. I turned to head back to the barn and the others, when I spotted a structure in the dim light. I started towards it, waiting for Xander to catch up.

"Where are you going? The barn's the other way!" he called.

"To see what sort of other hospitality our friends can offer us for our trip," I replied and took off at a run, a sudden burst of energy spurring me onward.

Mud clung to my shoes and the cuffs of my pants, but I didn't care as I tracked it into the warm cabin. It was only one level, but it seemed like the pair was the place's only occupants. I flung cabinets open, revealing stores of canned and jarred meats and vegetables. There was a fire nearby over which a spit spun, weighed down by a large animal carcass. I prayed it didn't belong to a shifter.

"Grab as much as you can," I told Xander when he stepped inside.

"Smart call."

"Leave some for our friends," I ordered.

'Aiden, those lunatics tried to kill us. They can starve."

"If we treat them like they're worthless, we're no better than they are. And we need to be better than them."

He held his hands up in surrender. "Fine. But I'm taking the good stuff." He bent over and nudged a few empty bottles out of the way. "Well, looks like Mels isn't the only one fond of making shine."

"Water would be more useful," I reminded him.

He still swiped a couple bottles. As I found a knife and carved chunks of fresh meat from the spit, I heard the floorboards creak as Xander went exploring. I laid the meat in a cloth to make it easier to carry.

"Come check this out!"

I set the food aside and followed the sound of his voice to the back corner of the house, where the biggest bed I'd ever seen took up the entire space. I wondered if Jimmy and Earl were more than just roommates. Xander flung himself onto the mattress with a sigh. "I could get used to this."

"We don't have time for this," I protested.

He responded by grabbing my hand and pulling me down onto the bed beside him. "We'll make time." He propped himself up on one arm and leaned over to kiss me.

The mattress was soft, and the emotion I felt in the kiss was a nice distraction from our present situation. For just a little while, even if only a few minutes, I let the worry fade and held on tight, kissing him back. Soon our bodies entwined, much like the image I'd seen in my head only a few short weeks ago when first trying to remember Lorelei. His hand slid beneath the hem of my shirt, coming to rest just above my heart. I could feel it beating double-time, blood pounding in my ears.

"This is what I want to remember," Xander whispered against my cheek. "The way you feel against me."

"When all of this is over, we'll have all the time in the world to feel like this," I promised, hoping it wouldn't turn into a lie.

I didn't want the moment to end, but I knew if we didn't return soon Mels would mount a search party. I let out a sigh. "We should get back to the others. We need to regroup and get out of here now that the rain's gone."

"Those guys won't bother us, and the sirens are too busy treating their wounded. Just stay here with me a little while longer. Please."

The burst of adrenaline that had pushed me to the cabin faded and I yawned. Maybe just a few minutes' rest couldn't hurt. I nestled against his shoulder and let the softness of the bed buoy me into sleep, unaware of what the man I was falling for was about to give up for me.

THIRTEEN

THIRTEEN

LORELEI

I stopped myself from glancing at the barn door for the thousandth and second time since Aiden and Xander left. Instead, I forced myself to sit next to the fire. Staring into the depths of the flames calmed my mind somewhat, but not completely. What if there was a whole enclave of shifter-hunting local yokels nearby? What if they recognized the boys as phoenixes and went for the big credit payday? I doubted Aiden was healthy enough to hold his own in a fight, and I didn't know Xander's style well enough to know if he could take on a group of shifter hunters by himself or not. They were in danger every day of their lives just from who and what they were. We all were to some extent, but phoenixes more so than any other shifter trying to survive in this crap-hole society. The exception to that rule was hybrids. I lay a hand across my stomach. "Don't worry, Little Accident. I'll protect you. Always."

"Getting used to being a mother?" Constance, still in half-shift, slithered over and parked her snake butt next to me. "I won't lie—for a while I thought you might cause yourself to have an 'accident' to get rid of the responsibility."

I took a second to realize what she meant. Hurting myself to hurt the baby wasn't something I would come up with on my own. They had fed me preventatives since I hit puberty at the Siren Academy. It was the same as taking a vitamin every day. *Here, take your preventative.* The government wanted to control us.I never questioned it. None of us did. I'm not sure why I left the pills in my apartment before my last bounty when Aiden's case crossed my desk, but maybe—somewhere inside—I didn't want to be controlled anymore. I wanted to be free to make my own choices. I only did what I wanted a handful of times in my life. Run off with Kegan. Start what everyone else but me called a relationship with Douglas. Help the Magical Creature Underground. My sisters and the government called me a traitor. I preferred to think of it as exerting freewill.

"I don't mind it so much now," I said to Constance. "The responsibility, I mean. It's scary as hell, but maybe it's what I need, you know? Someone to depend on me. I don't think I've ever had that before."

"Being a mother is the scariest, most exhilarating, thing you will ever do," Constance said.

"Are you a mom?" I knew the inner circle must have pasts—potentially tragic pasts—or they wouldn't be so up on fighting for magical creature rights, but I didn't give it much thought what with our latest run-ins with my sisters and the yokels.

"Was a mother," Constance corrected. "No one should outlive their children. I, unfortunately, did."

"I'm sorry to hear that." I stared into the fire so I didn't have to look at her. "How long ago?"

"Nothing is ever long enough ago to forget," she said. "Before the MCU, my mate Charles and I hid in plain sight. Instead of human form, we chose our full cobra form. Humans are at least scared of cobras. They gave us a wide berth. If we needed to, we'd venture out in the City in human form. Half shift—true naga form—was reserved for only us. One day, a pair of humans very much like our Earl and Jimmy found our nest. They smashed our eggs before we had time to strike. Charles sacrificed himself so I could live." Constance shook her head as if trying to banish bad memories. She reached out and patted my arm in that maternal way of hers. "I believe you are better equipped to protect your children than I was. All mothers fight for their young, but not all mothers have your knife-throwing abilities."

"I'm also great at kicking people in the face." I tried to lighten the mood.

Constance laughed. Mission accomplished.

"Your leg sweep is also truly fabulous," Douglas joked, appearing next to us, fresh from his recon mission to check the security of the barn perimeter. "How I haven't broken an ankle by now is beyond me."

"That's because I hold back."

"For me?" Douglas placed both hands over his heart, pretending to swoon. "I'm touched. Truly."

"What do you want, Doug?" I cut to the chase. Joking around and me don't mix well.

"Is that how you talk to your baby daddy? We will need to work on that." He sat down next to me. Constance slithered away to give us privacy, though neither of us asked her to.

"What do you want, oh annoying one who, for some mysterious, unknown reason, I'm incapable of saying 'no' to so am now stuck with?"

"Better, but still needs some work."

I nudged his shoulder with mine. "Seriously, Doug, what do you want?"

"Loads of things, but for now I'll settle for I want you to take more care of yourself when we're in dangerous situations." He reached down to take my hand in his. "Before you protest—and I know you will—just think about it, please. As the bairn grows, it throws everything off kilter. Yes, you're used to defending yourself, but not with an extra thirty pounds in your mid-section."

"Thirty pounds?" I glanced down at my abdomen. "Have I gained that much weight? Pregnancy blows."

"That's not the point I'm trying to make here." Douglas forked his free hand through his coppery hair. "Your balance and center of gravity are off. Defense won't be as second-nature as before."

I shook my hand free and struggled to my feet. Douglas popped up like he had springs on his shoes. "Okay, I admit getting up was harder than it should be, but I can still take on anyone or anything that comes at us. I know I can."

"What makes you so sure?" he asked.

"Because they trained us in all forms of combat —even fighting while injured."

Douglas sniggered. "You're not injured, Lorelei, you're pregnant."

I pulled a hairpin from my braid and executed a leg sweep in one fluid motion, knocking Douglas on his back—and not in the good way—in five seconds flat. I straddled his hips next, the sharpened point of the hairpin pressed against his throat. "Say I can't defend myself one more time and I'll cut you."

Douglas raised both hands in surrender. "Fine. I give, I give! Will you at least allow me to help more or clear your plan of attack with me before executing it?"

"If there's time, I'll think about it." I scrambled to my feet and held out a hand to help him up.

"And you wonder why I always ask you to take your hair down when we're alone." He glared at the hairpin still clutched in my hand.

I stuck the pin back in my braid. "Just trust I can take care of myself, okay?"

Douglas crossed his arms over his chest. "And *you* trust I say these things out of good intentions, yeah? I've always only had good intentions with you, Lore."

I rolled my eyes. "I can still stab you, you know."

He pulled me against him, wrapping his arms low and loose around my waist. For the moment, I felt like everything else in the world fell away and it was just me and him. Maybe that's why I stuck around. To continue to feel this connection between us.

"Try to remember to be careful, please," Douglas whispered, accent thickening with his sincerity. "I wouldn't want to live if anything happened to you or the bairn."

"I'll try," I said. "But I'm not very good at keeping promises."

FOURTEEN

FOURTEEN

AIDEN

I felt the bed shift beside me and rolled over to feel the warmth Xander's body had left behind. I opened my eyes to find myself alone in the bed. The sky was dark which could mean it was turning to evening, or I'd slept far longer than I'd intended. I stretched, feeling rejuvenated in a way I hadn't in days. Weeks even. Pushing myself to my feet, I staggered in the direction of the kitchen.

"Xander?" I called, but got no response. The fire beneath the spit had been recently stoked, the flames crackling.

"You're awake," he said from behind me.

I turned to see pieces of wood tucked under one arm. "How long was I asleep?"

"An hour. Don't worry, our friends haven't

come back and neither have the sirens. For now, at least, we're safe."

"Where's everyone else?"

"Still in the barn, I think." He tossed the wood onto the fire, making the orange flames swell.

"You're not trying to burn the place down, are you?"

"No. I guess I felt a little bad for those idiots. I mean, in a way they're just living their lives. Besides, it's getting cold out there and they'll need to warm up when they come to."

"Who knew you had a soft spot for mundanes with ill intentions," I teased, and repacked the food I'd gathered earlier.

"You're rubbing off on me," he replied, and kissed me. His hands slipped into mine and he pulled me close.

I expected the burns from the rain to react to the heat our bodies generated when aroused, but there was no pain. I pulled away and looked down at my arms. Smooth, unblemished skin appeared where, only hours ago, angry red blotches had marred it. I felt my neck and cheeks and found that those, too, had vanished. I studied Xander's face. While his expression betrayed nothing, I could see the bags under eyes were more pronounced and his skin had taken on a slight ashy quality. "You didn't."

"I had to. It would have taken longer than we

have for you to heal, and that was assuming the blood graft didn't interfere with the healing process. So, yeah, I helped it along a little."

"I didn't ask you to do that," I replied.

"You don't have to. That's what people who care about each other do. They sacrifice for the ones they love."

I let the word 'love' hang between us in silence. It was the first time either of us had uttered the word, and it took me by surprise. We'd known each other a few months, and yet he was telling me he loved me? Then again, Lorelei and Kegan had fallen just as fast for one another. Maybe I attracted those who fell fast into love.

"You know how dangerous it is to expend tears like this. It takes a physical and emotional toll," I reminded him, deciding to act as if I hadn't heard his declaration.

"Maybe, but I'm strong enough to bear it for you. I told you I'll get you to Sanctuary. We'll get you cured, and if that means I have to give up tears along the way so be it. I'm not going to stop."

""You will if you want this to work," I countered, my tone rising.

"Oh no, you don't get to hold this relationship hostage like that. Did you forget you'd be dead if I hadn't used my tears to help you come out of shift? Twice?"

"No, I didn't forget. You just don't get it. Our tears? They're precious. My owner forced me to give mine up over and over to keep that horrible woman young. I had no choice in what she took from me. Maybe if she hadn't done that I would be stronger now despite the blood graft. But I'm not. I can't change that. But you can't weaken yourself to strengthen me. I won't let you."

"Why not?" he shouted.

"Because I can only deal with one of us being on the verge of dying," I answered before I could stop the words from spilling out. I hadn't realized that was how I felt until that moment, but the words felt true. I had resigned myself to the possibility that I wouldn't see our journey to its end. But I was okay with that if the others made it and could find a safe haven.

He glared at me, sputtering nonsense syllables for a solid minute before he turned, grabbed the food I'd gathered, and stormed out and back toward the barn. I stayed rooted to the spot and watched the door close behind him. I raked my fingers through my hair to collect myself. This day hadn't gone at all as I'd expected.

I left the house and its warmth behind, returning to the barn. The fire Micah had started had died down—or maybe I was just expecting a blaze like in the house—and everyone was quiet. Constance met my gaze, cocked her head in Xander's direction, but I shook my head. I wasn't ready to talk about what happened.

"We thought you got snatched," Lorelei said, hands massaging her growing belly.

"Sorry, we were getting supplies and I needed to rest."

She touched my face. "Looks like it did you some good."

A gust of wind blew in through the open barn door, bringing with it the warning of our siren pursuers. Lorelei and I shared a look. "Looks like we've overstayed our welcome."

"Everyone out the back. Follow the path of the road away from here. I'll stall them as long as I can," Lorelei said, stomping out the flames with her foot.

"You will do no such thing," Douglas protested.

"He's right," I said, and gave her a solid shove toward the back of the barn. Douglas looped one arm around her torso and dragged her out of sight. Constance and Micah were next, leaving Mels and Xander staring at me. "Go. I'll be right behind you," I said.

"Last time that happened we almost lost you, birdie," Mels said.

"Just trust me. Go!"

FIFTEEN

FIFTEEN
LORELEI

"What the hell do you think you're doing!" I struggled against Douglas' grip on my torso, but it was a losing battle. The baby sapped my strength, making simple things an effort. "Aiden needs us! We can't leave him behind!"

"We can do exactly that," Constance said. "Aiden wanted us to."

"Aiden wanted us to let him sacrifice himself? Bullshit." I dipped down and slid out of Douglas' grasp. He grabbed me again before I could run back to the barn.

"Stop and listen for once, Lorelei." His accent thickened, which meant his emotions were running high. "We all make sacrifices in this world. That's just life. We may not like it, but there's no way around it. We all need to do things that others don't agree with. Your parents gave you up to the Academy. You gave up your job—the one thing you've trained your whole life for—for us. I gave up my country to come to a new one ... We all have stories. We all make sacrifices. Let Aiden do this. This is how he wants his story to go."

"He told me before we even began this journey that if anything happened to him, he wanted us to keep going," Constance said. "He wanted us to be safe. Honor his wishes, Lorelei. Please."

I pulled free from Douglas' grasp for a second time and got out of range before he could stop me. I swiveled toward Xander, standing silent and stoic near a tree. "Why aren't you tearing this place apart to get back to Aiden, Free Range? Do you even care about him? Or is he just some fuck buddy to you? Another body in a long line of guys to mess with and discard. I'm sure Aiden will love to hear how emotionless you were once he gets back."

Xander shrugged. "You're one to talk, fish. Isn't fucking with guys part of Siren Academy training? Gingers seem to be your type, right? Kegan, Aiden, Douglas. Or am I getting the order wrong?"

I yanked a knife from its hiding place in my boot but didn't throw it, no matter how much I wanted to. "Fuck. You. Talk shit one more time and

I won't be responsible for which part of you this knife takes out."

Xander spread his arms wide. "Go ahead. I already screwed things up so royally with Aiden I doubt he'll forgive me. What do I care about dying? It'll be better to forget with the rising."

I sheathed my knife. "Great. A suicidal phoenix. Like we don't have enough to deal with already without you going fatalistic on us."

"Can we skip to the part where we go back and rescue Aiden?" Mels said. "I'm tired of the talking and not doing anything."

"For once I agree with you, doxy." I crossed my arms over my chest. "We need to take Grady and Aria out, but Darya is soft enough we should be able to threaten her and she'll back down."

"You are *not* going back to face off with the sirens." Douglas forked both hands through his hair in frustration. "You may not care about your life and safety, but I do."

"Aiden said—" Constance began. Mels cut her off by spitting doxy venom in her face to paralyze her ability to talk. *Nice move.*

"Enough with what Aiden did or didn't say," Mels said. "I'm sure he thought nothing would *really* happen to him, which means he didn't expect us to need to make this choice. What happened to leaving no one behind? Did you all forget that? I say we go back."

"The longer we spend arguing and not deciding, the higher the chance Aiden won't be there when we get back to the barn," I pointed out. "If the rest of you aren't helping, Mels and I will go alone."

"Don't do this, Lorelei." All the urgency had drained from Douglas' voice, replaced by sadness.

"Watch me, Douglas."

I turned my back on him and motioned for Mels to follow me. We didn't wait to see if the others would come or not—we just left.

Mels was as silent as I needed her to be as we retraced our steps back to the barn. We didn't need to alert anyone—sirens or random locals who may lurk in the woods—that we were coming. I raised a finger to my lips in a signal to stay quiet when we reached the barn's back door. I pointed at the knife stuck in her waistband and pulled mine from my boot. I held up three fingers and counted down. *Three, two, one...*

I kicked the back door open, hoping for the element of surprise. What we found was an empty barn.

"Fuck." Mels pivoted in a circle, scanning the room for any sign of Aiden. "What do we do now?"

I dug around in my pack until I found what I

was looking for. I showed her the phoenix feather. "I can still track him with this."

"Well, get on it then," she urged.

I held the feather tight in both hands, closed my eyes, and hummed.

SIXTEEN

SIXTEEN

AIDEN

I tried to put the rest of the group out of my mind as I allowed Lorelei's siren sisters to lead me away from the barn. The one with the staff—Grady, I had to keep reminding myself—insisting on binding my hands. As if that would stop me if I'd wanted to escape. But that wasn't what this was about.

"Can't you lull him into shift and tranq him? I want out of this wasteland," Aria whined.

Grady eyed me over her shoulder, staff keeping a rhythmic 'thump' as she walked. "He seems compliant for now. Not worth the effort."

"Not that I get a vote, but I'm sure your bounty on me is to bring me back alive," I commented.

"Relax, bird; we won't kill you. We know a live bird is better than a dead one," Aria replied.

"Although, toting a bird would be much less conversation," Grady murmured.

Darya was silent, walking beside me. It surprised me they'd been able to catch up to us so quickly. Grady looked a little pale thanks to Mels' venom, but I wouldn't bet on her being down too long in a fight. I had to hope that Douglas and Constance could keep Xander and Lorelei from coming after me. They needed to be safe. No matter how angry I was with Xander, I still didn't want him to get hurt.

"I shift, you lose your money," I said matter-of-factly.

"That's bullshit," Aria snapped.

I shook my head. "I swear I'm telling the truth."

"Why would you die if you shifted?" Darya asked, voice low.

"The woman who put the bounty on my head thought it was a good idea to drug her prized possession. To keep me docile. Funny thing about a poison- like blood graft? It's killing me right now, but in bird form I'd be dead and you'd be returning a stranger to her."

"That isn't a real thing," Aria argued.

"Yes, it is. I've seen its work before," Darya replied, her tone a little stronger. "I was supposed to bring back a phoenix, but when I found her she was dead. The PLA cut my fee because I brought back a dead bird. They examined her before she rose and found blood graft. I heard them talking about it. They didn't think I knew."

She could have been lying, but there was no point in doing that. There was nothing gained by seeming to take my side in the argument against her sisters. But this was what I'd been hoping for. She understood what I was going through to some extent, and seemed sympathetic.

"Fine, no shifting. And don't get any ideas about a suicide run," Grady grumbled.

I held up my bound wrists. "I don't have a death wish."

We continued on the road back the way we'd come for a while, in silence. I thought I could hear a distant song on the breeze, but Lorelei wouldn't be foolish enough to track me and risk another confrontation with her sisters. I tried to ignore the sound and its alluring call. If the others heard it, they didn't react. Maybe they figured they would let her come and take both of us back, fulfilling the bounty.

"WE'RE STOPPING FOR NOW," Grady announced after we'd been on our feet for almost two hours.

I said nothing but I was grateful for the chance to stop and rest. Xander's healing tears had gotten me this far. Perhaps I shouldn't be so hard on him. If he wanted to give me this gift out of love, how could I say no? Darya kept a loose grip on the rope around my wrists. Grady lowered herself to the ground, wincing as she did so. Aria turned her back to us, rifling through a pack.

"Your doxy friend did a number on her," Darya said in a hushed tone.

I couldn't help but smile. "She's a little overprotective of me. I don't think she's gotten to have any real fun in a while."

"I get running, in a way. You don't want to go back. But why Lorelei? And where are you running to? There's nothing but wasteland out here."

And rifle-toting yokels. "We're looking for a better life. All of us. And we think we're getting closer." It was as close to the truth as I would give her. Until I knew I could trust her with our true agenda.

"I always thought what we were doing was necessary. It's what we're bred and raised to do. But now I'm not sure that's right."

"Lorelei felt the same way. She realized that

she was just as much a captive as I was. Sure, she didn't have bars to keep her locked away, but she might as well have with the PLA and what they forced her to do. You can't tell me you enjoy dragging shifters back to humans who don't understand us."

Darya twisted the rope between her fingers. "I've always been weaker than my sisters. They knew that when they sent me. I think they wanted to see what I'd do. I feel guilty sometimes."

I nodded my head in Grady and Aria's direction. "What about them?"

"They're firm believers. They think the government has given us some divine purpose. They embrace the hunt."

"Sounds like you should join us, then," I whispered.

"And end up with a bounty on my head?"

"With you on our side, we can take them. Subdue them or make them forget they were even hunting us."

"How is that even possible?"

"Because there are so many other types of shifters out there that you haven't met yet. People who just want to live in peace without the fear of their loved ones being ripped away from them because humans don't understand our dual nature. Because the humans think they're better than us."

"For a dying man, you're pretty persuasive," she said with a smile that reminded me of Lorelei.

"Help me. Help us find our real place in this world. Claim your freedom. Trust me, it feels good."

"That's what she did, wasn't it? All those years ago. She was on assignment and she vanished for months."

"She found someone who made her believe that her own happiness could be real. And for a time it was. We all deserve happiness."

She chewed her lower lip in thought as Grady and Aria spoke in low whispers. It seemed they hadn't noticed our conversation. I had to hope that Darya had enough strength to stand up to her sisters. Otherwise, I would never see Sanctuary.

"Do *not* move," she told me, setting the rope down at my feet. She pulled out a tranquilizer gun from one pocket in her vest, aimed at the back of Aria's neck, and fired. The dart hit its mark and she collapsed forward. Grady had just enough time to look in our direction before Darya felled her with a second shot. Darya lay the weapon on the ground and pulled out a knife. Just like the one Lorelei carried and the one Mels had stolen. She slid the blade between my wrists and freed them. "You'd better take whatever supplies you can carry. We won't slow them down for long."

Between the two of us, we made off with extra food and water and their weapons. I caught her pull something small from Grady's pocket, but she stowed it away before I could ask what it was. I suspected it was what they'd used to track Lorelei.

We retraced the path toward the barn. I hoped they hadn't gotten too far ahead of us. It turned out I didn't need to worry. Lorelei's siren song erupted in my head as we got closer, and I almost had a heart attack when Mels leapt out from a bush, teeth bared.

"Stand down!" I yelled, putting myself between her and Darya.

"What sort of mind fuck have you done to our dear birdie, fish bitch?" Mels spat.

"She's with us," I said, catching sight of Lorelei. It looked like her belly had swollen to twice the size in the time I'd left.

"What do you mean 'with us'?" Lorelei questioned.

"Your phoenix friend makes a great argument. I guess you aren't the only siren to take him up on his offer of freedom."

SEVENTEEN

SEVENTEEN

LORELEI

I knew we wanted Darya on our side, but the fact that Aiden had flipped her by himself with no glamour was impressive. That was Kegan-level negotiation shit right there. I crossed my arms over my chest, watching them.

"How do I know you're on our side and not a plant?" I asked.

"Would I have taken the tracking focuses if I were a plant?" Darya reached into a pocket on her vest and pulled out a handful of stuff. It looked like letters and a small gold object. She offered them to me. "Here. Take them. They're yours anyway."

"Do I still get to bite someone?" Mels looked around, hopeful.

"Darya tranq'd the others. Both of them, and

without me telling her to." Aiden kept his gaze trained on me, though I suspected his words were for Mels' benefit. Tranq'd sirens meant no fun for our doxy ally.

I uncrossed my arms, but didn't take the focus objects Darya offered. There was one more test I needed to do first. "What's the safe word?"

She frowned. "Excuse me?"

"The safe word," I repeated. "The one we came up with as kids. Say it now and I'll let you come with us. Don't, and Mels bites you."

"*Wahrheit*," Darya said without hesitation.

I glanced at Mels. "Sorry. You're not biting anyone today. She comes with us."

"Damnit," Mels muttered. "Spoil all my fun."

"I told you we could trust her. Shouldn't that be enough?" Aiden walked past me and continued down the half-overgrown trail to the barn. The rest of us followed.

"You don't understand siren dynamics like I do," I pointed out once I caught up to him. For a guy always on the brink of death, he could book it when he wanted to. "Spying and double-crossing is like second nature to committed members. I needed to know we could trust her."

"You should trust me," Aiden said. "Isn't my judgement worth anything?"

"It is, but I—" I stopped, not in the mood to argue. "You did good back there, okay? Kegan could convince anyone to do anything just by talking to them. I'm glad to see that didn't disappear in the burning."

Aiden looked down at his body as if it belonged to someone else. "Certain ... skills ... seem to always remain."

"You did good," I repeated. "Made my job a helluva lot easier, so I appreciate that."

His face clouded over. "Your job isn't to rescue me."

Darya jogged up to walk beside me before I could think how to respond to what felt like an accusation from Aiden. I knew he wasn't helpless—none of us were—but that didn't mean he shouldn't accept help. Working together was the only way to make it to Sanctuary, not going off on some suicide mission to buy the rest of us extra time.

"Hey, you forgot these." She held out the focus objects again. Up close I could tell they were letters from Douglas that I kept stuffed in my dresser at home and a small gold locket. The locket was all I had left to remember my parents by.

"Gimme those." I snatched them back and jammed everything into my pockets. "You had no right to ransack my apartment."

Darya cowered at my angry tone. "Macy gave the okay. She said we needed focus objects. You were smart and cleaned out your work desk. Your apartment was the only place to find anything of value."

"These are personal." I patted my pockets to make sure the letters and locket were still there, even though I'd just put them there myself. "I don't like to think of Grady and Aria pawing through my stuff."

"It's all part of the job requirement."

"Say that when it's your things you're going through."

Darya chewed on her bottom lip, lost in thought. "I bought us time, Lore. Whether the shiver tracks you or tracks me, they still need to go back to the City to find more focus objects. That buys us a week, maybe more, before they're back on our trail."

"I know, I know." I blew out my breath in a puff of air. "Thanks for thinking far ahead plan-wise. Smart move."

"I can't be a screw-up all the time."

"You're not a screw-up, Darya—just too soft for the PLA."

I walked faster when the barn came into view, hoping the others had circled back and waited for us there, yet hoping they'd left us behind and put as much distance between them and the shiver as possible while we were gone. Aiden was in the lead, followed by Mels, with Darya and me bringing up the rear. Aiden opened the barn door and stuck his head in. He looked back at us, smiled, and gave a thumbs-up/all clear signal. The smile turned to distress in an instant when he was yanked into the barn by unseen hands.

"Aiden!" I screamed.

"I got this." Mels sprinted ahead, disappearing into the barn.

I pulled a knife out of my boot and approached more slowly, not wanting to be surprised by whatever danger awaited us inside. "Wait for my signal," I hissed to Darya. She nodded, removing her taser from a pocket on her vest. I took a deep breath before kicking in the barn door.

"Hold! Stand down!" Aiden shouted as I tried to acclimate to the shadowy darkness of the barn. "It's our group."

My eyes adjusted enough to make out the rest of the MCU inner circle. I kept my knife in hand just in case anyone was still upset about Mels and me running off without a majority vote. I doubted anyone would jump me, but I'd learned you can never be too careful in life. People you think are your friends could turn into your enemies without a moment's notice.

"We picked up a second fish." Mels told the

group, motioning to Darya. "Aiden talked his way out of captivity ... again. Birdie's got skills."

Darya stepped forward, scanning the confused faces of the inner circle. "H-Hello. I'm Darya. Lorelei and I work together." She squeezed her eyes shut when she realized her mistake. "Worked together. We worked together. I guess shooting tranquilizers into Grady and Aria is kind of like my resignation notice like, um, running off was Lorelei's."

"Can we trust her?" Xander looked to me instead of Aiden for confirmation.

I nodded. "We can. She gave the safe word."

"Having a second siren along may be useful," Constance mused. "Especially when Lorelei's time comes."

Darya turned wide eyed. "Time for what?"

I lay a hand across my stomach. "Time for the baby to be born."

She laughed—not the reaction I was expecting. "That's not a disguise? I thought for sure you were just putting on a prosthetic to throw off the locals itching to turn in a shifter to collect the bounty."

"Why does everyone think I'm faking this pregnancy?" I glared at Douglas, who stood apart from the others. Judging by the fact that he wasn't rushing up to make sure I was okay, he was still mad that I ran off against his wishes. "Unfortunately, it's real."

Darya stifled a laugh. "Wow. I'm, uh ... do you want me to congratulate you?"

I kept my gaze trained on Douglas. "No. It's not a happy event. It's a hybrid accident."

"So, who's the dad?"

Douglas stepped forward. "Good to see you again, Darya." He extended his hand to shake. "That would be me. The hybrid accident's father."

Darya glanced back and forth between us so fast, I thought she'd get whiplash. "Oh, wow. That puts those letters in total context. Um, can I congratulate you, Douglas?"

"But of course." He grinned. "I'm happy for the blessed event." I couldn't tell if he was attempting to flirt with my siren sister to make me jealous or if he was being obnoxious because he was still mad at me. Maybe it was a mix of both.

"Congratulations, then," she said. "I hope your, uh, happiness continues."

"The longer we stand around, the easier it is for the sirens or locals to find us." Micah watched the half-boarded-up window for signs of life outside. "If we want to get to Sanctuary before the blood graft finds its way to Aiden's heart, we need to keep moving."

Xander stomped out the fire's dying embers. "You heard the doc. Let's roll."

"You're walking?" Darya looked to me for confirmation.

"The PLA froze my account, remember? We have enough money for the train, but it's not safe with two of the seven of us having a price on our heads," I said.

"I can help with that." Darya pulled out her government-issued phone, punched a couple buttons, and waited for whoever was on the other end to pick up. "Clancy? It's Darya. I need to call in that favor you owe me. I need two private sleeper cars. Enough to hold eight people. I have a large group heading west. Can you help?" She listened as the person on the other end answered, nodding along to whatever they said. "Great. Great. We'll be there in ten. Wonderful. See you then." She clicked the phone off and stored it in her pocket. "Forget walking. You're riding to Sanctuary."

EIGHTEEN

AIDEN

I watched the rest of our group eye Darya with skepticism. Despite passing Lorelei's test and me vouching for her, they didn't trust her. But I had to believe she was on our side; she was giving us a way to get to Sanctuary faster, after all. Fast enough that I might make it. We walked in a tight clump with Mels at the back, her stolen knife clenched in her hand. How Darya knew where to go in this area was beyond me, but before long—as night overtook the daytime hours—a looming structure appeared before us.

"We've got two cars and our passage should be free," Darya repeated for the third time since we'd begun walking.

"We heard you the first time," Xander muttered

under his breath, but still loud enough for her to hear.

I saw no trains that would carry us farther west, but trusted that Darya's contact wouldn't sell us out. As we entered the station, I caught sight of Lorelei pressing her hands to her belly and wincing. Douglas spared her a concerned look but stayed silent, still keeping his distance from her. I darted behind Micah and pressed a hand into the small of Lorelei's back. "What's wrong?"

"I think it's growing again," she replied, her breath catching on the last word.

I ushered her to a bench just inside the station and helped her sit down. I'd be lying if I wasn't grateful for the chance to rest, too. She gave me a grateful smile and leaned her head on my shoulder.

"We can rest once we're on the train," Mels snapped.

"Just give her a minute," I replied.

Mels glowered at me, but said nothing else. Darya disappeared from the group and Constance trailed her, but stopped when a pair of uniformed men walked toward us. They eyed us for all of thirty seconds before moving on without a word. Either we weren't suspicious-looking or they weren't surprised to see people waiting for the train.

"We need to be down on track seven," Darya said, and returned with a fistful of tickets.

"I'm okay," Lorelei said when I opened my mouth to protest. She stood under her own power and started after her siren sister.

The rest of us followed the two blondes in silence. I had been nowhere this exposed since my initial escape two months ago. I didn't like it. There were too many places to plot an ambush. Every step we took toward the train only heightened my worry. There were so many things that could go wrong. But the train pulled up and Darya ushered us inside, into two adjoining cars with long bunks stacked on top of each other.

"We should get close to where we need to be within two days. Three days at most," Darya announced once we'd all crammed into one train car.

"That's a long time to go without being discovered," Micah commented.

Before anyone else could respond, the door at the far end—the one that linked to our second car—slid open and a silver-haired man approached us. Both Mels and Lorelei reached for weapons. Darya stepped up and gave the man a smile.

"Nice to see you again, Clancy," she greeted, and offered him a hug.

He pulled her in tight. "Glad I could help. Let me see the tickets."

She handed them over. He scanned them and handed them back. "You're set. No one will be through here now, and I booked under false identities. No trace to you or your employer."

Which meant the PLA didn't know we'd booked passage out west. She flashed him another smile. "You have no idea how much this means to us."

"We have to look out for our own, right?"

She nodded and Clancy gave us all a small wave before retreating through the door he'd entered. Darya stuck four of the tickets into the four beds in the car and darted after our savior to leave the other tickets marking our spots. When she returned, Lorelei fixed her with an impressed smirk.

"So, you have your own informants, I see."

"You aren't the only one who can cultivate relationships," Darya quipped with a nervous hiccup of laughter.

"Well, whatever he owed you, I'm grateful."

"He's a shifter, isn't he?" I asked.

Darya nodded. "Believe it or not, he can turn into a ferret."

I wouldn't have assumed such a tall man would shrink to something so small. But then no one expected Mels to shrink to the size of a thumbnail. Micah stifled a yawn and crawled into one of the lower bunks. Lorelei started for the door to the next car and paused with her hand on the handle. "You coming, horse face?"

Douglas glanced around the space and followed her. He didn't look pleased to be going with her, but I suspected he assumed we would pair off. This left Xander, Mels, Darya, Constance, and me in the cramped space.

"You two had better not be loud." Mels darted off after Lorelei and Douglas.

Constance shifted the lower half of her body and slithered up to the bunk above Micah. Darya left without a word, and I settled on the lower bunk. I wanted to talk to Xander. I knew we'd left things in a bad place back at the barn, and I didn't want to fight with him. But it wasn't a conversation I wanted to have in front of other people. He climbed into the bunk above me and slid the small curtain closed to block out the rest of the car.

SLEEP ELUDED me as the train trundled through barren fields and wooded areas. It was more nature than I'd seen in a long time, and all of it made me miserable. It should have been a comforting place. Shifters were meant to be free and live on the land and in nature. It was as much a part of our DNA as our ability to change shape. I climbed out of the bunk and stretched, only to find Xander climbing down from his bunk, too. "Can we talk?" I whispered.

"Not here."

We tiptoed into the next compartment and found it populated by a few passengers, curled up in seats rather than bunks. I crept past them until we found what appeared to be the dining car. Long tables were lined with seats, and I could smell the lingering scent of baked bread and cured meats. My stomach rumbled at the scents. Xander must have felt the same, because he darted behind the serving station and rummaged through the contents.

"What are you doing?" I hissed.

"Taking advantage of their amenities," he replied.

"We have food from the barn," I reminded him.

He popped back up with what appeared to be a bottle of something and two glasses. "I didn't say I was hungry." He poured two generous helpings and passed me one glass.

I wasn't interested in getting drunk. He tossed his back in one swallow. I shifted the glass between my hands. "I'm sorry," I said.

"What?"

"I said, I'm sorry. I guess I might have overreacted earlier." I didn't want to be mad at him anymore. Not with the prospect of healing and good health in sight. And maybe I'd been overprotective of my own tears, given how I'd been abused.

"I mean, you were kind of right. It drains me, and I'm finding they take longer to replenish," he said, averting his gaze. He poured himself another drink.

"I don't want to see you get hurt," I said, and took a sip from the glass. The amber liquid burned as it went down, leaving a nutty aftertaste.

"Neither do I. You terrified me, going off with those sirens like that. I thought you'd gone crazy or they'd hurt you."

"I didn't have time to explain what I was doing. I knew we needed to even the odds; Darya was the weak link, based on what Lorelei said and what I witnessed when Mels and Douglas came back to get me. I knew I had to win her over. Besides, the bounty on my head is still higher than hers. They would have been fine leaving her behind." I downed the rest of the drink, trying not to grimace at the taste. "And it should have given you all the chance to get away."

"Constance said you made her promise to keep us going if something happened to you. We assumed you didn't mean it."

"I want to live. Believe me, I do. But I had to be realistic. The chances of me making the journey alive were slim to begin with. If we didn't have

Darya's help, we wouldn't have been able to get on this train. We'd still be wandering the wilderness for weeks. I know we started this to save me, but you all deserve a chance to be at peace. Lorelei and Douglas' child deserves a chance to grow up without a target on its back just because of what it is."

Xander set down the bottle and his glass and rounded the bar. He pulled me close and hugged me tight. "We'll get there together. All of us."

"I believe that now," I whispered against his neck.

He pulled back just enough to look at me. His cheeks flushed and the look in his eyes told me we would be okay. He leaned in and kissed me, conjuring the memory of our impromptu nap at the farmhouse. His arms circled my waist and he pulled me closer. I could already feel his arousal pressing against my thigh. I tugged at his shirt, sending it fluttering to the floor. He gave me a flirty smirk and sent my shirt to join it. In the dim light of the car, both our sigils shone bright and alluring. I took the time to trace the markings along his biceps and trailed my fingers down his chest and abdomen, until they rested above the waistline of his pants.

"We don't have to do this," he said, catching my hesitation.

I shook my head. "I want to. I ... haven't done this with a man before."

He slid one finger beneath my chin and tilted my head up so we were eye-to-eye. "Don't worry. Something tells me you're a quick learner."

Before I could respond he was on his knees, tugging at my pants. I flashed back to the bungled attempt at intimacy with Lorelei at MCU headquarters. The look on her face as she, too, hovered so close, offering pleasure. This time, I wasn't afraid of what I would feel or whose name might escape my lips.

His hands were gentle and sure, having done this many times before. That comforted me. I closed my eyes, enjoying the growing sense of arousal at his hands. I could feel myself getting closer to release. It had been so long. I wasn't ready for this to end so quickly, and I wasn't sure I'd be able to go another round in my current condition.

"Wait," I rasped, and opened my eyes.

He looked up at me with concern tugging at the corners of his lips. "I thought it was working."

I let out a shaky breath. "A little too well. I, uh, was getting close, but I don't want this to end yet."

"No argument here."

I offered my hand to him and pulled him to his feet. I wasn't sure what overtook me, but the urge to be in control took over and I pushed him back against one table. I pushed his pants down around his ankles and gave him the same treatment until we were both erect and breathing heavy.

"What do you want to do?" he asked.

I knew the answer before he'd even finished the question. "I want you."

He kicked off his pants and pressed his body against mine, kissing me hard on the lips. His fingers tangled in my hair as his lips broke free from mine to trail kisses down my jaw and neck. Just as he was about to travel lower, I spun him and he braced against the edge of the table.

I may not have been intimate with anyone in this lifetime, but some things were ingrained. Before long we were moving as one, Xander's hands gripping the table, knuckles going white as he let out a moan. I reached around, grasping him and stroking in time to my movements until we both found release.

"I needed that," he said when we'd separated and pulled on clothes.

"Me, too," I agreed. Much like back at the barn, the exertion caught up with me and I staggered sideways into the bar.

Xander wrapped one arm around me to steady me. "Maybe we should head back and get some rest. We could both use it."

"I think that's a good idea." I glanced at the bar and the open bottle of alcohol.

Xander grabbed it with a shrug. "Consider it a thank-you gift to Darya. Or, you know, a peace offering for Mels."

The train swayed, threatening my balance with each step as we made our way back to the sleeping compartments. I could hear a soft hissing sound, which I assumed was Constance, and a deeper snore from where Micah had ended up. I eyed the bunk I'd been in and Xander climbed in, patting the small space beside him. I smiled and climbed in, pulling the curtain partway so no one disturbed us. I curled against his chest and twined my fingers with his, pressing them against my chest. It felt right having his weight pressed against me. Like an anchor keeping me tethered to this world.

"We're okay, right?" he whispered.

"Yes. We're okay. And I have a feeling we'll be even more than okay soon."

NINETEEN

NINETEEN

LORELEI

Douglas may have disappeared with me into one of our two sleeper cars, but he left soon after with some thin excuse about needing to find the washroom. After ten minutes of waiting without him reappearing, I went looking for him. The easy way of finding him would be to hold the little copper coin I snatched from his stuff the first time we met, but tracking in such an enclosed location was dangerous. I didn't need to blow our cover because Douglas lied about going to the washroom. Instead of tracking, I walked up and down the hall twice before returning to the sleeper car. I opened the slider door and stepped inside, hoping to see Douglas. Three bunks were empty, but Mels sat on the bottom right bunk. She grinned at me.

"Hey, roomie."

"You have got to be joking." I threw my pack near the bottom left bunk. There was no way in hell I planned to waddle my way up a ladder to a top bed.

"Hey, you have fighting skills, which I respect," Mels said. "This doesn't mean I want us to braid each other's hair and gossip about boys, but I can be semi-okay with being around you, fish."

I rummaged around my pack so I didn't have to look at her. "Thanks, I guess."

"Is Douglas gonna squeeze in with you on the bottom bunk or take the top?"

"I don't know. We're not on the best of terms right now." I pulled out my cream-colored silk camisole and shorts set. While on the road, sleeping in our clothes was the best option to stay warm. Now we were on a heated train I looked forward to being a little more comfortable and, if I was honest, sexy. A little sexy time was the best way to make Douglas not mad at me. I smiled as a memory of one of our non-work-sanctioned vacations flitted through my mind. I doubt either of us got dressed for a whole week. It was the best vacation ever. My smile turned to a frown when I examined the skimpy camisole and shorts. Did they shrink? There was no way I was fitting into that without my belly being on full display. That did not sound comfortable or sexy.

"I think I can help you out." Mels noticed my dilemma. She dug around in her pack and produced a black lace nightgown. Even with my stomach stretching the material, it looked like it would still reach my knees.

"Where'd you get that?" I asked.

"A little five-finger discount in The City." She held it out. "I may be tough, but I like to feel pretty as much as the next girl. I just have no one to wear it for. You do. Take it."

It felt weird accepting any gift from the doxy, but I did so anyway. "Thank you. This is strangely nice of you."

She hopped off her bunk. "I'll go find Douglas and tell him you want to talk to him."

I wanted to do more than talk, but Mels didn't need a play by play of what I planned for Douglas and my much-needed alone time. After she left I changed into the nightgown, pulled the pins out of my hair, and unbraided it. It fell to my waist in thick waves. I tried to arrange it over my shoulder and back to look alluring. Every little trick helped when I had trouble seeing my feet, thanks to Little Accident growing at double time. I turned when I heard the door slide open, smiling in the way they taught us at the Academy.

Douglas sucked in his breath at the sight. "You look ... nice. Is that new?"

"Mels stole it from some Booshie chick in the City." I fidgeted with the lace on the left sleeve, self-conscious. "She said I could have it."

He took off his plaid overshirt and threw it on the top bunk before shimmying out of his pants, clothed only in his white short-sleeve undershirt and plaid boxers. I smiled. If we already moved on to the undressing part, we might fit more into our alone time than I thought. I lifted the hem of my nightgown and gave Douglas my best siren, come hither, look.

"Like I said, you look nice. Goodnight." Douglas was up the ladder and pretending to sleep before I processed the fact that he'd turned down my unspoken offer. I was standing in front of him in a damn negligée for God's sake, and he turned me down. This called for a trip down memory lane. If he remembered how much fun we had in the past, it should lead to fun in the present.

"Remember that time we went to Malabar together?" I asked. "We cheaped out and didn't buy a sleeper car. We spent almost two days crowded in the cheap seats."

Douglas sat up, feet dangling over the bunk. "We saved all our credits for the hotel." He grinned.

"We made good use of the small space in the train washroom, though."

I smiled at the memory. "Those poor people waiting in line."

"And I said 'let them wait. Some things take time.'" He jumped down and crossed the small space between us. It was my turn to hold my breath. Douglas cupped my face in his hand. I sighed, leaning into his touch. "A week alone with you was never enough time, Lore. I always wanted more."

I pressed against him to make it clear I was wearing the silky nightgown and nothing else. "Do you remember that feather bed at the hotel in Malabar? We talked all day, lounging under the canopy. I was afraid to close my eyes in case it was all a dream."

"It was the first time I felt you let your walls down," he said. "It was heaven."

"I wished we could freeze time and stay like that forever." I rested my hands against his chest. "No work. No responsibilities. Just us. Forever."

Douglas smiled, the gesture tinged with sadness. "Forever. I like the sound of that."

I stretched up on my toes to kiss him, doing my best to convey without words how much I needed this. How much I needed him. He moved his hand from my face to my waist, the other curling into my hair.

Time faded to nothingness. We could have stood there for five seconds, five minutes, or five hours. I didn't know, nor did I care. I wanted to feel like this forever.

I broke away first, turning to lead him to the bed. I jerked to a stop when I got to the end of his arm's length. I looked over my shoulder and frowned at him. Douglas didn't try to follow me.

"What's going on?" I asked. "If you're worried about Mels or Darya interrupting, they both know to stay away. We have time."

Douglas released my hand. "We don't have forever though, do we, Lorelei?"

My brows knit together in confusion. "What do you mean? We have an hour, two tops, before Darya and Mels will want to use their bunks. Let's make it count."

"I'm tired of snatching moments with you," Douglas said. "I want something constant. You've only given me inconstant."

I sighed. "You need to explain yourself a little better, Doug, because I have no clue what you're going on about."

"I've given you time, Lorelei," he began. "Sometimes I think more time than I should have. When we're alone I'm convinced you care and, perhaps, maybe even love me back. We can't live in a world of just us, though, no matter how much I want to. I can't keep questioning your commitment to me. To us."

I pointed at my ever-growing abdomen. "What do you call this if not commitment?"

"You said yourself the bairn was an accident." Douglas stepped forward and kissed the center of my forehead, expression sad when he pulled back. "No one wants to start life knowing they're an accident. The fact you're putting all that blame—all that guilt—on the bairn? I don't know how I feel about that. I don't know if I forgive you for that."

I blinked back tears. "So, what are you saying? Are you ending things with me?"

"What's there to end? You can't stand to admit we're even in a relationship."

"Doug, wait." I grabbed his hand when he tried to return to the bunk. "You know how I hate labels. I let other people call you my boyfriend without correcting them. For me, that's huge."

"But it's not enough. Not anymore." He shook free of my grasp and climbed back to the top bunk. "I've loved you since the second you walked through the doors of that grimy shifter bar, looking for help on a case. Can you say the same for me?"

I bit my lower lip, wanting to focus on that pain instead of the pain in my heart. "No, but that doesn't mean I *don't* love you. It just means I didn't fall as fast." I tapped my chest twice with my fingers. "You're here, Douglas. I promise you, you're here."

"Promises mean nothing without words or actions to back them up." I caught the glint of tears in his dark eyes. "Promises aren't good enough for me anymore, Lore. I can't stand this half-life. I need you to be all in or not at all."

"How am I supposed to prove something like that to you?" I sank to the floor, my legs no longer willing to support me. "Just tell me what to do and I'll—"

"You'll what?" he interrupted. "You'll do it? I highly doubt that, *M'eudail*. Besides, it's not for me to tell you how to prove your love for me. You should already know what you need to do."

I couldn't stop the tears any longer. I sat on the floor, body heaving as I sobbed. I jammed my fist into my mouth, trying to stop the near-foreign sounds of my own emotions breaking free. Douglas turned his back without another word and zero offer of comfort. He knew how sirens were raised before we got into our arrangement. He knew expressing my true emotions was as foreign as the Scotch Gaelic he spoke. He knew labels—especially relationship labels—were out of my comfort zone. He knew all this yet still stuck around, chipping away at my walls until I had trouble remembering a time when he wasn't the most important person in my life. I knew there was a "before Douglas" because, if I searched long and hard enough, I could pull up my half-forgotten feelings for Kegan. But even those felt like a dream instead of reality now. I wanted to hate Douglas for making me feel—for making me emotional—but I couldn't. I couldn't hate him.

I loved him too much to hate him.

TWENTY

AIDEN

I woke to the sound of low voices beyond the curtained barrier of my bunk. Xander still snored against my shoulder. I did my best to extricate myself without waking him. He was adorable when he slept. I peeked out beyond the curtain to find Constance and Micah sitting side by side on Micah's bunk. Constance was the first to notice I was no longer asleep.

"I'm sorry. We didn't mean to wake you," she said, the 's' coming out normal. Having legs again robbed her of that unique speech pattern.

I hated that she had to stay fully human while humans surrounded us. Just another reason we needed to get to Sanctuary. I slid the curtain back and stood, stretching the aches from my body. "You didn't wake me," I added.

Without a word Micah stood and checked my vitals, pressing his fingers to my throat to check my pulse. "You seem a little better today," he commented.

I took a minute to consider his assessment. I felt better. I could still tell I was ill, but death didn't feel so imminent. The whispers of the rising had died down. *When did that happen?* I glanced over my shoulder at Xander's slumbering form. Perhaps the angst and tension between us had been taking more of a physical toll than I'd realized. "We're in a good place now. I think that's helping," I admitted.

"If only everyone was as content," Constance sighed.

"What do you mean?"

"Douglas and Lorelei had quite the spat over the fact that she and Mels went off to find you after the sirens absconded with you from the barn," Constance answered.

"He begged her not to put herself in danger and she disregarded his concerns. I know you don't know Douglas well, but we do. And when he's hurt, he can hold a grudge," Micah said

"And she has been toying with the poor man's heart for a long while," Constance added.

I nodded in understanding. "I'm sorry we brought all of this into your lives."

Constance stood—a sight I was still not used to—and squeezed my hands. "Do not apologize. Life and love are messy, but always worth it. We should see about some food."

I was about to lead the way to the dining car, when the adjoining door to the other sleeper compartment opened and Lorelei appeared. Her hair was thrown into a messy braid and I saw dark circles under her eyes signaling that she'd barely slept.

"We were about to eat," I told her.

"Oh. Right." Her tone was flat, uninterested.

Micah pulled out the food we'd nabbed from the barn's owners and parceled it out as Mels, Darya, and Douglas joined us. The smell of the meat roused Xander from bed, too. There were too many people in this tiny space and it felt like there wasn't enough air for all of us. I could see Lorelei was uncomfortable, and nodded my head in the direction of the now-empty extra car. No one seemed to notice as we slipped away.

"Thanks," she said when we were alone.

"It was getting to be too much for me, too."

I noticed a black nightgown discarded on the floor. She kicked it out of sight and wiped away a tear. I wanted to tell her about my night with Xander. Not to rub it in that he and I had made up, but just to share the news like a friend. I didn't know how to bring it up without it coming across as if I was flaunting it.

"I heard you didn't have a great night. I'm sorry things are tense between you and Douglas," I offered.

"I don't know what he wants from me. He knew who I was when this all started. It's like he expects me to change to fit what he wants."

"I don't really know what to say," I admitted.

Her cheeks flushed with embarrassment. "Sorry—this has to be weird for you, even if you can't remember our time together."

"I want to support you. I want to tell you it will work out, but I can't see the future. False hope is dangerous in our world."

"Just you listening is enough. How are things with you and Free Range?"

It was my turn to blush. I could feel the heat burn all the way down my neck. "Better. We, uh, made up last night."

She arched a brow. "Details."

"I mean ... we had sex."

"Wow."

"I didn't mean to make you upset or rub it in your face," I said, hoping I could recover from what was a mistake in oversharing.

"You're not. I'm glad you sorted it out. He figured you'd never forgive him."

"If he can come around I have to believe Douglas can, too. Maybe he needs time."

She looked down at her growing belly. "Time isn't really on our side."

THE NEXT TWO days passed by in monotony. We stayed mostly to the sleeper cars and, as Clancy had promised, none of the staff bothered us. The mood among the group was an uncomfortable mix of Lorelei and Douglas' tension and the cautious excitement that we would actually make it to Sanctuary. I sat with the map in my lap, trying to figure out where we were and where we still needed to go. Darya wandered in and caught sight of the map.

"You look confused," she offered.

"When we were walking it was easy enough to figure out where we were. Now, I have no idea."

She sat beside me and plucked the leather-bound map from my hands. "I've been monitoring the train. We stopped at a town that used to be called Kent. According to one of the ticket-checkers, the last stop is a place that used to be called Bellevue." She pointed to a label on the map. It didn't look to be that far from the 'X' marking Sanctuary.

"How far is that?" I traced the distance between the two with my fingertip.

"A few miles maybe?" She held the map closer and studied something on the bottom right. "Okay, this says one inch is ten miles." She measured the distance on the bottom and lined them up with Bellevue and the 'X' over a place called Seattle. "Looks like about ten miles."

"That's still a long way."

"We can make it in a day if we only stop for short breaks," she commented.

"Thank you again for understanding what we're trying to do."

She passed the map back and studied her hands. "I'm not like my sisters. I'm not good at being ruthless. I don't know what happened, or what's wrong with me, but I don't have it in me. I think Macy sent me on this mission just to get rid of me. She figured Lorelei would fight her way out of being captured and that it might just mean one of us didn't come back alive."

"Well, that was her mistake. You care about other people. That makes you a good person. So what if you aren't the best siren? There's more to life than the roles we're placed in."

"I see why Lorelei fell for you before. You really are great at selling the whole freedom idea."

"I guess we all have our gifts."

"This will be a fresh start for all of us," she said just as the door opened and the rest of our group crowded in.

"The train is slowing down," Mels announced, as if we couldn't feel the speed decreasing.

"This is our stop," Darya said and we gathered our packs.

I stood beside Xander, slipping my hand into his and giving it a squeeze. We were close to getting what we'd been hoping for. I needed to be strong for a little while longer. Lorelei shifted from foot to foot; I could swear she'd grown overnight again. Douglas stood a little way off from her, looking miserable.

The train came to a halt and the outer doors opened. Mels led the charge this time. I could see the hilt of the blade in her waistband, within easy reach in case she needed to act fast. Micah climbed off next and offered a hand to help Lorelei down. Constance and Douglas followed behind her, leaving Darya to bring up the rear behind Xander and me. We moved into the shabby, run-down train station as the train hissed and settled. I expected other passengers to disembark, but no one else had come this far west. We watched as the train chugged back in the direction we'd just come without waiting to pick up any new passengers. Apparently, they assumed no one would get on this far from civilization.

"Where are we?" Mels demanded, making grabbing motions at me for the map.

I passed it to her and pointed to Bellevue. "We've got about ten miles to go before we get there."

Micah turned his head skyward. Dim daylight was grey, and heavy with another threatening rainstorm. "We'd better hurry, then. Something tells me we aren't likely to find shelter from the rain out here."

Without another word, we started out toward the road. It was dusty, but I could almost feel a different energy out here. It wasn't the same desolate desperation as the wilderness we'd left behind with Jimmy and Earl. It almost tasted electric, and I could swear I heard a buzzing in my ears to go along with it.

We'd walked maybe half a mile, when I stopped short and stared up at the sky above us. "Look at that!"

The rest of our small group stopped and craned their necks to see what I did. It had to be a mirage or a trick. Bright blue shimmered in the dim shadows of day.

"We all see that, right?" Lorelei commented.

"What the fuck is it?" Mels asked.

"That's not the largest of our concerns right now." Constance pointed at something ahead of us.

At first the shock of color in the sky blinded me. I blinked away the dark spots and took in the dark forest ahead of us. Then I spotted them creeping out toward us, teeth bared and hackles up.

Wolves.

Their sleek grey and brown fur shone beneath the strange patch of sky as they advanced on us. None of us moved. I couldn't if I'd wanted to. The sight of the wolf pack froze my body in place. Sirens may be our only natural predators, but that didn't mean other animals weren't dangerous.

"Who are you? Why have you come here?" a deep voice boomed from the forest. A tall, dark-skinned man with long hair and a bare chest appeared, standing among the pack as if they obeyed him. *What was happening?*

TWENTY-ONE

TWENTY-ONE

LORELEI

Mels, Darya, and I each drew our knives, palming the blades to keep them hidden until we decided if we needed to use them or not. I looked around the group. Everyone else seemed frozen in place. The man in the center of the wolf pack spoke again.

"Identify yourself. Who are you and why have you come here?"

Aiden was the first to find his voice. Considering his track record of talking his way out of almost any situation, that was a good thing. "We're travelers. We seek Sanctuary."

"For what purpose?" The man leaned against a primitive-looking spear. As rustic as his weapon looked, I didn't doubt he knew how to use it.

"I'm dying," Aiden said. "Blood graft is working in my system right now to stop my heart. The only cure is khalas root. Legend says it grows here."

"We're shifters," Constance added, voice soft. "We want a place to belong. The world outside your borders isn't kind to us."

At the word 'shifters', the wolf pack transformed into a mix of men and women. They stared at us with the same dark, glittering eyes as in wolf form. I didn't know which was worse—cold wolf eyes, or cold human eyes. Both groups watched each other, waiting to see who made the first move.

"Lycans," Xander murmured. "Shit. I thought those freaks were extinct."

Lycans, lycans, lycans. I wracked my brain to pull up Academy training on how to deal with lycans, but nothing came to mind. We learned lycans were wolf shifters who fought to the death with primitive weaponry, instead of surrendering to anyone or anything. They wiped out the entire Laporidae race with zero effort. The Vulpes weren't far behind during the reign of terror when the lycans just vanished. One day they were offing other shifters for sport, the next they were gone. The official story was that something in the post-wars' atmosphere caused them to die off. Judging by the fact there was a pack of lycans standing in front of us now, that was a lie.

"You claim to be shifters? Then shift." the tall man at the center of the pack said.

"Why?" Darya slid her knife back into her boot and reached for her taser instead. Smart plan. Even with our superior training, we'd be useless in hand to hand combat with the lycans. If it came to a fight, our best shot at survival would be to slow them down with tasers and tranquilizer guns.

"Not all who seek Sanctuary are worthy," the man said. "We have devised a series of trials. The first is to shift. If you wish to gain entrance and the cure you seek, shift."

We huddled together to discuss our non-options. Shift or go home seemed extreme, but I'm not surprised that's how things turned out if lycans came up with the stipulation. "What if they're lying?" I asked. "They could wait to see what we shift into and pick us off one by one."

"Can we go as a group?" Micah asked. "There's power in numbers, and we have a distinct skill set in and out of shift."

"Doc has a point." Mels ran a finger along the blade of her knife. "We got a lot of birds, too. Why not just say 'fuck this shit' and fly into Sanctuary?"

I shook my head. "I bet they have a stash of bows and arrows somewhere nearby. Do you want one to shoot you out of the sky 'cause you went against their dumb-ass trials?"

"Why don't you say that a little louder?" Douglas grumbled. "I don't think the lycans in back heard you call their tradition dumb."

"Oh don't even start with me, horse face. If I wanted your opinion about anything I say or do, I'd ask for it."

"Oh goodie, Mom and Dad are fighting again," Mels said.

"Again?" Douglas laughed harshly. "We never stopped."

Constance lay a hand near my elbow to quiet any retort I planned to lob back at the stupid kelpie. "Now is not the time or place, dear. We need to decide: shift individually or as a group?"

"I can't shift," Aiden reminded us, as if we could forget. "We need another plan."

"Somehow I don't think a pack of lycans will take no for an answer." Xander eyed them over his shoulder. "I vote one at a time. If the first person gets through without being killed, we know they're telling the truth about trials or tests or whatever they call them."

"So who wants to volunteer for a possible suicide mission?" I looked around our huddle. "No volunteers? Fine. I'll go. Even if it's a trap, what kind of asshat would hurt a pregnant chick?"

"Lycans," Xander said. "Lycans would."

My gaze flicked to Free Range. "You seriously

have an irrational fear of lycans. They're wolf shifters. Big fucking deal. Nothing I can't handle if they're looking for a fight."

"Absolutely not." Douglas mucked up my plan again. "It's clear you don't listen to reason for yourself, but I have a 50% say in what happens to the bairn. He or she will not be collateral damage in your piss-poor plan."

I pivoted toward Douglas. "While this kid is 100% in my body, I have 100% say in what happens to it."

" This kid', as you so eloquently put it is a child, not an 'it' or a thing." He lifted his chin in a show of all too familiar kelpie stubbornness. "In your body or out, you will not put him or her in danger."

"I'll go," Darya volunteered, I suspected just to get us to stop arguing. "If you can handle the lycans in a fight I can, too, right?" She forced a shaky smile, but I noticed how much her hands trembled.

"Darya, you don't have to—" I began.

"No, I want to," she interrupted, voice stronger. "That weird guy with the lycans talked about trials. Maybe this one is two-fold for me. I get into Sanctuary and I prove I'm on your side."

I gripped her by the shoulders and looked into her eyes. "Are you sure?"

Darya nodded. "I'm sure."

She shook free of my grasp and walked in slow,

measured steps toward the lycan pack. Once in front of them, she took the ever-polite Darya approach to meeting strangers.

"I'm-I'm Darya. A siren. Nice to meet you. I don't know your name."

The tall man with the spear cocked his head to the side, as if unsure what to make of an introduction. "Hunter. One of the guardians of Sanctuary."

Darya nodded. "Nice to meet you, Hunter. I'm ready for the first trial."

Darya sat on the ground so she wouldn't fall after the shift to siren form and removed the bottom half of her clothes. She hummed to speed up the process. Soon her legs fused together up to the waist, golden, shimmering scales covering her from caudal fin to waist. When the transformation was complete, Darya looked up at Hunter.

"Do you need to see more?"

He shook his head. "Welcome to Sanctuary."

With Darya safe on the other side the others took turns one by one, passing the trial. The only two left were Aiden and me.

"What am I going to do?" Aiden hissed. "I shift, I die."

"We'll get you in," I said, another one of my so-called piss-poor plans forming. "Leave everything up to me."

I stepped forward and gave Hunter the biggest,

most insincere smile I could muster. "Hey. I'm another siren." I pointed at my stomach. "This is my kelpie-siren accident. Hybrid pregnancies are a bitch, aren't they? I'll shift, but I don't know how it will affect little accident here."

I sat on the ground and removed my boots. While I was leaning over, I winced and wrapped my arms around my stomach. I cried out and grit my teeth to make the fake labor pains more believable. Hunter's tanned face turned pale and Douglas and Aiden were beside me in an instant.

"Lorelei!" Douglas wrapped an arm around my waist and helped me stand.

I grabbed a fistful of his plaid overshirt, leaning in so he and Aiden were the only ones close enough to hear me. "It's not real," I whispered. "We need a distraction to get Aiden in. This is the best I could come up with on such short notice. Now, help me distract them."

Aiden squeezed my hand to show he understood. "Quick! She needs a doctor!" he yelled. "We need a doctor, clean linens, hot water. The longer you delay, the higher the chance this baby won't survive."

Hunter and the lycans became a blur of motion. They ushered us down a hill toward a large metal building with a clear domed roof. I kept up my end of the act—stumbling and pretending to be in pain every couple of minutes. I held tight to Douglas' hand, Aiden trailing a step behind. One of the lycans opened the bronze doors to the building and led the way down a clean, well-lit hallway to a room in what I assumed was their hospital ward based on the medical equipment hanging on the walls. Douglas helped me into the raised bed.

"I hope you know what you're doing," he murmured.

I ran my fingers down the length of his arm. "Thanks for playing along. I appreciate it."

I played my labor pains game until I was sure Hunter and the lycans forgot neither Aiden nor I shifted for the entrance trial. We were in. Now the real healing could begin.

TWENTY-TWO

TWENTY-TWO

AIDEN

I stayed by Lorelei's side as the lycans retreated, leaving Hunter to keep an eye on us. I took stock of the medical facility. It was far more advanced and clean than I would have expected from a mythic shifter haven. I had so many questions, but my mind only focused on the most important: what did I have to do to get the cure? Micah moved toward Lorelei, but Hunter put a hand on his arm.

"Our doctors will examine her," he said.

"I'm a doctor and she's my patient. Unless your people have intimate knowledge of multi-shifter hybrid pregnancies, you'd better let me look."

Hunter didn't seem happy at Micah's response but stepped back, allowing him to approach. Micah shoved his way in between Douglas and the edge of the bed and checked Lorelei's pulse. She motioned for him to lean down.

"It isn't real. I needed to get us in without shifting," she hissed just loud enough for those of us standing close by to hear.

"That was risky," Micah chided. He continued to check her out, probing her belly. I swore I saw a tiny hand press through near her navel. After another minute or two, he turned back to Hunter. "It appears to have been false contractions. They occur more with hybrid gestation. She will need rest and monitoring."

Before Hunter could speak a dark-haired woman walked in, dressed in loose pants and a long tunic. I could see faint markings on her cheeks and throat that looked almost like bloodstains. Her eyes glittered like the other lycans.

"They told us one of you is ill with blood graft?"

I stepped forward. "Me."

"Follow me."

"Where are you taking him?" Xander protested, reaching for my hand.

"We have to be certain he's telling the truth."

"Why would he lie? Look at him!" Xander argued.

"We cannot treat the disease if we aren't certain what it is."

I turned to Xander, placing a hand on his chest.

"It's okay. I'll be fine." I leaned in and kissed him, hoping to provide extra reassurance.

"If they hurt you ..." he breathed.

"I'll be fine," I repeated. I then followed the woman, leaving the rest of our group behind.

She led me down a short hallway to a private room, complete with equipment I didn't recognize. She gestured for me to sit on the examination bed.

"Roll up your sleeve," she said, and pulled on thin gloves before picking up an empty syringe.

I obeyed and watched as she pierced the vein below my elbow and filled the vial with blood. It looked no different. What was I expecting? Black bile? She shook the vial twice and set it in a machine that whirred at a rapid pace.

"Please describe your symptoms," she said, not meeting my gaze.

"Uh, fatigue, inability to stay in shift or come out without serious help," I replied. I couldn't stop staring at the markings on her face.

Behind her the machine beeped, and a readout appeared on a screen next to her. "Well, it looks like you're telling the truth. How did it happen?" Her tone changed, softening.

"I was kidnapped by a human woman three years ago, forced to stay in shift so she could harvest my tears. She poisoned me. I only realized what she'd done after I escaped and found the others I arrived with. We made the journey together, looking for our freedom." After a moment, I reached out and grabbed her wrist. "You can help me, can't you?"

"Yes. We have what you need to cure the disease. I am curious, though, from what I've heard about your kind, is it true that any ailment burns itself out when you rise from the ashes?"

"It is, but I wouldn't be me. We lose our identity and memory of the lives we've lived. I've barely lived this life. I'm not ready to give it up."

She nodded. "Stay here. I'll be back with what you need."

Now that the cure was in sight, the other questions swirling in my mind took over. What were we going to do now that we were here? Would the lycans let us stay if we asked? And what about all the shifters out in the world still being exploited by the human elite?

The woman returned before I could follow that last thought down what was likely a dark path. She carried a bag of fluid and another needle. "I need you to lie back and get comfortable."

"What is that?"

"Distilled khalas root, with some other nutrients mixed in to help boost your system."

"You know, I never got your name," I said as she slid the needle into my arm and hung the bag on a pole above my head.

"Serena," she replied.

"You're a lycan, too, aren't you?"

"There will be time for questions later. You should rest," Serena said, and started the flow of the medication.

I could feel the khalas root mixture hit my system with an icy balm. It lulled me toward unconsciousness. I only hoped the others would still be there when I woke up.

WHEN I WOKE, everything around me seemed brighter. I took a breath, and realized that the fatigue I'd felt for the last two months was gone. I looked around at my surroundings to find the bag hanging over my head was empty. Xander sat slumped in a chair beside the bed, snoring. As he slumbered, I took stock of my body. I felt stronger than I could ever remember. I didn't ache, and the tiny ember of fear that had ruled me since we began our journey had been stomped out. There was no more threat of my body betraying me and rising from the ashes to rid me of the poison.

It worked.

I pulled the needle from my arm, wincing at the pain of it, and sat up. Tears came unbidden to my eyes and I dabbed one onto the spot that was now bubbling with a pinprick of blood. The tiny wound healed far faster than I'd ever seen.

"Xander, wake up," I said, nudging his shoulder.

He mumbled something in his sleep and I shook him harder. It was enough to rouse him; he blinked the sleep from his eyes, sitting up straighter when he saw me. "You're awake," he said.

"That stuff knocked me out, I guess."

"Aiden, you were unconscious for two days."

I stared at him, mouth agape. "I was?"

"Yeah. They made the rest of us undergo medical tests to make sure we weren't carrying anything that could hurt their people before they'd let me see you."

"How's Lorelei?"

He shrugged. "Fine. She and Douglas still aren't speaking, but their doctor has let her get out of bed so she won't murder anyone for now."

Speaking of murder ... "Has there been any sign of Aria and Grady?"

"Nope. Lorelei thinks we put enough distance between us and them. They most likely didn't have what they needed to track us, so they went back to the City empty-handed."

That was a relief. I got to my feet and started for the door. "Is there anything to eat? I'm starving."

"That's a good sign," Serena said, appearing in the doorway. She pointed to the smooth skin at the crook of my elbow. "I see you're not a very patient ... patient."

"I feel fine. Better than I have in a long time," I said, hoping a smile would persuade her to let me find food.

"I'll be the judge of that. Sit back down a minute—I need to run another test."

I slumped back against the exam table and let her poke and prod me again. The machine beeped at her and she nodded. "We've purged your system of the graft. You're good to go. I'll take you to see your friends."

Serena led us down a series of brightly-lit hallways to an outdoor eating area covered by large tarps. I could even feel a breeze. It felt like heaven against my skin and called to the bird within me, begging me to fly. I turned my gaze skyward, expecting the dullness of our world, yet it was blue and bright.

"I don't understand," I said, pointing upward.

"You will. Come and join us for a meal. I promise it will be illuminating."

We followed her to a long table where Douglas, Micah, Lorelei, and Darya sat. As warned, Douglas sat as far from Lorelei as he could get. Constance sat coiled on her snake's tail at the far end of the table. A few of the lycans roamed among humans. I couldn't quite tell who among them were also shifters—I'd never had a talent for that—but they appeared comfortable with those of us who could change our shape. Most were darker-skinned and I noted a few bore the same facial markings as Serena. I took a seat beside Constance, who pushed a tray of meats and fresh fruits my way.

"You look so much better," she said, and patted my arm.

"I feel better. I can't believe we made it to Sanctuary."

"Neither can I. I must admit I had my doubts that this place even existed. But I am so glad it does."

I piled food high on my plate and no one seemed to object as I ate. Xander scooted in beside me, picking at a bowl of warm grains. I spotted Hunter at the far end of the table, keeping an eye on our contingent.

"What have I missed?" I asked, pushing away the empty plate fifteen minutes later.

"Well, the tests," Mels said, growing larger at

my side and making me jump. "Glad you're not dying anymore, birdie."

"Me, too," I said, and tried to get my heartbeat to slow.

"From what Hunter has said, the lycans retreated to this place decades ago. They were not equipped to survive in what had become of our world," Constance added.

"My people lived on this land before the wars," Hunter said, his voice carrying effortlessly down the table. "We sought to protect it because, to us, this land is sacred. It was our duty to honor it. So, we kept it safe. We built air purifying systems that remove the ash and pollution from the air. Our engineers built the dome above us to protect us from the acid rains."

"He's trying to make us think not all humans are Booshie assholes," Lorelei said.

"You live so openly with shifters. We aren't used to that," I commented.

"The lycans came to us and sought our protection. We granted it on the promise that they, too, would become this land's protectors. As time moved on, we realized that if we were to survive we needed to integrate. We had mixed children. Some of our young ones now can no longer change," Hunter answered.

"You never explained the markings," Darya interjected.

"They're a way to honor our ancestors. The wolves who came before us, who are no longer among the living. It is a reminder of our heritage, given when we first undergo the change," Serena replied.

"We're so grateful for you taking us in and looking after our people. We want to be a part of your community, if you'll let us," Micah said.

"You can stay, but we have rules. Everyone must tend to the land. We do not deal in credits or items of that nature. We measure your worth by your contribution to our society. Can you agree to those terms?" Hunter queried.

I looked at our mismatched band of outcasts. We'd all come to the Magical Creature Underground looking for something our world couldn't give us. This place was offering us a chance to be at peace with those we loved. How could we say no? One by one, our group turned toward me and nodded. Somehow, I had become our leader. "Yes, we can abide by your rules."

"Good. Now please take your fill of food and explore. We will house you together until we can agree on more permanent arrangements. We do not wish to disrupt any family units."

In that moment, I realized that they could consider Xander and me a family unit. I couldn't re-member having a family, and I had no way of knowing if the parents who'd conceived me even remembered me or were still alive. But these people could be my family now. I reached over and squeezed his hand. This was a new beginning.

TWENTY-THREE

TWENTY-THREE

LORELEI

"'Pull your own weight,' they say. 'Why don't you collect firewood,' they say," Mels grumbled as we followed the stream that ran through Sanctuary, looking for kindling. "Why do you think they made us go together? I can carry shit, and you'll only slow me down."

I put a hand on my lower back and attempted to hide the wince when another round of what I hoped were false labor pains rippled through my body. Mels was too busy bitching about chores to notice my discomfort. "There's nothing wrong with my hands or my aim." I surprised myself by being able to keep my voice normal and not pitched to 'Gods, I think I'm dying' level. "I can still throw knives at anything or anyone that comes at us."

Mels tilted her head to the side. "Can you teach me to throw like you? I mean, I've got the siren knife, right? I need to know all the ways to use it."

I sat next to a shallow pool the river created in the forest. I didn't tell Mels I needed to sit before I fell down. Dampness spread through my undergarments and down the inside of my pants, but I forced myself to ignore it. No matter how fast this pregnancy was progressing, it was still too early for Little Accident to make his or her debut. An image of Douglas joking that kelpies come out in horse form flashed through my mind. I really, really hoped he was joking. Birthing a foal was *not* on my to-do list. Birthing anything was not on my to-do list till a couple months ago.

"Did you ask me to help you with something?" I focused all my attention on Mels to take away from the rhythmic pain rolling through my body. "Is the world ending?"

"Naw, just thought I should go to the source," she said. "Siren plus siren knife equals learning opportunity." She flitted closer, still unaware of how I felt like my body was being torn apart from the inside. "I got hand to hand combat covered. However, I'm not great at long range."

I breathed in deep through my nose and let it out through my mouth. It helped with the pain a little. At least it gave me something to focus on and feel more in control. Mels frowned.

"You okay, fish?"

I held out my hand for the knife to show her a throwing technique. I needed a distraction besides breathing and cursing my stupidity. Not long ago, I had a job and a life—not a great one, but still a life—in the City. Why the hell did I throw that all away? Now I was alone with a doxy who'd rather bite me than help me, and a kid trying to evacuate from my body. I grimaced, imagining a hoof instead of a hand pressing against my abdomen. What if Little Accident shifted mid delivery? Would either of us survive?

"You're too quiet," Mels announced. "What's wrong?"

I pointed at my stomach. "It's time."

"Time? Time for what?"

I jabbed a finger at my stomach this time. "The baby. Not fake. Real."

Mels mouth dropped open. "Wh-What can I do?"

"Go. Get. Someone," I panted. "Douglas. Aiden. Micah. I don't care. Someone."

"I can't leave you alone," Mels said. "Douglas would kill me."

I grabbed her hand and squeezed tight. My

knuckles turned pale from the effort. "I want Douglas! Get Douglas!"

She shook her head, blueish tears sparkling in her eyes. "I can't leave you alone. I won't. I'm sorry I'm not Douglas but, right now, you're stuck with me. I'm all you and the baby have."

I tipped forward, pounding my fists on the ground until they were dirty and bloody. "Just make it stop," I begged Mels. "Make the pain stop."

Her face lit up. "I've got it! I can bite you. In this case, doxy venom acts as a nerve blocker. You'll be numb from the waist down. You won't feel a thing."

I nodded consent. I didn't care what she did as long as the pain stopped.

"Okay. This works best if I can get at your lower back, near your spine."

Mels helped me undress down to just my camisole. I didn't realize how over-heated I felt until the breeze cooled my bare skin. Mels tapped at my spine till she found the spot she wanted. She spit into her hand and rubbed the venom on my skin to numb the injection spot. She counted down from three before sinking her teeth into the sensitive area of my lower back. Thanks to her prep work I only felt a jab, like getting a shot. I sighed as the venom spread through my system, bringing much-needed and appreciated numbness from the waist down. I sat up, feeling almost normal again. I smiled before holding out a hand to Mels again. "Thank you."

She sat next to me, my hand gripped in hers. "What do we do now?"

"Hope nature takes over and my body knows what to do, 'cause my mind doesn't." I closed my eyes and leaned back against the nearest tree. "The government gave us preventatives for a reason. They never wanted us to be in this situation."

"They never allowed me in the nest when a baby was on the way," Mels said. "Mom sent me out to play or bite something ... there's not much difference." She shrugged as if the memories belonged to someone else. "Some stupid human snatched me on a day like that. I thought he wanted to pluck off my wings and bottle my venom to sell on the black market, but I was worth more to him alive than dead. You talk about being raised to be a weapon. So was I. They called it a shifter fight club. They kept us in cages and forced us to fight each other for entertainment. Humans bet credits on who they thought had the best shot at surviving."

"I ... I didn't know that." I felt more respect for the doxy than even an hour before. "I thought the feds shut down all the fight clubs."

"Making something illegal doesn't stop the humans from doing it." Mels shrugged again. "I survived. I escaped. End of story."

"Maybe what you call the end is just the beginning."

She laughed. "Yeah. Maybe. How are you doing, fish?"

I ran my fingers down my stomach. "Ready to be done with this ... and I hope Little Accident doesn't shift mid-process."

Mels squeezed my hand. "You might want to come up with a better name than 'Little Accident'."

"I was thinking Douglas if it's a boy." I squeezed my eyes shut as an urge to push overtook me. "He's been good to me, even if I haven't always been the best, um, girlfriend to him."

She nodded approval. "He'd like that."

"Mels?" I made eye contact. "I'm scared."

"So am I, but we got this. Now, push."

I took a deep breath and pushed. Time seemed to stand still. Everything and nothing happened all at once. Progress slowed before it ground to a halt. I couldn't keep this up. My strength was gone and the doxy-venom spinal block was wearing off.

"Water." I crawled toward the shallow pool. "Water will help."

The water soothed my exhausted body. I wished for sleep, but I knew there was still so much work to do before this kid was in the world. Little Accident wasn't making this easy on me. Still, nothing worth having was ever easy. Our journey to

Sanctuary wasn't easy, and neither was this birth. Both were worth it, though. I needed to believe both were worth it.

I'm not sure how long I was in the water. Time remained a blur. The one moment that stood out was Mels shouting, "You did it, Lorelei! You did it!" She scooped something up from the water. I was slow to register it was the baby.

"Boy or girl?" I asked.

"Boy. You have a son." Mel bit through the umbilical cord with her sharp incisors and carried him over to the clothes I'd shed earlier. She found my shirt and wrapped him up in it.

I blinked hard, feeling dizzy. I lifted a hand from the water. It was red with blood. My blood.

"Something's wrong," I called.

"I think he's just cold." Mels chafed his bluish hands, blowing warm breath on them. "I think he'll wake up if we get him warmed up."

My mind was hazy, not noting the baby's lack of cries. I crawled out of the pool and toward Mels and the baby. "Something's wrong," I repeated.

"No. No, I think I can get him to cry." Mels looked up at me, her face draining of color. "Oh. You mean with you."

The grass was wet with a mix of water and blood. I felt the darkness overtaking me, but I needed to tell her one thing. I needed to make sure Douglas knew...

"Mels, tell Douglas I ... tell Douglas I—"

Darkness claimed me, enveloping me in the sweet rest of oblivion.

ETERNITY

CAPTIVITY BOOK 3

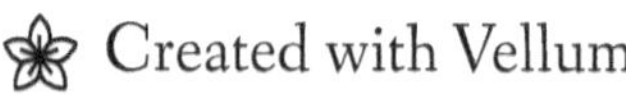 Created with Vellum

ONE

ONE

AIDEN

Xander and I strolled through tall rows of sweet-smelling crops waving in the breeze. I'd grown used to the sky above us changing colors with the sun. It was so bright—even brighter than the light Micah let off—and warm. How we could feel the warmth through the protective dome still baffled me, but I had decided not to question it. The Guardians and Lycans had built this place to keep themselves safe and that was all that mattered.

"What are you thinking about?" Xander asked, lacing his fingers between mine as we walked.

"How much I want to fly," I replied without thinking.

He made a show of looking around us. "I don't think anyone will stop you."

I pulled him close and kissed him. "Fly with me."

"I thought you'd never ask."

We disrobed amidst giddy laughter. This was nothing like the first time we'd flown together. There was no hiding our existence. It was just pure joy. He grabbed me and held me close, pressing our naked bodies against one another, a promise of what was to come. Just as I felt the stirrings of arousal, he pulled away, skin melted into feathers and he took off like a shot into the air.

I followed suit, welcoming the change as it slid through me like water. There was no tension or resistance to taking on beak and wing. My heart sang as I relished the feeling of freedom. I flapped my wings twice and was airborne in seconds. This was truly what happiness felt like. We darted through treetops, wheeling on the warm swells until below us, I spotted a wolf racing from the brush below. It let out a howl that called to the human part of me— a warning.

I swooped down, landing on the soft grass before letting the skin and bone take over. The wolf changed, too, becoming a lithe young girl. She had dark brown eyes like so many of her people. The markings on her face—red like blood around her cheeks and mouth—were fresher, maybe only recently applied.

"The siren. You must come," she said, tugging on my arm.

"Lorelei?" I prompted.

"Come. Hurry!"

Behind me, Xander landed and shifted back to human. I looked at him. "Find Douglas. Now."

Xander sprinted off, forgetting his clothing, as I pulled on my pants and shirt. The girl paced nervously back and forth, as if she were eager to return to all fours.

"What's your name?" I asked, trying to calm her down despite my own panic mounting.

"Luna. Please, come."

"Where is she?" Douglas boomed, cresting the hill.

Luna led us back into the woods and toward the river that ran through the heart of Sanctuary. Douglas trotted faster, outpacing me as we darted through brush and ducked under low-hanging branches. I skidded to a halt when I spotted Mels sitting beside the riverbank. Her hands were rust-colored and something lay in her lap. Lorelei was slumped against a pile of clothes motionless. The grass and the skin of her legs was angry and red, as was some of the water.

"What happened?" Douglas rasped.

"It came too early. She thought ... she thought

the water would help, but .... He's not breathing and she won't wake up," Mels murmured.

Douglas stood immobile, gawking at the baby in Mels' arms. Luna remained silent, shifting from foot to foot. We didn't have time for this. We needed to act now. I rushed forward and took the baby from Mels, cradling him close to my chest. I looked to the others. "We need to get her back to the medical area now. If we don't, we will lose them both."

I'D NEVER RUN SO FAST. My heart hammered in my chest as I looked down at the tiny life in my arms. Lorelei and Douglas' child was on the verge of turning blue when I slammed through the outer doors to the medical facility.

"What's going on?" Serena asked, appearing from a doorway.

"He's not breathing. He came too early. Lorelei's right behind us. It looks like she's lost a lot of blood," I said in one breath.

She reached for the newborn, but I couldn't relinquish him. "Tell me what to do," I said.

"Lay him down. We need to warm him up and clear his airways," she said.

I followed her into one of the empty exam

rooms and laid the baby on a clean blanket. My fingers trembled as I rubbed the infant's skin, praying silently for him to be okay. Slowly, he regained normal color and one tiny hand moved against mine. "Hang in there," I whispered, bending low and let a few of my tears escape to land on his forehead. I rubbed them in while Serena wasn't looking.

The tears helped. He began to move more freely, but he was still struggling to breathe. Serena appeared at my side and ushered me aside. She placed a small suction device over his nose and mouth. With a soft 'whoosh' she expelled fluid and mucus, at last he gave a hearty cry.

"Help!" Douglas' voice echoed in the hallway. I didn't have time to feel relieved about the baby. We still had to help Lorelei.

I wrapped the baby in the blanket and nestled him in the crook of my arm before following Serena out into the hall. Lorelei continued to bleed and she was deathly pale. Douglas was panic-stricken. His hair was matted to his head with sweat and I could see his hands shaking. Mels trailed behind him and Luna, her gaze fixed on her hands. She was shaking her head and muttering to herself.

"Bring her in here," Serena ordered.

I could see a crowd gathering at the entrance to the medical facility. Constance, Micah and Xander peered in along with Hunter. They could wait. I placed myself in Mels' path, forcing her to look up when she bumped into me.

"He's okay," I told her and showed her the wriggling newborn.

Mels stared at me and the baby glassy-eyed for a minute until the baby let out a howl. She blinked and broke out into a wide grin. I passed him to her and she held him gently to her chest. "You gave Auntie Mels a scare," she whispered against the top of his head.

Hunter burst through the doors trailed by the rest of our group. "What is going on?"

"Lorelei had the baby early. She's lost a lot of blood. Serena is with her now," I answered.

"Show me."

I led the way down the hall to the room where they'd taken Lorelei only a few days ago when we first arrived. Serena had a device pressed to Lorelei's belly; her brow furrowed in worry as she studied something on the screen beside her.

"Please, you have to save her," Douglas pleaded.

"The placenta ruptured. It's why she's lost so much blood. I need to deliver it, but I can't do that if she's not awake. Her body doesn't seem to respond to what it needs to do."

"I bit her. She was in so much pain, I thought it would act as an anesthetic," Mels said.

"Using doxy poison in that way is dangerous. You could have paralyzed her," Serena said.

"I ... I was trying to help her." She looked at Douglas. "I swear."

"Maybe phoenix tears can help things along?" I volunteered.

"She'd say not to waste them on her," Douglas said with a hiccup of bitter laughter.

"I'll help, too," Xander offered.

"I might be able to give her something to counteract the poison and get her body to remember what it needs to do, but she will still need a transfusion," Serena continued. She held up a hand before I could speak. "You just got the blood graft out of your system. Besides, I don't' think she needs shifter blood."

"Then what does she need?" Constance asked from the doorway.

"Mundane blood," Micah supplied.

Before any of us could object, Hunter settled beside Lorelei's bed and rolled up his sleeve. "Let's get to saving her then."

Douglas' eyes brimmed with tears. "You would do this for her? A stranger?"

"Our people have accepted you. You are no longer strangers. Go, be with your son. We will do everything we can to save his mother."

Mels stepped forward to hand Douglas the

baby. He accepted the boy's weight effortlessly, the sadness and worry in his eyes momentarily replaced by the utter joy of meeting his son. "Hello there, wee bairn. I'm your daddy. I will always be there to protect you. No matter what." After kissing the baby's head, he bent low to kiss Lorelei's forehead. "Come back to me, *M'eudail*. Come back to me."

TWO

TWO

LORELEI

I opened my eyes, not sure what I expected to see. I stared at the white panels of the ceiling and let myself slowly adjust to consciousness. A monitor beeped somewhere off to my left and my arm felt sore. I looked down, noticing an IV taped to my skin. *What happened?* I rewound my mind back to collecting firewood with Mels. How long ago was that? Yesterday? Today? Days ago? Going into labor caught me off guard and the baby—

The baby!

I sat up, the room spinning from the motion. Once my equilibrium righted itself, I scanned the room for anything that could help me figure out what had happened to the baby. Mels said it was a boy. Was he even alive?

My gaze found Douglas sleeping in a chair across the room. He cradled a swaddled bundle in his arms as if he didn't dare let it go. I saw a tiny hand pop out of the blanket and wave around before the bundle wailed for ... I'm not sure what. Comfort? Food? Me? Were they real or a trick of my imagination?

"Douglas?" I tried to call out, but it sounded more like a whisper.

He started awake before rubbing his eyes with his free hand. He noticed the baby was crying before he noticed I was awake.

"There, there, now, bairn." Douglas rocked the little bundle to soothe him. "I'm here. I promised I wouldn't leave you, and I haven't. Are you hungry? Here now, let's find you some grub." He rummaged around in some sort of baby supply bag under his chair and pulled out a bottle. He brought the empty bottle to the sink, all the while cooing to the baby in his arms. Douglas scooped some powder into the bottle, added water, put the lid on, and shook it. He replaced the cap with a bottle nipple and swiveled to return to the chair. In that same instant, he noticed me sitting up watching them. His face paled before the bottle fell from his hand.

"Lorelei? Are you really awake? *Mo Dhia, M'eudail,* I've wished and hoped for this moment and now ... are you real? Am I dreaming?"

"I thought I might be dreaming, too." I put a hand on my throat. It was sore from lack of use. "Are you real?"

Douglas smiled. "I am." He bounced the baby in his arms. "We are. Do you know we have a son?"

"That's about the last thing I *do* remember." I ran my fingers through my hair, trying to untangle some of the knots. "Can I hold him?"

"He's hungry," Douglas warned. "I was just making a bottle."

I gestured at my swollen breasts. "Hey, I'm a one-woman milk factory here. I think I got the food thing covered."

Douglas crossed the room and handed the squirming baby over to me. Someone had changed me into a hospital gown sometime between the woods and now. It was open in the back, but also had hidden slits in the front to make breast feeding easier. I closed my eyes, trying to remember how the younger siren sisters were nursed. A hazy memory came to mind of the time when my life was still my own. Before the Academy, PLA, and everything that came with working for the government. It was the happiest memory I had up until now.

"Don't worry, little one," I whispered to the baby. "I know what to do."

I adjusted myself in bed until I was sitting cross-legged. I put a pillow across my lap and laid the baby on his side facing me. This way, I didn't need to lean down and he didn't need to reach up too far. He latched on almost immediately, sucking with a strength I didn't expect from someone so little. I winced.

"Dougie! Dougie, slow down!"

"Dougie?" Douglas pulled a chair up next to my bed and sat down. "Short for Douglas? You named him after me?"

"I ... I thought you'd like it." I grimaced as Dougie pulled so hard, I was sure he'd leave a bruise. "Douglas, I know our relationship wasn't in the greatest of places before. It was my fault. I know that. I've always known that. I just didn't know how to fix it. The one good thing about fighting with you is it gave me a lot of time to think."

Tears glittered in his dark eyes. "The worst moment of my life was when they told me something was wrong with you and the baby. I know you can be ... difficult ... and intensely private. That doesn't bother me. When I dream of the future, you're always in it. In that instant when Hunter and the others said we might lose both you and the bairn, my world shattered." He raised my hand with the IV to his lips and pressed a kiss to it, before letting go. "I want you, Lorelei. I want our family. What do I care of titles or labels if you're not here to share my life with?"

I took a ragged, emotion-heavy breath. "I love you. I love you, Douglas. I should have told you *so* long ago, but I was stubborn. I didn't know how much of me was tangled up in you until I thought I had lost you. I'm sorry. I wish I had realized that sooner. It would have spared both of us a lot of heartache."

Douglas kissed my hands, then my forehead, and finally the top of Dougie's head. "*Ar theagh-lach.* This is all I need to be happy."

"I'll be a better girlfriend," I promised. "Just promise to be patient with me, okay?"

"I'll be patient," Douglas agreed. "We have all the time in the world, *M'eudail.*"

I scooted over so there was room on the bed for him to join me and Dougie. Once he did, I rested my head against his shoulder. "Ahr hy-lock," I attempted to pronounce the unfamiliar Gaelic words. "What does that mean?"

Douglas tightened his arm around me, his fingers resting on my hip. "Our family."

"*Ar theaghlach,*" I repeated. "I like that. Our family is all I need, too."

THREE

THREE

AIDEN

L ife in Sanctuary settled down once Dougie came along. It felt as though everything we'd been fighting for had finally come to pass. I sat alone at the long communal table at the heart of the compound, staring up at the rising sun turning the domed sky above beautiful shades of purple and blue. I would never tire of seeing it. The soft creak of weight shifting on a seat nearby broke the tranquility. I turned to find Luna sitting beside me clad in a short dress that matched the markings on her face.

"You're up early," I commented for lack of a better thing to say.

"I like the sunrise. It's peaceful."

"So do I. We don't really get anything like this where we're from."

I had expected her to pepper me with questions about our existence beyond their borders, but she stayed silent. After a few moments, she sighed and said, "Were you really forced to stay in your spirit form against your will?"

This wasn't the first time I'd heard her people refer to being in shift as donning a spirit form. "Yes, I was," I replied, my tone flat.

"Some of our people don't believe that the humans beyond our borders are bad, but our ancestors wouldn't have built the dome to protect our land if they weren't dangerous." Her mouth hung open, as if she wanted to say more, but no words came out.

"Not all humans are bad. There are some—like your people—who don't see us as objects to be possessed," I said.

"I want to believe there is good in the world, but ..." Luna bit her lip as she trailed off.

"What's going on? You have something you want to say, I can tell. Just tell me."

Her dark eyes sparkled with fear. "They don't know I heard. I wasn't supposed to be there, but I heard them talking.'

"Heard who talking? About what?"

She shook her head. "I'm not supposed to know."

I reached over and took both of her hands in mine. "Luna, if something is happening that shouldn't be, if it puts the people I care about in danger, I need to know. Please. I won't mention I heard it from you."

She chewed her lower lip again and I realized how young she truly was. She couldn't have been over thirteen or fourteen, still a child in so many ways. Finally, she squeezed my hands back.

"There is a room in the main compound where they watch the outside world. They don't think I know about it. They have been keeping a secret about the people beyond the border."

Secrets were never a good thing in our world. They had a nasty habit of making situations worse. "Thank you for telling me." I stood and headed back to the barracks that had become our group's sleeping quarters. I tried not to let my mind chase down the darker possibilities of what sort of secret our new allies harbored. I found Darya coming out of her room.

"Glad I'm not the only who likes to get up early," she said upon spotting me.

"I need your help," I said.

"Okay."

I gestured for her to follow me down an empty corridor. "It appears our new friends are keeping secrets about the outside world."

"What does that mean?"

"I'm not certain."

"They've been nothing, but kind to us since we got here. They saved yours and Lorelei's lives."

"I'm not saying that they haven't been good to us, but they are hiding something. I need to know what it is."

She crossed her arms over her chest. "Why do I get the sense you are one of those people who isn't happy unless he has something to fix?"

I wasn't expecting pushback from Darya. She'd been so easy to convince to join our cause. She had sympathy for our kind. Sympathy that wasn't often seen in sirens. "I won't lie. Coming here and seeing what these people built, it made me wonder what will happen to the people we left behind?"

"Other people?"

"Come on, Darya. You had to know there were others in the underground who couldn't come with us. We may be safe now, but who will protect them from the Booshies intent on keeping them prisoners?"

"I understand your desire to help them. But what can we do? Do you have any idea how many shifters there are on this continent alone?"

"I bet we outnumber the humans. Don't we owe it to them to try?"

"What do you want me to do?"

"Just be a look out for me. Please."

She shifted from foot to foot and wouldn't meet my gaze. "Okay, fine. Promise me we aren't going to take action without thinking it through."

"We won't do anything until we have all the details. I swear."

WE HEADED BACK OUT into the ever-brightening morning and across the empty central space to the main building that housed what Hunter had mentioned as the tech hub of Sanctuary. All of the systems that kept the atmosphere outside were situated in one place.

"I saw Lycans patrolling this area the last few days," Darya commented.

The entrance sat unguarded. If birds had hackles, mine would be raised at the change in routine. As it was, the small hairs on the nape of my neck prickled. Darya stepped in front of me and slid out her taser from its holster. It said something that she hadn't felt safe enough to leave her weapons behind. She peered through the window in the door before trying the handle. It swung inward on silent hinges.

"Where are we going exactly?" she whispered.

Luna hadn't given me an exact location. It had

scared her enough passing on what she'd told me. "I'm not really sure. We'll just need to check everywhere."

"This place is huge. Maybe we should get backup."

"We can do this," I answered and nudged her forward.

The interior wasn't as expansive as I'd first believed. We found a medical supply room and a few other rooms that appeared unused, leaving the large space in the dead center of the building. Darya crept forward with her back pressed to the wall. She craned her neck to peer in through the partially open doorway.

"What do you see?" I hissed.

"Hunter, Serena, and a few others I don't recognize."

So many of the Lycans remained in shift it was hard to know what they looked like in human form. I crouched low and darted across to the other side of the doorway to get a better vantage point. Inside I could make out large monitors with images from the City. I recognized the train station we'd used in our bid to cash in on my bounty.

"We already discussed this. It isn't relevant," a balding man with grey temples said, leaning over documents laid out on the table.

"Why, because this is all the way on the other

side of the continent? It will reach us eventually," Serena argued.

"Years. Decades maybe," the older man replied.

"We've made modifications to the air and water purifying systems to account for it. Even if it makes it here, it won't affect our people," Hunter added.

Serena shook her head. "Have you become so blinded and isolated that you can't see the dangers this poses?"

"He was an isolated incident. You said so yourself," Hunter said.

I got the feeling our group had appeared in their conversation. Darya's brow furrowed which told me she'd picked up on it, too. Serena picked up some of the papers, shuffled through them and slammed them down on the table again in front of Hunter. "That poison came from somewhere, Hunter. They nearly killed him just because he was more profitable to them in a cage. They did not care about hurting him. If our information is accurate, every shifter out there is at risk of the same fate, free or caged. Humans may be immune to the graft, but those who can shift shape will all die. Don't let your humanity blind you to their cruelty."

"I am not blind. I know exactly what they are capable of. We will not let them hurt our people."

Serena's mouth hung open and she stormed toward the door. Darya darted to my side of the hallway and we both held our breath. Serena slammed through the door and marched down the hallway we'd come from. She hadn't noticed us. We let the door ease closed behind her before slipping back the way we'd come.

"We need to tell the others," I said once we were outside. Luna had been right to be worried. If the conversation we'd overheard meant what I thought, the entire population of shifters was in danger.

FOUR

FOUR

LORELEI

Knock, knock, knock.

I rolled over in bed and squinted at the view from Douglas' and my window, trying to gauge the time of day. The sun streaked the sky with colors I'd forgotten even existed. Seven in the morning? Maybe, eight?

"Tell whoever it is to go away." Douglas pulled his pillow over his head. That move might block out the sun, but it didn't block out the knocking.

Knock, knock, knock.

I sat up and swung my legs over the side of the bed. It still felt weird sleeping in a comfortable bed with plush pillows and blankets. It reminded me of the fancy resort in Malabar by the ocean. We had saved for four months to afford the trip. I didn't even correct Doug when he called it a vacation. I called it a 'work related recon mission' when I put in for the time off. I should have admitted to myself then I had real feelings for the kelpie. You don't spend a week alone with someone you don't like.

Knock, knock, knock.

"Coming!"

I spared a glance at Dougie, sleeping in his bassinet, on my way to answer the door. Had it really been only three weeks since his dramatic entrance into the world? Both of us were on the mend thanks to siren rapid healing. I used to think the Academy had fabricated the line "you were made to fight harder and heal faster." Both Dougie and I proved it to be true, though.

"We're both fighters." I couldn't resist smoothing his downy soft hair. It showed more signs of red than gold now that he wasn't so fresh out of the shoot. He was proving to be the perfect mix of the best of both of us.

I opened the door, frowning when I saw Aiden and Darya standing outside. They were *not* who I had expected. Hunter or Serena, sure, but Aiden and Darya together? No way.

"What's going on?" I asked.

"And why does it have to be so early in the morning," Douglas muttered from bed.

"Hi, sorry ... we're sorry, but can we ... uh, come

in? To talk?" Darya's cheeks flushed pink with embarrassment. "Aiden and I overheard ... uh, saw something that needs, uh, discussing."

"Right now?"

"It's important," Aiden said. "I'm afraid our hosts may not be as altruistic as we thought."

I opened the door wider and ushered them in. "Who else knows what you're about to tell us?"

"You're the first." Aiden sat on the couch near the window. Darya scurried to follow him. "We thought it might raise suspicion if the whole group was together. Plus, your room is closest to the tech hub."

"Lucky us." Douglas sat up, deciding to join the conversation. His hair stuck up in all directions and he refused to look for a shirt. Still he was awake which was about all anyone could ask from him in the morning.

"Why do you think our hosts are hiding something?" I double checked that Dougie was still fast asleep before I joined Douglas on the bed, facing Aiden and Darya on the couch.

"They have monitors in the tech hub watching the outside world," Darya said in a rush. "I bet they knew we were coming before we did."

"They've also been turning a blind eye for who knows how long to shifters' fate outside of Sanctuary," Aiden added. "*They're* safe, so why bother with the rest of us?"

"Because they don't have to." I shrugged. "If I lived my whole life in a mystical land where the sun still shines and the sky is blue, I wouldn't give a shit about what happened outside my border either."

"But they're not just watching, they're ignoring a very real threat." Darya waved her hands, seeming agitated we weren't as worried about this supposed 'threat' as they were. "We overheard them saying the Booshies planned to put blood graft in the water supply. You know what that will do to any shifter that drinks it, right? Why would the Guardians and Lycans ignore a shifter genocide?"

"Because they feel they're safe," I said. "Safety makes people complacent."

"But we can't just sit back and do nothing," Aiden insisted. "Who knows how many shifter species will go extinct if we do. It's not a perfect world, but it's still our world."

"Normally, I'd be up for a little Booshie ass kicking, but things are different now." I hopped off the bed and lifted Dougie from his bassinet when he began to wail. "If the Guardians and Lycans don't care about some supposed plot to poison shifters, I don't either."

"So that's it?" Aiden's words were frosty with a

mix of anger and disbelief. "You're choosing to be just as complacent as they are?"

"Yup."

Aiden turned to Douglas. "Do you agree with her?"

"Helping all shifters and magical creatures is why the MCU was founded," Douglas said. "We can't just ..." He trailed off, watching me a moment in silence before adding: "I'm sorry, Lore, but if what Aiden and Darya overheard is true, we have a duty to protect those we left behind at the base and, well, everywhere. Aiden is right. It's not a perfect world, but it's ours. Do you want Dougie to grow up knowing his parents did nothing to stop a genocide or do you want him to be proud we took a stand against the human elite?"

I nuzzled Dougie's soft little baby face. "I just want him to grow up, period. We're safe here. Why isn't that enough for everyone?"

"We're safe, yes, but for how long?" Darya asked. "You and I never quite fit in at the Academy or PLA, Lorelei. You saved my butt more times than I can count. Here, I'm not just some screw up. I can be more than that. I can be whatever I want to be. I'm free. I will keep fighting, because I want everyone to have the same chance you all gave me. I owe the other shifters that."

Helping those beyond the Sanctuary borders

might mean saying good bye to Dougie for however long we needed in order to complete this proposed plan. As much as I didn't want to be without him, I knew it was unrealistic to tote a baby along on a dangerous mission to the City. I didn't want to say good bye. At the same time, I didn't know how to put all those thoughts and feelings in words that the others would understand either.

"Fine, but we gotta get more proof than just be-cause-I-overheard-the-Lycans-say-so before I'm in," I said.

"We can do that together," Aiden said. "All of us. I believe the guards at the tech hub change shift at eleven. We'll meet outside ten minutes before. Let's go tell the others, Darya."

Aiden smiled at me on his way out the door. He looked so bright and earnest and Kegan-esque, I forgot where I was for a second. No matter how much I loved my little family, a small piece of me still would do anything to make Kegan happy. If that meant returning to the City and fighting the good fight, I'd do it. Gods help me, I'd do it.

FIVE

FIVE

AIDEN

I left Darya to pass on the news to Constance and Micah. I needed to tell Xander the plan myself. I slipped back into our room to find him sprawled in our bed, taking up most of the space. He snored into the lush pillow beneath his head. I knew I needed to wake him up, but I watched him sleep for a moment longer, memorizing the peaceful look on his face. Perching on the edge of the bed, I ran my fingers through his hair.

"Wake up," I whispered in his ear.

He mumbled into the pillow and tried to roll over. The sunlight filtering through the window hit him in the face and he moaned. "What time is it?" he said through a yawn.

"Earlier than you like, but I need you to get up. There's something I need to tell you."

He pushed himself into a sitting position with his back pressed to the pillows. "This sounds serious."

I wet my lips to buy enough time to figure out how to break the news. His demeanor had changed in the short time we'd been in Sanctuary. He was lighter, freer than he'd ever been in our world. He no longer hid his true nature. Gone was the constant need to dye his hair and to cover his sigils. Going back to the City would change all that. "Darya and I overheard some things this morning that the Lycans don't want us to know."

"What things?"

"They can monitor what goes on in the City. We saw the tech. They have information about a Booshie plan to infect every shifter out there with blood graft."

"That's not possible."

"It is when you poison the water supply. It doesn't affect normal humans. They can drink gallons of the stuff without a problem."

"Why would they want to do that?"

"I don't know. To ensure their pets stay put? Does it matter? We can't sit back and let this happen."

"Maybe we can. Aiden, we nearly lost you to

that shit and it kills me to even think about. But we saved you. We accomplished what we set out to do. We're safe now."

"Lorelei said the same thing. We are safe here, but we owe it to everyone out there to make sure they don't end up dead in the streets."

"If what you're saying is true and they are planning to do this on a massive scale, that's millions of shifters."

"Exactly!" I exclaimed.

"We aren't responsible for every shifter on the planet."

"What happened to fighting to keep our people safe? That's what the MCU stands for. You can't tell me three weeks in the lap of luxury has changed you that much."

Xander rubbed his face with both hands. "No." He heaved a sigh. "I was getting used to not having to hide who and what I am. You realize if we go back out there you and Lorelei still have targets on your backs."

"It's worth the risk. Anyway, we aren't doing anything until we confirm for ourselves what we overheard. We're meeting the others by the tech hub right before eleven when the guards change over."

THE LYCANS who'd been patrolling near the hub were still absent when our group gathered outside just before eleven. I tried not to let it bother me as I led everyone inside.

"I thought you said there were guards," Lorelei whispered, Dougie clinging to her in a sling.

"There usually are. I don't know why they aren't around today," I answered and headed straight for the central area of the hub.

"Does this place make anyone else uncomfortable?" Xander asked.

"Reminds me of the City," Mels grumbled, her wings lifting her feet a few inches off the ground.

"It's in here," I said and waved everyone onward.

The door sat ajar but when I peered through the small window, I found the space empty. I eased the door open enough to let us in and we looked around at the large monitors. Images flickered across them of the City, different areas highlighted on each one. I watched as figures moved in and out of view of whatever surveillance the residents of Sanctuary relied upon. Most appeared human, but the people were too small to pick out any defining characteristics that would signal shifters. Besides, most free shifters avoided the central nexus of the City.

"I'm not seeing anything to signal some nefarious plot," Micah commented.

I turned my attention from the screens to the table at the center of the room. The papers Serena had shown Hunter and his colleagues sat scattered haphazard over the surface. I rifled through them, unsure what I was looking for until I found a document outlining the plan. "Look at this."

I passed it off to Lorelei. She inspected it as she rocked the baby. "They wouldn't be this stupid to put it all down in writing," she scoffed.

Mels plucked the paper from Lorelei's fingers. "They didn't. Someone else sent this information. Like someone's been spying for them. But, birdie's not wrong. This says whoever sent this has heard that there's a wider plan to use blood graft to subdue and control the shifter population." Poison sizzled on the edges of the paper as Mels scowled. "That Booshie bitch who nearly killed Aiden is at the heart of this bullshit."

It was Xander's turn to snatch the paper away. "We're going back and stopping her for good. Before she can hurt more people."

"As much as I agree we need to take action, if we are to go off on this mission, we can't bring the wee bairn with us," Douglas chimed in.

"We can't all go. It would be too obvious," Micah added.

Constance remained silent; her gaze trained on one monitor to my left. I let the rest of the group squabble over who would join us on this mission and moved to stand beside her. "What's wrong?"

She turned with tears in her eyes. "I have fought so hard to keep our kind safe and give them a chance at freedom. I did so because of what I lost. My children. My mate, Charles."

I placed a hand on her shoulder. "We know what you've sacrificed."

"I have to go with you."

"I'm not arguing, but why?" I replied.

She pointed to a figure on the screen. "I thought he was dead."

I studied the monitor more closely, this one close up enough to show detail. The man swayed from side to side beside a rail-thin woman. I didn't spot it at first, but she held a length of something in one hand. Rope? A chain? It didn't really matter. She was restraining him. He turned and I saw the same snake tongue dart out of his mouth and the slit-like pupils Constance sported. "Your mate."

"I never dreamed I would have a chance to save him. I have to go."

"You aren't supposed to be in here," Hunter's voice boomed from behind us.

Constance and I turned to see him standing in the doorway, his greying hair hanging around his face. Mels darted forward with venom dripping from her mouth. "You better have a good reason for abandoning all those shifters out there. And if you don't, well I can't promise I won't rip your throat out."

SIX

LORELEI

"And how exactly do you plan to do that?" Hunter crossed his arms over his chest, unimpressed by Mels' threat.

"Enough." Serena pushed past Hunter to check the monitors and jotted down notes on a pad of paper. She looked exhausted, her skin was pale and sallow under the dark markings across her cheeks. "No one is ripping anyone's throat out today. Both of you need to stand down. We don't have time for games. There's too much at stake."

Hunter opened his mouth to protest, but closed it with a click when Serena cast him a withering glare. Even though we had lived in Sanctuary for a little over three weeks I never noticed until now that Hunter and Serena seemed closer than your average work colleagues. We'd had our own drama to worry about without taking on theirs, too.

"You dismissed the guards to make it easy for them to find our monitoring room," Hunter said, his gaze never leaving Serena's pale face. "You wanted them to know what was occurring in the outside world, didn't you?"

"Just because you're complacent, doesn't mean I am, Hunter." Serena threw a stack of loose papers at him. They bounced off his chest and fluttered to the floor. "We are not an island. No matter how much you want to stay locked away from the outside world, it is just not possible. You have a responsibility to your ancestor's lands? Well, I have a responsibility, too. Blending our kinds together does not mean we forget where we came from." She motioned at the screens. "Those are my people, too. Outside in the world. Completely unaware catastrophe is coming for them. Why do you insist it is not our fight? Their fight is our fight ... it always has been."

"This is really awkward," Darya whispered next to me. "Like, I want to look away, but can't."

"Hunter didn't know we were coming today, but Serena did," I murmured. "She wanted us here. She's the one that set the whole thing up."

Serena stumbled, weakened, and grabbed for

the counter top for support. Hunter rushed to her side, but she waved him away. "Don't touch me."

"You've been experimenting on yourself, haven't you?" he accused. "Serena, why? You know the risks."

"The shifters out there deserve a chance to live just as much as we do." She rolled up the sleeve of her lab coat to show needle marks, her veins were enlarged and purple as poison raced toward her heart. I had seen those same track marks on Aiden during his illness. Aiden recognized them, too.

"Blood graft," he said. "As a doctor, you know the danger. Why?"

Serena grimaced before pushing her sleeve down to cover her wrist. "I need to find a broad-spectrum cure. Khalas root is effective in individuals, but we need something wider reaching if the Booshies contaminate the water supply." She watched the monitors silently before motioning at one that showed the inside of Madame Faberge's mansion. "She—your former owner, I believe—has been planning this for years. She's experimented with her own pets to get the dosage just right before unveiling it on a broader scale. At best, shifters will be docile. At worst, they'll die. Either way, the humans keep control of the City and beyond. We could never grow enough Khalas root to counteract such a large amount of blood graft. It's just not possible. Yes, I have been experimenting on myself. We need to find something to enhance the root's effects if we have any chance of diluting the poison in the water supply."

"You should have told me." Hunter's voice was quiet and thoughtful, far from the booming, confident tones we were used to. "Why would you keep something like this from me?"

She threw him another withering look. "Why do you think?"

"As much as we appreciate the blood graft in the water supply heads up," I began. "why did you take so much effort to make sure we'd be here? Why us?"

"Because you—unlike him—" Serena jerked a thumb toward Hunter, "will do something about it. Your group understands we are not an island. We are in this life—good and bad—together, ALL of us."

Micah sucked in his breath when a thought struck him. "You knew we would come. Not just today, but before when we were still in the City. You knew we would come. You wanted our help. That's why you accepted us into your society so easily."

Serena motioned at the monitors again. "We have an extensive network of spies in the City and across this country. Yes. We have watched you. We knew the MCU was different. You cared where others did not. I wanted to remind others in our society that caring for others still existed no matter how dark the times or circumstances seemed."

"What can we do to help?" Douglas spoke up.

"Hold up. *We* aren't doing anything to help ... not yet." I repositioned Dougie in his sling to try to relieve my sore muscles. "We already stumbled into the middle of their relationship shit. How much further do you want to ride this crazy train?"

"Lore, we talked about this," Douglas warned. "I thought we agreed—"

I raised a hand to silence him. "We didn't agree to anything. Or, I didn't, at least. We both know the City isn't a place for a hybrid baby. Are you really okay with leaving Dougie here while we run off to save the shifters or whatever shitshow everyone is proposing? I didn't almost die bringing this kid into the world to let a bunch of Lycans babysit him."

Douglas forked both hands through his hair. "Of course, I'm not okay with leaving the bairn. What choice do we have?"

"Now whose relationship shit did we stumble into?" Mels said in a loud whisper. She stuck her finger in her throat and made exaggerated gagging sounds.

"Are you aware that blood graft is more potent to hybrids?" Serena asked. "Our filtration systems are good, but not that good. We may survive once the poison reaches us, but not the children. If we do nothing, we just delay the deaths of our children. Do you want that for your son?"

"No," I admitted. I looked around the group, making eye contact with everyone. "Back at the MCU base, you liked to take votes to see where everyone stood. Should we do that now?"

Constance slithered forward to lead the vote. I remained neutral. I didn't want to put myself in danger again—not with Dougie depending on me for his every need—but I didn't want the Booshies to enact a shifter genocide either. Maybe it was a cop out, but I would go along with what the group decided.

"All those in favor of returning to the City to stop the humans from poisoning shifters?" Constance asked. A chorus of 'ayes' echoed in the tech hub. "Those opposed?" Silence. "The ayes have it." Constance trained her eyes on a monitor in the upper left corner where a skinny guy shifted to cobra form and slithered into an aquarium style cage. "We return to the City."

Darya touched my arm to get my attention and she smiled. She was much more self-assured since she broke free from the PLA, but was still the ever-sweet Darya I remembered from the Academy. No matter how hard the government tried, they never took that from her. "I'll stay behind with Dougie," she offered. "You can use my credentials and PLA account for travel expenses. If people don't look hard enough, they'll never know the difference between you and me."

"I'll stay, too," Micah said. "I've been the boy's doctor since before birth. I won't let anything happen to him. I promise."

"But what about us?" Xander said. "You want us to infiltrate a Booshie blood graft plot without a medic?" He rolled his eyes. "Yeah, that's smart."

"We'll send one of our own," Serena offered. "Bader asked just this morning for some field experience. Time is of the utmost importance. Get what sleep you can and ready yourself for the journey. I wish there was more time ..." She scribbled something on a scrap of paper and held it out to Aiden. "We have a group posing as a Booshie family. Here is their address in the City. Go there first and ... thank you."

I gazed down at Dougie, trying to memorize every tiny detail of his dear little face. Would I see him again after tomorrow?

SEVEN

SEVEN

AIDEN

$\mathbf{M}$uch like when we started out on this journey, I didn't have much to pack. Despite how much I'd pushed to go back and face the Booshies, I couldn't deny the worry building in my chest. I stood in the middle of the room Xander and I had claimed as our own when someone knocked on the door. I turned to find Luna standing there wearing the same dress I'd seen her in last.

"You're leaving," she said.

"We have to. You were right that Hunter was hiding things from us. There are a lot of lives depending on us out there."

She wrapped her arms around her torso. "It scares him."

I nodded. "I'm scared, too. But we would be just

as bad as the people who are hurting shifters out there if we sat back and did nothing."

Luna shook her head, her dark eyes shining with unshed tears. "He's afraid, because something happened to me."

"Everyone here is close, aren't they?"

A half-smile quirked on her lips. "He's my father."

I didn't remember my parents, but I'd seen how Lorelei and Douglas protected their son. I could understand why the situation would terrify Hunter, especially given that his own daughter, Luna was a shifter. "I can see why he would worry, then. You mean so much to him."

"He thinks I can't take care of myself. I can though." The tears vanished and determination hardened her facial features. The red markings on her face shone in the overhead light.

"You're young and he's your father. It's his job to look after you," I replied just as Xander appeared with extra clothes and packs in his arms.

"Sorry to interrupt," Xander muttered, not making eye contact with me.

"Come back," Luna said in a whisper before she turned and left the room.

"You're still mad at me," I said and shoved clothes into one of the packs he'd set on the bed.

"No, I'm not," he answered.

"Then why won't you even look at me?"

Xander sighed. "I'm scared, okay? I'm scared that if we go back, I might lose you again."

I pulled him into a tight embrace. "You won't lose me. I am healthy and I won't let that woman hurt me or anyone else I care about ever again. Besides, we aren't in this alone. We have more allies than we did before. We know what they're planning and they have no idea we're coming."

"I just had to fall in love with someone who was so noble, didn't I?"

I kissed him. "I get it from you."

It was then that I noticed his bare arms bore no signs of the sigils that marked him as a phoenix. He'd also darkened his hair. He nodded his head toward one pack. "We better get yours covered up, too."

I relinquished my grip on him and let him apply the dye and the concealer to make me appear fully human. When he'd finished, we each slung a pack over our shoulders and I took one last look around the room. "We'll be back."

We made our way out into the hall to find Constance with a pack of her own, her cobra tail rattling impatiently against the floor. I approached and put a hand on her shoulder to draw her attention. Her slit-like pupils tracked me.

"We will find your mate and save him."

"After everything I have seen in this world, after what you had overcame, you would think I would be surer of the outcome. Yet, I find myself so filled with anger and revenge it hurts."

"You are the reason I made it here. You took me in and gave me a home. I owe you my life, Constance. We'll get him back. We'll make the world better for all shifters out there."

"Thank you."

Slowly, the rest of our group gathered. I could see the red rims under Lorelei's eyes as she kissed Dougie's chubby cheeks over and over again. Douglas kept his composure as he whispered something in the baby's ear. Darya held the boy tight and rocked him when he fussed.

"So, where's this medic we're taking with us?" Mels asked, her feet hovering a few inches off the ground.

"He has a name, you know," a baritone voice said from behind us.

We turned as one to see a young man—barely an adult by the fuzzy stubble on his face—with dark skin and sharp green eyes standing in the hallway, a bag slung over his shoulder.

"You must be Bader," I said, offering a hand to shake.

"Doesn't look like much," Mels grumbled.

Bader smiled. "Looks can be deceiving. We

should get going. Hunter and Serena filled me in on the plan. I won't let you down."

"You have my ID and account numbers, right?" Darya asked, eying Lorelei.

"Yeah. We just have to hope Aria and Grady didn't nark on you to the PLA."

"Yes, we will," she agreed.

STEPPING beyond Sanctuary's borders was a harsh reminder of the world we'd left behind only a few short weeks ago. My lungs protested the ash in the air and I could see the rest of our group—save Mels who seemed immune to almost everything— had similar reactions. Bader tied a cloth over his face to ease his breathing as we made our way to the train station. As we walked, the small hairs on the nape of my neck prickled, signaling danger. Every time I glanced over my shoulder to find the source, nothing obvious jumped out at me. When we arrived, the tracks were barren.

"Are we sure there is one coming soon?" Xander asked.

"We bought passage for today. They wouldn't have let us do that if they weren't running," Lorelei replied, fiddling with one of the sharpened hairpins she kept hidden in her hair.

We huddled in the station for nearly an hour until a train pulled into the station. Knowing we had a small window to get onboard before it began the return trip, we piled into two of the sleeper cars and waited for the conductor to come through. None of us bore obvious signs of being anything other than human. Constance had shifted into her full human form and sat in one of the bunks, knees pressed to her chest. She looked meek in that position.

"What do we do if someone recognizes Lorelei?" Mels piped up.

"I have Darya's credentials. To most humans we all look the same," Lorelei answered.

Before Mels could respond further, the door to our compartment slid open and a familiar face peered in. Clancy stood before us looking tired. "I didn't expect to see you back so soon and heading in the direction you'd come from."

"Neither did we," Lorelei said and held out the tickets.

Clancy punched and slid them into the slots on each bunk, disappearing momentarily to claim our second car before returning. "Where's Darya?"

"She stayed behind. But something tells me she reached out to you before we left."

He nodded, his expression turning sad. "I hope she's okay."

"We'll let her know that you miss her," I offered.

"Thank you."

"So, what do we do now?" Bader prompted.

"We keep a low profile until we arrive at our destination."

The train pulled out of the station and I watched the bleak sky and surroundings pass us by as we picked up speed. Still, that sense of foreboding nagged at me. Bader, Lorelei and Douglas left us in the car with Mels and Constance. Constance pulled the curtain closed over her bunk and I turned to Xander.

"Why don't we get something to eat."

He nodded and we wound our way through the cars until we found the dining car. Unlike our last trip, it was bustling with people. I spotted the table where we'd made love for the first time and I couldn't hide my knowing smile.

"Bringing back some fond memories?" Xander whispered in my ear. His hand brushed against my thigh.

"Not with all these people around," I hissed and approached the bar.

In short order, we'd gotten enough food to last us several days—the duration of the trip back to the City—and returned to the compartment. I knocked on the adjoining door to pass off some of the food to the rest of our group before settling on the bunk beside Xander. Mels sat on the upper bunk across from us, her legs swinging back and forth in time to the movement of the train.

"You've been quiet," I said.

"Just busy thinking. When we stop those Booshie bastards from committing genocide, then what?" There was no hesitance in her statement. She knew we would succeed.

"We go home. Back to Sanctuary," I answered.

"They don't have enough space for all the shifters in this country."

"No, but they have the technology to expand their borders to make the space."

"They didn't seem particularly willing to get involved," Mels muttered.

I wanted to argue with her, but knew it was a waste of time. I would not change her opinion of the Guardians—especially Hunter. I just hoped we weren't too late when we finally made it to the City.

BY THE MIDDLE of the second day of our journey, the nagging feeling had only intensified. Nervous energy coursed through me like a current, making every muscle seize until I forced myself to get up and walk the length of the train. On one of my loops, Mels fell into step with me.

"You hate being cooped up," she said with a knowing nod.

"You, too."

"I don't know why, but last time it seemed different, not as claustrophobic. We had a purpose and a mission."

"We have one now, too. But it means facing more Booshies than we've had to deal with before."

"The stakes are higher." She twisted her fingers together and for a moment, I glimpsed the flutter of her gossamer wings. She stopped walking, her nose twitching. "We're not alone."

I looked around the empty compartment two down from ours. "There's no one here."

"I can smell it." She bent down, following an invisible trail I could neither see nor smell. She stopped at a closed compartment for baggage, her hand poised over the handle. "Stand back," she whispered and threw open the door.

A dark-haired girl in long pants and a shirt tumbled out of the space. She looked up and I spotted the familiar markings of a Lycan. "Luna."

Mels looked from me to the girl and back again. "They said nothing about taking the kid with us."

Luna struggled to her feet. Her cheeks were pale and her lips cracked. If she'd been hiding in this space for the last two days without food or water, it would explain her state. "You shouldn't be here," I reminded her.

"I'm not letting you fight them alone." She swayed on her feet.

I caught her and settled her in one of the seats nearby. "Your parents are going to be worried about you. And we aren't alone. You know that."

"They think I'm still a child, but I can help. I know I can."

"What do we do with her?" Mels asked from behind me.

"First we find her some food and water and then we decide as a group."

I led her back to our sleeping compartments, careful to keep her face in shadow so we wouldn't attract attention. Lorelei, Douglas, and Bader had crammed into the space I'd shared with Xander, Constance, and Mels.

"What is she doing here?" Douglas asked as soon as the door slid shut behind us.

"Looks like we've got a stowaway," Mel grumbled.

Bader moved to put an arm around the girl. "You aren't supposed to be here, Luna."

"You're not that much older than me and they sent you. I can help. Let me help."

"We need to send her back to Sanctuary," Lorelei said.

"We are two days away from there. We can't afford to turn back now," Constance chimed in, the first words she'd spoken all day.

She was right. We'd reach the City in less than a day. It made no sense to go back now. "Constance has a point. She's already come this far and she's determined to see this plan through. We can use the extra set of eyes and ears."

"We didn't agree to babysit," Mels protested.

Luna bared her teeth and let out a low growl, even though she still appeared human. "You aren't the only thing around here that bites."

"Look, I will vouch for her. I've been teaching her about medicine. I know she can bandage wounds and handle triage. We can use her," Bader interjected.

"We take a vote," Xander said. "Everyone who thinks we let the girl stay, say aye."

A chorus of "Aye" went up around the cramped space. Mels was the odd person out. "Fine. But if she's the reason we get caught I'm going to bite every single one of you."

EIGHT

EIGHT

LORELEI

I laid half reclined against Douglas, our legs stretched out on the bottom bunk. His arms were wrapped loosely around my waist, hands resting on my hips. The last time we were on this train, he had broken my heart—shattering it into a million pieces when he had finally grown tired of waiting for me to commit to calling our relationship a real relationship instead of a work partnership. Looking back, I don't blame him. Two and half years in relationship limbo would break almost anyone. Since Dougie's birth, we were solid; a real family. Now if Bader and Luna stopped staring at us from across the tiny sleeper car, everything would be golden. I don't know why we got stuck with the kids. Just because we have one doesn't mean I want to parent anyone else's offspring.

"Have something to say?" I asked them. I didn't care one way or the other, but I needed to break the creepy silence.

"You're the ones with the hybrid," Bader said. It was a statement, not a question.

"What's it to you?" I burrowed my back further into Douglas' chest. His eye lids drooped, already lulled to a half-sleep by the motion of the train.

"We're hybrids, too." Bader motioned between himself and Luna.

"I can shift, he can't," Luna added.

"Has your baby shifted yet? Do you know if he can?" Bader asked.

I scowled. "What is this? Twenty questions? Why do you care?"

Luna chewed on her bottom lip; her teeth sharper than normal thanks to her Lycan blood. "You are part of our tribe now. We care about all members of our tribe."

I sighed, relenting. "Fine. No, Dougie hasn't shifted yet. He's only three weeks old."

"It might be soon," Luna said. "Mom said I first shifted when I was a month old. I didn't enjoy being confined to human limitations. Our spirit forms are much more liberating."

"It's not liberating when the government uses

your 'spirit' gifts as a weapon," I said. "Have you ever wondered why we've been part of your tribe for a little over a month and I've never shifted? I hate it. I hate being reminded of what they made me do. For me, shifting is not freeing. It's another reminder of the shackles the humans placed on me."

Bader frowned. "But you're free now."

I closed my eyes. "No, I'm not. I'm not free from my past. I'm not free from my memories. Maybe one day I will be. That day's not here yet."

Luna jumped off the top bunk, landing nimbly on her feet. She turned to Bader. "Let's explore. I've never been on a train before."

"Dinning car and wash room only!" I warned as they slid the sleeping car door open. "And be back in an hour!" I grimaced. Gods, I *did* sound like a mom.

"I thought they'd never leave," Douglas muttered once Bader and Luna's voices faded.

I twisted to face him. "You've been awake this whole time? Asshole! Why didn't you step up when they started asking hybrid questions?"

"I wanted to see how you handled it." He leaned in to kiss me. "Good job, Mum. Plus, you gave us an hour alone. We can do a lot in an hour."

I grinned, my anger evaporating. "I remember.

What are you waiting for, horse face? An invitation?"

Douglas pulled the privacy curtain closed. "Come 'ere, fish fins."

THE CLOSER THE train rolled toward the City, the more on edge everyone appeared to feel. As we neared the final stop, everyone gathered together in one sleeper car, not talking. There was safety in numbers. Mels attempted to play off the unease by tossing the knife she acquired from Grady into the air and catching it. We fought so hard to leave this place, and here we were going back.

The train lurched to a stop as it pulled into the final station at the center of the City. I pulled Darya's PLA badge out of my pack and clipped it to my jacket. I didn't know how far impersonating Darya would get us, but I hoped to avoid detection until we met up with the undercover operative group from Sanctuary. How long had they been among us, reporting back to Sanctuary? Days? Months? Years?

Clancy stuck his head in through the sliding door. "End of the line. Everyone has disembarked. It's safe to go."

Aiden held out his hand to Clancy. "Thank

you. You've done more to help us than you'll ever know."

Clancy shook it and tipped his hat with his free hand. "Happy to oblige."

We filed past him, each of us shaking his hand as we went by. We'd been lucky so far. We found shifters on the inside willing to help. *How long will our luck hold?*

Once outside, Luna and Bader recoiled from their first whiff of the City's pollution and ash filled sky. It was more concentrated here. Bader tugged his bandana over his nose and mouth. Luna cupped her hands over her face, only her red-rimmed, watery eyes showing.

"Do you want to give us away?" I hissed. "Act like you belong here and no one will pay us any attention. Parading around with half your damn faces covered is suspicious."

They lowered their hands and bandana. Neither looked happy about it.

"So where are we supposed to meet your group?" Xander asked. "I hope you know, because no one told us."

"The thing about surveillance, is we already know everything we need to know," someone called out. "Welcome to the City ... or should I say welcome back?"

We turned as a group toward the sound of the

voice. Three figures emerged from the dimness; two men and a woman. All three were tall and slender with dark hair and high cheekbones similar to Bader and Luna. Bader grinned, recognizing the group.

"Bastian! Noemi! Kyle!" Bader embraced each in turn. "I didn't know you were the operative ... uh, meeting us," he corrected his fumble. *Smooth, kid.* All we needed was for everyone lingering at the train station to know we were meeting a group of spies.

"Where did you think we've been this whole time?" The woman, Noemi, ruffled his hair. "C'mon home. You can introduce us formally to your friends there." She gave our group a tight smile before motioning for us to follow them.

NINE

NINE

AIDEN

Our group didn't look as out of place as I'd feared we would. This deep in the heart of the City, people were more focused on themselves than surveying the people around them for possible escaped shifters, or those hiding in plain sight. The more distance we covered, the more familiar the setting felt. I glanced over at Luna to see her clinging tightly to Bader's arm. By the rapid rise and fall of her chest, I could tell she still struggled to breathe the polluted air.

"It feels weird to be back here," Lorelei said, falling into step with me.

"I know I've said it before, but thank you for coming. I know it must have been devastating to leave Dougie behind."

"I'm doing this for him," she said, sweeping her braid over the other shoulder. "We have no choice, but to stop them. Besides, would I really pass up a chance to stick it to the Booshies?"

Our group turned down a series of side streets until we reached what most would consider a modest home. The Booshies no doubt considered it tiny, but it still had the gold filigree that denoted it as belonging to the wealthy. A shiver ran down my spine. It wasn't the same place that had been my prison for three years, but it might as well have been.

"Please, come in," Bastian said, gesturing to the open gates.

I swallowed the lump of fear in my throat and followed Lorelei and Douglas into the house. It wasn't nearly as gawdy as I had expected. Compared to what I could remember from Madam Faberge's mansion, their space was simple. It had only a few places to sit—and all of them appeared comfortable—and no cages in sight.

"Doesn't look very Booshie on the inside," Mels said with a wary glance around the room.

"We are playing the part of the newly wealthy," Noemi replied. She gestured around the room. "We have another room we use for entertaining guests, but this is where we feel most comfortable."

"How'd you infiltrate them?" Xander pressed.

"We came here several years ago, when our people first suspected there was trouble brewing. You have to understand we were isolated from everything else around us," Noemi responded.

"You still are," I muttered.

"We needed to know what was going on, just in case we needed to take action to protect our people. So, they sent us to pose as newly wealthy."

"Are you all human?" Mels asked, sniffing the air as if she could tell the difference. Then again, there was much about doxies I didn't know.

"Bastian is. I am several generations removed from the ability to shift. Kyle is capable of shifting, but does not take that form. They believe him to be our son."

"He's my cousin," Bader offered. I caught the look of longing in his gaze. Not for finally reuniting with his family, but with the fact he could not shift and his kin could.

"How does that work, exactly? With some of you being able to shift and others not?" Lorelei asked.

Before any of them could respond, I caught sight of Constance slithering to the far window, taking in the view beyond us into the City. "As fascinating as genetics lessons are, we came back here with a purpose."

Seeing her mate alive and still in bondage had

hardened her. I missed the nurturing mother figure who'd taken me in without a second thought, cared for me and guided me to freedom. I moved to stand beside her. "We will find him and we will save him. We'll save them all," I whispered.

"To your friend's point, we have information vital to the mission you intend to undertake. Madam Faberge is hosting a gala in four days' time. All of the City's elite will be there and we believe it is where she plans to unleash the graft into the water supply," Bastian answered.

"We need to get into that party," I said.

"They've got rules. Like lots of them," Kyle answered.

"Well then we find a way to bend them." Mels hovered several inches off the ground, her teeth glistening with poison.

"Every guest must come with a ... pet," Noemi explained.

"You mean a shifter," Lorelei spat.

"Unfortunately, yes."

I glanced around our small group. "We can manage that. Those of us who have smaller forms, can pose as pets. The rest can go as party guests."

"We will have to secure invitations for you all. Also, we'll need to vouch for you," Bastian replied.

"How do they feel about the PLA being

present? If everyone is coming with shifters, they have to be concerned about security," Lorelei pointed out.

Bastian and Noemi exchanged nervous looks. "After what happened with you … Madam Faberge doesn't trust the PLA any more. She's hiring private security. From what we've been able to gather, they are humans willing to do anything for credits. I have a feeling their orders may be shoot to kill any shifter trying to escape."

Lorelei's hands balled into fists. "Let that bitch try."

"Say we get into this party and none of us get turned into jerky, how are we supposed to stop them from dumping blood graft into the water supply?" Xander interjected.

"We were hoping you would have some idea. Our last communication from Sanctuary mentioned you had plans to widely disseminate the cure," Bastian answered.

"I'm sorry, what?" Douglas finally joined the conversation.

Bader stepped into the middle of our gathered group and held up a small device. "Serena gave me all of her research. I'm not nearly as advanced as her, but I think she may have found a solution."

I'd entered this place with trepidation, but still

clinging to a sense of hope. Now, we were pinning our success and the continued existence of all shifters on unproven and untested research. I wanted to stay positive, but the realization we had no clue what we were doing soured my mood. We needed an actual plan, and fast.

TEN

LORELEI

"So, let me get this straight." I scanned the room, looking at each person in turn. I stopped to glare at the spy network from Sanctuary in particular. "We traveled three days back to a place that absolutely hates us or hunts us and no one has any idea what to do besides show up at a fucking party?"

"These things take time," Bastian, the 'dad' of their fake family insisted. "We've spent years ingratiating ourselves into the Booshies' lives. I will not ruin that by letting any of you destroy our hard work."

"All of our intel says everything revolves around the upcoming party." Noemi talked a lot with her hands. They waved around like crazy now. "Madame Faberge loves a spectacle and this will be her biggest one yet. The man-made stream that runs through her property is fed by the City water supply. Our intel shows she plans to hold a ceremony during the party ushering in a 'new era' of human-shifter relations." She made a pouring motion. "Big speech; dump the poison in the water."

"Once she dumps the graft, it travels back to the source and we're all screwed," Kyle added.

"Then we'll just need to stop her before that happens," Aiden said.

I pivoted toward him. "What are you thinking?"

Aiden turned toward the group from Sanctuary. "What does your intel show on *how* she's putting the graft in the water? Is she pouring it or is it in some sort of capsule that dissolves when it hits the water? Tell me what we're working with."

Bastian shuffled through a stack of papers on a desk. He held out a black and white photo of a large pill shaped capsule. It looked like a cross between an hour glass and a preventative. *Yeah,* I thought — *Preventing shifters from living free ever again.*

"Madame Faberge loves showmanship, remember?" Bastian said. "The graft goes in this vessel. The countdown starts when the first guest arrives."

"When the time runs out, it's ceremony time," Noemi said. "Once in the water, the outer layer dissolves. That's all the information we have on that front."

"Stealing it would be too obvious." Xander crossed his arms over his chest and leaned back against the wall. "What about breaking it?"

Aiden shook his head. "Too risky. How do we know she doesn't have other ones sitting around just in case something happens to the first one? She keeps shifters in cages, Xander. She kept *me* in a cage for three years."

"I know that," Xander mumbled.

"With Madame Faberge, there's always a backup plan." Aiden continued as if he didn't hear Free Range. He shook his head as if trying to shake lingering memories of his own captivity away. "There is no way she's put this much planning and thought into something to leave success up to one capsule of blood graft. There's got to be more some- where, maybe even within her estate."

"Then we find all of the other capsules," I said. "How hard can that be?"

"Harder than you think." Kyle flipped over the picture of the vessel. There was some writing scrib- bled on it, but I couldn't read it from here. "There's no notes about decoys or spare blood graft vessels. If she has them, they're hidden really well."

"That doesn't mean they aren't there," Aiden insisted. "We just need to find them."

"So, we send a group in." I pulled a sharpened hair pin from my braid, the weight of the weapon felt comforting in my hand. "Half of us would go as a distraction. We can sip tea and make small talk with Madame Faberge or some shit. The other half would find the extra vessels. Once we know their location, we destroy them during the party. Problem solved."

"One problem solved, but not all," Douglas said. "Who goes in with the first recon mission? Who poses as the pets and who will play Booshies at the party? Did Serena send any medical or scientific intel that will help us? For every answer, there's at least ten more questions waiting in the wings."

He leaned against the couch cushions before growing silent and moody—neither typical Douglas traits. I thought back, trying to pinpoint when his mood change had occurred. One week ago? Maybe two? What was bothering horse face? I opened my mouth to ask, but closed it a second later. I didn't want to drag out our personal business in front of everyone.

"I'll check Serena's files to see what she sent with us," Bader promised. "I know she was working on an antidote before we left. Maybe she perfected it."

"I'll help." Luna was quick to jump all over the medical research train. I hid a smile behind my hand. Poor kid had it bad for the medic and he didn't have a clue. It wouldn't surprise me if he was the reason she stowed away on the train. I thought it might be something more than just rebelling against her parents. Love made you do crazy things sometimes.

"If we have the antidote and a way to make it, why don't we just swap it for the thing filled with blood graft?" Mels swiped something off the ornate end table and hid it in her pocket before I got a clear look at what she snatched. "We wouldn't mess with her ceremony or anything. It just wouldn't have the oomph she was shooting for."

"Excellent idea." Aiden nodded in agreement.

"Of course, it's excellent." Mels grinned. "I thought of it."

"Then it is decided," Bastian said. "We need to hurry. Time is of the essence."

"If I may ..." Constance slithered to the center of the living room to make sure all eyes and attention were on her. She seemed worn out and tired, almost defeated. It was a huge change from the naga with the warm maternal streak I had first met months ago. "I know a chemist who can help us with compounding the antidote. His name is Charles and he's my ... he's my mate." Tears glittered in her eyes. She took a shaky breath before continuing. "I thought he was dead, but I saw him on one of the security cameras at Sanctuary. I'm not sure which one or what location it showed, but I want the chance to save him. I failed once. I won't fail again, I can't."

"Take the naga to our surveillance room," Bastian instructed Kyle. "Rewind all of the footage to how many days ago?" he asked Constance directly. "Three days? Four?"

"Four," she confirmed, her eyes still glistening with unshed tears.

"Rewind the footage to four days ago," Bastian reiterated. "Once we identify the location of her mate, we can stage a rescue."

"Uh, thank you." Constance's hands shook as she placed them over her mouth. "Thank you, thank you, thank you. We won't let you down. Any of us."

"I'll show the rest of you to rooms." Noemi stood. "Rest while you can. I doubt we'll have that luxury going forward."

ELEVEN

ELEVEN

AIDEN

Despite Noemi's suggestion to get some rest, I couldn't sleep. The room was nice enough, but the gilded walls still reminded me of the prison I'd escaped only a few short months ago. Xander lay beside me, snoring. I envied his ability to sleep anywhere. I stood before the window overlooking the view of the City. It was surprising how quickly I'd become accustomed to the changing colors of a morning or evening sky and the clean air.

I left Xander to gather his strength and wandered about the house. I found Constance coiled in one of the chairs in the room we'd been briefed in earlier, her gaze far off into the distance.

"How are you doing?" I asked in a gentle whisper, not wanting to startle her.

She blinked and turned to look at me. "We found him. His owner takes him out every day. We checked the surveillance recordings going back two weeks." I caught the disdain in her tone and the glint in her eye.

"Being predictable is not such a good thing for his owner," I commented and settled in the seat across from her.

"No. Thankfully it is not."

"We're going to get Charles back to you."

She gave me a sad smile and it almost looked like the woman who had been so kind to me. "I know. I also know that he will not be the same man I loved. Captivity changes people."

"I have faith you will find a way to reach him."

"You are going to tell me I cannot go on this mission."

"You are angry and you have every reason to feel that way, but if we can get him back with as little attention as possible, we need to be strategic." I couldn't voice the fear prickling at the back of my mind.

"You believe if I go with you, we will leave a corpse behind," she said, as if reading my mind.

I wanted to deny her statement, but she knew me well enough to tell when I was lying. "Yes."

She glanced down at the thick, muscular coils of her lower half. "You are not wrong. Take Mels with you. If I can't bite the monster who has kept my Charles like a slave, at least I can live vicariously through her."

I smiled despite the grim image popping into my head. "Mels will love that."

"I'll love what?" Mels appeared in the doorway, hovering several feet above the ground, as had become her default state since returning to the City.

"Getting to bite the Booshie who has Constance's mate," I answered.

Mels gave a wicked grin. "With pleasure."

Constance eyed a tall clock in one corner, her lips turning down at the corners into a frown. "You will need to leave soon."

"Tell Xander we'll be back as soon as we can," I said and started for the front of the house.

I was halfway there when Lorelei appeared. "You heading out?" she asked.

"We are. You?"

"Here's hoping that Booshie bitch doesn't recognize me. And that I can restrain myself and don't just stab her to death on sight."

I pulled her into a tight hug before she could react. She stiffened for a moment before relaxing into my embrace. "Be careful. You know how dangerous it is out there for the both of us," I whispered.

She leaned back and tousled my hair. "Good

thing you'll be camouflaged."

I'd had the sense to reapply the dye to my hair and Noemi had helped me cover my sigils again. I still wore a long shirt just in case. As I stood there with Lorelei relaxed against one of my arms, I could almost remember the feeling of loving her. It was fleeting—like the partial memory I'd kept from my life as Kegan.

"What's that look for?" she prompted.

"Nothing," I muttered and let her go.

"No, it was something. Tell me."

I could feel the hint of her glamour wash over me. "For a moment I almost remembered being Kegan."

She nodded and gave me a sad smile. "Sometimes, you'll do or say something and I swear you're him. And then I realize it's just a coincidence, making me sad all over again."

"The price we pay for love, hmm?"

She nodded again. "Don't get caught out there. I'm really not in the mood to hunt you down for a third time."

I gave her a small salute and went to join Mels outside. As I approached the open doorway, I caught the sound of raised voices.

"You are staying here, pup!" Mels said.

"Don't call me that," Luna growled. I could see the barest prickle of fur rippling over her bare arms.

She'd also donned concealer to cover her Lycan markings.

"What's going on?" I interrupted, placing myself between them.

"Tell the little wolf she's not coming with us."

"Mels is right. You don't know the City and our mission needs to be carried out with as much anonymity as possible," I said.

"But I can help. And I want to know this place. I want to see what you have faced. My parents are so scared of what I'll find. I'm not scared though."

This girl was so desperate to prove her worth to her family, she would risk getting caught just to say she'd done it. "Your people said you can't survive in this atmosphere in shift. Can you promise you will stay on two legs?"

Luna chewed her lower lip, but the fur vanished pulling back into the depths of her body. "Yes."

"And do exactly what we tell you? No questions or arguments?"

She nodded. Mels scowled, but didn't put up any more of a fight. Besides, we didn't have time for bickering. We were operating in a tight window and we weren't likely to get another chance before the party.

LIKE CLOCKWORK, CHARLES' owner appeared on the street with his captive on a leash. I stood on the corner with Luna, pretending to show her something in a shop window as the woman approached. This close, I could see the glazed over expression on Charles' face; obviously drugged. With blood graft or something else, I couldn't tell. He staggered forward until his owner ushered him into a tank.

"Stay here," I hissed to Luna and started forward. If we could knock out the owner, absconding with Charles wouldn't be too hard. I pulled the hood of my coat up to obscure my face and felt Mels flit out of my jacket. "Only enough to paralyze her," I whispered.

Despite her tiny size, I could still see Mels stick up her middle finger at me as she zoomed through the air undetected. I just had to wait until the Booshie was taken care of to scoop up a shifted Charles and head back to the safety of our latest refuge. The woman was too busy staring at Charles in the tank to notice she was about to be neutralized by a doxy.

"Come on, Mels. Hurry up," I breathed even though she couldn't hear me.

I took my eyes off the scene for a split second—I felt the tiny hairs on my arms prickle and I turned to find the source. It was just long enough for the woman to let out a scream of terror. My head whipped back around, expecting to find her on the ground and immobile. Instead, I found a snarling wolf advancing on her.

Damn it, Mels was right. Luna shouldn't have come. The woman's jaw worked as if she was trying to form words, but nothing came out. She back pedaled up the street, her captive completely forgotten.

"Wolf!" she yelped, just as a tiny speck landed on her throat. She tensed and keeled over.

I didn't have time to worry about whether they would spot us. There was no way news of a wolf in the City would not make its way through to the Booshies or to the PLA. I leaned into the tank, scooped up the lethargic snake and took off at a run. I stopped at the end of the street, expecting to find Luna and Mels behind me. They were nowhere to be found.

"Damn it!" I swore and I started back. I was almost to the tank when I spotted an unconscious wolf floating through the air. Mels shifted to human size, hefting the lupine body in her arms like it weighed nothing. "You were right," I said as we carried our unconscious charges back to the mansion.

"At least I still got to bite something," Mels said.

I had to hope Lorelei's mission went off better than ours. Otherwise, we were about to lose the element of surprise.

TWELVE

TWELVE

LORELEI

I didn't enjoy splitting up to run two missions. While Aiden and Mels were off attempting a rescue mission, Douglas and I were prepping to run recon at Madame Faberge's estate. Noemi would introduce us as her "out of town guests" at afternoon tea. I just hoped that dressing up and wearing my hair down were enough of a disguise to fool that old toad. Our MCU group got this far by sticking together. The City was huge. Would anyone even care if we went as a large group versus two smaller ones? It would look suspicious to bring so many "out of town guests" to a tea party, but I couldn't shake the feeling that splitting up just meant more chances to get caught.

"I hate this," I griped to Douglas.

"The dress Noemi lent you or the party?"

Douglas sat on the edge of the bed and held out his arms to show off the suit Bastian had loaned him. It was a little short in the sleeves and pant legs, but was the best we could do on short notice. He looked dapper wearing something other than plaid. I blinked hard, my mind skittering to non-mission related thoughts. Douglas grinned when he noticed my reaction.

"Maybe I should dress up more often, yeah?"

"No plaid," I stated the obvious.

He pointed at his waistband. "Still got my own boxers on."

I turned away before I could say "show me." I needed to focus on the mission, not getting Douglas out of his clothes. The dress Noemi lent me was a white, Grecian style number with gold accents that zipped up the back. It reminded me a little of what I had worn when doing the circus act with Kegan. That dress had pulled over my head. This one was a bitch thanks to the zipper that ran all the way from my waist to my neck. No wonder Booshies had maids. No one could dress themselves with these types of clothes.

"Zip me?" I looked over my shoulder and pointed at the zipper.

Douglas stood and crossed the small room. His breath warmed my bare back and neck as he stood behind me. My own breath caught in my throat. *Mission, mission, mission*—I reminded myself. *I need to focus on the mission.*

His hands guided the zipper up my back before coming down to rest on my hips. "That okay?"

"Yeah. Thanks." My words came out in a raspy whisper. I turned to face him. "What do you think?" I motioned at the dress. "Not bad, right?" I touched my unbraided hair next—anything to keep my hands busy. "Although I feel naked without my hairpins."

"Interesting choice of words, *M'eudail.*" Douglas brushed my hair away from my neck, before kissing the sensitive junction by my shoulder. I shivered. *Mission, mission, mission. I need to focus on the mission.* "I love the dress. You should wear it to our handfasting."

"Our *what?*" I jerked away, whirling to face him in the next heartbeat.

"Our handfasting," Douglas repeated. "I know how you feel about weddings. It's not a wedding. It's an ancient Celtic tradition of—"

"I know what it is," I interrupted. "Shit's still legal, Doug."

"Why is that a bad thing?" he asked. "I *want* to be legally committed to you, Lorelei. It would give Dougie more safety if something ... if something happened to one or both of us. I want to protect you

—both of you—and if that means making our messy, complicated shit legal, we make it legal."

"You forgot to mention love." My hands shook. "Love" was the single hardest word for me to say. "Protection is noble and all, but most people get married, because they love each other."

Douglas cocked his head to the side, studying me. "Did you just say 'married' and 'love' in the same sentence?"

I stepped forward, deciding to fiddle with his tie to focus my nervous energy. "If we plan to build a real life in Sanctuary for Dougie, I suppose a hand-fasting is ... uh, is a good thing to consider. How long have you been thinking about it?"

"A couple weeks," he admitted. "I thought it was a more realistic possibility after Dougie was born. We were getting on so well. You seemed more receptive to commitment talk. Before then?" Douglas shrugged. "It was only something I allowed my-self to dream of."

I tip-toed to kiss him lightly, lingering on his lips. "A girl likes to be asked, you know, not told she's getting married."

A bright grin spread across his face. "Wait. Are you on board with the Hand Fasting?"

"Ask first," I said. "And I expect some jewelry. I'm not normally a jewelry kind of girl. In this case, I'll make an exception."

Douglas backed up until his knees smacked the bed. He looked floored that I was—yes—on board with his plan. "Anything," he promised. "I'll buy you anything you ask for."

"Doug! How many fucking times do I need to fucking tell you to ask me already?"

He laughed. "Well, can't get much more romantic than being cursed at by your future wife. Here goes ... Lorelei, will you hand fast to me?"

"Yes," I said, marveling at how such a simple word could change so much in my life.

"WHERE DID you say you were from again?" Madame Faberge asked.

"Caledonia originally." Douglas smiled, mixing a little glamour in with his words to lull the bitch into a false sense of security. "After that, a little town outside of Philadelphia in Pennsylvania. Quite a lot of shifters who escape the City head down that direction."

It surprised me that Douglas went for the truth, though it was a stretch to call the rooms for rent above the shifter bar a "little town." I just smiled and sipped my tea, not trusting myself to say anything now that I was face to face with Madame Faberge again. She had destroyed my life once when she kidnapped Kegan. The bounty on Aiden and my own head was also her doing. Now the horrible toad of a woman planned to poison all shifters just because she could.

"Do you have any unique pets down in Pennsylvania?" Her eyes widened at the thought of the untapped shifter market outside of the City. It wouldn't surprise me if she was into dealing and buying.

"Some." Douglas shrugged. "I'm sure our selection isn't nearly as varied as you have here."

"I see you've built your collection back up." Noemi motioned at the multiple gold cages hanging around the parlor. "I was so sorry to hear of the theft of your precious pets. How long ago was it? A month? Two?"

Madame Faberge's lips pressed into a thin line. The last time we were here, we had sprung all the captive shifters. I wasn't happy she had replenished her collection, but was happy to know the rest weren't recaptured.

Noemi stood and tucked her hair behind her ear. Our signal to start Part B of the recon mission. "Pardon us, Madame. Where is your powder room?"

The mission itself was fairly straight forward. Noemi and I would snoop around for the spare blood graft capsules under the guise of using the wash room. Douglas would glamour his way into Faberge's good graces and keep her talking until we returned. After that, we excused ourselves and were home free. At least we hoped.

"The powder room is the last door on your right near the garden," Madame Faberge instructed. Leave it to a Booshie to design a house with a wash room as the last room on the main floor. That way, you had to walk through and admire all her other crap while searching for it. I balled my hand in a fist, trying not to snap. I managed to smile, curtsey, and follow Noemi out of the parlor.

"We've been working the Faberge angle for months," Noemi whispered as we moved toward the back of the mansion. "We've bugged almost every room. If she has spare capsules like your phoenix friend thinks, our vid feeds show the most likely locations to store them are the two offices." She pointed up at the ceiling. "One on the second floor. One down here near the wash room. We need to search both. How long can your kelpie boy talk? We need time."

I almost laughed. "How long can Douglas talk? All day and night if you need him to."

"Good." She motioned at the ceiling again. "I'm more familiar with the estate. I'll take the second-floor office. You take the ground floor."

"Got it."

We split up. I tried not to look at the cages lining the hallway and overflowing into room after room. Looking reminded me of my role in putting shifters in cages. I had left the PLA, but what I did in their name would never leave me.

"Hey, pretty lady, help a bro out, will ya?" A tiny hand snaked out of a hanging cage and grabbed my sleeve. The hand was small, but the creature's strength was not. I jerked to a stop.

"What the hell are you doing?"

The creature pressed his face against the bars. "You can't hide your true nature from me. I know what you are."

"What I am? I have no idea what you're talking about, pet." I attempted to play off his accusation. I didn't need one of the captive shifters narking me out to Madame Faberge.

"Sure, you do," he insisted. "We're the same, you and I. I'm just locked in this cage and you're not. We both can be free if you just open the door." He motioned at the tiny padlock. "Pick the lock if you have to. I'll wait."

I looked closer at the insistent little creature—black hair, glittering dark eyes, and gossamer wings—shit, a doxy. I always thought the smudges on Mels' face was dirt, but this male doxy had the exact same markings. "Who are you?" I asked. "Why should I help you?"

He grinned, his pointed teeth glittering in the chandelier light. "Because I know what you're looking for and—better yet—where to find it. I heard you talking in the parlor with She. I hear everything anyone talks about with She. I can help you. Just open this cage."

"If I open the cage, you'll show me where the capsule is?" I dug a lockpick out of my handbag before I realized I had already made my decision to free him.

"Of course," the doxy agreed. "There's two of them. Your friend is looking in the wrong spot. There's only one hiding place." He pointed toward the direction I assumed the first-floor office was.

"You better not betray me, doxy." I picked the lock and swung the small door open. He flew to freedom before shifting to boy form. He was short, but still would be several inches taller than Mels. Madame Faberge had so many "pets", she wouldn't miss one doxy. I doubt the bitch even knew all the species she'd collected over the years. They were a status symbol, nothing more.

"Do you know other doxies?" he asked. "I haven't seen any of my own kind since I left the nest. I'm Alejandro, but you can call me Alec. And you are?"

"Lorelei," I supplied. "If you help me, I'll take

you with us. We're from the MCU and there's a doxy in our group."

"Well, now you have two." Alec darted toward the office. "Come on! I'll show you what I know! You can trust me."

I followed, hoping I had made the right decision. He better not double-cross me.

"Come on!" Alec repeated. He opened a drawer on Madame Faberge's over-sized desk. There was nothing inside, but a bunch of papers.

"What game are you playing at, doxy?" I snarled.

"Just wait." He felt around the top of the drawer until he heard a click. A second compartment—this one with two objects that looked like the surveillance photo Noemi showed us—rose from the drawer. "Best to leave them here or She will move them again." He watched me, as if trying to decide if he proved useful or not. "Can I come with you?"

I opened my loaned handbag. "Get in and stay quiet."

Alec grinned. "Thank you." He shifted to tiny form and flew into the bag. I closed it most of the way, leaving a little crack for air.

I met Noemi in the hall as we both retraced our steps to the tea parlor. "Any luck?" she asked.

"They're both in one spot," I said. "There's a

hidden compartment in the ground floor office desk." I opened the bag to show her Alec lounging on the bottom. "Also, we have a stowaway. He helped me find the capsules."

Noemi nodded toward the doxy. "We are in your debt."

"Debt repaid if you take me with you," he promised.

"He could be useful later," Noemi mused. "The more members we send to the fancy-dress party familiar with the layout of the estate, the better."

"I'll help," Alec said. "I'll do anything you ask. Just take me with you."

It was impossible to miss the desperation in his voice. We might be his only way out of this house of horrors.

"He comes," Noemi decided. "Now let's get your boyfriend and get out of here before we all end up in cages."

THIRTEEN

THIRTEEN

AIDEN

W e'd almost made it back to the mansion when I spotted images flickering in one of the shop windows. I stopped long enough to glimpse mine and Lorelei's faces. The bounty was still out for us and it noted that we would more than likely be spotted together. We would need to address that sooner than later.

"What's wrong, birdie?" Mels asked as she nearly walked into me.

"The bounty is still out on our heads," I answered and gestured as best I could with my hands full of unmoving snake to the window.

Mels spat venom at the window, making the glass sizzle and pop. "Booshie bastards."

I didn't disagree. "We can tell the others once we are back at the mansion," I commented and took off at a sprint.

We arrived back to find that Lorelei, Douglas, and Noemi had not yet returned. I tried not to think the worst. *Madam Faberge didn't get them*, I repeated in my head as we stepped through the ornate front entrance. Bastian and Constance greeted us before we got very far. Constance took in the reptile looped around my body and tears fell glistening against her cheeks.

"We had a little problem with the plan," I announced and tried to set the snake down on the ground. Constance scooped him up, cradling him close to her bosom.

"We saw," Bastian said just as Kyle stuck his head out of one of the adjoining rooms. "If we witnessed what transpired then there is little doubt the authorities are aware as well."

"Where is she?" Bader bellowed, shoving his cousin out of the way and making a beeline for the unconscious wolf in Mels' arms. "You shouldn't have let her go with you," he said, eying me.

"She swore she would stay on two legs," I countered, aware of how lame my words sounded.

"Can you get her back to human form?" Kyle asked.

Bader glanced from the four-legged creature at his feet to the snake resting in Constance's arms. I could see the look of indecision in his eyes. He was supposed to be our medic and able to prioritize the greatest need for attention, but Luna was his kin. "She needs clean air to rouse her. It should be enough to allow her to shift on her own. The naga needs more immediate care."

"I can draw him back to two legs, but I cannot treat the poison in his body," Constance replied in a hushed tone.

"If you can do it quickly, fine. We have no idea how long he's been poisoned. Unlike your phoenix friend here, he might not get a second chance," Bastian said, taking charge of the situation.

Constance slithered into the less ornate parlor and set the snake in one of the chairs. I watched Bastian and Kyle take Luna still in wolf form from Mels and usher her off to another room, hopefully to give her the air she needed to wake up.

"What's going on?" Xander asked, finally putting in an appearance while awake. His dark red hair was still mussed.

"We rescued Constance's mate, but ran into a little complication," I answered as Bader disappeared, returning a few minutes later with a pack slung over one shoulder.

"Why am I not surprised," Xander replied and placed a hand on my shoulder. "Nothing in this fight is ever easy."

We moved to the doorway of the parlor as Constance worked. The top half of her body was still mostly humanoid, although now it was covered in scales. She lowered herself down and rested her forehead against Charles' body. I could hear hissing noises coming from her mouth, but could not comprehend their meaning. They weren't meant for us. She transferred her weight so that her tail could intertwine with his, giving him another connection to his own kind.

Slowly, the snake in the chair stirred, flicking its tongue out to test its surroundings. It blinked and finally opened its eyes. While we watched the creature gained mass and limbs, until a fully-grown man lay curled into the chair. Constance pulled her tail away and the scales on her upper body disappeared.

"Oh, my dear Charles," she whispered, stroking his cheek.

His eyes were glassy and his skin ashen. He was thinner than a man of his size should be. His tongue still darted out of his mouth like a snake. Constance turned to our assembled group.

"Get him clothing and water." Coming from anyone else, it would have sounded like a harsh order.

Mels flitted away, returning moments later with the requested water and clothing. I grabbed Xander by the arm and turned him around so we were no longer facing the reunited couple. Fabric rustled behind us as Charles dressed.

"C-Constance," Charles finally said, his voice weak.

"You are alive and you are safe," she answered.

Out of the corner of my eye, I caught Bader step forward. I chanced a look over my shoulder to find Charles fully clothed and sipping water from a glass. Bader moved to examine him and pulled out medical equipment I wouldn't have suspected would fit in his tiny pack. He hung a container of liquid above Charles' head and secured the other end to a long tube.

"This will hurt for a moment and it will probably knock him out for a while. But it will cure him of the graft," Bader explained, producing a syringe.

"Do what you must," Constance answered for her mate.

With Charles in good hands, Xander and I retreated in the direction Bastian and Kyle had gone with Luna. Xander's hand slid into my own and squeezed tight.

"You're worried about Lorelei," he said.

"They should have returned by now," I answered.

"They've proven they are resourceful. They will be fine," Xander said and gave me a quick kiss on the lips.

We found Bastian and Kyle holding a mask over Luna's muzzle. I could see her flank rising and falling as she breathed. Slowly, fur receded, melting effortlessly into dark skin. Someone had already placed a blanket over her body to provide her some modesty when she finally returned to human form. Bastian sat beside her when Luna weakly opened her eyes and stroked her hair.

"You gave us quite the scare, little one," he said.

Luna turned her gaze to me and she paled. She tugged the mask from her face. "I should have listened. I'm sorry."

"We got him. But, next time, you need to do as you are told," I replied, hoping my words didn't carry too much judgment. A part of me couldn't blame her for wanting to lash out at the human elite for their cruelty to shifters.

A commotion cut the conversation short and those of us who could move under our own power rushed back to the front hall to find Lorelei, Noemi and Douglas hurrying through the entrance. Mels flitted into the room just as Lorelei opened her bag.

"We found an ally," she announced as a tiny figure zipped into the air, increasing in size to hover opposite Mels.

"Hi there, gorgeous," the doxy said.

Mels' cheeks darkened and she slammed her fist into his face. "Don't call me gorgeous."

I looked to Lorelei. "We've got a lot to catch up on."

FOURTEEN

LORELEI

I glanced at Douglas to see if he wanted in on Aiden's "lots to catch up on." He was busy filling Bastian and Kyle in on our afternoon adventure at the Faberge Estate. I bet he wouldn't even realize I was gone.

"Come on." I motioned for Aiden to follow me to the back-bedroom Douglas and I shared. Once inside I shut the door, before realizing how alone we were. Aiden had everything of Kegan's except for his memories. Three years ago, I would have given anything to be alone in a room with him. Now, it felt strange—like a dream and I couldn't quite remember all the details.

"Why are you looking at me like that?" Aiden asked.

I shook my head before sitting on the bed. "I thought I'd be used to it by now. You looking like Kegan, I mean. I feel like even my memories of him are out of reach. Sometimes—it doesn't happen very often—you say and do something so like him, everything comes flooding back," I said, repeating our conversation from earlier that afternoon.

The mattress shifted as Aiden sat next to me. "Does remembering hurt?"

I shrugged. "It's more like I'm mad at myself for giving up. If I hadn't stopped looking, I could have saved you from years of torture in that cage. I've never said 'sorry', have I?" I touched his hand briefly before pulling back. "I'm sorry. I hate that they stuck you in a cage, because of me."

"They stuck me in a cage, because my owner wanted to harvest phoenix tears," Aiden said. "You did nothing wrong, Lorelei."

Sadness and regret mingled together before welling up into tears. I swiped a hand across my face before Aiden saw them. "Maybe if you say it enough, I might actually believe it."

"You did all you could," Aiden insisted.

I combed a hand through my loose hair, looking everywhere, but at him. I still wore the fancy dress from afternoon tea. I'd need someone's help to undo the obnoxious back zipper. For a brief second, I thought about asking Aiden, but changed my mind before I even opened my mouth to ask. There was no fucking way I wanted Douglas to walk in with that going on. He and I were in a good place. Engaged even. I didn't want to ruin that with yet another misunderstanding between us.

"You said we had a lot to catch up on?" I circled back to the reason I brought Aiden to the bedroom. "What kind of intel did you get?"

"We found Charles," Aiden began. "Once he's rested, he can help create the blood graft antidote. We swap that with the real poison in the capsules and then ..." He trailed off, as if afraid to say "we go home" after so long of not having a real home with a real family.

"On our end, we found the capsules," I said. "The witch kept them together. How dumb is that?"

"She's confident," Aiden said. "No one has ever ruined her plans before ... well, besides me."

"I think we should get the doxies to swap the poison for the cure," I said. "They're the smallest in shift. They could fit through the keyhole if needed." I toyed with the ends of my hair again. "That is, if Mels doesn't murder the new guy first."

Aiden laughed. "I think Mels enjoyed being the only doxy."

"Not my problem." We sat silent as I ran the plan through my mind. There were so many moving pieces. We needed to make the antidote, masquerade as party guests with half of us shifted and half of us not, swap the cure with the poison in the capsules before, finally, getting out of the party undetected. It sounded simple, but getting everyone in and out unharmed would be tricky. "I just hope it all goes off without a hitch."

"Speaking of hitches ..." Aiden spread his hands out in front of him, examining each finger as if he was still not used to what he saw in front of his own eyes. "Coming back, we saw some wanted bulletins. They flashed through pretty quickly, but I'm positive I saw your face and mine. The government knows your siren sisters failed. They may not still be actively looking for us as far as we know, but someone is."

"We can't be seen together." I followed his train of thought to its conclusion. "Fuck that. I'm not sitting here waiting."

"Neither am I," Aiden said.

"Still you need someone who can glamour just in case we get caught and the Booshies need persuading to let us go."

"You're not the only one who can glamour." He'd already put a lot of thought into this. I should have known I'd be overruled before I had even opened my mouth.

I chewed on my lower lip as Aiden's words sunk

in. "Douglas ... I *really* can't sit here and wait if both of you go in to the heart of danger. Don't make me. I need something to do, Aiden."

He sat silent, as out of ideas as I was.

"How tight is security?" I asked.

"Bastian and Kyle say it's mostly private hires," Aiden said. "Not quite human mercenaries, but close. And she doesn't trust the PLA after what happened with us, but something tells me she might have them on hand, too."

"What if I cause a distraction?" I liked the idea the second it popped into my brain. "If I show myself enough to get the PLA on my trail, it will thin out security for you. If needed, it will be easier for you to get away from humans than trained PLA agents."

Aiden considered my suggestion. "I like it. But I want you to take Xander along."

"Free Range?" I blinked, surprised. Although at the same time not, realizing that he'd want Xander far away from the main action at the party. "Uh ... We don't exactly play nice together."

"Now is a good time to learn." Aiden nudged my shoulder with his. "I promise I'll take care of Douglas for you."

My mouth tipped up into a half smile. "Deal. And *I* promise I'll take care of Xander for *you*."

FIFTEEN

FIFTEEN
FIFTEEN

AIDEN

Lorelei and I may have been in agreement on the diversion, but that still left Xander and Douglas who needed to be persuaded. I suspected the idea of splitting up would thrill neither of them. Although, this wouldn't be the first plan that part of our group objected to. I left Lorelei to undress and went looking for Xander. A loud commotion drew me to the large room where I'd last seen Constance and Charles.

Furniture lay strewn about the room as if something—or someone—had blown through in a frenzy. I heard a low growl from my right and spun to find our newest doxy sporting several gashes to his cheeks and a fat lip. Mels advanced on him, teeth bared and fists raised. Her grazed knuckles were her only sign of injury. She'd been doing most of the beating.

"What the hell is going on?" I demanded, stepping between them hoping to diffuse the situation.

"I was only being friendly," Alec said, flecks of blood and spittle dotting his chin.

"What makes you think I want a *friend*?" Mels snapped.

I cleared my throat and turned my attention to Mels. "Do you think maybe he really is just trying to get to know you?"

She rolled her eyes. "He tried to touch my wings, birdie."

"It's a sign of respect and admiration," Alec protested.

I had no way of knowing if his words were genuine. I had no idea what doxy culture or interactions were supposed to look like. Perhaps Mels had forgotten, too. I stepped closer and lowered my voice. "I know you haven't been around your own kind in a very long time. Maybe there are some mating rituals you don't remember?"

Mels spat venom on the floor so that it sizzled into the floorboards. I had to remind myself that our Sanctuary allies were only in this place spying on the Booshies. They likely weren't attached to any of the objects in this room. Still, for a moment I worried about ruining the floor. "Seriously ... Why would I want to mate with him?"

"I'm not saying that you have to or even should, but maybe you were reading his signals wrong. Maybe he really is just lonely and looking for a friend. Neither one of you has seen another of your kind for a while."

Mels gave a huff, but lowered her arms. She peered around my shoulder at Alec, who still remained quiet. "Maybe I could use a reminder of what it was like." She pointed a finger at him. "But that doesn't mean I want to nest or some shit like that."

Alec held up his hands in a show of surrender. "I swear it. Only friendship."

Mels flitted off in the opposite direction and I turned to Alec. "Just don't touch her again. She doesn't like it," I offered.

Alec's head dipped in a small nod before he went off in the opposite direction. Having stopped the doxies from killing each other, I still needed to find both Douglas and Xander to fill them in. Lacking a siren's innate ability to track whomever they wanted, I went searching down one of the longer corridors until I happened upon a room with its door ajar. I heard voices coming from within and pushed it open.

I found Constance and Charles both in half-shift, their tails entwined together. I knocked on the doorframe to announce my presence, unsure what I was interrupting. Constance's head swiveled in my direction and she gave me the first genuine smile I had seen from her in weeks.

"I don't mean to intrude," I said.

"You are of course welcome. Besides, we have you to thank for our reunion," Constance answered.

Charles remained focused on whatever they'd been discussing before my interruption. Constance slithered just far enough away to still keep physical contact with her mate, but engage with me at the same time.

"Charles has gotten most of his human faculties back. He is working on amplifying the antidote Serena devised."

At the sound of his name, Charles set his tools down and looked over at me. He was brighter eyed than he had been only a few short hours ago. Still, I spotted the telltale markers of fatigue—sagging under the eyes and pale skin—marking him. Perhaps the Khalas root had been less effective in treating his blood graft poisoning.

"Given more time to rest, I would appear more invigorated than my physical symptoms would suggest," he said as if reading my mind. Just like Constance, the slight fork of his tongue elongated the 's' sounds of his words.

"Sadly, time isn't something we have in ample supply," I said.

"Indeed. I believe with a few more tweaks, the antidote will be viable."

At least that part of the plan was still coming together. We only now had to get it into the place of the actual blood graft capsules. "I'll leave you to your work. Have you seen Xander or Douglas?"

"I believe they were in the kitchen," Constance answered.

Sharing the plan with both of them at one time would save me having to repeat myself. But it also meant having to manage both of their objections. Not having been given a tour to the kitchen, I wandered aimlessly through long hallways—passing the room where Luna still rested with both Kyle and Bader by her side—and the surveillance room which stood eerily empty and quiet. Finally, I found the kitchen with its fully stocked shelves and cooking elements. Xander and Douglas sat across from each other, gazes focused on the plates in front of them.

"There you two are," I said and leaned on the end of the table.

"Aye, here we are," Douglas said, giving me a glaring side eye.

"I don't like that look," Xander said and set his

food down. "You look like you're about to tell us the plan's off or going to blow up in our faces."

"No, the plan's still on," I said slowly.

"I'm sensing a but coming," Douglas remarked.

"There's a slight wrinkle. I know that we thought the PLA wouldn't be in attendance, but it sounds like they will be now. Lorelei thinks she can lead them off on a bit of a distraction, but she's not going to do it alone." I looked at Xander. "You're going with her."

"And why would he do that?" Douglas asked, his accent thickening along with his defensiveness.

"Because we will need someone who can glamour at the party and since we don't have any other sirens in our arsenal right now, that leaves you," I answered.

"I don't like splitting up," he grumbled.

"I know you want to be with Lorelei and protect her, but I promised I'd look out for you. She'll do the same for Xander. Lorelei and I may not be lovers anymore, but, trust me, we would do anything for each other's happiness. Now, I don't want to hear any arguments from either of you. I've already had to stop Mels from slaughtering our newest addition."

Douglas sighed, set his plate aside and left the kitchen. I assumed he was going in search of Lorelei to convince her to change her mind. Xander stared at the remnants of his food.

"What aren't you saying?" I prompted him.

"We don't get along, your ex and me."

"This will give you the opportunity to get to know each other better and play nice. I care about both of you. I am trusting you with her safety as much as I'm trusting her with yours." I leaned down and kissed him as I swiped the rest of his food. "Now, come on. We should take advantage of the little time we have before we storm that gilded dungeon."

SIXTEEN

SIXTEEN

LORELEI

After Aiden left, I unzipped my dress low enough to shimmy out. It took some major contortionist moves where I felt like I might need to dislocate my shoulder to reach the damn zipper, but somehow, I managed. I changed into my own clothes and re-braided my hair. I felt more like myself instead of some flashy Booshie. I turned when someone knocked on the door, instinctively reaching for the knife hidden in my boot. The City wasn't safe, no matter where we stayed. Friends could easily turn into enemies for the right amount of credits. I relaxed when Douglas slipped into the room, before shutting the door behind him.

"Aiden told us the plan," he began without preamble. "I wish we had all agreed on it together. The

MCU is and always has been built on group decisions not one or two members leading the charge."

"You think I enjoy relying on Free Range to have my back against whoever the PLA sends to the party as back up security?" I asked. "He's far from my favorite person. I mean, I don't even know how good he is in a fight. He's done nothing, but stand around when we could have used some extra muscle." I flipped my braid over my shoulder, twirling the end around my finger. "I'm not happy about this either. I'm sure I'll be carrying his dead weight across the entire City."

"Then why did you agree to it?" Douglas sat on the bed. "You can tell Aiden no, *M'eudail*."

I considered joining Douglas on the bed, but needed to focus on the mission. Me and Douglas together on a bed would destroy whatever concentration I had left. My feet took a step toward him automatically before I stopped. I needed a clear head, not one muddled up by desire.

"It was my idea to lead whoever the PLA sends away from the party," I said. "Please don't blame Aiden for that one."

"I just think we're stronger together, versus apart," Douglas insisted. "You know how I feel about you and rash decisions, Lore."

"And you know how I feel about being questioned over every damn thing I do," I snapped. I sighed before softening my tone. "Doug, it will take all of us working together to pull this plan off. There are no leaders here. Everyone will be playing an important role. Even without your glamour, you can charm your way in and out of any situation. You're going to be needed at the party."

"Well, when you put it that way ..." He patted a spot on the bed next to him. "If all goes as planned, we only have one more night in the City. Care to have a proper send off?"

I grinned. "You have such a one-track mind."

Douglas shrugged and flashed his own bright grin. "You think strategy, I, of course, think of you. It's not such a bad combination, is it?"

I shook my head. "No. It definitely has its benefits."

He patted the bed again. "I don't know how much more of an invitation you need here, Lore. Let's make tonight count."

Screw focusing on the mission, I decided. I could talk to Xander tomorrow morning.

THE NEXT MORNING, I awoke before Douglas. The constant blackish-gray of the sky I saw from the fancy high Booshie style window was a lighter color, signaling daytime. I watched Douglas sleep for a moment. He looked so peaceful like there wasn't a care in the world. We had found peace and safety at Sanctuary. And Dougie. Dougie was a precious gift. Would we return to him after this mission ? Would we return to the new life we all found in Sanctuary? I leaned over and kissed Douglas' tousled hair before climbing out of bed. I found my clothes, dressed, and padded barefoot to the kitchen. Aiden and Xander were already there, two steaming cups of coffee cooling in front of them. They looked ... content.

"You have a good night, boys?" I teased. Aiden's cheeks colored in response. Xander stared at me almost defiantly. His attitude better change if we were expected to make it through today without me accidentally letting a weapon slip and hit him on purpose.

"Hey, Aiden, can you give Xander and I a minute?" I asked. "We need to strategize."

"Of course." He stood and grabbed his cup of coffee before leaving. I eyed Free Range a moment longer before sitting across from him in Aiden's vacant seat.

"We don't have to like each other, but we need to at least trust each other," I said.

Xander clutched his coffee mug tighter, staring into its liquid depths. "What makes you think I don't like you?"

I laughed. "You mean you're this cold and standoffish with everyone?"

He scowled. "You're one to talk. Standoffish is practically your middle name." Xander glanced up. "You have baggage, right? And issues? That's what makes you act that way? What makes you think I don't have baggage and issues too?"

I arched an eyebrow. "Do you?"

"We all do. You can't be a shifter surviving in this shithole world without collecting some. I've done some ... things ... I'm not exactly proud of. Things I wouldn't want Aiden to ever know about. He's so *good* and I've been so very *bad*. I can't explain any of my past to him. And that's just this time around. Who knows what I've done during my other Risings."

"I put shifters back in cages for a paycheck, remember?" I reminded him. "How bad could your past be?"

"Do you really want to know?" he asked.

"Only if you want to tell me." I settled into my seat, ready to wait him out. "I won't tell Aiden if that's what you're worried about. I'm not going to pretend like I understand what he sees in you, but you make him happy. I respect that."

"You know I have black market connections, right?" I nodded and waited for him to continue. "Well, you don't get black market connections if you don't pull a con or two yourself. You need to be one of them to earn their respect. I sold anything I could get my hands on. If I couldn't find it at the MCU base, I'd steal it." He took a long pull from the mug in his hands. "Vials of Phoenix Tears were easy and those were always in high demand. Doxy venom was popular too. Mels was happy enough to spit into a reinforced test tube. I never told her what I was doing with it. I doubt she would have cared, but still ... honesty and me don't exactly go hand in hand. I stopped my side gigs after Mels brought Aiden to the base. I wanted to be better. I wanted to *do* better. Partially for him, but also for me. The dirty dealings eat away at your soul after a while, you know? I didn't want that dark shit hanging around anymore. I'm not a good person, but I'm trying to be better."

"We're all trying to be better," I told him. "You feeling guilty about the past shows there's goodness in you, Xander. I don't care what you did in your past, as long as you don't screw us over in the present. Can I count on you to have my back when we break off from the rest of the group?"

"You won't tell Aiden what I just told you?" He watched me through a curtain of his hair.

"It's not my story to tell, Xander. It's yours," I said. "Do I think you should tell him eventually?

Yeah. Am I going to speed up the process by narking on you? No."

"Thanks," he mumbled.

"How are you in a fight?" I asked. "A physical fight, I mean. Chances are pretty high we'll need to take out a couple of my siren sisters tonight."

"I can hold my own," he promised.

"Good." I nodded my approval. "You'll need to if you want to make it back here alive."

SEVENTEEN

SEVENTEEN

AIDEN

Despite agreeing with Lorelei's plan to split up, I still had reservations about working with Douglas. Sure, he'd had my back against the sirens on our cross-country trek to Sanctuary, but I still couldn't help feeling as though there was a lack of trust between us. I didn't doubt his dedication to the mission—he had a child he longed to return to—but his past wasn't entirely noble either.

As afternoon dimness faded to the deeper shadows of evening, I found Douglas in the main room, righting furniture from Mels' and Alec's disagreement. "Here, let me help you," I offered and hefted one side of a large, wing-backed chair.

He eyed me in surprise. "I keep forgetting you aren't sickly anymore."

"I'm not sure how to take that," I replied as we set the chair down.

"When our paths first crossed all those months ago, you were wounded. You gave Lorelei something to focus on other than myself and perhaps I acted out of jealousy."

"I should have realized asking you for advice on how to win her over was a bad idea," I agreed. It seemed he wanted to clear the air as much as I did.

He laughed and I swore I picked up the faintest of neighs. "Aye. Blame it on the poison?"

"You'd spent three years falling in love with her. I was a threat to that, even if I wasn't the man she remembered. Even if I wasn't real competition."

"I see why she fell for you in the first place. You inspire goodness in others. I've seen it in Lorelei and in Xander."

I cocked my head to one side. "What do you mean, in Xander?"

Douglas gave a fake cough and cast his gaze about the room, no doubt searching for some diversion. "It isn't my place to say anything. Just know that you make us all better, laddie. And that is a good thing. We need to be reminded that there are people and causes worth fighting for in this world."

A familiar sense of jealousy rose in my chest like it had when I'd asked Xander about his past with Micah. I pushed the feeling down and tried to focus on the mission at hand. "I appreciate you saying that."

He studied his hands for a moment and then said, "I know you don't remember being Kegan, but I feel a bit responsible for pulling Lorelei's focus away from finding you."

"What happened wasn't your fault. We can't know for sure how long I was being poisoned. Lorelei finding me sooner may not have made much of a difference. Besides, we need to focus on the future now. To make sure we still have a world where we can safely exist. Where you can raise your child in peace."

"Indeed." Douglas smoothed his shirt, looked me in the eye and extended his hand. "Bygones, then?"

"Sure," I replied and shook on it.

WE ASSEMBLED in the front foyer of the safe house an hour later. Lorelei, Constance, myself and Noemi were dressed in expensive outfits. I couldn't help noticing the low cut of Lorelei's dress. She caught me looking and blushed. Xander arched a brow at me and I felt my own cheeks flush with embarrassment. Mels and Alec both hovered a few inches off the ground; human sized. I wasn't sure if doxies had rapid healing abilities or not, but Alec's face already appeared less bruised. Luna and Bader hung back with Kyle and Bastian. Charles rested against the wall; the capsules tucked under each arm.

"So, the plan is clear?" Lorelei asked, fixing her eyes on the group.

"We go in, we switch the capsules and watch as the Booshie bitch inoculates the entire water supply," Mels replied with an almost disinterested shrug.

"Remember we can't do anything to arouse suspicion. There will already be security patrols. Those of you who will pose as pets will need to shift before we leave," Noemi responded.

"Wait ... Don't you think it will be a tad strange to see a kelpie traipsing through the streets?" Douglas asked.

"No stranger than a wolf," I muttered.

"I still don't understand why I can't go," Luna argued.

"Because little one, you nearly died from exposure," Bader answered, patting her on the shoulder.

She shrugged him off. "I'm not little. I can do this."

"We'll have enough moving parts and people to keep track of. Your parents would never forgive us if anything happened to you. Believe me," Constance said, her tone soft.

"Let me be a look out. I swear, I won't take on my spirit form," Luna begged.

I knew we wouldn't win this argument. If we forbade her from following us, she would do it anyway and likely put herself in more danger. "Fine, but you will stay with Bader and out of sight," I said.

"I'll keep her safe," Bader agreed.

"We've confirmed that there will be a PLA presence at the gathering," Bastian interjected.

Lorelei glanced at Xander. "We've got that covered already. We'll slip away from the party and make sure they follow us."

"What will you do if you run into Aria and Grady? Something tells me they will not be particularly forgiving of our last encounters with them," Douglas commented.

The sharpness I associated with the Lorelei I'd first met in this life made the angles of her face into razor edges. "If they come, I'll handle them."

"Can you kill them?" Douglas pressed. "I highly doubt they will let you escape with your life."

"If I have no other choice, I will do whatever it takes to protect the people I love."

"Then we better get moving. Madame Faberge detests lateness," Noemi announced.

Those of us posing as guests stepped into the ashen night air. I closed my eyes, envisioning the sunset from Sanctuary. I had to remind myself what we were fighting for, if only to keep my mind from drifting to the fear I had yet to voice to anyone. I may have been in bird form the last time I entered this jailer's prison, but I could still recall the feeling of being locked away. I wouldn't say it to anyone, but it terrified me to face this woman—this monster again.

"What's wrong?" Xander asked, nudging my shoulder.

I opened my eyes and looked to find him still fully clothed. "You're supposed to be shifting."

"It won't take long. What's bothering you?"

"I ... I'm scared that this won't work. Worried I'll need to face the woman who stole my life."

He reached down and squeezed my hand. "You aren't alone and she can't hurt you anymore. I promise."

"I love you," I whispered as he leaned in to kiss me.

"I love you, too," he breathed against my cheek.

In short order, he'd stripped down and shifted

into the beautiful bird who'd captured my heart. I swallowed the lump in my throat as the others joined us. I would not let my fear rule me. I had beaten her every step of the way. I wasn't about to let her win now or ever.

EIGHTEEN

EIGHTEEN

LORELEI

The easiest way to get to the Faberge party would be by hover taxi. It wouldn't be the flashiest arrival, though. Booshies were nothing if not flashy. We all had our roles to play. We needed to show off. We needed to parade down the street with our heads held high acting like the shifters beside us were our most prized possessions; not our comrades, friends, and lovers. We needed anyone passing by to believe our Booshie cover story. If they did, the real Booshies at the party would too. Or so we hoped.

As usual, I walked next to Aiden. We seemed to unconsciously gravitate toward each other. Maybe a hint of our shared past seeped through into the present, making us want to be near one another. I'd never been friends with an ex before, mainly because I never stuck around long enough to count anything as a relationship. First Kegan, and now Douglas were the exceptions to me not sticking around for any length of time rule I had always followed. They were different, but beyond that, I was different now. Something in me had changed the second Kegan asked for my help almost four years ago. I never went back to the person I was before that time. Even now I could barely remember her.

Douglas in kelpie form whinnied from my right, pulling me back to the present. I laid my hand against his auburn-colored flank, my palm rising and falling in time to his solid breathing. "Don't be a hero tonight, you hear me?" I told him. "No heroics. Only do as much as you need to get in and out alive."

"That's not the most inspirational of pep talks," Aiden joked from beside me. "Don't die! It doesn't exactly inspire confidence."

I turned my head toward him. "It goes for you too, you know. Making it to Sanctuary will seem easy compared to tonight's party. I've worked with these Booshies for years. We mean nothing to them. They'd kill a shifter as easily as swatting a fly. We're not safe, none of us. We never will be safe as long as they hold all the power."

"That's why we need to stop them from ever

harming another shifter," Aiden agreed. "It won't be easy though. Nothing worth fighting for ever is."

I motioned at phoenix Xander perched on Aiden's wrist. "Free Range isn't going to like it, but I'll need one of his feathers to track him if we get separated. Any one of them will do."

"Is that okay, Xander?" Aiden asked as if expecting a bird to answer him. Xander cocked his head to the side and bobbed it once. Aiden took that as a "yes." He gently plucked a small brightly colored feather from near Xander's talon and handed it to me. "You need to take your own advice tonight, Lorelei. Don't die. Your family would miss you if you did."

My family. For a second, my mind flashed to the hazy memories of my childhood with the siren shiver at St Goar. My parents had taught me my first song. It was a happier song, not the one used to lure men. That one had come much later after I was taken to the Institute. We had sung, swam, and *lived.* I didn't understand the government's interest in harnessing our natural abilities. They had wanted to make weapons out of girls. They had got their wish for generations. Even now, I'm sure there's a new crop of girls being trained at the Academy, waiting for their turn to join the Phoenix Location Agency. What would they do if there were no more escaped shifters to hunt? Would we all be left alone? Would the Booshies form another government agency to use our abilities to their advantage? The five innocent years I spent with the main siren shiver was the last time I had felt safe and loved. That near-foreign feeling of belonging to someone or something returned when I had joined the Magical Creature Underground. The MCU members were my family now—every single last one of them.

"Thanks," I mumbled. "I don't plan to." *But anything is possible*, I added silently. I needed to show the brave 'what-the-fuck-ever' face I had worn all these years as a mask. Feelings and emotions were a hinderance after all. I needed to stuff those so far down they wouldn't bother me at all tonight. The less I thought of Dougie, Douglas, Aiden or even the rest of the team, the easier it would be for me to fall back on my government training. It would be like flipping on a light switch. We were taught at the Academy that emotions equaled weakness. You couldn't survive if you were weak. I'd been surviving all these years, but I had never really lived until I let emotion in.

I patted Douglas' soft flank again. "I can't wait to get out of this hellhole and see Dougie again."

Douglas nickered in agreement. I heard his thoughts as clearly as if he spoke them. *Me too, M'eudail. Me too.*

A LINE WAS ALREADY FORMING at the front gate of Madame Faberge's estate as we drew near. Security was tight. Big burly guys who looked like the yetis who'd kidnapped Kegan all those years ago checked invitations at the gold gate and again at the front door to make sure no party crashers slipped in. Noemi pulled a handful of gilded envelopes from her handbag.

"Some of these are forgeries, but don't worry our guy is good enough to fool the gatekeepers." She nodded toward the security detail. "I'll go first. Bastian, take the rear. Everyone else, act like you belong."

"Luna, Bader, and I will stay outside the gates," Kyle said. He motioned at me and Xander. "We can create a diversion if too many come after you. It evens the odds of you getting a fair fight."

"Don't do anything stupid," I warned. "Remember you're just kids."

"Yes, Mom!" Mels called in a sing-song voice from inside Noemi's handbag.

"And *you* shut the hell up!" I snapped.

I heard snickering from inside the bag. Who knew shoving two doxies into a dark, enclosed space would help them bond instead of wanting to murder each other—Sadists.

The wolf kids moved off to the side, near a topiary phoenix or some shit. The rest of us waited in line, invitations in hand. Noemi was first. She handed her invitation to the guard with flourish.

"Where's your pet?" the security guard on the left asked.

Noemi opened her handbag to show off Mels and Alec. "Doxies. Aren't they just too precious? Be careful though, don't get too close. They bite. Doxy venom will knock you out for days if you're not careful."

The guard didn't look very convinced that any creature so small could cause such drama. He waved Noemi inside anyway. Constance sauntered up like she owned the place. She held out her invitation nonchalantly while Charles coiled around her neck like a naga necklace. Aiden shuffled his feet a little, betraying his nerves, but made great eye contact with the guard as he presented his invitation.

"You look familiar." The guard frowned. I held my breath, waiting to see if Brawn Before Brains recognized Aiden from the wanted posters or his previous stint in Madame Faberge's house of horrors.

"I must have one of those faces," Aiden said. "I dyed my hair to match my pet." He jiggled his arm to get Xander to flap his wings. "Isn't he a magnificent creature? Phoenixes are so rare now. I'm lucky to have one."

"Madame used to own a phoenix too," Guard number two said.

I caught a glint of pain in Aiden's eyes before they turned steely. "Yes. Word travels around. He sounds like quite the troublemaker."

"Escaped ten times, he did," Guard number two said. "Still he only got out of the compound once."

Aiden's smile was as icy as his eyes. "It only takes one time."

I kicked Aiden's heel. He looked over his shoulder, mouthing "what?" "Don't ruin things," I hissed. "Go inside. Now." I mimed walking motions with my fingers and pointed at the front door. Noemi and Constance were already inside. Aiden squared his shoulders and focused on putting one foot in front of the other. I didn't have time to check if he made it indoors. It was my turn with the security guards.

I presented my invitation. Guard number one squinted at Douglas. "A horse? What kind of pet is that?"

"Don't be ridiculous he's a kelpie, not any old regular horse." I forced my voice into a bright I've-got-money-and-not-a-care-in-the-world tone. "I know. I know. Before you say anything, you're probably wondering why I picked a kelpie to bring to

Madame's gala. Believe me, I wondered the same thing." Douglas snorted in protest. I laughed to cover up his displeasure. "A girl's gotta have a way to stand out from the crowd, right? How am I expected to do that if I bring just any old pet? I needed to stand out. My kelpie is my answer to that dilemma."

"Is he going to break shit?" Guard number two asked.

"Only hearts, boys," I promised as I breezed past them without waiting for an okay. "Only hearts."

Once Bastian was through security, we found an empty parlor on the first floor for one last group meeting. Douglas, Xander and Charles shifted to humanoid form. No one would miss a couple of 'pets' in this crowd. They dressed in the clothes I'd stored in my oversized bag as Noemi passed out com link ear pieces to everyone.

"This is the best way to communicate. We can't risk visual, so only have audio on. Keep your ear piece in at all times. One tap connects you to the main channel." She demonstrated with her own com link. "We're each other's eyes tonight. Report any suspicious activity. Getting caught is not an option."

I swapped my fancy high heels for a pair of flats. I stored the heels in my bag. I appreciated that the sharp points of the shoes were weapon ready, but I wouldn't miss wearing them any time soon. "When do you want us to lead the sirens away?"

"Let's all run a perimeter check first," Bastian said. "We need to know exactly what we're dealing with at all times. Find your partner?"

"You're with me, Free Range," I called when Xander instinctively moved closer to Aiden.

"Already?" Xander grimaced. "I thought we'd have a little more time."

"Nope." I crossed my arms over my chest as if I could hold in everything I was feeling. "You and me now."

"I'll be fine," Aiden promised. "We all will. Bastian, Noemi, and Kyle have been planning this for months. They have a system in place." He hesitated, looking like he wanted to kiss Xander good bye, before deciding against it. Sappy good byes didn't fall in line with 'we'll be fine.'

Douglas brushed his fingers against my arm, forcing me to look at him. "Whoever the PLA sent as backup, I hope you give 'em hell, *M'eudail*."

I cracked a smile. "I plan to." I didn't dare say more to him. I couldn't risk my emotions bubbling up to the surface. Instead, I motioned at Xander. "C'mon. Let's go, Free Range." Xander sighed and cast Aiden one last silent look before following me out of the parlor.

XANDER and I stuck close to the wall, slipping un-noticed from room to room as we ran our leg of the perimeter check. I tapped my ear piece, inundated with chatter from everyone with their com links on. I almost pulled it out of my damn ear, before re-membering Noemi's warning. This was the only way to keep in contact tonight.

"Rooms four, five, and six are clear," Xander said to the air.

"Not a siren in sight," I added. "Are you sure your PLA intel is accur …" The words died on my lips as I caught sight of Grady in the crowd. She was wearing the all-white PLA dress uniform; the kind worn for special government functions or pri-vate security detail. I grabbed Xander's wrist and pulled him against the wall. I brought my left finger to my lips in a "shh" gesture.

"Over there." I pointed at Grady. "I doubt she's alone."

"Who did they send?" Douglas' voice crackled over my com link, his accent thick with concern. "Talk to me, Lore."

"Grady." I scanned the room, picking up five other uniformed sirens. "Aria too and four others. I've seen them around headquarters before, but have never worked directly with them. I don't know what their fighting styles are like."

"Try to lure Grady and Aria," Aiden's voice piped over the com link. "Leave the others for Bader, Luna, and Kyle."

"Lycans versus sirens. Is that even a fair fight?" Xander asked.

"Bastian and I will join them once we check our rooms," Noemi promised.

I locked eyes with Grady. "Let's go," I said to Xander.

Once outside the main gates, I popped my com link out of my ear and held out a hand for Xander's. He put it in my palm.

"What are you doing?" he asked. "We need those."

"It'll get intense tonight." I tossed the com links on the ground before smashing them with my heel. "The less the others know what's going on with us, the better. If he thought you were in danger, would Aiden try to rescue you?"

"Absolutely," Xander said with complete confidence.

"Douglas would do the same for me," I said. "Trying to rescue us puts them in danger. We need to rescue ourselves." I turned to Bader, Kyle, and Luna when they joined us. "We need you to distract four sirens. Think you can handle it?"

"Point out who and we'll do our best," Kyle promised.

I pointed at four of the six uniformed sirens. "Those four. Divide and conquer is our plan for tonight."

"Got it." Bader frowned at Luna, who looked a little green from atmosphere exposure. "Think you can stay out of shift, little one?"

"I'm not little," she insisted before puking in the bushes. "I'm just ... I'm just ... I'll be okay."

"You don't look okay," Bader said. "Maybe you should sit this one out. Serena would ..."

"My mother isn't here! Stop saying what I can and cannot do. I can handle anything you can!" Luna lifted her chin in a show of defiance I had started to associate with the little wolf. "Just watch." Without warning, she shifted to wolf form and ran inside.

"Luna, wait!" Bader yelled.

I grabbed his arm to stop him from following her. "No time, kid. Help us, not her."

He didn't look convinced, but followed my directions. The six sirens had elbowed their way through the crowd awaiting entry to the party and were heading straight toward us.

"Now?" Xander asked.

"Now." I nodded.

Bader and Kyle created such a commotion, for a

second, I thought all six sirens would follow them. In the end, Grady and Aria split off from their group to trail us. I knew they couldn't turn down the chance to get another crack at the bounty on my head.

Xander and I led them on a winding chase through the City's back streets. We made sure never to get too far ahead though and to maintain line of sight.

"Where are we going?" Xander looked over his shoulder to make sure Grady and Aria were still trailing us.

"My place," I said. "Or, it was my place before all this shit went down. You'll see."

I stopped outside my former apartment building. Grady and Aria would know where to go after this. Xander trailed me up three flights of stairs to my old apartment. I found my spare key right where I hid it and opened the door.

Xander looked around at the spartan furnishings and drab walls once we were inside. "This is what government pay gets you? Shit. I'd defect too."

Before I could answer, Grady's boot connecting with the door blew it off its hinges. Even if we weren't looking for a fight, it had found us.

"You ready?" I asked Xander.

He cracked his knuckles. "Let's do this."

NINETEEN

NINETEEN

AIDEN

The siren shiver following Lorelei and Xander out of the party should have relaxed my nerves. But I couldn't shake the feeling that danger still lurked around every corner.

"You don't look so good, lad," Douglas said as he moved to stand beside me, offering me a glass of something amber colored.

"I never thought I would be back here," I answered. I didn't dare taste the contents. I wouldn't put it past my former captor to poison even her rich guests. An easy way to steal their pretty pets.

"Aye, I don't think any of us did," he agreed and surveyed the party-goers.

As discreetly as I could, tapped the com in my

ear. "How are we doing swapping out the capsules?"

No response just silence.

I caught the nervous energy rippling off Douglas beside me as he shifted his weight from foot to foot as he, too, realized we weren't getting any answer. Before I could voice my concern, a familiar figure caught my eye, sending icy tendrils of dread down my spine. *Madam Faberge.* My throat went dry and I couldn't move. The human part of me knew she no longer had control over me. I had defeated her poison and I had my freedom. Still, the part of me she'd kept captive for three long years, had forced to keep to one form, remembered the cruelty and panic. Thoughts that she would once again lock me away, rooted me to the spot.

"Might I suggest we make ourselves scarce?" Douglas hissed in my ear.

I wanted to agree with him. I *wanted* my limbs to do my mind's bidding and move far away from the wretched woman who was so intent on hurting shifters. But, I couldn't.

"Go check on the others," I finally rasped.

"I promised Lorelei I wouldn't let anything happen to you," he protested.

"And I promised her the same about you. It doesn't make sense for both of us to get caught."

"And the entire reason I'm here is to glamour

our charming host if necessary. Which I cannot do if I am not present," he whispered.

We didn't have time to argue more. Madame Faberge descended upon us, her gaze intense and full of suspicion. She wasn't a stupid woman. She had to know who I was.

"I don't believe we've been introduced," she said, her tone silky and devoid of any of the cruelty I'd expected.

"Forgive my friend, here. He's rather in awe of your grand home," Douglas said, covering for me.

"Is that so?" She arched a brow at me and turned back to Douglas. "As I recall, when last you graced my parlor, you had a beautiful wife in tow. Where is she this evening?"

"We have a problem," Noemi's voice crackled in my ear. "There's only one capsule in the first-floor office. She must have moved the other after our visit"

"Charles and I will check upstairs," Constance's response came through the earpiece.

"I'm sure I saw her around somewhere," Douglas said, pulling me from the conversation in my ear.

"Why don't I go find her for you," I offered, intent on no longer being under Madame Faberge's watchful gaze.

"Certainly, her husband is up to the task,"

Madame Faberge said and unceremoniously grabbed my arm, dragging me away from Douglas.

"*What do you want me to do?*" I heard Douglas' voice in my head.

I gestured toward the door, hoping he understood that it was imperative he tend to the mission. I watched him vanish from sight and tried to quell the anxiety rising in my chest, urging me to change form and take flight.

"So, I don't see your pet. I hope you haven't lost it," Madame Faberge said coolly.

"No, I know exactly where he is," I lied. I only knew that Xander was far away from this charade.

"You may have fooled my idiotic doormen, but you will not fool me, *Aiden*," she whispered.

Did I lie and try to throw her off the scent or did I admit my identity? If we changed out the capsules, there was still a chance I could get out of this with my freedom still intact. "I just had to see your face after I heard what you were planning," I finally answered, opting for the truth.

"You were always a bold little bird. But I never pegged you as stupid. You really think my guards will let you leave?"

"And you really think I came alone? You are the one who is underestimating me," I quipped. The confrontation loosened my lips and I couldn't hold in my feelings any longer. "No, you didn't consider me at all, did you? Not as a person. To you, we are just objects to possess not people with lives, loved ones, and dreams. You made me feel like I had no value beyond what nature gave to me that you could strip out for your own vanity."

I stepped closer to her. "I know now I have worth as a man. That I am worthy of love and affection and that no one deserves to be kept in bondage. I would have thought your kind realized that a long time ago. But maybe you've wrapped yourself in so much material wealth you forgot what it means to truly be human. To care for others around you simply because they are your fellow man. You will not get away with this."

I caught noise coming from a small device sticking out from a bag on her wrist. I picked out the words, "intruders" and "upper level". The security she'd hired had found our people which explained the problem Constance had reported. Madame Faberge eyed me as she retrieved the device and said, "Stop them. Permanently."

I opened my mouth to protest when a woman in the large ballroom let out a high-pitched scream. Both Madame Faberge and I turned to see a grey wolf leaping into the crowd. I immediately recognized the markings; Luna. She snarled at the humans in the room, sending shifters scattering from her presence. Somewhere in the din, I swore I heard the familiar cackle of two excited doxies ready to wreak havoc themselves.

"Aiden, get up here now!" Douglas shouted in my com, making me wince. Leaving Luna and the doxies to terrorize the Booshies, I darted for the upper level. Just as I reached the first landing, the pop of gunshots rang through my com, cranking my anxiety all the higher as I raced upward, unsure of what horrors awaited.

TWENTY

TWENTY

LORELEI

"You shouldn't have come back, Lorelei." Grady pulled a small nightstick out of her inside uniform pocket. She pressed a button on its base, extending it to a full-size staff. "Seriously. You must have a death wish or something. Why didn't you just stay gone?"

"Why are you helping that Booshie bitch poison shifters?" Out of the corner of my eye, I saw Xander get into a fighting stance, his hands up in a weird flat palm, fingers bent fist. He better know what he was doing, or I just signed my death sentence by picking a fight with my siren sisters. I kept talking to stall for time. "Tainted water would kill you just as sure as it would other shifters. Why help her?"

"We weren't helping, just guarding the joint," Aria said while she drew a tranq gun from the holster near her hip. "Why do you even care? You made your choice the second you abandoned the PLA."

"Are revolutionary phoenixes and lovesick kelpies more important to you than your family, Lorelei?" Grady's tone made it sound like half question and half taunt. "Don't worry. Once we're done with you, we'll kill them, too."

Xander stepped in front of me. "No, you fucking won't."

Before I had time to fully process what was going on, Xander sprang into motion. He smashed his palm into Aria's nose at an angle. I heard crunching as blood sprayed over her once pristine white uniform. While she screamed about her nose being broken, Xander landed a chest kick that sent her flying into the wall. Aria never once had time to use her weapon. Xander next attempted a leg sweep on Grady. She jumped over his foot before extending her staff toward him. Xander dodged back, blocking the intended blow. The staff wobbled in Grady's hand, but she maintained control. Even if she lost the staff, she would be far from weaponless. Sirens always came armed to the teeth, no matter the occasion.

I checked on how incapacitated Aria was while

Xander sparred with Grady. I dodged shuriken throws meant for Free Range as I moved across the room, jumping over my broken table and crumbling couch to where Aria lay slumped against the wall. Her eyes fluttered as she slowly regained consciousness. I pulled a knife from my stocking garter and waited.

"L-Lorelei?" Aria's gaze lost some of its glassiness. "Why do you fight so hard for a world not worth our time? Just do your job and forget the rest. That's what they trained us for. Fight first, ask questions never."

"There's a better way, Aria." I crouched down next to her, my knife at the ready in case this was a trap. "The human minority have kept us captive for far too long. Isn't it time to fight back?"

"But what is so worth your time and effort?" She winced as she touched her bleeding, broken nose. "What's so important? What do you fight for?"

"My family," I said. "Just because we didn't inherit a perfect world, doesn't mean we can't make it better for others who come after us. I want my son to live in a world where he doesn't have to worry about a price on his head or hunting his own kind just to put food on the table. He deserves better than that. We all deserve better than that too, Aria."

"Your son?" She smiled. "Tell me about him." I

noticed blood on her teeth. This felt like a good bye. *How hard had she hit the wall?*

I glanced toward Xander. He had somehow disarmed Grady. They were circling each other now, hands up, ready for a fist fight. Grady fought dirty, but so did Xander. I wasn't sure why Free Range waited until now to bust out his street fighting skills, but I was glad he did. He wasn't kidding when he said he could hold his own in a fight.

I turned back to Aria. Her breathing was labored. I frowned. Maybe she broke some ribs or punctured a lung with the chest kick. "My son's name is Douglas, after his father," I said. "We call him Dougie. He's the best of both of us. He didn't ask to be born, but you better damn well believe I'll do everything in my power to make sure he doesn't need to do the shit I did to survive. I don't want him to just survive, Aria. I want him to live."

"Where's Darya?" Aria coughed up blood. If we didn't get her some medical care soon, she'd die.

"Taking care of Dougie for us back home in Sanctuary. Don't worry. She's safe."

Aria's brow puckered in confusion. "Sanctuary? I thought that place was a myth."

"It's real." I reached for her hand with my free one. Aria's return squeeze was weak at best. "You can come with us, Aria. There's a place for everyone who wants to be free."

"It's too late for me."

"It's never too late," I promised.

"Hey, Lorelei, what do you want me to do with her!" Xander called.

I whipped my head in his direction. He stood behind Grady, one hand wrapped in her hair, pulling her head back. He held one of her own shuriken to her neck.

I opened my mouth to say "kill her" but couldn't get the words out. Instead, I said, "Do whatever you want."

"Don't bother." Grady tugged a small pouch from her jacket pocket. I knew what it was before she popped it in her mouth. The PLA called it our fail safe, but it really was instant death—*cyanide capsules*.

Xander threw Grady to the ground once she foamed at the mouth and went limp in his arms. "Fucking buzzkill."

"Why didn't you tell me you could fight like that?"

He shrugged. "You didn't ask."

Aria's coughing ended with a hiss of pain. She was still alive, but I wasn't sure for how much longer. "She wants to be better," I told Xander. "Help me carry her. We need to get her to Bader *now*."

TWENTY-ONE

TWENTY-ONE

AIDEN

"**D**ouglas, talk to me," I hissed, praying my com link would carry my concern to wherever he'd ended up. I continued up the stairs, anxious to find him and the others. *Where did those shots come from?*

I got no answer from any of our allies, but I picked up on the sound of muffled shouts and took off at a sprint down the corridor to my left. I had no recollection of ever being in this part of the mansion, though that didn't mean much. I'd been confined in more ways than one during the torturous three years I'd spent in this living hell. My heart hammered against my ribs and my lungs ached, reminding me that even within the boundaries of this mad woman's abode, the air was still tainted. It made me long for the clarity and beauty of Sanctuary's protective dome. We were so close to returning to what had quickly become our home.

I finally found the source of the shouting as I rounded a sharp right turn. The tableau in front of me was grim. A single mercenary had his weapon trained on two motionless figures as a second guard lay splayed on the ground at his side, very distinctive hoof marks imprinted on his sternum. I couldn't pick up the rise and fall of a living, breathing person. The mercenary, his hands shaking, turned to look at me, eyes wide with fear.

"It ... it just attacked," he whimpered.

I had some idea of who had done the damage to his partner and suspected Douglas would take great offense to being called 'it'. Luckily the guard didn't believe me to be a part of the sabotage effort, playing in my favor. I approached slowly, trying to exude an air of superiority like any good Booshie.

"It looks like you have things under control now," I said.

"It went that way. We caught these two trying to steal from Madame's private office."

I focused on the two bodies on the ground and my blood turned icy in my veins. *Charles and Constance.* I swallowed the lump forming in my throat.

Had they been able to switch the capsules before the guards discovered them? I bent down, spotting one of the large capsules by Charles' arm. It didn't bear the small demarcation of our antidote so perhaps he had succeeded.

"It doesn't look like they succeeded," I lied. "Why don't you go report that everything is secure. I can take care of this mess," I said, not facing the man. If I did, I would give away my true agenda. I could feel the grief welling up in me as the words left my mouth.

"Right," the man mumbled and shuffled back the way I'd come.

I waited until his footfalls receded before calling out, "Douglas, he's gone. You can come out now."

I heard snuffling and huffing from down the hall. I didn't want to leave Constance and Charles alone, but I needed Douglas to tell me what I'd missed. We could still salvage the mission. I followed a small trail of blood down the hall into a large room where the coppery-coated kelpie lay, flank rising and falling as blood oozed from a wound in his side. I raced to him, pressing my fingers to the edges of the wound. It didn't appear to be deep and I couldn't feel anything lodged beneath the skin. For the moment though, he couldn't shift back to human form while injured like this.

"Hold on, I've got you," I whispered, patting his neck.

He shook his head and settled against me. Conjuring my healing tears wasn't difficult. No longer were they turned bitter by the trauma I'd endured nor were they tainted by the poison that had nearly claimed my life. They flowed freely down my cheeks and onto the wound. It fizzled and the edges mended together. Within a minute, the only evidence of his injury was the blood on the floor leading into the room.

"You need to tell me what happened," I said and got to my feet, giving him room to shift back.

Slowly, Douglas stood on all fours and returned to human form. He didn't seem bothered by his lack of clothing. His skin was far paler than I'd seen it before. "We need to check on them," he said and pushed past me.

I followed him back to where Constance and Charles lay. I heard a soft moan and bent beside Constance. I brushed locks of dark hair out of her face and found her snake-slit eyes were hazy with pain.

"You're going to be okay," I said, preparing to check her for injuries.

"Charles," she rasped, the end of his name trailing off in an elongated hiss.

Reluctantly, I turned my attention to her mate. I

knew before I even laid hands on him that he was beyond my healing touch. Still, if I could give her a tiny grain of hope, even for just a moment longer, I would. I probed him and found the two bullet wounds in his chest. His skin was already clammy to the touch.

"Constance, I'm so sorry," I whispered. "He's gone."

"No," she moaned and threw herself back across his prone form.

Douglas nudged me with his foot and I stood, giving Constance a moment to mourn in private. "They exchanged the capsule. Noemi and Bastian were supposed to get the other one."

I pointed to the downed mercenary. "What about him?"

"I got here after they'd already fired. I don't take kindly to people trying to hurt my family." He touched his side where the bullet wound had been. "At least I got a good kick in."

I tapped my com link. "Noemi, did you get the other capsule in place?"

I heard crackling in my ear and then, "Yes. We had to subdue some guards along the way."

Beside me, Constance raised her torso, only to fall back against the floor with a grimace. I bent down and pressed my hand to a wound in her belly. "Lay still. I can fix this."

She shook her head, pushing my hands away. "No."

"Constance, you'll die if he doesn't heal you," Douglas argued.

She blinked and looked at me through tears. "I know. Perhaps it is my fate. I lost my children to creatures who did not understand my kind. I thought I had lost my mate and so I found a new family to protect. And then, I was blessed enough to find the love I had lost again." She coughed, blood dribbling over her lips. "But he is gone and my new family has found safety and peace. It is time for me to join my children."

I shook my head, refusing to let her give up. "I'm not letting you die," I proclaimed, letting the tears fall onto my hands before I pressed them back against her skin. She had just enough energy left to take hold of my hands. I met her gaze and immediately knew I shouldn't have. Her hypnotic lure snagged me.

"Let me go," she hissed.

Every fiber of my being protested, but my mind could only obey her command. Her hands went limp in mine and she slumped backwards. Anger quickly replaced the sadness of loss at the monsters who'd done this to us; to our family.

"We need to regroup. Lorelei and Xander are

back and they aren't alone either," Bastian said over the com link.

Douglas hauled me to my feet. "Come on. The mission isn't done yet, lad."

TWENTY-TWO

TWENTY-TWO

LORELEI

You couldn't exactly be stealthy while carrying a wounded person through the City. Xander and I didn't even try. I didn't give myself time to wonder how the others had fared on their part of the plan. I was focused on getting Aria to Bader so he could fix her. I didn't want to consider the alternative. Her, Darya, and even Grady were the closest thing I ever had to real sisters. We were taken from our home, came up through the Academy, and joined the PLA all at the same time. We had seen and done so much together. I couldn't stand by and do nothing when Aria needed me the most.

"Bader!" I yelled for the kid as the lights from

Madame Faberge's compound came into view. "We need a medic! Now!"

Bader materialized from near the bushes. Kyle was next to him. I didn't ask what they had done with the other sirens from the party. My focus was on Aria.

"What's wrong?" He knelt on the sidewalk next to where we laid Aria, already checking her vitals with equipment from his pack.

"I don't know," I said. "Ribs. Maybe lungs. A broken nose for sure. Can you help her?"

Bader placed a device on her chest, listening to her breathing. "I don't know. I don't have the equipment to fix anything internal."

"Then we take her to the hospital," I insisted.

"Are you trying to get yourself captured?" Kyle asked. "You still have a bounty on your head, remember? Taking her to the hospital guarantees the feds will nab you. We came to bust up a party, not bust you out of a jail cell."

It took several moments for his words to sink in. I needed to get home to Dougie. I couldn't do that from inside a fed prison. "Don't you have field training or something?" I asked Bader. "We can't just stand here and do nothing for her."

"Lorelei?" Aria opened her eyes and reached out a hand toward me. "Whatever happens, it will be okay."

I squeezed her hand. "Bader's a medic, Aria. He can help."

Her labored breathing wheezed and rattled as she struggled to sit up. I pushed my free hand against her shoulder to keep her still. "I want to help you," she rasped.

"Save your strength. We got this one," I promised. "You can help our next mission."

"Do you remember when you came back after being off grid?" Aria's voice was low and urgent. I had to lean in close to hear all her words. "You were different. You pretended like you weren't, but we all saw it. I wasn't surprised when you ran off again. Remember what you told me the first time you went off grid?"

I shook my head. "No. Tell me."

Aria smiled. Her face had that unearthly glow about it I'd seen so many times when death was near. "You said it's easy to put animals back in a cage, but not people. Once shifters show their human side it's a ... it's a ..." She trailed off and her eyes fluttered closed.

I sucked in a ragged breath. "We'll get you help, Aria. I promise. We'll get you help."

"She's gone, *M'eudail*."

I looked up, not realizing the others had joined us until I heard Douglas' voice. "No ... She's just sleeping," I insisted. "Just sleeping. We'll find her help and-and-and—"

"It's not the kind of sleep she'll ever wake up from, Lorelei," Aiden said, his voice soft. "I'm sorry. She's gone."

"She's gone?" I repeated, not ready to believe it. My voice sounded hollow and lost. First Grady and now Aria gone too. How could half of our team from the Academy be dead?

"I know we've sustained some losses tonight, but we still have a mission to complete," Bastian reminded us all. "We've come too far to let it fall apart now. Switching the capsules was a success. Now we need to make sure the guests know what Faberge had planned from the start. We need them to turn against her."

"But how?" Xander thumped Grady's stolen staff into the ground and leaned against it. "If they cared about their shifters' safety, they wouldn't have come to the party in the first place."

Something Aria said floated back to me. "It's easy to put an animal back in a cage, not a person. That's it!" I jumped to my feet. "We need to get the guests to see their shifters as people. Not pets!"

"How do we do that?" Noemi asked.

I paced back and forth as I tried to work out the next step of our plan as quickly as possible. "We need them to shift en masse. Hurting humans ..." I shook my head again. "Even Booshies wouldn't do that. Well … Not unless they're completely depraved."

"How do we reach them all at once?" Kyle asked.

"I know a song," I said. "I'll weave what we want them to do into the melody. Anyone who hears it will obey." I looked at Aiden. "Kegan understood how to be seen as human, he needed to look human. Now we do the same thing for every shifter at this party." I found Douglas next, falling into his waiting arms for a hug I didn't know I had needed until that exact moment. "After that, we all go home."

TWENTY-THREE

TWENTY-THREE

AIDEN

The losses were piling up, but I was determined to stop Madame Faberge from continuing her oppression. I walked back into the party to find Luna snarling at the remaining guards. Clusters of Booshie attendees cowered as I spied two tiny winged creatures flitting around their heads, venom droplets hissing against skin. At least Mels and Alec were having fun. Madame Faberge stood at the center of the room, a haughty expression on her face.

She didn't realize she'd lost. She was about to learn the hard truth. Behind me, I could hear Lorelei's siren song calling out to every shifter in the room and for once it wasn't aimed at me. I was already in human form. The notes held no power over me.

"Someone shoot that filthy beast," she snapped and gestured toward Luna.

Xander jumped in front of Luna, brandishing Grady's staff. Electricity crackled from one end and he deftly swung it, taking out two armed mercenaries in one swing.

"Anyone lays a hand on her, you deal with me," he announced, planting the staff on the floor between his feet.

"You fools think you have ruined the evening, but you have simply proven my point," Madame Faberge said, spreading her arms wide. "Good pets are obedient, respectful—"

"You don't know the first thing about respect," I snapped, unable to stay quiet any longer. I closed the distance between us, not caring whether her mercenary guards took aim at me. "You held me prisoner in this place for three years. All because you wanted to stay young and to show everyone you had the power to keep me. Not once did you consider what I wanted or that I was really a person. So, don't you dare speak of respect."

Out of the corner of my eye, I saw shifters taking on human form. If Madame Faberge noticed, she said nothing. Her guests peered between her and me, waiting for whatever came next.

"You were always the most defiant," she said and produced the two capsules. "And yet, I made you obedient for quite some time."

"She poisoned me," I shouted and pointed to the naked shifters around the room. "You really think she cares about your pets?"

A few of the overly dressed Booshies turned. Their mouths hung open at the sight of their precious pets wearing their human faces. Mels and Alec descended, landing on either side of me, growing to full size as their feet touched down.

"You will never have to fear losing another pet. They will be docile," Madame Faberge argued and inched closer to the water supply.

"She will poison your pets with blood graft," Lorelei called, joining the conversation.

At the mention of the poison, the shifters who had returned to human form turned toward Madame Faberge. For the first time, I spied real fear in her expression.

"But, won't that kill them?" exclaimed one Booshie woman who wore a hat full of ostrich feathers to match the ostrich shifter she'd brought with her.

"Yes, it will," I answered.

Horrified gasps went up around the room. Madame Faberge turned and lobbed the two capsules into the water. The casings dissolved and the water frothed. "He is lying to you. It will just make your pets docile."

Owners grabbed their naked shifters and pulled them clear of the water. Not the response Madame Faberge had been expecting. Her eyes widened at the behavior of her guests. "It won't hurt *you*, you fools!"

Before anyone could get another word in, the doors to the room burst open and armed government officers appeared. "She tried to poison us," one of the guests shouted.

"And our pets too," another announced.

"No. This is ridiculous," Madame Faberge protested as the officers descended on her, dragging her from the room.

I stepped into their path and leaned in close to her. "You failed. You just inoculated the entire water supply. You could dump gallons of blood graft in and it still wouldn't harm a single shifter."

I could hear her protests long after they had removed her from the premises. The guests finally came to their senses and some of the shifters reverted to their animal forms, fleeing the party. I prayed none of them would be pursued.

Xander set aside the staff and pulled me into a tight embrace. "I'm so proud of you," he said in my ear.

"Where'd you learn to fight like that?" I asked and returned his hug.

"There's a lot I need to tell you when we are home."

Home. We were really going back to the safety of Sanctuary. Even those of us who hadn't survived our mission. We would bury Constance and Charles under the warmth of sunlight and the vivid blue of a cloudless sky. They would rest in the world that they both had fought so hard for.

EPILOGUE

LORELEI

Three Years Later

"Uncle Aiden! Uncle Xander! Watch this!" Dougie stripped off all his clothes—something he liked to do whether or not we wanted him to—and shifted into a pony sized horse with tawny scales. He whinnied before galloping off.

"That's my boy!" Douglas grinned. "I better go after the wee nipper." He leaned down to kiss me. "Meet you out front?"

"I'll be right there," I promised before turning back to our two phoenix babysitters. "Please remember to put Dougie to bed by eight. And no swimming for a full hour after eating. And sing him a lullaby at bedtime. He likes that. And—"

Xander rolled his eyes. "Just leave already. We

got it covered. It's not like we haven't watched the kid before."

"But never overnight." I twisted the gold band on my left-hand's ring finger. Sometimes its weight still felt foreign to me and other times it was like I'd never been without it. "If you don't want to sing to him, tell him a story. And no sweets two hours before bed and –"

"Just go already!" Xander bellowed.

Aiden leaned against Xander's side. Free Range was quick to wrap an arm around his waist. "What Xander meant to say is, hope you and Douglas enjoy yourselves."

"But don't enjoy yourselves too much," Xander added. "One hybrid kid is enough."

"Oh, ha ha."

We hadn't left Dougie since our last mission to the City. Things had changed for the better since Madame Faberge's failed attempt to poison all shifters. The Shifters Rights Law passed two years ago. Recognizing shifters and Magical Creatures as equal to humans. We'd been afforded all of the same rights as mundanes, humans. If shifters stayed in their former owners' homes, the law required they be provided paying jobs, not cages. Last year, Sanctuary shared their clean air technology with everyone. Blue sky and sunshine still sometimes felt like a novelty. At the same time, I was glad Dougie would never know burning rain and an ashen, dim sky. We cared enough to create this world for him. We could all live without fear of cages or poisons like blood graft. We were free. No one could hold us captive ever again.

THE END

Ready for more magic? Enter the halls of Celestial Academy, where even the saints aren't perfect. Grab Celestial Academy and binge the series today.

Join Sarah's Newsletter for all the latest news and receive your copy of Menagerie as a gift for signing up!
Subscribe here!

Join Molly's Newsletter for all the latest news!
Subscribe here!

ABOUT THE AUTHORS

Sarah Biglow is the USA Today Bestselling author of several urban fantasy series. She is a licensed attorney and spends her days combating discrimination as an Investigator with the Massachusetts Commission Against Discrimination. Sarah is a lover of TV and runs a recap blog with her long-time friend, Jen. She lives in Boston with her husband and son.

Read More From Sarah Biglow

www.sarah-biglow.com

Molly Zenk was born in Minnesota, grew up in Florida, lived briefly in Tennessee before settling in

Colorado. She writes many genres including Young Adult, Historical Fiction, and Romance. She is married to a Mathematician/Software Engineer who complains about there not being enough "math" or info about him in her author bio. They live in Arvada, CO with their daughters.

Read More From Molly Zenk

https://mollyzenkwrites.wordpress.com/

9 781955 988032